K.L. Vincent

POISONED

PAWN

THE BLUESTOCKING TRIO

To my father, who fostered my imagination by reading bedtime stories.

PRONUNCIATION OF FREQUENTLY USED CHARACTERS

Æri: air-ee
Brennos: bren-ose
Belisaur: bell-i-sar
Brynja: br-ee-nya
Cuthbert: cooth-bert
Dahlia: doll-ya
Eydis: ee-dis
Gratian: grass-ee-an

Gyr: gear
Ildrid: ill-drid
Knjal: nall
Marlena: marr-len-a
Nicomedes: nik-o-mee-des
Oisin: oh-sheen
Odoacer: odo-ACE-er

Rione Aulius: ree-own ow-lee-us
Remus: ree-muss
Signe: seen-ya
Toril: tore-ill
(Tye)grieve: tie-greeve
Yrsa: err-sa

Gods/Goddesses
Hesól: he-sole
Nynth: ninth
Skathi: ska-thee

PLACES

Dianeane: die-an-eene
Fíronbec: fee-ron-bec
Hælsgade: hells-gade
Erynelleth: air-en-ell-eth
Kostros: kose-trose

Larkærseim: lark-air-sheem
Méritras: mair-i-tras
Særenfell: sair-en-fell
Vallantheia: vall-an-thee-a

Other
Acuslasor: ah-cuss-la-sore
Deinoplore: dee-in-O-ploor
Scitator: sit-at-or
Specuformae: spec-U-form-A

Poisoned Pawn includes content that might not be suitable for some readers. Triggers involve hand-to-hand combat, battles, violence, poisoning, oppressive language, torture, abduction, addiction, and trauma recovery. Welcome to the aftermath of the Split.

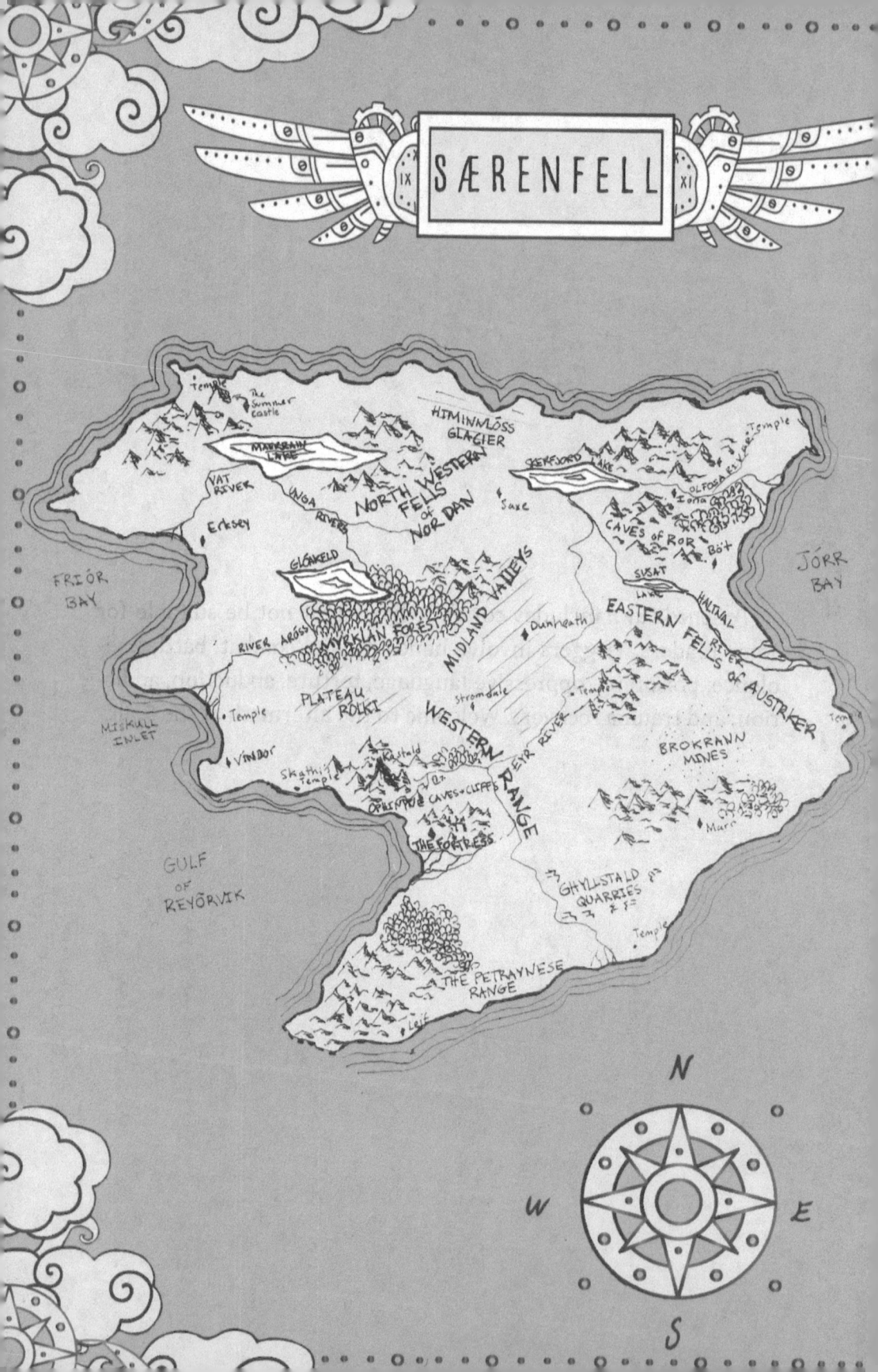

A Children's Rhyme from Særenfell

Eyes of ice blue, loyalty is our virtue

Eyes of brown do not bow down

Eyes of silver long remember

Eyes of green are serene

Eyes of violet hold a secret

Eyes of blue and yellow tell of tomorrow

Eyes of gold do uphold

Eyes of red bring the dread

And faded tones are left unknown

A Vow from the Deities

We *Split* their world into a thousand pieces. They did not listen, and now they scramble to survive on a broken earth, damned to live an existence of chaos and ruin. They have forgotten. They have forgotten who they were and what they have done. So, we ask what they value above their fates. Another soul? A queendom? A kingdom? A world? Let us see what they choose, and maybe then they will remember.

~ 1 ~

ÆRI

The Bogs

Heat and ash smacked into Æri's face. They rippled over her leathers as her aircraft sliced through the Bog's choking black haze. The impact stole her breath. Her head spun as her lungs fought the smoke surging into the cockpit. Æri swallowed the sick that threatened to paint her windshield. *Focus.* She had to stay conscious—for her queen, for her people. They all depended on her to prevail.

Æri jerked her cowl up with a free hand and covered her nose and mouth, desperate for the thin relief of filtered air. The Skimmer shook, hitting air pocket after air pocket. Adrenaline seared in her veins as the hellish earth rushed at her, its fissures glowing amber. Her muscles locked in the seat, teeth gritted with determination, hands gripping the shuddering controls as if sheer will would keep the Skimmer from shattering. She had survived worse. She would see this through.

Sweat beaded at her temple. In the rearview, Gyr closed in, darting like an arrow in pursuit, cutting straight for her.

She slammed the throttle. Hot gushes of air whipped overhead. The drag force pulled on loose strands of her dark cropped hair.

Gyr tucked in his white wings, a predator gaining ground. Within an instant, he caught her tail.

Come on. Yield.

Sulfur burned her eyes through the flight goggles. The geysers' boiling water flicked her exposed skin. Æri blinked to clear her tears, enduring the discomfort. She lowered the Skimmer's crystal windshield to feel the wind. A swoosh, and she twisted, evading a torrent of steam.

Closer and closer, the earth loomed, its roughened details blurring with sweat. Her hands slipped around the control stick. She wasn't giving in.

A bird's screech—and the falcon flared his wings, falling back. *Finally.*

Æri yanked the stick and lurched the Skimmer up, leveling her aircraft just above the lava field. She trusted the falcon's instinct over her own to find an opening.

Thanks, Gyr. Æri saluted her companion.

Gyr trilled his reply and swooped to somersault.

Shaking her head, she adjusted her speed and flattened her smile. *All right, Gyr. The fun's over. Time to hunt.*

The air was clearer closer to the Bogs. With the red sun to her left and Gyr in tow, Æri banked hard toward the south.

The sight never grew old: A mixture of pumice stone and quagmire moors covered the uninhabitable lands. Something about the ancient, torn-up world kept her balanced, reminding her there was some other place outside her realm of ice. She could only imagine what it looked like before the Split, recollecting images from the old scriptures.

When the realms detached from Glasterra, giant lesions pocked the earth, leaving a molten red and orange. Its wounded terrain oozed magma. As the oceans pooled over and cooled the crust, their waters created a heated black marshland that bubbled and popped.

"Kak-Kak," Gyr squawked in warning. Though Æri hunted, it didn't mean she was at the top of the food chain. Unusual beasts roamed the Bogs, either altered survivors from the lost oceans or things that lurked under the earth ere the Split.

She steered the Skimmer into the cloud cover.

Ash floated like lost memories, suspended in the air after the Split's destruction.

Gyr moved to her left, then beat his wings and rolled over the Skimmer's lift, repositioning himself on her right.

Had he seen something?

Impatient, huh? Take the lead.

She dipped the Skimmer to follow her companion. A giddy thrill tingled through her chest reaching her toes as she maneuvered past rifts, through arched rocks, and up again.

Careful, Gyr, don't get too close. Those geysers are unpredictable.

Descending into the Bogs' lower atmosphere, she listed away from currents rising from wells of melted rock. Their rumbles thrummed in her ears as the Skimmer's controls juddered.

Æri's eyes combed the lava field, marking the holms—dry patches on the earth if she needed to land. One could walk on the Bogs' crust with the right gear *if* they knew where to step. Many-a-prey fell victim to the copious sinkholes and tar pits, hidden to the untrained eye—which is why she chose to do most of her hunting from the skies.

Her falcon flapped his spotted wings, pushing ahead, and vanished into the haze.

Gyr, wait! She attempted a whistle, but he was already gone.

Æri chased the billows of disrupted smoke betraying his flight path.

The heat rose, forcing her to re-tweak her straps and crank the curved windshield to block the fiercer gusts.

Where'd he disappear to?

Diverting the Skimmer onto a smoother trajectory, Æri tapped the supplies with her foot, ensuring they hadn't moved during the drop—all safely packed in place.

Her falcon's blue eye flashed bright, a beacon in the diluted light.

What did you find?

His winged form soared above a shape, but the mists muddled the view.

Æri drew in, lowering the Skimmer.

Her flight goggles snapped open with a click, and she tuned the monocle. It zoomed and focused.

A man.

Details of his sleek, form-fitting clothes and the small sack bouncing on his back sharpened.

A man from Fíronbec? But why so close to our borders?

Gauging by the fuel in the cell tank, they hadn't traveled far from Særenfell.

Æri reached for the lever, ready to release the netting, but idled. The man crisscrossed nimbly, skipping past hot spots and breaks on the surface, knowing where to step. Not a runaway then—a good sign. He'd last longer. Runaways floundered, unprepared for the terrain's dangers, and were often left frail—even if they made it out this far, they rarely survived the trip back to her fortress.

Shifting her wrist, she leaned on the throttle.

Maybe a seeker? Too wiry to be a hunter. Despite the gurgle and fizz of the Bogs, a skilled tracker would have heard the muffled whizz of her craft and been running by now.

Why didn't he move faster? No one was fool enough to linger in the Bogs.

A tingle of uncertainty flitted through her, but the lure of prey outweighed the doubt. She'd snare and put him in one of the cages kept on the holms while she sought more feed. The sooner this hunt was over, the sooner Æri could go home—and continue a more important pursuit: finding a cure for the Blodlyst.

She switched the Skimmer to autopilot, dropping the speed to hover.

Balancing her weight, Æri unlatched her straps and retrieved the crossbow. Her hands moved automatically over the mechanism, having hundreds of years to practice. With the stirrup pointed down, she waited for the double click as she pulled the string back, cocking the bow, and loaded it with a web arrow. The dart would stun and release a net on impact but not kill.

Firming her stance, she adjusted the buttstock to rest on her good shoulder. Æri locked her eyes on the target.

Steady...steady...

A light breeze fluttered the straps on her archer's gloves. She deviated slightly to the right. Her monocle re-centered—a perfect shot. Taking a controlled breath, Æri angled her head and squeezed.

Whoosh! A gust of wind hit her seconds before a faint whirring echoed her own glider's buzz.

"What the—" Her arrow skewed. The net deployed around a cluster of rocks, missing the target by several feet.

A blur of light flashed, and a smaller craft skirred above, its body shaped like a wild hog. Her Narkrye crew member rode atop, blond hair peeking out from a leather helm.

"*Yrsa.*" Æri hissed under her breath, rocking her Skimmer to the left just as Yrsa shot by, her Boar nearly colliding into Æri's hovering aircraft.

By the gods—she wasn't supposed to be here, not this far from Særenfell's patrol line. Æri shoved the Skimmer's controls back into manual, not bothering to fasten herself in.

Yrsa's Boar whined while it undulated ahead.

The man had vanished.

"Draug's blood!" She couldn't jeopardize losing her prey when she was so close, not after her queen's desperate command—*her sister's* command.

Æri scoured the surface.

There!

He'd picked up his pace to a running hop through the Bogs' sod, getting farther and farther away.

Yrsa crouched lower on her craft, homing in on Æri's target.

The man darted into a sunken ravine, Yrsa rashly following his steps.

Æri's ears pulsed. "Yrsa, stop!"

Something wasn't right.

Trailing her crew member, Æri whistled to Gyr to intercept the rogue huntress, hoping his call would bring her back to her senses.

"Kak, kak, kak!" He flew higher, angling himself behind the Boar, but his efforts were pointless. Yrsa surged forward, ignoring his cries.

"No, no, no." Æri zigzagged through the winding chasm, dodging cliff edges and the sporadic spray of magma.

Yrsa closed the distance, near enough to reach and grab the man, but the rocks made it impossible. He seemed to know where to tread, vaulting from ledge to ledge, all too aware of the footholds and crevices to duck into.

Their prey was getting away. Yrsa was going to ruin the hunt.

Without slowing his pace, the man extracted an object from his sack. A spark escaped from his hand. Æri flinched, expecting him to direct it at her or her Narkrye, but it jetted upward into the sky, flaring through the murky clouds.

Then it clicked.

"YRSA!" The scream ripped from Æri's throat.

Bait. The man was bait. They were headed into a trap.

Cold fear pealed through Æri. The pressure on her eardrums swelled to bursting as alarm bells shrieked. She flailed her arm, but Yrsa didn't turn. Her determination fixated on the man who leaped and readily navigated himself through igneous rocks.

Æri's finger flew over the control switch. Should she release one of the stun grenades? No—too dangerous in the tight passage.

A rushing note tore past Æri's ear.

"No!"

The arrow zipped by, swift and sure, lodging into Yrsa's side. The huntress jerked, and the Boar rammed into the cliff face. Losing equilibrium, the volatile craft bucked wildly as it barreled toward Æri. She swerved, but not fast enough. It clipped one of the Skimmer's wings, crunching under impact. The wing tilted. An ear-piercing screech of metal filled the ravine as it scraped against the wall, sparks flying. Then it broke off completely.

With the uneven balance, her aircraft nosedived. Cracked turf and lava swamped her vision. She thrust her right arm up to shield her eyes from the blistering heat; her bionic arm latched like a vise to the aircraft's controls.

As Æri careened downward, her last thought was of her sister sealed away in the fortress's keep.

~ 2 ~

BRYNJA

The Day Afore

Sœrenfell

Shivering, Brynja pulled her heavy pelts close. Outside the keep's tower, the wind wailed like a trapped soul. Morning's steel-blue light tried and failed to break through the embrasures. These skinny windows hardly let in any sun.

The fortress's many turrets pierced the ethereal mists, like fingers of a god reaching toward the heavens—toward Vallantheia. Carved out of a towering mountain range, its battlements extended from a sheer cliff face, the silver stone born from the fell itself.

Yet the gray rock did little to block the ice, and Brynja was always so cold.

Whom could she blame but herself? She had done this, locked herself in one of the highest towers and removed herself from her people—*to protect them*—to keep them away from her bloodthirsty court.

She rotated the still-beating heart in her hand. Blood coughed out of the remaining arterial in gurgled bursts and trickled down her wrist. Her silver nail stroked the flesh. Its ore-clad tip sliced into the atrium, and the heart's muted thumps guttered to a halt.

A second stream of blood spilled over Brynja's palm into the griffin-claw goblet beneath.

An iron tang permeated the air, its rusty scent making her salivate. The goblet brimmed full of red liquid. A fleck of its fluid sprayed the corner of Brynja's mouth. Her tongue snaked out to lick it, immediately putting her senses into a heightened frenzy.

A desire for more crawled up her throat, the muscles squeezing.

Drink it all. All of it. It's ours to take, the voice coaxed.

Brynja wrapped her fingers around the claw-shaped vessel, shaking with restraint.

Control. We must practice control.

She clenched her teeth, holding her breath to gather every ounce of strength, but her resilience weakened.

Brynja lifted the goblet. The itch at the back of her throat—that want to down it all—mounted.

No.

No? Why ever not? Nothing's stopping us. The voice tempted, threatening to splinter her stability. It would be so easy to give in, to not fight it.

Her lips traced the rim. Touching the liquid, they parted. Her sips grew into mouthfuls, arms lifting the goblet higher. Blood poured into her, quelling the thirst. She gulped and gulped, then licked the goblet's shell. Tossing the empty griffin claw aside, she sucked at her ore-tipped fingers.

We need more.

There's nothing left—just the heart's flesh.

Saved for last, it held the most life.

Take it! The voice's fervor rose.

No.

Brynja waited, expecting the voice to demand again, but it slept, satiated.

Her fingers closed around the heart's shriveled pieces, squeezing. She despised this—this hunger that took innocent lives just to save her worthless crown. If another option offered itself, she would choose it, abdicate the throne and waste away in the darkness of the tower. But no one else in her bloodline wanted to rule—or knew how to. No one else wanted to guide and manage what was left of her people, a decimated population. And she did not intend to let it fall into ruin, crumbling as it was.

But this lust...this disease that ravaged her lands and subjects—she felt it gradually taking over her mind, like talons scraping at the doors to her sanity.

Brynja inhaled and let a controlled breath diffuse from her nose, its pressure rasping against her ears.

Sucking drew her attention to the other end of the table, where a man's body slumped. The same being whose collapsed heart she held.

Her court—just two of them today—knelt on the floor, lapping at the man's wrists. Wrists marked with lacerations, some scabbed, others fresh, cut again and again while he lived, done to make him last. He *had* to last. Only one remained in the crypts; this man had survived just two weeks. The one before lasted a month. It wasn't a good sign. Either the men were becoming weaker, or she and her court drank too quickly. Death was not an easy choice. She dreaded summoning for another hunt.

"Ladies, please. We are human. Be dignified." She gestured to the plates laden with sweet mountain fruit and pheasant meat, untouched on the vast table, and scowled at the drops staining the floor. If she had any humanity left in her, at the very least, she could prevent excess. "We cannot waste...as you are doing now."

The two moonlight-haired women scarcely twitched in her direction, continuing to feed and suck. Her jaw tightened, and an icy burn spread through her limbs.

"I said, *stop it!*"

"Y-yes, Your Majesty."

They bowed their heads while their eyes alternated between their queen and the corpse.

Brynja calculated.

"Dahlia."

"Yes, Your Majesty?"

Brynja raised the withered heart. "When you've finished with this..." She hesitated, her throat aching, then bit down on her resolve and flung it at them. They tore at the remnants like beasts. "Send for Æri."

Æri

A chill breeze weaved its way through a cracked window. Scents of pine and fresh snow curled in and out of the room, mingling with the fire's smoke.

Æri tugged the bear fur tighter. Its warmth kept the arctic air from reaching her limbs. Limbs she currently draped across another inviting body.

"Close the damned window, Æri," the languid form mumbled into the pillow.

"Mm-mm." Æri squeezed an arm around Signe. She enjoyed sleeping with the window open, exposing her face to the alps' storms and biting torrents while, of course, piled under mountains of furs and down coverings.

"*Please.* It's cold."

"Then do it yourself. My room, my rules."

Signe didn't move.

Æri pried her lids open, glimpsing Signe's voluptuous form. Her corded muscles were smooth and long, the dip of her waist curving up to her breasts, adorned by a cascade of flaming red hair.

She nuzzled her nose into Signe's waves, soaking in her scent, sweet and bitter—like the lilliock berries that grew in the higher elevations of their mountainous homeland.

Then Æri placed her freezing hand on Signe's exposed back.

"Eeeek! You didn't just do that!" She kicked a foot, deftly finding its mark on Æri's thigh.

"Oof. Okay, okay...no need for violence." Æri rubbed at the spot and rolled over to hoist herself from the bed, right hand landing on a griffin-head post. She rummaged blindly for her tunic, remembering how and who took it off. The memories brought a coltish grin to her lips as she threw the woolly fabric over her head.

Æri's toes squished into the shaggy ryas covering the stone floor.

The round chamber only possessed essentials. Natural beiges and browns juxtaposed the gray of the sparse walls. Her bed rested at the center, the solitary embellishment. Its carved wooden posts depicted two abstract heads of griffins with swirled and knotted bodies.

"I love this room."

"I don't." Signe melted into the furs. "And I won't be coming back here if that window stays open."

Æri rolled her lips, holding in a chuckle, and tiptoed toward the lead-paned window. Cames held each diamond shape in place, partially obscuring the view outside. Through the crystal panels, lace-like snowflakes dwindled.

Her favorite time of day was in these early hours as the blizzard settled and a calmness fell upon the alpine terrain, swathing it in a suspended peace. Like after a hard run in the crags, the energy and madness from the storm expelled, and all that remained was blissful exhaustion. The late night left her like that too. Sleep evaded her, but forgoing the necessity was worth it.

Signe burrowed herself deeper, covers now pulled to hide her head.

Æri furtively eased the window open wider, letting one last gale fill the room. The tunic whipped at her thighs, and her dark silken strands danced, their fringe tickling her chin. She had recently cut her thick hair short to the jawline, not liking the weight of her former braid.

"Snowfall's stopped, Signe. Come and see. The weather's clearing up nicely too. We can run a flight check with the controls."

"Feel free. Your arm's there." Signe pointed toward Æri's bionic arm, hanging over the headboard, then slipped her fingers back under the furs.

Æri reached for her metallic device.

She'd allowed Signe to remove it the night afore, watching her carefully unlatch the harness and roll down the sleeve. Æri's face heated as she recalled Signe's soft fingers grazing her residual limb. A tantalizing sensation heightened by the old wound.

Æri didn't like being touched—especially not there. It was more than the physical pain—she just didn't trust others enough to allow it. The memories that came barreling in every time someone else touched that tender spot were far from welcome. She had lost that part of her arm so many years ago but still sensed her fingers, the palm that once held swords and bows and cocked arrows.

Signe was an exception. Their long friendship had turned into something more.

Æri dragged the sleeve up and slung the harness over her shoulder. Supporting the bionic arm and hand, she clicked it smoothly into the socket with a chink. Her muscles tingled and twitched as tiny electrical currents raced up the nerves of the elbow, shoulder, and into her spine. She never got used to that odd awareness, the vibrating tremble of her limb and mind relinking but not quite regaining the full sensation in the lower arm, the fingers not feeling entirely solid or real.

Wriggling the myoelectric joints, she stretched her forearm out the window into the rising mist. Her lips pursed, and a sharp whistle penetrated through the settling storm.

His high-pitched call echoed. In an instant, a gyrfalcon, coated in white feathers and black-speckled wings, swooped into view. Her shoulder muscles strained as Æri leaned farther out. Black talons secured their perch on unyielding metal. His blue bionic eye blinked at her.

It connected them: two beings held together by a device of science, sharing a part of themselves so that one could predict the other's whereabouts or sense danger.

When she straightened, Signe was out of bed, getting dressed.

"Leaving so soon?"

"It's my fault for ambushing you last night. I should have remembered you were an early riser." She finished lacing her fur-trimmed boots and tucked in her leather braies. "And you'd have that *thing* accompanying you."

Æri feigned a hurt expression. "Gyr is *certainly not* a thing."

"Right, then we are *certainly not* lovers." Signe smiled sweetly, a dimple forming in her right cheek. She flung on her elk vest and headed for the vaulted door.

Gyr puffed up his feathers, sensing Æri's intentions, and stretched his wings. In a wisp of air, he flew out the window into the fog-covered landscape.

With three strides, Æri was at Signe's side. She rested her hand along Signe's hip, anchoring her; the other moved slowly over her ribs and chest until her fingers slid up Signe's neck, holding her in position. Her lips grazed Signe's ear. "I beg to differ." Æri tipped Signe's face backward, snagging her gaze. She broke it to trail her lips down. "Shall we challenge that statement further?"

Signe arched, but a knock rapped the pine door before she could respond.

Both swiveled toward it.

"Yes?"

"The queen requests your presence."

Æri let out a huff. "Not now..." She placed her lips onto Signe's.

Her second-in-command pushed away and flicked the tip of Æri's nose, laughing. "Maybe it will be your turn to ensnare me tonight. You can trap me in those long limbs of yours." Signe's blue eyes sparkled as she gathered the rest of her things.

"Is that an invitation?"

"Definitely not in this chamber." Signe slid the bolt free. "Let's go. You mustn't keep *the queen* waiting."

Why had Brynja summoned her so early? Æri's mind raced through the possibilities as the sentinels fumbled with the locked door leading to the keep's southern tower.

Upon entering the throne room, the alloyed scent of blood hit her in a sickening gust.

"My Queen." She dropped as low as her knees would take her, exaggerating the bow to hide the wrinkle in her nose. Despite her duties as Særenfell's huntress, blood never boded well with her stomach.

"Get up, Æri." The queen jeered. With a flick of the hand, she gestured toward her court. "The two of you—out. Take the body with you." Women with the same moon-white hair as the queen's shuffled from the tower room, stiffly hauling the mutilated corpse behind. Blood streaked the floor by the table. A red line trailed out the door.

"And do not call me *queen*. Not you of all people, *Liværi*."

The queen sat high on her ore throne—a flash of light in the low-lit chamber. Her snowy mane was arranged loose and gossamer, clinging to her shoulders and upper arms like spider silk. A silver crown, long with thorns, perched upon that ethereal white. Despite the hearth's blazing fire at the north end, ink-black pelts enwrapped her. Iron-tipped gloves remained on her hands, stained with rust, tools she used to pull out that man's heart.

"I thought you appreciated the title."

Howling winds echoed off the walls, and Æri exhaled visible puffs of air—none formed in front of her queen.

"Not from you."

"How are you, Brynja?"

"I am fine."

"Any new changes to report?"

Brynja studied her gloves, then removed each spiked finger one by one to reveal ordinary, if not a little pale, hands underneath. Tossing them aside, she pensively rolled her black velvet sleeve to expose a silver-blue torc around her upper arm. A white fingernail traced the intricate threads of metalwork, spun into place to create a solid band. Her eyes shot to Æri's right arm.

"You're not wearing it."

"No."

"*Our* mother gave us these," she said, glaring, "and you refuse to wear it because it associates you with *me*."

Æri broke the queen's ice-blue glower. "It reminds me of her as well."

"Just because she and I shared the Blodlyst does not mean you should forget we, too, share a familial blood."

"It is for what she *did*, Brynja," she retorted. "I do not wish to be reminded of that every waking hour."

"Wear your birth band."

Æri opened her mouth to protest, but Brynja held up a hand. "That is a command from your queen."

A pause and the queen's tone softened. "The Blodlyst killed her too. Should that not be enough for you to forgive?"

"Forgive?" Æri shut her eyes. Forgive whom? Her sister or her mother? A familiar burn vibrated through her limbs and stung her throat. It was too soon to be talking about this.

Their mother, the former queen of Særenfell, who shared Brynja's ghost-white hair, had died less than a year ago—sealed in another tower within the keep, the Blodlyst devouring her mind. At night, Æri thought she still heard her screams on the wind.

"Ironic, is it not?"

Æri opened her eyes at her sister's words.

"Our mountains burst with ore, and yet it is lacking in our own flesh."

The unnecessary reminder rankled.

"Not for everyone," Æri whispered. She had been fortunate; Æri was born with lightly tanned skin and black-brown hair. This did not change in the many, many years following the Split. Her sister and mother did not have such luck.

Both born on the night of the Split, Brynja was pulled from their mother's womb before the quake occurred and Æri minutes after. Perhaps something in those moments, that urgency of time, of life and birth, exposed Brynja but not Æri. At first, they appeared identical, but as Brynja grew each day, her hair and skin changed, the Blodlyst taking its form. Now it was almost impossible to tell they were sisters, let alone twins.

"Why has my queen summoned me?" The smell of metal and blood made Æri impatient.

"I told you not to call me that!" Brynja bared her teeth, rising. She stepped toward Æri, rage now possessing her features.

Rather than maintaining Brynja's stare, Æri diverted her gaze as if faced with a threatened creature. "Remember to breathe, Brynja."

After a moment, fabrics rustled, then came the methodical breaths: two in, one out. When Æri lifted her head, Brynja had sunk back into her throne. Her features pinched, fingers hooked, jabbing into the armrests.

"The court is emptying the ironbloods faster than they are being caught. We need more."

"Is the Blodlyst spreading again?" Æri met her sister's eyes. Blood vessels webbed into the whites. Did she see red amongst the blue irises too?

"I don't know...possibly."

Brynja had enacted stringent rules after the king was killed. Those hunted must be fully settled and foreign. Under no circumstances were they to cull children. These rules kept the Blodlyst at bay—kept those inflicted from destroying their realm.

"Is there anything I can—"

"I have it under control. What I need you to do is hunt."

"We are doing our best, Brynja. The prey seems to be avoiding our usual hunting zones. I can't scour the entire Bogs—our fuel cells would run out." Æri held back her thoughts on how she had grown to hate herself. She'd stopped looking at the men's faces when she snared them. They were the enemy, yes, but they had lives—pasts, presents, and futures—and she took that from them.

"Best?" Brynja's face crumpled. "*You're* not ruling with this illness, with this burden. You're not the one locked in this tower. You have no idea what it's like."

"We'll find another way—a cure."

"Right now, there isn't one. *This* is what keeps our court satisfied, what keeps them tame. It's been this way for centuries." The red in Brynja's eyes shined clearer now.

Brynja did not kill for amusement, Æri knew this...but she saw the duress of it, how it eroded her sister's conscience—more so than the Blodlyst. Yet what choice did they have? A stranger's life or the collapse of their queendom...thousands upon thousands of lives. Until they had a cure, it was all they could do. All the same, Æri detested the thought of going into the Bogs so soon. She'd just started rereading the archive's scrolls—convinced an answer to the Blodlyst was hidden within the ancient texts.

"Prove you are loyal to this land, to your people, Æri."

"You know I am."

"Then do it for them if not for me. Fly out tomorrow."

~ 3 ~

ÆRI

Æri cursed as she descended the staircase, sliding her hand down its balustrade. Its icy glaze nipped the tips of her fingers. She'd have to spend the day preparing for a week or more of tracking.

And it meant Signe would have to wait.

The two of them bore an arrangement of sorts. It passed the endless time and made life—this never-ending life—amusing for both of them. Besides, the redhead shouldered her own duties to keep her plenty occupied. She'd survive having a cold bed for a few nights.

Æri didn't know if she preferred women to men—perhaps both? It was circumstantial, hardly having an opportunity to compare. After the internal war engendered by the Blodlyst, Særenfell had been visibly wiped clean of men—the disease targeting anyone with higher amounts of iron in their systems—and on the hunt, her mind was in a different place. She compartmentalized herself—her thoughts, emotions, and behaviors—all focused on the task.

Her feet padded each stone step, down, down, down. The stairway spiraled through the fortress's keep and out to lower chambers, heading directly to her workrooms.

It amazed her how the old stones retained their shape after all these years—frozen in time like the rest of them. An endless winter outside and a stone-cold palace within. She knew every twist and turn like the back of her hand, all the gaps and passageways carved into the mountainside, all the dips and secret tunnels hidden behind moth-eaten tapestries. Granted, she'd had a thousand years to learn them, the millennium fast approaching.

When the nine realms ripped from their home world, Glasterra, time had warped. Not stopping per se; some people aged, others did not.

She and her sister ceased aging after their eighteenth year—or maybe nineteenth? Æri couldn't remember. They relied on physical appearance alone, not the passage of time.

She looped behind a stone wall and onto an exterior bridge. Like a saddle between two mountain peaks, the chiseled walkway connected the two lower sections of the fortress. The snow was picking up again, and a bitter wind snapped through her tunic.

Out across the wild landscape, fog tendrils clung to the basins of silver mountains, hiding the broken edge of her lands. Scattered evergreens poked their triangular heads from the white blanket, contrasting the dark stone houses that speckled the small plateau below, bringing to mind Gyr's spotted wings. Beyond that, tiny blue veins of a frozen river mouth twisted in the foothills.

She spun toward the north. Over the Ophinyne Cliffs, Kastald, the tallest mountain in the Western Range, could just be seen. A new layer of crisp snow capped its angled summit.

A whistle pierced the eddying skies, and Gyr flapped into view, leaving small vortices in the mist. Soaring in, he hooked his talons onto her bionic gauntlet and screeched, reminding Æri she had neglected him earlier.

All right, all right, no need to fuss.

She rummaged in her sack for his sunrise treat. Once satisfied, he found a firmer perch on her shoulder, and she trotted to the indoor gallery to get out of the blistering cold.

The expansive bartering hall that once burst with voices of merchants and tradespeople was now devoid of sounds besides the pattering feet of mice. Her heels tapped as she wended her way between its columns and went down another staircase into the base of the fortification.

Æri heaved open the heavy door blocking the way into the workrooms.

The drafting space, a large room packed with parchment, inkpots, and a hodgepodge of vector drawing tools, was mostly empty. Well...except for...

"Morning, Otta." Æri kicked the back of the bench where a lanky woman slept.

"Wha—" Otta shot up in her seat. "Oh...Æri."

Otta's freckled limbs covered a set of unfurled scrolls. The woman possessed a copious amount of unkept mousy-brown hair, and despite it being plaited into two long braids down her spine, whisps of it stuck out in odd places. She rubbed her eyes and prodded the desk for her reading spectacles.

"Up late again?"

Otta expelled a yawn, then chuckled. "And you weren't?"

"Ah, touché."

This castle rarely held secrets. If any existed, her and Signe's nightly rendezvous were not one of them. "I have to go hunting tomorrow."

"Already?" Otta sighed. "I thought you were just out two weeks ago."

"I was, but the queen requires replenishing. They're down to one ironblood in the crypts." Æri suppressed the shudder that riled under her skin every time she thought of those frigid cells, relieved Signe was the one who delivered the men to the tower.

Otta gave her a sidelong glare. Leaving the queen's court without human blood for too long risked havoc.

Ignoring Otta's warning, Æri flipped through some of the open scrolls. "Is the Skimmer fueled up?"

"Yep. I checked it last night." Otta stretched her arms and rose from the bench.

Not only an indomitable researcher determined to find a cure for the Blodlyst, Otta was also a mighty fine engineer.

In the aftermath of the Split, leaving the floating island became impossible. Særenfell, once bordered by oceans, now hovered high above the Bogs. For years, her people were stranded on their own lands, unable to access the old world below.

That was until Otta discovered how to amass energy from their tempestuous storms—fuel made by ether in the glacial lakes, a hydrogen gas. Though precarious to produce, it powered their aircrafts and allowed them to reach the Bogs to hunt.

Æri's bionic arm operated on the same power. Recently, Otta had installed another type of reaper that harnessed the sun's energy, which was convenient when it ran low on the gas created by the storms.

"The Skimmer is all ready to go. But you might want to double-check the undercarriage. You scraped the belly up pretty rough on your last trip. I did what I could, though I think your eyes might catch anything I missed."

While Otta was the brains, Æri participated in the mechanics. She'd developed a knack for mending broken parts. After her father died, they transformed his old hobby shop into their workrooms. The adjacent space expanded into a network of caves under the fortress, which functioned as a perfect dwelling for their flying machines.

Æri strode toward the hangar as Gyr flew to his coop at the lip, finding a good resting spot to preen his feathers.

The Skimmer, a one-person glider, could haul three to five ironbloods in its net. But her crew, the Narkrye, used the Boars.

She pushed herself under the Skimmer's body, the wooden dolly sliding to the area where she had scuffed its metal shell. As she ran a hand over the refurbishments, it felt even as ever. Just some minor scratches remained on the exposed belly. Better than she expected.

Æri smirked. When Otta requested to learn how to mend her inventions, Æri taught her what she knew. Now it was Æri's turn to master some of Otta's knowledge...if only she could convince herself to study more of the old scriptures. Sitting for long hours deciphering ancient languages was not exactly how she liked to spend her days.

Despite this, she forced herself to do so, if only to unearth a clue to the Blodlyst. And though Otta wouldn't admit it, Æri knew she welcomed the company in the dingy archives. Situated on the floor just above the hangar, the rooms were grimy and cold, containing row upon row of rotting tomes. She often found a furry rodent or two gnawing on a leather spine.

Æri half believed the ancient folk still haunted shelves—people who inhabited the caves in days of yore, prior to the fortress's construction.

Otta was munching on a nut roll and drinking a steaming brew when Æri stepped back into the drafting room. "You better go and grab some breakfast before the rest of the womenfolk get to it." She swallowed a chunk of the roll. "Are you thinking of taking the Narkrye tomorrow?"

Æri shook her head and wiped some of the propeller's grease onto a ragged cloth. "I'm not planning on picking up more than two. And that's if we're lucky. I'll send a signal if I catch more."

Their temporary cages in the Bogs should hold the ironbloods for a few days until the Narkrye could come and assist. However, on the last bout of hunting, she hadn't been able to find more than that. Her crew would be disheartened—they lived for the hunt—but the Narkrye would have to satisfy their hunting itch another way.

This was why Æri hesitated outside the doors to the warming kitchen, debating whether to skip breakfast and let her stomach rumble until noon. Hearty smells of the morning meal wafted from the doors' gap. Boisterous chatter rose from within.

Sighing, she jerked on the wrought-iron handle.

Signe, Disa, Eydis, and Toril lounged around the battered refectory table. Though initially meant for royal food preparation, the room had been requisitioned by the Narkrye since their inception.

A giant concave oven took up one of the walls, and heat radiated from its roaring fire. Chopped pinewood sat tucked away in a separate nook. Sap leaking from hacked ends, the new wood contrasted with the seasoned kindling—meaning at least one of her Narkrye woke ere dawn.

The women laughed around plates of wild pheasant, nut rolls, and fried eggs half-eaten.

"Where's Yrsa?" Æri stole some eggs off Signe's plate.

"Either sleeping in or throwing knives in the courtyard." Disa shrugged, combing her fingers through her cropped black hair.

"I wager she's sleeping," Toril said, and flipped wild honey-blond tresses from her eyes.

Eydis, a chestnut brunette with a wicked scar down her right jaw, scrunched her mouth to the side. "Nah, she looked like she wore a temper at supper last night. She's definitely throwing knives."

"Good, well, either way..." Æri was satisfied. She did not want to deal with Yrsa's irritability when she told them they would not be needed.

"We heard a little rumor that the queen wants you to go out again." Signe broached the topic nonchalantly.

News traveled fast in the fortress. Æri should have known they were informed.

"Will you require our services, or will it be like the last two hunts?"

"She's already had *your* services, Signe."

Signe kicked Toril in the shin hard, causing her to grimace. Toril lunged to knock the tea out of Signe's hand, but Æri intercepted by blocking the third-in-command's arm. Disa rocked her stool back and smirked at the almost brawl.

Æri cringed. Gods and goddesses above, they needed a release.

"No, I won't be needing the Narkrye, not for this one."

Disappointment glistened in her crew's ice-blue eyes, and she exhaled. "It's too dangerous to take out all the Narkrye. There may only be one or two ironbloods to catch." She gulped down some lukewarm tea. "Eydis, you, Toril, and Yrsa can run patrol around the island tomorrow. And Signe and Disa can snare some elk or crag boar—in case I come back empty-handed."

"I think the queen prefers bear," Disa said, "when men cannot be had."

"If you can snare a bear, all the better. We need more blood. But abide by the laws. No youth, no mothers, and make sure enough are on the lands to warrant a capture. I haven't seen a bear out of the caves for a few months, but it might be because of the storms."

The Narkrye nodded in unison.

Æri fell into silence while sipping on her tea, rubbing her thumb back and forth over the embossed surface of her pewter mug as she smoothed her tongue over a chip on her incisor. The abrasive texture of it helped her focus. She was priming her mind for the hunt tomorrow. Her crew knew how much concentration it necessitated. It was imperative to have all her senses alert if she was to succeed.

Bright light reflected off the snow, flickering on the outer lip of the hangar.

Signals and instruments, lights, fuel cell, propellers, and autopilot—all in working order.

"Before-takeoff checks complete!"

Æri strapped the harness and pack securely to her back and pulled down the monocle to cover her right eye—another one of Otta's inventions, allowing her to see from afar in the murky light of the Bogs. It also gave her access to Gyr's robotic one, programmed to function with her arm.

Her torc circled the other, hidden beneath her leathers and hugging her skin. It felt foreign there, but her queen demanded it. Worn by the last surviving heirs, or so their mother had said, it was a symbol of their old world.

Lastly, she sheathed a dagger in her boot in case of close combat, although most of her hunting was done from above.

The Narkrye—Eydis, Toril, and Yrsa—were poised in front, straddling their Boars. Swirling blue motifs of their hunting paint adorned their faces. If someone or something tracked Æri, the crew patrolled the main island. Another reason to leave the Narkrye behind. They weren't the only hunters out there.

Æri couldn't find Yrsa in the barrack's courtyard yesterday, nor was she sleeping in the quarters. Nonetheless, she showed up today, her ash-blond hair tied into a low knot.

She seemed different. A streak of her hair glowed lighter than the rest.

Suspicion niggled its way into Æri's thoughts as she fixated on that strand of white. Most with the Blodlyst had already turned on Særenfell. Marked by the loss of the color in their hair and skin, their personas shifted, senses heightened. A new case hadn't emerged for centuries, the Narkrye confining those afflicted to the queen's court.

Æri blinked, immediately dismissing the idea. The sun was out—perfect weather for entering the Bogs. She ought to take advantage of it and focus on the hunt.

She raised her arm. The Narkrye flew out first.

Gyr dove from his coop, his spotted wings spreading wide to lead the way.

Then her turn.

Æri relished the sharp drop. Her stomach flipped as they dove past the cliff wall. Brisk currents lashed at her exposed face.

This was freedom.

She soared through the high peaks of the Western Range, passing the Ophinyne Cliffs and over scattered villages. Their shale-roofed houses shrank into toy-sized dwellings. Mountains floated around them in tiny islets, having detached and fractured farther into the skies during the Split.

On one, the forgotten temple of Skathi gleamed in the morning light, its silver spire still standing after years of neglect. Now too treacherous to land on, it bore no visitors, save for Æri's infrequent outings with her Skimmer.

As a custom, she sent a silent prayer to Skathi, goddess of the winter, the hunt, and the mountains, before plummeting into the Bogs' thick mists.

~ 4 ~

ÆRI

Present - Crash

The Bogs

The world spun in an angry flurry of blacks and reds. Her hands fumbled for the ripcord and yanked. Spans of plumy fabric unfurled, rapidly tugging Æri from the cockpit. Her neck snapped back as the parachute ballooned.

It would have worked outstandingly well *if* she had not crashed in a narrow ravine.

Its fabric snagged on a protruding rock above. The ropes attached to her pack swung, slamming Æri into the sharp wall. She swallowed a yell when something in her side cracked. Her inhalations came in fast and shallow. It felt like a knife had pried her ribs apart.

Intense heat and a lick of pain rolled over her body. Her lower limbs dangled above magma, which sizzled and hissed. A wave of vertigo overtook her—not from the height but from the wreckage.

At the bottom of the ravine—about twenty paces below—the ruins of her Skimmer stuck out of the semi-fluid. Her supplies burned in the cockpit, and the metal shell warped against the heat, gradually sinking into the earth.

Another shiver stole through her.

She drew in a breath and regretted it. Sulfur stung her throat, and the scent of rotting pheasant eggs pervaded her nose. Her eyes watered, and she coughed, hiking up her wool cowl. Its carbon-infused fabric provided immediate relief, and the scratchy burn eased.

Æri scanned the base again. No trace of Yrsa or her Boar. She doubted her Narkrye had survived the crash, assuming she lived after that arrow. Æri kicked herself for not heeding the first warning signs; irrationality was one of the first precursors of Blodlyst.

She arched her head to the murky sky. The arrow had come from atop the ravine. But from whom? And where did the bait go? No sign of him scaling the serrated walls.

Æri weighed her options. She could unlatch the pack, but doing so risked another fall, and she would likely break a limb if she attempted it. Aside from that, magma covered the ravine floor. Her only choice was to head up.

The ascent looked precarious, but the honeycombed rocks might provide a good foothold. Some even created makeshift ledges, one of which held her parachute. She had little option unless she wanted to be found hanging, a treat for whatever creatures prowled the canyon at night. And Æri did not care to glean which beast claimed this rift.

She flicked a switch on her bionic arm, intending to shift her vision to Gyr's.

Thank the gods she still possessed that and the monocle.

It jammed—no signal. "By Skathi's Spear!"

Where was Gyr?

Not circling above...but pillared rocks obscured most of the view. He wasn't senseless enough to try to fly down here like she had been. His absence pulled, the pressure of it rattling at her skull's base, unbalancing her.

She cursed again. It was stupid to follow Yrsa like that, but she was her kin, not by blood but through the sworn oath of the

Narkrye. They did not leave their sisters. She would've done the same over again, even into a pit of bubbling tar or the powerful jaws of a Bog beast. Æri never abandoned her own.

Prodding her waist, she winced as she identified her cracked rib—one of the lower ones. Everything else was intact: some bruising and scrapes but nothing more. She swung her body weight toward the wall, latching her bionic hand to a fissure; the other hooked onto a lip in the stone. Pausing a moment to find her footing, she inhaled tersely as the rib throbbed, then began to ascend.

Though her hands were calloused from days of combat training and scaling the Ophinyne Cliffs, she took caution. Æri was built for climbing. Her arms and legs were lean with muscle, but she neither had the right gear nor was the toothed pumice the same as Særenfell's rock. It cut and scratched her palm like tiny shards of glass.

Lifting herself onto the perch, she caught her breath and unhooked the parachute's fabric from the extended rock face.

Æri tore at her undertunic's hem and wrapped the rough fabric around her bleeding hand. Sweat dripped between her shoulder blades and under her breasts.

Estimating the distance from the base, she calculated she had climbed a third of the way. Diluted sunlight seeped through the haze.

It must be past noon.

Tucking the durable fabric of the parachute away, she anticipated its value for later—one of her only forms of protection against the Bogs' elements.

Fortunately, her pack contained some basic supplies. The water skin and a handful of dried meat weren't sufficient for the entire trek back, but it would help her get out of this gods' forsaken hole.

Prior to this point in the ascent, she'd used the parachute's ropes like a belay. Now, without the cord's security, she'd have to free solo.

Her muscles shook with fatigue every time she stretched her arm. Æri forced herself to be attentive, watching her handholds and maintaining the weight close to her torso, hyperaware that one misstep could send her plummeting.

Grit fringed her eyelashes, and she fought to keep from rubbing them. Her nailbeds bled, cracked from digging into the stone, and her side ached.

With one more push, she hoisted herself over the rim. Her vision reeled in and out, blurring around the edges. Slumping onto the dry earth, Æri gasped, filling her lungs with the muggy air, relieved she'd made it with some daylight to spare.

But relief was short-lived as a set of scuffed black boots entered her wobbly frame of view.

Skull pounding from exertion, her mouth tasted sour, and her stomach's contents undulated up and down her throat. Æri hurled her sparse meal all over those scrapped-up boots. The Bogs' relentless heat made her stomach bubble, and she heaved again.

As Æri raised her head, a dark brown eye slammed into hers, the gaze so terrorizing it felt physical.

She choked back the sour bile that climbed her throat once more.

Æri strained to refocus, scrambling for her senses to right themselves.

A man, clad in black-and-russet leathers, loomed over her. An armored chest plate covered a sleeveless tunic. Its burgundy fabric hung open at the sides where leather chaps shielded his legs. His long dark hair was pulled from his face in coiled back rows. Old wounds riddled his muscular arms, the skin dark from days in the sun.

From his right eyebrow to his thin mouth, a silver laceration disfigured his face, a patch hiding the presumably mutilated eye underneath. His nose looked as if it had been broken once or twice.

He could be twenty-five or five hundred for all she knew, though his physical age put him at the former.

When Æri's vision finally settled, her heartbeat doubled. She was in the presence of not one man but *four*. Save for the cowls covering their noses and mouths, the three others, all of whom varied in size, were clothed like the first. Each brandished a seared V on their right forearm. She instantly recognized the wiry man used as bait.

Curse the Draug and her luck!

Hunters. These men were hunters. And not just any by the looks of their uniforms, but from Fíronbec—the Realm of Man.

Panic twitched in her gut, and she wobbly scrambled to her feet. Swiftly unlatching her pack, she tossed it between them, knowing she'd have to leave it if she was to outrun them. Æri withdrew the sheathed dagger in her boot, throwing the one with the eyepatch—undeniably their leader—an unyielding glare, prepared to fight.

The men glowered at her with predatory intent, scorching her face like the brand on their arms. She refused to surrender. Her pulse sped wildly, her empty core clenching with what they could do to her. Fíronian hunters were brutal, unbending beings. Those caught were never seen again.

"A Lamiæn," the huntsman with reddish-brown hair whispered to the leader, his tone somewhere between wonderment and hate.

Lamiæn was what the Fíronians called her kind—all of those from Særenfell. No doubt she was recognized by her ice-blue eyes and what remained of the painted patterns across her face. The Narkrye ritually adorned their ancient battle symbols before each hunt.

"There's little use, girl," the leader said in Særenian, his accent heavy and rich, like pine sap. The brown eye glimmered.

She didn't flinch from her fighting stance, not giving in to his sneer. Æri sensed he liked this, seeing his prey cornered. His eye paused on her bionic arm, probably weighing what she could do with it.

Words of a childhood rhyme taught to her by her father surfaced from memory: *Eyes of brown, do not bow down.*

Well, neither would she.

"I don't intend to leave this world on my back," she bit out in the same tongue. Æri knew their language well enough. She had been tutored in it as a child, and then had it reinforced from her years studying with Otta, but she was not about to let them know that.

His mouth twisted. "Well, too bad. Because that is exactly how you'll be leaving *this* world." The leader raised his hand and signaled to one of his men.

Before she could advance her blade, weighted ropes flew from the man's hands. They found their hold, twining her arms and waist. She grimaced as the binds squeezed into her injured rib. A stinging flared across her skin as if she lay in a bed full of poisoned nettle, and her blade fell from her grip. Whether it was the electric bolts, the exhaustion from the climb, or simply the Bogs' heat, Æri's body could not hold out, and consciousness faded.

The rumble of wheels nudged Æri awake. She opened her eyes to darkness, and panic stormed through her as if a god had ripped into her rib cage. Her throat clogged, the air stopping, incapable of reaching her lungs. Her arm pulsed.

Not real. It wasn't *real.*

Taking a shallow inhale, she nicked her hand over splintered wood, remembering where she was—the Bogs' humidity reminder enough that she wasn't in an icy cell. The fractured memory receded with her slowing breaths.

With its wane, other physical aches became apparent. Æri winced when she tilted her head. A throbbing pain radiated from the back of her skull down to her shoulders. She tried to move her arms, but a rope still bound them. Mercifully, they no longer tingled. As she moved her fingers on both hands, some of the tension in her chest relaxed. They hadn't taken her arm.

She probed the shadowy interior of the wooden box. Two iron-barred windows, one in the front and one in the back, let in a negligible amount of light. Pushing her body upright, she attempted to stand, but her legs gave in.

Spent. Thirsty. So thirsty. Her throat scratched, and the muscles stuck there when she swallowed, too sore to move. The remaining hunting paint itched, flaking on her cheeks, and she scrubbed her face against the wall to quell the irritation. Her head pulsed—undoubtedly from retching out what little she ate.

Something sloshed in the corner—a trough. *Water.* It had to be.

She dragged herself to the basin. It smelled a little like dry grass, but otherwise, nothing rancid or foul. Like a farm animal, she dunked her head in, not caring what might be floating in it. It was water, somewhat earthy, but nothing out of the ordinary. She gulped large mouthfuls, satiating her throat and belly. When she had her fill, she flopped back against the wooden wall.

Reason slowly returned and her senses cleared.

Why was a trough in this cell to begin with?

Of course.

The Narkrye left water in cages for the ironbloods. The huntsmen wanted whatever they trapped to *survive.* But for what? She didn't want to know if it was anything like what her Narkrye did.

The notion of it brought back the pursuit in the Bogs, of Yrsa...How had she turned so quickly? One of her best Narkrye sisters died because of the cursed Blodlyst. It made her doubt her judgments, her mind as jumbled as her body felt trying to pinpoint the root cause.

She lay there for a time, between sleep and consciousness, willing strength back into her legs. With the replenishment of water and the short respite, she bit through her pain and propped herself against the tottering wall, lolling her head toward the front window.

Æri squinted, unsure what she was seeing, some movement...animals...but scaled? Her breath caught.

Through the bars, two powerfully built beasts towed her wooden box. They were unlike any other animal she'd seen in her realm. Three—possibly four times the size of elk, they marched on four limbs covered in black iridescent scales.

These animals must originate from the Bogs—or in any case, partially from them. Most Bog beasts didn't walk but rather crawled or slithered.

Their massive hooves treaded on a kind of road that only revealed itself seconds after they stepped down on it. If the Fíronians built this hidden road, what other things had they constructed? Her mind whirled.

Beyond these beasts, she counted three more wooden cages, one for each huntsman to manage.

Another jolt of terror shot through her, the tips of her fingers prickling. These beasts, the wagons they towed, all of it...she needed to escape. Her bionic arm tingled up her shoulder as she struggled against the ropes.

Her arm! How had she forgotten?

Though useless strapped to her side, she remembered long ago, Otta had added another defense mechanism within its frame: tapered fins hidden in her forearm's lateral side. They were forged from their strongest ore, arium, extracted deep from within their mountains.

Æri had never had any use for them before but sent Otta a prayer of thanks. As instructed, she angled her forearm, tensing the muscle in her upper arm to free the blades.

Nothing.

Maybe she signaled the wrong muscle? Which one was it?

She strained her biceps, trying to isolate one that would trigger the release. There, a small click from the arm. Blades sliced through the rope.

Her arms wriggled free. This small success renewed her vigor. She moved toward the back window: only one wagon stocked with hunting gear. No men. If she snuck past it undetected, she might have a running start. As a swift sprinter, she could make it to the outcropping of rocks beyond the path—a good cover and well worth the shot.

Her blades sliced through the locks on the door, shearing the metal as if it were butter. Soon, it swung on its hinges.

She edged herself down the bumping wagon, earth moving beneath the wheels.

Æri jumped. Expecting to fall into tar or marsh, she rolled to lessen the impact, but her back scuffed a sure ground.

Ignoring the throbbing at her side and her screaming muscles, she found her footing and bolted onto that unseen road. She'd have no other opening if she didn't push herself now. This was it.

Æri made it ten paces on the road before hearing a heavier stride. Adrenaline pumped through her body. Whoever they were, they were catching up quickly—too quickly. She pushed harder. Her legs and arms shrieked in protest. She begged them to move faster. *Ignore the pain. Ignore the pain.* Her erratic breaths accelerated.

She flicked her eyes around the rugged terrain. The outcropping was still too far. Beyond the road, only a flat marsh fizzed. Sweat dripped into her eyes, and she swiped it with her fingers.

The thuds grew closer.

She'd have to fight.

Æri reeled around to face her pursuer.

The lead huntsman was a step behind. Her arm whipped out, aiming for his leather-armored abdomen. He moved quickly, but her blades made their mark, carving through the plated material. The blow reached skin—just a surface scratch, the glint of blood indistinguishable against his burgundy tunic. He snarled, showing teeth, but whether in anger or in pain, Æri couldn't tell. She recoiled, ready to swing again, this time aiming lower. Again he evaded her, jumping out of her arm's path.

They leaped in and out of each other's reach. The huntsman was wearing her down—a cat playing with its food. Just like any skilled hunter would, she'd give him that credit. The set vehemence in his eye stripped her bare, and she wanted to look away. Why did he look at her like that? Like he needed to rip her guts open.

He hardly made a sound as he escaped her blows. Despite his size, he moved as a snow leopard stalked its prey, deliberate and agile. Her slashes became more frantic and less fluid as she fatigued.

Seeing her falter, he went in. Æri careened back, attempting to avoid his lunge, but it was too late. He pinned her to the heated ground, gripping her bionic arm in his large hand while avoiding the blades. Effectively immobilizing and twisting it away, he slammed the arm onto the road's surface, its fins lodging into the dark earth. His powerful thighs blocked her outer legs. He loomed ominously above her, their chests heaving against one another.

Terror spiked, her vision wavered, and her lungs constricted. She was trapped.

No, not a cell. Not darkness.

Irrational. This feeling was irrational.

With her human arm, she made a last attempt to reach for his face, clawing for his right eye. But he turned his head, and her hand hooked the patch, tearing it away. He pinned that one, too, shifting his weight forward, holding both her arms in an iron grip with his legs.

Æri writhed, kicking with her legs. His grasp was firm. It produced no pain besides her own exhausted body and aching side. But inside, inside, she screamed, her fear racing up her spine.

The huntsman leered, panting, his undamaged eye scanning her face. His other, a grotesque, hollowed space of misshapen skin where an eye ought to be, drilled into her. She turned away, finally unable to look at it.

He drew his face close. "Coward. Too gutless to look at your own work?" The huntsman laughed bitterly, and the resentment in it went to the pit of her stomach, making her cringe. "Did you think I wouldn't remember?"

She blinked, not understanding.

"*Look at it.*"

Still twisted away, his breath blew hot on her face.

Æri wasn't a coward. She suppressed the rising anxiety. Her nostrils flared as she bore her eyes back into his—out of defiance and hate for this man who made her powerless.

Why was he forcing her to look at the gruesome thing?

He let out another vindictive chuckle. "Don't you see it? I was the one that got away."

Then she understood. It hit her like a thunderbolt.

He was the hunter.

A mixture of guilt and hatred battled through her. It happened maybe two or three hundred years ago. She couldn't pinpoint the date, her memory muddled with the lost time. His hair must have been shorter then, but something else had changed—possibly his composure, the way he held himself...

Nonetheless, he had escaped *her*.

Æri had sliced right through that eye when she captured him, right to the bone, not bothering to take a close note of his face or his other features. Like every other prey, he was a blood source for her queen and court. Looking at their faces required empathy and compassion, and she had lost that years before.

Æri's squirms waned as he kept his weight on her, trapping her to the earth, until another huntsman came to his aid. The leader hauled her to her feet, maintaining that death grip. Then, before she knew what was happening, he pulled up her tunic's sleeve and unlatched her forearm.

"I'll hold on to this."

Shackled this time with heavy iron manacles, Æri felt like a mass of ore, barely able to move. Her left limb seethed from the abrupt dismemberment. The huntsman shoved her into the wagon cell again, the door fortified with new bolts thanks to the strange technology they possessed.

Her head panged again. She hadn't sensed Gyr...perhaps for the better. Æri willed him to stay away despite the dull whirl in her skull that began when they were separated.

Maybe he would send for the Narkrye?

Under her leathers, she felt the torc rub, secured around sticky skin—the one thing left that may identify her. As the day faded into night, and the wagon's rumbling through the Bogs brought her farther and farther away from Særenfell, the more she lost hope of returning.

The huntsmen pitched their tents overnight, making sure at least one of them stood guard in front of her wagon, rotating shifts throughout the darkness. They threw some bits of dried jerky into her cell—like she was one of their animals. She debated refusing the food. Then, by the time they reached their homeland, she would be worthless, too frail to be of any use. This thought quickly dissipated when she remembered the ironbloods they caught who'd done the same. Her court just devoured them faster, their deaths no less inevitable.

Æri decided if she were to go down, she would fight until the end. So she stomached the scraps of meat.

The caravan jolted to a halt, rousing her from a half sleep.

How long had it been? Four, maybe five days? She couldn't recall.

During the trek, she identified one thing. The leader bore a name, *Rione*. His men used it when they yelled for directions or orders. Although the other wagons obstructed her view of the pack's leader, she recognized his cadence in his answering calls.

"Prohibere!"

The men's strange tongue carried over the Bogs' pops and gurgles and resonated in her cell. Æri strained her ears, picking up bits and pieces, but her knowledge of the Fíronian language was rusty. Something about hunting...a nest...maybe a gully...not much use out of context.

The locks clunked on her door.

"Out," a voice commanded.

When she did not obey, two rough hands yanked her from the wagon, her chains clinking like the strikes of a blacksmith's hammer. She blinked several times as her eyes adjusted to the new light. Little sun peeked through the overcast clouds, but it was brighter than inside that wretched box. She welcomed the weak rays on her paling skin.

"You're coming with me."

Rione dragged her onto a vast field of black rock. It looked out over the Bogs, the terrain all the same with subtle variations; dark hills rolled on the horizon—a stark ocean of black and molten red. No sign of any floating islands, of Særenfell nor Fíronbec.

Steam burst from a geyser several strides away, reminding her of their precarious situation. The hot moisture cooked the side of her face. A brief shudder ran through her bones as she realized what they might want her for—a lure.

It made sense. They hadn't let her bathe, and gods knew she smelled.

But as if to dismiss her apprehension, Rione said, "You're to watch," his tone cold.

"Watch *what* exactly?" she countered, her pitch matching his stone.

"That." He bowed his head in the direction of one of his hunters. The man was riding into the black spans and toward those low hills on some odd creature, a beast akin to a horse—no doubt another half-breed of realm and Bog. Its legs were sheathed in similar black scales to the creatures who hauled the wagons, its stride so fast that it skipped over the Bogs' rough terrain.

How did they get these animals to breed?

True, time was more variable in the Bogs than on the islands, which allowed some creatures that once lived here to adapt to their new surroundings, but the quick changes and shifts made it impossible for humans to settle. Had the Fíronians discovered a way to control this?

She had little time to speculate, for shortly after disappearing into those hills, the rider re-emerged, his satchel now round and bursting with something inside.

His mount was in a full-blown sprint, and with good reason. Behind the huntsman, a creature ten times the size of any man slithered across the black pitted rocks.

"Gods above..." Æri widened her eyes. Flitting them back to Rione, she expected him to prepare for aid. Surely, the rider could not outrun the monster.

"Watch," Rione said, his eye unwavering from the approaching huntsman.

The creature's body stretched impossibly long, covered in thick scales that glimmered like black armor. Its predecessor may have once been a swamp animal, but now it was something entirely new. Despite its short, stocky legs, it ran at an incredible speed. The rider was just paces from a jaw wide enough to devour the man and mount in a readying snap.

Æri tensed as Rione's voice bellowed to the other two huntsmen who lay in wait.

The rider reached back into the satchel, withdrawing a large, oblong stone. Its creamy coloring contrasted against the black of the land.

No. Not a stone, but an egg. He stole the mother's *eggs*. No wonder she was livid.

The rider headed directly toward Rione and Æri, a wild grin plastered to his face while anticipating Rione's command. Rione eyed the other two men, ensuring they were in position—just two men, *two men* to capture a thing that size.

Rione hurled another shout, and the rider threw the egg right back into the crazed beast's jaws. To Æri's surprise, the creature slowed, catching the large egg in its maw as if catching a snowflake. The ruse was enough to distract it. Prepared, the hunters circled the beast with their stinging nets.

It ended all too fast.

The Bog beast, its long snout and squat limbs bound, closed its sad yellow eyes. It didn't attempt to fight back as they loaded it into one of the larger wagons.

Something inside Æri broke then, to see a beast like that resigned to its fate.

Rione jerked on her chains, indicating a return to her wagon. This time, his eye stared right past her, indifferent, his tone soft and all the more lethal for it. "That's why you shouldn't run. It would be in vain."

~ 5 ~

BRYNJA

Sœrenfell

"What do you mean 'she has not returned?'" Brynja dug her fingertips into the ore throne.

Æri's second-in-command averted her gaze to the floor. Her eyes appeared red-rimmed, her face splotched.

"We lost her signal about a week ago. This often happens in the Bogs, so we did not think anything of it. But after the second week, when we didn't receive feedback, we went out to locate her Skimmer. It took some time, but we managed to find it."

"And...?" she pressed, the suspense unbearable. Gripping the armrests, she did everything in her power not to yell at the auburn-haired Narkrye. What went wrong?

"And there were remnants of a wreckage—Æri's Skimmer."

Brynja swallowed hard, trying to keep a level head with this information. Æri acted as her eyes and ears outside of this damned fortress. She was everything Brynja could not be. Her huntress. Her sister—*missing*? Or...No. Not dead. She wasn't dead.

In the thousand years Æri lived on this island, her command over the Narkrye and the hunt was flawless. A few times, she had returned a little beaten around the edges. A nicked lip, maybe a bruised eye, yet alive and well. But now...*now*...

She's finally left us, the voice baited.

"No sightings of a body were reported, and from what we re-trieved from the site, we know she deployed her parachute." Signe's words cut into Brynja's thoughts.

The queen's chest eased, and her grip slackened—a sliver of hope, a chance her sister survived.

But will she return?

Again Signe interrupted her musings. "However, in our survey, we traced other markings—a Fíronian hunting pack. We believe this might have been the cause of the crash." The second carried a restlessness about her, a nervous twitch under the skin. Though she firmly planted her feet, her fingers fidgeted, her hands clasped and unclasped. She withheld something, some information. Æri would not make a mistake like that and fall into the hands of the Fíronians so easily, her skills as a hunter and pilot far superior. And what were the huntsmen doing so close to Særenfell—less than a day's ride from the borders?

The queen cocked her head, beckoning the Narkrye to come closer.

Signe took a few halting steps as if her boots snagged on the stone.

Her smell wasn't right either. Særenfell's sovereigns held keen senses; they were from the wild alps, after all, said to be the de-scendants of the ancient folk, a people who originated from the mountains and forests. The Blodlyst enhanced this acuity, break-ing them from their mortal barriers. Brynja picked up emotions just through the scent that hovered in the bitter air.

The only reason the second-in-command wasn't sprinting down the tower steps was because the Blodlyst had been anchored for the day. Brynja and her court fed that morning. The remaining man lived, but death's door knocked.

"There is more. What are you not telling me, Signe?"

Signe closed her eyes and exhaled. "Your Majesty, I apologize, I—"

"Out with it!" Brynja's shoulders strained as the irritation wormed up her spine. She did not need nor have the time for the Narkrye to hide information.

"Our sixth-in-command, Yrsa, violated directives." Signe's words spilled out. "She did not appear at her post when Eydis and Toril went out on their patrols. Her ruined Boar was discovered close to the Skimmer's wreckage."

"And her body?"

"None found, but the report states she neglected to wear a harness and pack when they took flight. Magma beds were sighted in the ravine where they located the wreckage. We believe she did not make it....and may have been involved with Æri's crash."

The queen nodded. That made more sense. Fiercely loyal to her crew, Æri strove to protect them no matter the cost.

Curse it. How had she lost two of her best Narkrye?

An inkling of remorse tapped on Brynja's thoughts. Once, years ago, Yrsa visited her in her private chambers, defying any ounce of rationality. She seemed to be the only one of the Narkrye to dare it—to brave the ice queen and her lust for blood. Brynja had welcomed her, if just to feel the warmth of a human's touch for one night. But in the subsequent days, Yrsa did not come back.

Brynja sucked in a breath, smoothing her lips together. She debated the worth of risking more Narkrye to locate her sister. If she hazarded a rescue, they'd have to wait. They needed to build another Skimmer and find some way to infiltrate Fíronbec. This could take time. Time she may not have, depending on how much the Blodlyst progressed. And without more ironbloods...she needed the Narkrye to find more feed, to subdue the progress of the disease.

They brought in a bear the other day, which gave Brynja and her court a little leeway but at the risk of breaking the peace. Unchecked hunting on their lands ruined the balance of the island. If they increased it, all her and Æri's hard work would be lost.

"See if you can attain a signal from either Æri's arm or that bird of hers. Tell Otta to start constructing a new Skimmer." Brynja refrained from asking the Narkrye to hunt. She wanted to know if they could find a track on Æri first.

Curse the heavens above! Vallantheia! Why had Signe not come to her sooner? They were days behind.

Though her people took priority, Brynja vowed she'd find a way to get her sister back. She would not—*could not*—abandon her to the Realm of Man.

~ 6 ~

ÆRI

A sharp snap woke Æri from a dreamless sleep. The lid had collapsed over the water trough, and the procession had halted. Another hunt?

Her wagon rocked, then abruptly lurched. Æri slammed into the rear wall, her chains rattling and entangling her limbs. Steadying herself, she planted her knees on the wood, her hand clinging to whatever it could. Æri crawled to the window.

The wagon dangled above the Bogs' basin and continued to rise higher and higher.

Below, sentinels in polished black armor corralled the beasts that once pulled the wagons into open pens built directly on the Bogs' surface.

So this was how they managed to breed the hybrids; raising them down in the Bogs allowed the crossbreeds to flourish.

Æri had long lost track of how much time they spent in the Bogs—she guessed several weeks, possibly a month. Her greasy hair itched against her scalp. She'd probably acquired some nit that nested in the hay from a previous creature. Her torn, stiff leathers, now loose, had blackened further with grime and her own filth. A small hole in the floorboards of the wagon allowed her to relieve herself so she didn't have to sit in her waste, but it also meant the hunters rarely let her out. The men mostly ignored her, save for the flit of brown eyes at the door and food scraps dropped through the slats, left for her to pick through the hay and darkness.

Her Narkrye had not come. She didn't blame her sister for not sending them. Æri would have done the same. Even if they did end up tracking her, deploying the Narkrye this close to the heavily guarded borders of Fíronbec would be like signing their own death warrant.

Still, her chest throbbed with the sting of abandonment. She suppressed its burn—there was no use feeling sorry for herself.

Signe ought to make a fine replacement captain for now. But the cure for the Blodlyst...who would pursue that? If Yrsa had developed the illness, the disease must be spreading again, though it was impossible to judge how fast. Years? Months? Otta had to continue with her research, perhaps enlist Toril or Eydis for help. Neither of them enjoyed reading...but maybe...

An idea ignited, a small light in a dark room. Perhaps untapped information existed here, in Fíronbec. They must have archives comparable to Særenfell's. The light dimmed. If only she wasn't stuck in this gods-awful cell.

Æri slumped back against the wall as the wagon continued its ascension. Though the journey allowed her rib to heal, her muscles had weakened. Æri did what she could in the confined space, stretching her limbs with the chains. Despite reasoning her people would not come, she promised to survive—to escape this new world, and return home one way or another.

"Ouf." Æri flailed her arms as the cell turned, bracing for the whump of wheels hitting solid ground.

More sentinels waited at the top, ready to re-harness the wagons to oxen, as the hunting pack traded their riding beasts for horses.

At the threshold of the floating island, they passed a series of rickety watchtowers, crosshatched with long logs. She did a double take, studying the buildings again.

Strange...They appeared to grow out of the earth like living trees.

Impossible. Her eyes must be playing tricks. They ached with the new light penetrating the cell.

Outside, the sun heated a red stone road, and flaxen grasses edged the route. In the fields beyond, laborers rhythmically scythed crops. No mountains or snowcapped peaks gnarled the land. Instead, golden sun seeped over flat terrain, its rays touching every blade of bleached grass. Never had she seen land without a dusting of white—no cold storms or fervent winds tormented the skies. Without a cloud in sight, the sun baked down on the island.

Despite shedding her heavy pelts before the hunt, her remaining leathers stuck to her skin like glue. Sweat, built between the layers of dirt in her unwashed gear, dried and pulled at small hairs on her skin. She squirmed with the discomfort of it. Compared to the Bogs, the heat was different here, more arid. Her eyes scratched, and her lips peeled.

Æri rested her chin on the windowsill. Fieldhands slashed at the grasses. A curvy form dressed in a homespun robe stopped her work, straightening to watch the procession rumble by. Lines etched her face from long days in the sun, wrinkled and olive brown.

So they *did* have women on Fíronbec.

Æri blinked. She thought the Realm of Man meant exactly that, *man*, assuming women no longer lived in these parts, or at least so openly. Men did exist in Særenfell...they were just rare. Most, if not in hiding, identified as female—Eydis, one of her Narkrye, being one...though they kept her away from the queen's court.

Fields turned to orchards, ripe with familiar and unfamiliar fruits. Whiffs of citrus and apple blended with the pungent odor of horse and oxen excrement. Slowly, these agricultural lands morphed into rural villages, then into towns, their roads lined with tall, elongated trees. The breaks between each settlement lessened, and soon enough, they marched through a city that glistened a golden yellow in the afternoon light.

"Rione! Rione! Rione!" The crowd's uproar drowned the horses' clopping, the noise bounding off her wooden cell and crashing into her ears. Men and women alike yelled in delight at their hunters' return, waving burgundy flags in their fists, their faces full of excitement and awe.

However, as in Æri's realm, one observation remained clear: Not a single child ran or shouted within the festivity's fray.

Hands pinched her arms and shoulders as a pair of guards dragged Æri from the wagon, herding her out like a farm animal. Their hands left her head reeling. Her body buzzed testily as if insects scuttled up and down her back, overwhelmed by the unsolicited input.

She stumbled into a low-lit building that smelled of old hay and clay. The bulky stone walls seemed to compress inward. No sign of Rione and his pack.

The guards pushed her toward the room's center. Chains clunking, she tripped. Mercifully, Æri caught herself before falling onto packed earth.

Sniffs and gulps punctured the silence. Five other prisoners, fettered with shackles like hers, shared the space. As far as she could tell, she was the only woman. They all maintained a human form—short or tall, lanky or broad. One owned a set of slender ears, pointed at the tips and peeking from a shabby gray-green cap.

A guard neared the rumpled group bearing a strange cylindrical object. Ticks and sparks sputtered from the device like a flint striking ore. Before she knew it, he grabbed her right wrist, pressing the vibrating end to the inside. A prick, then a numbing sensation crawled up her veins. When he removed it, a thin red line of raised skin remained.

Succinct and deliberate footsteps came from the other end of the room, and an official materialized in the dim light.

"In the center! Put them closer!" He snapped his demands at the guards.

The official's thin maroon robe, like a sheet of folded paper, pressed tidy and crisp against his form. He ran a hand down the skirt, then raised it to flatten his slick hair. Beside him, a shorter man wearing similar maroon colors translated.

Her ears perked as she recognized an archaic version of her own tongue amongst the list.

"Listen carefully. You are now and hereafter under the ownership of His Royal Majesty, King Remus Cosmin Belisaur of Fíronbec and will be sold into his court and the Curia through the Auctioning. You are not to speak unless spoken to. You shall fulfill your duties without complaint and do as your designated overseer commands. You will be stripped of your current possessions, cleaned, and readied for the bidding process. The Auctioning is to take the course of one to two full weeks, depending on your allocations. If you try to escape during this process, expect to be severely flogged, and food will be restricted. If there is a second attempt, the authority on behalf of the king and Curia will order your public execution."

The prickling from earlier grew, and a wave of disbelief gutted through Æri.

Had she heard wrong?

Something wedged in her throat and her lungs squeezed as if a trussed again by those awful tinging ropes from the Bogs.

When captured, she expected to be a prisoner. Perhaps used as ransom, or even killed...but a *slave*?

Before the Split, an agreement between Fíronbec and Særenfell had long outlawed any form of slavery throughout the realms. Yet the translator just stated she belonged to the king's court. The phrasing had changed but it did not hide the intent. The abruptness of it—the official's words did not feel real. Any semblance of free will she still possessed evaporated. Gone. And now...that title bound her like a tightening noose.

They separated Æri from the others, transferring her into an adjacent chamber, two guards posted outside the door.

A maid with a haggard, austere face removed her chains then stripped off her stale linens and leathers. The woman's mouth crinkled further in disgust when she saw Æri's left arm. "A cripple...they bring back a cripple from the Bogs."

Understanding the maid's Fíronian insults well enough, Æri put her arms behind her back. Something about the way she said *cripple* unnerved her. It felt different. When they obliquely titled her a slave, it cracked that protective shell she had set for the hunt. Now this woman called her a *cripple*. Like a nail on thin ice, it pushed harder on that fractured shell.

Even before crafting her bionic arm, Æri never thought of herself as a cripple. Others had suffered much worse. She just thought of it as another challenge. Since the Split, she and her sister's lives had been chock-full of these tests. They survived them together. They made sure Særenfell endured.

Æri inhaled slowly.

The thought of ripping the maid's own arm off played around in her head, but she held back. They weren't going to kill her. She had that.

As the maid removed Æri's undertunic, the woman started to click her tongue at the flash of silver-blue. *Her birth band*—the torc that looped her upper right arm flared in the low light. With all the distractions, she forgot it was coiled there.

The maid motioned to pull the band off, but Æri jerked away. She had no intentions of letting this skivvy take the last link between her and her sister.

The maid continued tsking and shaking her head as she left the room, only to return with the official, the interpreter, and a brawny guard.

Eyes widening, Æri scrambled to cover her half-naked body with discarded pelts.

"Fabia has indicated you possess something of value." The official's voice was smooth and direct like ice sliding down her neck. He nodded at the guard, who moved to grab her arm. She lashed out, nails raking his face. The guard drew back, cursing as red lines developed on his cheek.

The official motioned again. "Seize her."

The guard leaped. This time, she managed to twist his outreached arm, pinning it between his shoulder blades. Then she planted a kick behind his knees, sending him to the floor. It gave her enough time to scurry to the farthest side of the room.

"Ah, a fighter...*and* you are adept, despite your...deformity." The official's face turned introspective. "We should have been notified ere your admittance." He paused for the interpreter to translate. "Well, it appears the Venators brought you here for a worthwhile purpose after all, contrary to their negligence." He scanned her half-clad form over steepled fingers. "And that torc on your arm...you are not of a lower class."

The man signaled to the guard who'd risen from the floor.

"Remove it."

Æri bristled as the guard reached for her again. She landed a boot to the groin, and he collapsed with an agonizing groan.

The official narrowed his eyes, calling in the two guards stationed outside. "Hold her down."

Æri hissed, her eyes darting between the men. The guards stalled, wary as though regarding a feral creature.

"Hold her down now, you idiots!" The official's face turned bright purple with the delay.

Eventually, they managed to restrain her, albeit not without a struggle. One donned a bruising red eye, and the other dabbed a sleeve to oozing teeth marks embedded in his hand.

The official slinked to where she lay pressed to the cool floor, his face wrinkled in revulsion. "You *will* obey my orders, *Lamiæn*. Let us see how well you truly fight tomorrow in the Arena."

She did not need the faint words of the interpreter to grasp the meaning.

Tomorrow...so soon.

The official pried the torc from her arm with two bony fingers and pocketed it beneath his robes.

They left her in the room with a bucket of cold, soapy water and a tatty sponge. The maid did not return.

~ 7 ~

ÆRI

Æri sucked air through her teeth as she gingerly applied a salve to her wounds. She had found the small jar behind the bucket, a handwritten label naming its purpose. The scuffle left her with a few scrapes, and the nicks started to puff and redden around the openings.

She smeared a glob onto her knee. The greenish-tinged gel smelled of garlic and possessed a limpid, smooth consistency. Her abrasions' itch cooled as the salve coagulated to create a breathable seal. She poked the flexible bandage in amazement—yet another remarkable innovation of this realm.

Following her wound care, she sponged off the caked dirt and dead skin that covered the rest of her body. She lathered her matted hair with a sharp, acrid soap that killed whatever crawled there and turned the water gray-brown. Water dripped from the ends in cold trickles past her legs and onto the floor.

The guards flung a bundle of cloth at her, watchful not to get too close—a modest smock that fell past her knees. Its fabric was finely woven, superior to any of the linens she wore in Særenfell. Æri smoothed her fingers down the garment. The smock's texture reminded her of her mother's old underskirts—items from foreign lands she obtained before the Split. Those, of course, were long gone now.

Unbidden, a memory of her mother's pale hands entwined in a similar fabric surfaced, hands that mended as much as they stung. She quickly pushed it away.

Three new guards came to escort her out of the room, ensuring her ankles and arms were re-chained, her feet left bare. They shuffled down a dark hall, their torches guiding the way to a small chamber.

Another cell.

A pang of homesickness expanded in her chest.

Was this to be her life now? Locked up in cramped and barren rooms? She longed for the openness of her mountains, the lead-paned window in her chamber, and cozy furs—the cool, awakening breeze.

Musty with disuse, this room held only a pallet shoved against yellow stone, a chamber pot, and a wooden water bucket crammed in the other corner. Rays of weak moonlight entered through a barred window in the back, squeezed close to the ceiling. She had a sudden urge to rush over and press her face through the bars, just to feel the air outside, but knew it would be too high to reach.

It remained balmy in the cell, and the simple smock clung to her skin.

The guards left her in the room with a rudimentary oil lamp made from hardened red clay. Tiny, winged insects swarmed the flame. Æri contemplated breaking it and using the shards to form a weapon but decided against it. The pieces would be too small, and she likely wouldn't be given any other light source.

One of the insects landed on her rounded elbow and nipped the skin. She slapped at it, leaving a smear of blood. The site immediately began to itch.

Sitting on the hard pallet, scratching at the new bite, she thought back on the official's words. She was to fight tomorrow. Her strength had diminished after weeks of captivity. Now, in this cell, it was all but impossible to move properly—the room so small that when she stretched her arms, she touched both walls, her left limb grazing the wall by the bed. Would she need to speak as well? Words felt random, untethered and decayed in her mind, like dead leaves. Her tongue clogged her mouth. She understood Fíronian, but since her capture, she hadn't spoken more than a sentence in her own language. She had endured silence before.

Æri pressed the heel of her palm between her brows and exhaled. She wouldn't succumb to her panic.

It wasn't the same cell. It wasn't the crypts.

This one had a window, a small mercy—unlike the one beneath the fortress.

Was this the same desperation Brynja felt in the tower? Her chin trembled.

How much time did her sister have? What if Særenfell had already fallen to the Blodlyst? What if they devoured each other and no one was left when she finally made it home?

No. Æri steeled her nerves. She mustn't think like that. Brynja wouldn't allow it.

She prodded her side and winced. Her broken rib still twinged. It would weaken her during the fight tomorrow. Maybe if she bound it somehow...She'd have to bind her breasts too.

There was nothing of use in the room. Well...except for that.

On the pallet, an unadorned sheet lay wrinkled over the lumpy hay-stuffed mattress. That should do.

Having fallen into a deep but brief sleep, Æri woke abruptly, drenched in a clammy sweat. Moonbeams played on the wall opposite, and it took her a moment to remember where she was.

She desperately wished for it all to have been a bad dream, to be in her bed of furs, Signe's warm body beside her. But the sheets felt wrong, the mattress too lumpy, and the pallet's planks too hard.

Her left arm tickled. She held it up to the moonlight. Bite marks puckered the rounded end. Æri tried not to scratch. They hadn't given her more of the green salve.

She stared at the wavering shadows until they disappeared, unable to fall back asleep.

At dawn, the bitter-faced maid entered, making yesterday's ordeal all the more real.

Fabia held a waxed cloth in one arm and folded garments under the other. Her eyes instantly went to the torn bedsheet, but rather than fussing, she gestured for Æri to remove her smock.

Fabia's scrutiny went to Æri's chest binding and her arm. Muttering something unintelligible, she continued with her task, unlatching Æri's ankle cuffs and handing her a pair of trousers.

"Braccae." The maid pointed at the clothing, then mimed pulling it over each leg, and pointed back to Æri. "You." She then forced a dull-gray tunic over Æri's head and grabbed her foot, strapping on flexible boots with looped fastenings and an open toe. Æri was perfectly capable of doing this herself, but the maid brushed off her attempts.

Finally, Fabia shoved the waxed cloth into her hand. "Food."

Unfolding the bundle, Æri found a stale chunk of bread and a thin cut of meat.

"Eat." She crossed her arms and tapped her foot.

This was barely enough to last the day. What did they expect her to do? Fight on an empty stomach?

But the maid's hard look told her to be thankful to get even the smallest scrap of nourishment. She picked every crumb clean, swallowing the last of it with a ladle of water.

Before leaving, and to Æri's dismay, Fabia re-attached the shackles.

Three guards lounged against the wall outside. They escorted her to a semi-open room that smelled of sweaty bodies and the biting odor of lye soap. At the other end of the room, a set of sliding doors opened out onto a training yard.

Blue sky beckoned. Her first real glimpse of it since she arrived. She could almost feel the warm rays of the morning sun on her skin.

Loud grunts and thuds took her attention back to the room. A handful of men wearing the same gray uniform stretched and jumped in the center; others sparred in the yard. Out of the twenty counted individuals, only two women occupied the space. One fought with the men; the other was binding her wrists on a bench near a wall that displayed combat equipment. Weapons hung like an art exhibit: throwing knives, spears, and crossbows she recognized, but others she was unacquainted with.

"I can take it from here."

A peculiar man about Æri's height approached the guards.

The guards wavered at her side, but after a stern look from the man clad in blue, they returned to their positions against the wall.

He rested a hand on his chin, which touted a well-trimmed beard ending at his jawline, not a single hair out of place, all of which was a bright, bold yellow. His face exhibited neither kindness nor cruelty. His nose was too large for beady, astute eyes. Æri could not tell if they were deep blue or purple. His tunic's sapphire hue reflected in their glassy surface, concealing their true shade.

He squinted, making his eyes even smaller, examining her head to toe.

"This is the first time I've seen your kind...." He spoke in her native tongue, surprising her. She didn't think many knew her language so fluently beyond the hunters and interpreters. Wanting to ask how, she opened her mouth but, recalling the official's words, shut it again.

He dropped his hand and circled her once, stopping his perusal an arm's distance away. Unlike the guards, he showed no fear, utterly unperturbed that she could loop her chains around his neck if she wished.

"What shall I call you?"

His accent was softer than the others, the lilt smoother as he pronounced the end of his words.

When she held back her response again, he did not scowl, merely appeared quizzical.

"I believe I asked you a question. What name may I address you by?"

This time, she did not hesitate. "Æri. You can call me Æri." Her voice came out raspy, broken from disuse.

"Thank you, Æri. You may call me Brennos. While you undergo the three bidding stages, I, Keeper of the fighters, will be in charge of your whereabouts during the day. Do you have any questions for me?"

Questions? Was she not supposed to ask these? Was this a ploy to get her to disobey?

"Let me clarify. This world"—he gestured to the room—"can seem somewhat overwhelming to a newcomer. I, myself, am enslaved. Hence the uniform."

Now that he pointed it out, the cut was comparable to her own. The vibrant blue had distracted her.

"I've resided in Fíronbec for many years, and my ranking falls under the officials who govern the Auctioning. You are not my equal, but the rules differ when you address me. My job is to answer questions. The officials think it helps with—" He took in a breath, rolling the words around on his tongue. "Well, it helps tame the severity of the circumstances."

Ah, so this was what made the process more "civil."

Æri's eyes contracted with suspicion but she spoke anyway. "You mean I can ask you any question I'd like?"

"Yes. Within reason. I will choose to answer how I see fit. So, I'd advise you to ask the right questions."

She considered, remembering the burn on her right wrist—hardly visible now. Just a single red line remained. "What was this for?"

"It is a tracking device. All those from outside of Fíronbec receive one." Brennos held up his own wrist, where a faint line replicated hers.

A tracking device?

Her last scrap of resolve to break free emptied out like a punctured water skin. She had no clue how to remove the thing that coursed through her arm—that's *if* she managed to run again, and Æri didn't want to lose another limb...not yet anyway.

Nevertheless, Brennos' admission told her something else. That he, too, was not from here. She might have guessed, given the color of his eyes. So she tried to focus on this.

"How do you know my tongue?"

"My time as Keeper and my previous life as a soldier gifted me with such exposures. I know many languages."

"And where are you from?" She had so many questions it made it difficult to think. They all overlapped now that she had a chance to ask them. This knowledge of who governed who, and their history, held importance. Knowing one's past was a window inside. It was their roots, the buttress to their future choices.

"I originate from Larkærseim. However, so far from the realm, my powers are limited to bindings and security. Thus my purpose as Keeper."

Larkærseim—the Realm of Magic. He was a *mage*. How in the gods' name did he end up here? Her father's rhyme came to mind: *Eyes of violet hold a secret.*

Æri ruminated over this information, not entirely understanding the cautionary message within. She moved on to the next question that popped into her head. "What building is this?"

"This is called the Castrum. It's a fort within the city walls that temporarily houses those enslaved during the Auctioning."

The Auctioning. Why "Auctioning"? And who were to be auctioned? The fighters? To whom? The king? His court? The official explained little before, and she had only been half listening, her attention focused on that label of slavery. Would the Keeper disclose these questions if she'd ask? There were too many unanswered questions for her to think straight.

"Tell me more about the Auctioning."

"That's not a question. You'll have to be more specific."

"What can you convey to me about the Auctioning? What is it for?"

"It's a multi-faceted system to organize labor and services in the realm."

It sounded like a generic answer. Was he trying to be vague? She'd pry again later when she wasn't so mixed up. She had to think. Her mouth and mind seemed to work in opposite directions.

"What city are we in?" Æri held a speculation. She often came across descriptions of Fíronbec's capital during her time with Otta.

"Méritras."

One of the biggest and most prosperous cities among the nine realms, it seemed to have kept the title even after the Split.

Æri examined her ankles. "When can I have these chains removed?"

"When you train in these rooms and when you fight in the Arena. All other hours you must be bound."

"Am I supposed to fight today?"

He turned to a sundial hanging on the exposed wall—another clue to how this realm operated. So, the Fíronians kept time in terms of hours and days here. Æri suspected the aging process paralleled Særenfell's too.

"Yes. The scrimmage is in two hours."

"How many rounds of the bidding process are there to be?"

"Three. Today is the first round of fighting. The day following tomorrow will be the second. And the last will be in six days—the finals."

"Finals?"

"Winners against winners. If you succeed to this stage, your bidding fee will increase immensely." Brennos smiled, giving a hint of amusement. "We'll see what surprises you have for us. Any more questions?"

Æri shook her head, a little edgy from that smirk.

"All right. Now the guards will remove your shackles, and you may mingle with the others. However, I do not recommend making friends. You will soon be fighting against them, and though we have a no-kill policy...accidents happen."

It was another cold warning, hidden in a set of insouciant rules.

Brennos nodded to the guards, and they reapproached to unlock the manacles around her ankles and arm. Relieved to have them off, she rubbed at the raw rim that emerged where they chafed.

"You are to keep to these rooms and Castrum's training yard. A horn will announce the hour of the fight."

Should she thank the Keeper? Æri didn't know their customs—all her readings pertained to history and what was here before. In the end, she simply bowed her head and turned from him.

Moving amongst the fighters, she eyed them steadily, observing her opponents' movements: the types of punches they threw and which sides they blocked—all while avoiding flying fists and knees.

Æri made her way toward the wall of weapons.

She reached out, intending to select a spear, but the moment her fingertips grazed the shaft, a cutting jolt shot up her arm.

"By Skathi—" Æri clamped down on her curse, not wanting to attract attention as she cradled her hand to her chest. The burn pulsed.

A chuckle broke from behind, and she twirled.

It was the woman on the bench, still binding her wrists. "That's Brennos's doing. He locked them up for the scrimmage. It's just hand-to-hand combat for the first round. No weapons allowed besides these." She lifted her fists, then glanced at Æri's missing forearm. "Or lack thereof."

This woman, too, spoke in Æri's tongue.

Why spend energy talking to Æri, yet not warn her about the ward?

The woman looked as though she could throw a decent blow. She had pulled her light brown hair back, securing it out of her face. It wasn't pretty, but not plain. Intelligence sparked behind her brown eyes.

"I'm Marlena." She held up a leather-bound hand and motioned for Æri to sit beside her.

"Æri." Charily taking the offered seat, she ignored Marlena's outstretched hand. "You're Fíronian..." Æri murmured. "Why are you in here?"

Marlena drew in her fist, unfurling and refurling her fingers as if she intended to do this all along. "My father sold me to pay his debts. Couldn't be married, so"—she shrugged—"I'm here. Luckily, he failed to have a son...trained me in some of his old war combating...Eh, kept them from putting me in the fields or the Lupanar—those pleasure houses. Never want to be sold there," she said shuddering, and indicated to the room. "Most of us here are indentured."

Brown did indeed flash in most of the fighters' eyes.

"You do get the odd dwarf or giant that comes through. Rarely anyone from Bolcán or a Fae from the Isles. I've heard they're a bit harder to catch. I thought the Lamiæn were too. Yet here you are."

Marlena's eyes narrowed in on Æri, looking at her inquisitively.

Was she going to ask how she came here? Not keen on letting strangers know, her hunter's instincts kicked in: Have others talk, reveal little.

"I think I saw an elf yesterday," Æri said, redirecting.

"Oh! Is he in the training rooms?" Marlena took the lure, her brows lifting as she gazed out to look amongst the fighters. "Usually, they save the Fae for the king's entertainment."

Æri pointed him out. The elf was practicing in the yard, keeping to himself. No longer wearing the cap, he had tied his long hair to cover his pointed ears, making it difficult to identify him as Fae. At least it averted Marlena's attention.

Æri mulled over Marlena's previous words. No harm in asking her own questions.

"You said you couldn't be married?"

In Æri's realm, the ritual represented a deep connection between two individuals. Partners never had to marry by law, making all couples, married or not, equally respected in Særenfell.

"I kind of fell for my tutor...and, well, he was already married." Marlena flapped her hands as if it explained what happened. "And let's just say Fíronbec can be...harsh on those matters."

Æri tipped her chin, vaguely understanding.

Marlena continued. "He taught me your language...Særenian, right?"

"Yes." Æri crooked her head, careful to deflect the questions again. "Do many people speak it here?"

"Only those with an education. It was the closest realm, so it's taught in the curriculum, but we have little chance to use it now. And the officials prefer to use their translators." Marlena leaned forward, looking at the sundial.

"Here. You should wrap some of this over your fist." Marlena didn't wait for Æri's reply as she picked up her hand in hers and began swaddling the leather strips across her knuckles. Æri flinched, but Marlena was quick, securing the covering and dropping her hand before she could pull it away.

"And we ought to start warming up."

They managed to get a lap in around the yard before a horn blared through the training rooms.

~ 8 ~

ÆRI

The light intensified as they approached the antechamber, making Æri squint and turn her head away. From the Castrum, they had traveled through winding tunnels that seemed to go in circles, disorienting Æri. And when the fighters finally stepped out onto the pit, a colossal complex glistened before them.

Statues resembling gods marked each level—lesser gods toward the top, and rows upon rows of vacant benches soared toward Vallantheia. Seated in the bottom tier was a sparse crowd of well-dressed men. Yet, a gilded section at its center remained empty.

"That's where the king and his advisors sit for the Games." Marlena leaned into Æri. "I don't think they'll be here today. Too early in the rounds."

"Have you seen any of the Games?"

"One or two. I sat in the nosebleeds. Way up there." Marlena pointed to the very top rim, which arched inward. "We seldom saw anything. Never expected to be on the Arena floor, though...A part of me wishes I was still in the nosebleed seats rather than receiving one firsthand."

Æri lifted an eyebrow. "I have a feeling you'll be the one causing nosebleeds."

"Let's hope so." Marlena grinned.

Æri skimmed the crowd again, attempting to familiarize herself with some of their faces. None of the men looked to be from the hunting pack—or what did the official call them? *Venators.*

Wait.

Her eyes snagged on a man in the rear, under the awning. Its shadow hid part of his hawkish features, but the leather eyepatch gave away his identity: the pack's leader, Rione.

He caught her stare, and Æri immediately looked away.

The snide-faced official from the night afore took a position at the podium, his interpreter glued to his side.

"They'll be pairing us with equally skilled opponents," Marlena whispered. As she said this, guards were already snaking through the group of fighters.

"But there are only three women."

Marlena didn't have time to answer. A guard took Æri's arm, placing her beside the woman she spotted warming up in the training rooms. Another guard positioned Marlena next to a lean man about her height and weight.

A curved horn resounded, and the fighters' fists raised.

The woman paired with Æri was somewhat taller than herself, her dirty-blond hair plaited from her face. She, too, had brown eyes like Marlena.

Those eyes went directly to Æri's missing limb. "Hah. They gave me a cripple. What bull's wool." The remark rankled, but Æri stood her ground. No use losing focus if she was going to survive this round.

The Fíronian woman took her first swing.

Æri veered her head to the side and deflected the blow. Still too weak to be on the offensive, she needed to play it safe.

Luckily, her opponent bore little experience in combat. Bouncing from toe to toe, she threw her punches at random—like a drunken miner striking the wrong rock. Her stance wasn't even stable.

Æri parried the next jab, slipping her opponent's wrist to the side and redirecting the attempt with her good arm. She quickly gained control of the fighter's upper limb and twisted it against the joint. With a kick to the knees, Æri had the woman on the floor.

The guard called it.

Relief made her lightheaded. The world tilted, and she reeled to stay upright. She dug her heels into the sand. Æri needed sustenance and recovery time but wouldn't get it in this round.

The smell of blood and perspiration tinged the dust kicked up from the pit. Fighters' grunts, snorts, and the occasional yelp filled her ears. Marlena seemed to be holding her ground amongst the ruckus.

In the next match, they paired Æri with a Fíronian man who sported a ragged chunk torn from his ear.

After she blocked and evaded several kicks, a hook to the side of her head and a stomach jab, he grew aggravated and went in for a choke. Æri ducked, swiftly stepping behind the fighter and twisting her body against him. It threw off his balance and he flumped to the pit floor.

"Lamiæn bitch."

The man lashed out, silver flashing in his hand, directed at her ankle.

Æri staggered back. She groped the earth for a defensive stance.

"AWHH!" A boot crushed into the man's wrist, and he released the knife.

"Disqualified!" The mediating guard hauled him out of the Arena.

Some scattered gasps and boos came from the stands.

Æri released a breath. That was too close. She needed to be more vigilant.

Not sure where this would all lead, Æri understood that she couldn't afford to lose. The losing fighters' crestfallen faces and creased brows said as much. Her stomach soured with the unknown fear of it. What would happen to them—to her?

For the ensuing bouts, Æri used the power of surprise—a bird feigning a broken wing to distract its predator. If her opponents wanted to think she was weak, fine by her. She dodged her attackers until they made a wrong move and then went in, all that time spent training with her crew proving its use.

It just hadn't helped her when she was snared twice by the man who undoubtedly scrutinized every move made on this arena floor. She sensed his gaze following her like the Fíronian sun, beating relentlessly on her back.

Æri grew dizzy, her stomach sore—the morning's light meal winning over.

The Fae, now opposite Æri, moved with extreme agility, ducking his fists with an ease she'd never seen before. His long ears poked through his black hair, which whipped around, trailing his movements and leaving arcs in the air. Lower limbs dancing in a way that enraptured Æri, the elf's legs and knees turned into weapons. Not even her Narkrye moved like that. He swerved behind her, performing some maneuver Æri missed, and she fell, face-planting in the sand.

The final horn blew to signify the end of today's skirmish.

Despite her loss against the elf, Æri somehow made it to the Auctioning's next round, as did Marlena, a Fíronian man, and a giant. She also managed to escape unscathed besides some minor scrapes. Others were not so lucky, including her first opponent, who nursed a swollen knot under her eye.

The official instructed the losing fighters to stand before the king's court, assigning each a number. Then the bidding began.

Nausea crept up Æri's parched throat as she was forced to watch along the rim with the other winners.

Courtiers yelled prices for the defeated—lower sums for those who fought poorly—all of them nothing more than prized cuts of meat, lugged away when their number was claimed. The sun sagged low when the last fighter sold.

As guards directed the five winners toward the tunnel entrance, Æri glanced back at the veranda, but the furtive Venator was gone.

Crammed plates of pork, mutton, and an array of poultry accompanied a rainbow assortment of vegetables and bowls of steamed grains, all arranged on the mess hall's massive farm table in no particular order. Sliced fruits and hearty blocks of cheese on large wooden boards decorated the ends.

Æri ogled the slabs of succulent meats as she squeezed next to Marlena. The sight of so much food nearly made her forget that her shoulders were sandwiched between two other bodies. This feast was an indulgence after weeks of stale bread and jerkies.

Æri shoveled buttered grains onto her plate, heaping roasted meats and vegetables sautéed in fragrant herbs next to them. Her mouth salivated in anticipation.

"It's custom for larger meals to be served in the evening...though, I think they threw in a little more as a bonus." Marlena passed a jug of wine to Æri, who took a swig.

Her hand flew to her mouth, almost dropping the jug whilst trying not to spit out the contents. It tasted like rancid lemon juice. Her lips puckered, throat burning, as she swallowed.

"Posca," Brennos said from across the table. "It takes some getting used to."

Æri chewed on some bread to lessen the burn, then took another tentative sip, seeing no other liquid offered. Her nose scrunched from the robust tang.

"Can you sing or write poetry, Oisin?" Observing the Fae's plate, Marlena questioned the elf in her native Fíronian. "I heard those from the Isles of Erynelleth are born with a talent for the arts."

Æri shouldn't be intrigued. She should distance herself from the other fighters, not sit amongst them like a comrade. But curiosity got the better of her. She'd never seen a Fae before; she had just read about them in the scriptures. And if she continued to listen, somebody might answer some of her questions.

The elf raised his head. Striking eyes of ochre yellow rimmed in teal caught Æri by surprise. Their color popped like the core of carmer, Særenfell's vibrant winter root.

Oisin fiddled with his food, pushing it about, then rotated his plate to show them. He had created an abstract composition that alluded to a natural world, with curving rivers and trees shaded over a bed of flowers. "I was a painter."

"Ah, the officials will be pleased to hear that. They can set your bidding price higher."

Now that Brennos had rejoined the conversation, Æri sought to inquire more about the Auctioning, making sure her question didn't sound like she'd been following his Fíronian response. "You said the next round of bidding will take place the day after tomorrow. Are we to fight as we did today?"

Brennos dropped a grape in his mouth. "No. The next round will include one weapon of your choosing."

"Would that not risk injury?" Concern emerged across Oisin's face, and his ears lowered.

"Perhaps..." Brennos mused. "But the rules still apply. The aim is to disarm your opponent. Not to wound or kill them. The king does not desire to have his property maimed in any way."

"That's reassuring," Æri mumbled. "So what's the point of all this? Only to be bid on and end up a slave regardless? What's the point of winning?"

Brennos sucked at his teeth, removing a lodged grape seed. "I would have thought the officials communicated that to you upon entering. But yes..." He stroked his beard. "You were not part of the initial fighting selection." He looked at Marlena to explain.

She swallowed, putting down the leg bone she was munching on. "It's advantageous because you'll have more value to your owner. The higher you rank in the rounds the better you'll be treated—finer clothing, food, and whatnot. If you win all the rounds, you serve directly under the king, fighting in the Games. And if you win enough Games, you can earn your freedom."

The table's lively babble fell silent as Marlena finished her sentence, the fated word hanging in midair.

It all made sense—*this* was Æri's way out.

~ 9 ~

ÆRI

Freedom.

The word circled in Æri's thoughts as Fabia tugged a clean tunic over her head. Her previous one was drenched in sweat and covered in sand.

Freedom.

It reverberated, carving at her attention. If she won, she could go home.

Before Fabia dressed her in a new uniform that morning, she had motioned to unwind Æri's makeshift binding.

Æri shook her head in protest, knowing she needed it for training. But Fabia made more frantic motions, waving her hands. In a final attempt, she unfolded a band of linen fabric.

"A strophium...for your—" Fabia gestured to Æri's breasts, still trussed with the torn fabric.

Æri cagily removed the soiled binding, and Fabia neared to wrap the new garment around her, knotting it between her shoulder blades. The snug cloth fit comfortably—much better than the sheet. This small nicety was indeed unexpected. Æri nodded and said thank you in Fíronian, assuming Fabia would think she picked it up the day afore.

In the training room, Marlena rubbed the sides of her temples. "I must have had too much of that posca."

Æri's lips twitched. "Glad I didn't take a liking to it, then."

Marlena managed a half-hearted smile.

The space looked empty compared to yesterday. Only five of them stretched about the room—an odd number. Strange the officials reserved five winners for this round...Æri supposed she'd bring the question to Brennos when she saw him.

Her scrutiny hitched on two guards by the hall entrance. No...one wasn't a guard; his clothing appeared different. No leather armor protected his torso, and the fabric was neutral, meant to blend and go unnoticed. And his hair, though raked into a twist, was too long. He had been speaking with the guard, or so Æri assumed. Her fingers curled and fisted.

Why, in Skathi's name, was *Rione* talking to the Castrum guards in the training rooms? Where she could see him? Was he paying a visit to ensure his wild catch sufficed? But before she could cross the room to confront him, he slipped out the exit. The ease with which he came and went from this prison riled her further.

She wanted to ask Marlena what he had been doing here but had no one to reference. The guard by the door stood alone as if there had always been just one and she'd dreamt the whole thing.

"What is it?" Marlena had observed her intent stare at the guard.

"Nothing." Æri sighed. "Want to spar?" She needed to occupy her thoughts with something else and use the day wisely. Testing out her offense against Marlena would be a good start.

"Sure, but after a decent stretch."

They positioned themselves on the bulky floormats that hid most of the yellow stone.

Æri fixed on prying out more information about the mess she was in. "Do you know how frequently the Auctioning takes place?" She rotated her torso and drew back her upper arms, broadening her chest.

"Best to ask Brennos...but the Venators go out three or four times a year. I guess it depends on what they bring back and how many are willing to indenture themselves." Marlena leaned over a leg. "There was talk last night that the king's going to come and watch the rounds tomorrow. He usually just attends the final stage, but given that a giant, an elf, *and* a Lamiæn are fighting...it might draw him out sooner."

"How much do you know of him?"

"Who?" Marlena moved on to the next leg, pulling it up to stretch the thigh.

"King Remus."

"Oh...hmm...Well, he was born after the separations...also not as favored as his father—King Lucius Alexi Belisaur," Marlena said, glassy-eyed and reverent. "He died about fifty years ago. Other than that, I don't know much. My family isn't noble, so we were never invited to any of the royal banquets. Ready to spar?"

They made their way to the palestra—what Marlena called the training yard. Oisin was already there and, to Æri's delight, volunteered some helpful tips in Fíronian as Marlena translated.

Æri hadn't let on she knew the language yet. Though from the way Oisin directed his instructions to the both of them, she suspected he saw right through her feigned naivety. Regardless of this apprehension, she was grateful to receive the fighting advice. The Fae were notorious for their ferocity as warriors.

"You're not so bad." Marlena blocked a strike.

"When you spend years cooped up in a castle with unruly housemates, you learn to throw a punch." Æri's lips arched, letting some rare coyness peek through.

"You lived in a castle?"

"I was an archer." Æri covered.

It wasn't an outright lie, and staying closer to the truth made it more believable. She withheld the obvious information, but if she didn't give Marlena something it would look suspicious. Besides,

Marlena didn't seem to be a threat—parts of her even reminded Æri of her Narkrye crew.

For the remainder of the morning, Æri, Marlena, and Oisin continued to spar, switching partners when one tired. The giant and the Fíronian fighter trained alone, running mat drills and lifting weights at the other end of the facility. They kept on like this as the sun's burning orb rose to noon.

A high whistle broke the routine.

"Gather, please, gather." Brennos stood out of the sun's rays in the cool cloister bordering the palestra, motioning to the five fighters. "Although the second round does not formally begin until tomorrow, your preparation for the match begins now."

Guards carried in bundles, their muscled arms straining under the load.

The fighters shared cagey looks as the men dropped sacks of sticks, rocks, and scraps of hide.

"I hope the task isn't to build a house to keep out the big bad wolf," Marlena said into Æri's ear. Æri returned a doubting smile.

Brennos ignored the low chortles and continued. "You are to make one weapon to implement in tomorrow's round. However, you can only use the materials you see here."

The small group's nervous energy was palpable while they scrutinized the pile; their arms all crossed tight, and the sporadic scratch of a foot on sand hardly broke the tension. To the untrained eye, it looked like a scrap heap.

The Fíronian man twitched as Brennos conveyed his final directives. His eyes glazed, oddly unfocused, and he kept rolling his shoulders as if attempting to loosen the muscles.

"Whatever you make this afternoon stays in these rooms. You may practice with the tools if time permits. Keep in mind that what you construct today will play a role in the bidding round tomorrow. However, it is not a deciding factor. Once you have finished practicing with your weapon, you may leave and join the guards in the mess hall for the evening meal."

Brennos held out a sack from which a set of thin rods poked out, their bottom halves obscured by the cloth. "Take one each. The selection is at random. Choose your materials carefully; you will only have this one occasion. Blue goes first."

Æri withdrew her rod, tipped in orange. The giant grasped the blue. He was double the height of the tallest man in the group.

"Cuthbert." Brennos angled his head, signaling the giant to come forth.

He lumbered over and took a moment to observe the heap. Nudging the debris with his foot, he uncovered a large branch equipped with a tripod prong at its head. He kept that along with a heavy rock and some twine.

Green was next.

"Pollux."

However, when the Fíronian man walked up to the pile, he just stared. Æri wanted to show him, call out and tell him to take the Y-shaped branch and leather scrap to make a sling or throwing stick with the branch next to his foot, but she didn't know if she was allowed to help. She didn't completely understand the rules, and the selection seemed so individual. Eventually, he took a piece of wood and some rope. The stick was big enough, but a split cut through the top. It wouldn't hold for very long.

Brennos called the next color.

Marlena stepped forward with her yellow rod, examining the hoard. She tested some of the longer, thinner branches and settled on one about her height. She also picked up a stone with a whetted edge Æri had eyed earlier.

Pollux, too, looked longingly at the serrated rock he'd missed, seeming to realize his choices may not have been to his advantage.

"Orange!"

She knew what she planned to make the minute the pile had fallen to the sandy floor. This was what Æri did. She built things. Her father had taught her, tinkering away in his hobby shop with similar items and oddments found around the fortress. *Learning these skills will broaden your mind,* he'd say to her. Though Marlena had taken the stone, Æri found another, not sharp, but it held a smooth surface and the texture she required. She scooped that up along with a smaller stone, rounder than the first. Then went about collecting leather strips, feathers, and a handful of willowy twigs.

Brennos called red last, and Oisin gathered some twine along with several round stones. He chose quickly, his actions deliberate like Æri's.

Given the rest of the afternoon to craft their devices, the fighters dispersed.

Æri settled in a shaded spot in view of the palestra. In spite of the heat, being cooped inside for so long had left her yearning for fresh air.

She spread the materials before her, sticking her tongue between her teeth in thought. Starting with the two rocks, she used the momentum of the smaller one to smash the larger. Æri grinned as it fractured. Repeating the motion, she continued to knap, chipping the stone until she had shaped a hand ax—a tool to help her with the rest.

Some of the twigs still bore leaves and spurs. She cut these down into smoother, more succinct boughs. Once finished, Æri arranged them so they bunched in the middle and tapered at the ends.

Expectedly, the giant, Cuthbert, left the training room first. Oisin and Marlena trailed him.

Just she and Pollux remained.

Pollux buried his face in his hands, his weapon half-finished and discarded. At the branch's base, he had secured a thin rope.

If he knew how to lasso, he could thicken it and just use that, she thought, but again Æri held back.

The sky turned a rusty mauve, and her stomach gurgled.

She'd probably missed the meal.

Carving her last shaft, she paused, a noise taking her from her work. It sounded like a moan.

Pollux had risen to his feet. At first, he drifted, walking from pillar to pillar. Then his head turned to one of the exits. Again, he looked at his rejected weapon, his hands clenching and unclenching.

Gods and goddesses above, he couldn't be attempting to flee, could he?

Pollux took one last look around the yard, fear wild in his eyes. He made a sudden jerk straight for the exit doors as if drawn in by a vortex.

She wanted to yell and stop him from nearing those doors, but her reaction was too slow. Her mind fogged with the hours of concentration.

A crack erupted.

Æri stood transfix in horror as Pollux lay on the ground convulsing.

Brennos emerged from the shadows, watching the man twitch, his expression unfazed. "He will be flogged, then saved for the next Auctioning...that is, if he heals." He rotated toward Æri. "It appears we now have an even number." Brennos' gaze flicked to her completed work. His purple eyes mirrored the twilight sky. "This will certainly attract some attention tomorrow."

~ 10 ~

ÆRI

Today, a more sizable flock populated the Arena. Æri squinted in the early morning light. A low chatter and some shouts susurrated as the guards ferried the fighters into the pit. The arid heat from yesterday had dropped, as had the dust, but the bright sun forewarned another hot day. The bottom tier, where the king's court gathered, was more than three-quarters full. Still, the royal dais remained empty.

Where was the king?

His absence only intensified her interest. A fleeting glance over the audience told her Rione wasn't present either.

A band of musicians assembled close by, most likely for the king. Their tuning of instruments droned over the crowd's racket; drums rapped and horns squeaked.

Guards stationed Æri and the other remaining fighters in a line facing the dais while they awaited the official's orders. Each of her opponents clutched their primitive weapon like a life source.

The giant gripped a bludgeon in his fists. Its three clawed prongs supported a massive rock—a good choice for close combat but not distance.

Marlena twirled her javelin, spinning it with what looked like a leather sling attached to the shaft. Æri guessed it would be used to help throw the crude-cut spear. Not a bad choice either.

Æri tightened the straps on her left arm, mimicking her harness. Leather and twine supported a basic arm extension. Not as functional as her bionic arm, but it would do for the fight. Where her hand should have been, collected sticks fastened together to create a rudimentary bow.

Her bark quiver, strapped across her back, light and portable, carried fifteen arrows, wood-tipped and purposefully blunt. It would have taken too long to carve each tip or fashion arrowheads with the stone. Anyway, the aim was to disarm her opponent.

A snivel came from the podium, and the official tapped his foot in impatience. His scowl deepened as the sun ascended, delaying his announcements. They all waited for the king.

Surveying the weapons again, Æri noticed the majority were not ideal for disarming. Instead, they seemed more suited for impaling or crushing flesh—except for Oisin's: a simple but effective choice.

Looped in his fists were corded strips of leather weighted by rocks at each end: four sets of bolas—perfect for capturing live prey.

Just as she began to mull over Oisin's ingenious idea, the bronze instruments blared, quenching the restless buzz of the crowd. The Arena seemed to shake with their boasting notes.

A herald lowered his horn. "His Royal Majesty, King Remus Cosmin Belisaur!"

The king stepped into the dais, appearing undeniably younger than most of his retinue—a cluster of male courtiers flanking him.

Tawny skin glistened in the late morning sun, looking as if the god Hesól himself had blessed him. His face, clean-shaven, was handsome, the jawline strong and the nose desirably straight. A crown topped his burnished head, crafted to emulate the sun's rays. Its fierce spikes hewn on the gold band jutted upward, reaching toward the sky. His cream tunic passed his knees, simple yet refined, while a crimson cloth etched in a gold brocade draped across his shoulders and encircled his waist. A signet flashed on his fourth finger, right hand.

Æri's scrutiny flicked to the man entering behind the royal, recognition inevitable: the same man she had defaced—the very one who had carted her to this realm. Their eyes locked. Something sharp cracked in his eye, then cooled. She threw as much animosity as possible into her glower. She wouldn't look away this time. Let him see what he'd done. His expression remained phlegmatic, but he broke their stare first. Her mouth twitched with gratification.

As soon as the king sat upon his throne, the official announced the rules. They were not to maim or kill; the goal was to remove all weapons from their opponent and neutralize.

Æri took steady breaths as guards sent the four to distant ends of the pit, Marlena and the giant stationed closest. She'd have to battle one of them first before getting to Oisin.

The herald inhaled, cheeks puffed—like two bubbles ready to pop—but halted, his lips not yet touching the bronze.

The heckling onlookers went silent, and all heads turned to the dais, where King Remus held a raised hand. He twisted to an advisor, a man with dark violet eyes like Brennos. The man nodded at the sovereign's inaudible words. In turn, the advisor waved at the official, who promptly scuttled over, kicking up dust along the way.

The official listened while the advisor leaned over the banister, relaying the king's message. His eyes went wide, and he threw a coded gesture to guards. They quickly departed into the Arena's ramparts.

Beads of sweat rolled down the official's forehead as he returned to his podium. "There has been a *minor* change in today's match." He dabbed at the perspiration with a square cloth and cleared his throat. "In addition to disarming your opponent, you are to further prove your abilities...by battling a Bog beast."

Whispers swelled over the Arena. Æri's heart jumped, unsure of what this meant. The other fighters' expressions reflected her confusion.

Behind the king, Rione's expression didn't change, but a fleeting twitch from his eye in her direction—so swift she almost thought she imagined it—had her pausing.

Then the ground shook.

A bloodcurdling screech pulled her attention to the center of the Arena. Sand bounced as a door slid open. Rising on a platform was a creature poised on two powerful hind legs. Its four arms revealed extended black claws, tipped like honed lances. A small dorsal fin flared with anger as it screeched a guttural cry, displaying its rows of serrated teeth, onyx black and drenched in a sticky film.

So this was how the king liked his games: improvised and lethal. Though not as large a creature as the one the Venators ensnared in the Bogs, it looked just as deadly.

"Cut the ropes!" The official signaled to the guards.

The beast snorted, swiveling its neck toward a guard who approached too close, and snapped. Teeth bit into the man's head, and with a jerk, tore it right off the body. The others leaped back. Frustrated grunts, drool, and blood emitted from the Bog beast's mouth. It tried to charge again, but its fettered legs restrained it.

Æri's mind swam. They didn't have much time before the guards severed those ropes, nor did she possess the right weapons to overthrow a beast like that. Maybe if her arrows were tipped in arium...but she doubted even those could penetrate the scales. They needed to work together, just as Rione's pack had done in the Bogs.

Stay alive. Then earn your freedom.

Her eyes met Marlena's, and as if she knew what Æri planned, she tipped her head in response. Now the matter of convincing Oisin and the giant.

The guards finished their hacking. Towing the headless body of their comrade, they fled to the ramparts.

The starting horn blew.

Before Æri could signal to Cuthbert, he stepped into the beast's range, his club in hand. One rope, half cut and fraying, kept the creature from lunging. Surpassing Cuthbert's towering height threefold, it snarled, setting its eyes on the giant. Viscous saliva dripped from its maw, pooling onto the sand.

His diversion provided the others with enough time. Æri and Marlena sprinted toward the elf. Still unaware of the plan, Oisin prepared his stance for battle. The elf's arm raised, bolas spinning above his head, as he aimed for Marlena—the nearest of the two. She stuck out an arm, yelling in Fíronian. By the time she reached his side, the elf had lowered his weapons.

Æri joined them seconds later, trying to even out her breaths. Without waiting another beat, she outlined her strategy.

Oisin's brows knitted together, ears angling. "Is this authorized?"

"To hell if it's not. I'd prefer not to spend my last hours in the belly of a Bog beast." The king had thrown this at them without warning; she was prepared to bend the rules.

Æri and Marlena covered one end of the Arena as the giant attempted few shallow swings with his club, but the strikes hardly scratched the beast's pelt. On the defense now, he blocked snaps from the beast's elongated maw.

Loosening her shoulders, Æri cocked an arrow and pulled the bowstring. The tension in her hand increased, her fingers finding the anchor point—and released. It hit just above the target, glancing off obsidian scales over the beast's eye as if she'd thrown a measly pebble.

"Draug's blood!"

Having no time to practice with her bundle bow, she knew it cost her, the effort to keep the bow steady compromising her well-honed accuracy.

The beast didn't blink her way, continuing to advance on the giant.

She aimed again.

This time Æri hit its eye straight on.

The Bog beast snarled in pain. Using its pincerlike forearms, it yanked the lodged arrow free and swung its head in Æri's direction. Blue-black blood oozed from its injured eye. The beast pawed at the sand and rushed toward her. A tremble of fear tingled down her limbs as it barreled at her, but she held steady, cocking another arrow as the beast blasted rancid breath over the pit. It crouched, readying itself to for a final lunge.

A spear spun through the air. Its pointed tip imbedded under the beast's arm—one of the few exposed points without scales. It roared, giving an ear-splitting shriek as it diverted, ripping toward the launcher. More blood leaked onto the dusty surface.

Before it could reach Marlena, a pair of hurled orbs twisted around the creature's legs. Seconds later, another set coiled its arms, and the last bound its enormous maw. The beast toppled with a mighty thud. It writhed to no avail on the pit floor, unable to free its limbs, the bindings deceptively secure.

A deafening wave of cheers burst from the crowd, and Æri's stomach dropped. Though the beast lay defeated, the ovation generated a new form of horror. This was all a game to them, a silly little game for entertainment, while the beast could have torn Æri and the other fighters to shreds. The Fíronians probably didn't care, so long as they got their show.

In Særenfell, prisoners had a purpose: to sustain another's life. Yet in this blood sport, life held little significance.

And the fight wasn't over.

Marlena was already racing to retrieve her javelin from the beast's arm. Her fingers stretched, almost touching its shaft when—*whomp!* She fell, the last set of bolas wound tightly about her thighs.

At that moment, a protracted shadow overtook Æri's. She spun. Cuthbert lumbered toward her, his club raised for battle, aiming right for her appendaged bow.

"Consummatum est!" The official's high voice called, and the ending horn rang off the stands.

The giant dropped his fighting stance.

Bewilderment washed over Æri. Why had the round been called? Oisin still stood.

The official spoke over the hollering crowd. "As there are only two fighters left with their weapons, we have our finalists!"

Then it registered. Oisin had used his last weapon. The rule was to *disarm* their opponent, not have them on the ground.

Unjust. This was unjust.

Æri wanted to shout at the official—to forfeit her standing in the bidding. Oisin was clearly the superior warrior. He had wielded his first three bolas to take down the Bog beast. If not for that sacrifice, he would have won the round. She caught the elf's eye, and he shook his head, showing his resignation.

He had done this intentionally, freely throwing his last set of bolas so she would win.

Why?

She didn't have a chance to ask. After the official's ruling, they broke the fighters apart like the first round. Guards flanked the victors, stationed to the side. More positioned Marlena and Oisin before the king and his court.

King Remus called for the bidders to rise. Then he himself conducted the bidding frenzy. Men shouted prices, thrusting their fists up to form peculiar signals—their fingers symbolizing an amount.

It sickened Æri: the relish in the bidder's faces, their shouts and intermittent wolf whistles. The way Marlena and Oisin held their heads up, their backs straight in valor, made it worse. Those men were all wolves devouring the fittest of a stolen flock.

In the end, the king auctioned off both losing fighters at obscenely high prices—if Æri translated her numbers right. Her sparring partners were ushered from the Arena.

Would she see them again? Æri prepared herself to be pushed into the twisting tunnels and back to the fortified Castrum.

"Stop. Bring the winners forward." The king's tenor resonated across the pit.

This was unexpected.

Æri and Cuthbert were steered toward the dais.

King Remus's eyes moved over the giant then to Æri. They lingered on her makeshift bow. It made her feel like an exotic curiosity—a shiny, new thing—and she fought to keep still under his stare.

Her eyes held the King's, the wolves' leader, only wavering to glance at the man standing behind the royal. But Rione kept his gaze averted, his face stoic, looking past her at something else in the distance.

"Congratulations." King Remus addressed each of the winners in their tongues. "I wanted to thank you personally for putting on such a fine performance. As is custom in the Games and for this round's reward, I invite you to stay at my villa. You may rest and recuperate there while preparing for your final bidding round."

Traces of a smile played on King Remus's ruddy lips. "I look forward to speaking with you both in more...comfortable quarters."

ÆRI

Æri spent the night at the Castrum with unease. She tossed and turned on her hard pallet, the dry heat making it especially unbearable, and scrunched the single torn sheet between the wall and the bed. The mattress's cover scratched, blades of straw poking at her skin—so unlike the soft pelts of Særenfell.

Why had Oisin forfeited the match for her? What did King Remus intend for them at his villa in the scant days leading to the finals? And Rione...The Venator was finding his way under her skin. What role did he play in all this? Had he orchestrated this—set her up to win the rounds so she could compete in the Games? If so, why?

These deliberations churned in and out of her dreams and had not receded by the time Fabia woke Æri with her customary scowl.

Horse hooves clopped on cobblestone streets while guards escorted Æri from the Castrum. Yet, this time, instead of shunting her into a wagon, they blindfolded and plopped her upon a steed.

A set of heavier treads and the low grunts of the giant, Cuthbert, came from behind as her horse bumped forward. Perhaps he struggled to stay atop his mount? She wasn't faring any better.

Her chains shifted and scraped against the leather saddle, adding to the racket. Æri strained her ears, trying to rely on her other senses. The city streets hummed with a cacophony of vendors crying out prices of fabrics, dogs yapping, and an occasional chambermaid shouting a warning from above. The stench of the streets alluded to the general uncleanliness of the vibrant town.

However, soon the clamor faded, the air sweetened with scents of dry grasses and freshly turned earth. Water sloshed nearby. A river? Birds began to sing, and a friendly breeze kissed her face.

Æri rolled her head back to glimpse the countryside, but the blindfold was bound too tight. A blur of blacks and grays stole her vision, varied by the light. She pictured the tall column-like trees along the road and wheat or rye fields beyond, their stalks ruffling in the wind.

Eventually, the horses slowed.

"Take them this way!"

The sun's harsh heat disappeared from her skin, and the odor of hay and animal dung permeated her nose.

A rough grip fastened around her waist and arms, pulling her down like a sack of winter potatoes. Æri's legs wobbled when her feet hit the earth, and she struggled not to fall to her knees. Fingertips fumbled at her blindfold, a jagged nail scraping her cheek. Once the cloth was removed, she squinted. They were in a stable, grooms ushering the horses to their separate stalls.

"Hurry up." A guard yanked at her chains.

The armed men propelled Æri and Cuthbert out and onto a sweeping landscape. Æri squeezed her eyes and opened them again, adjusting to the light. The scene before her rivaled a dream.

Bright pops of red, yellow, and white summer wildflowers waved through a meadow that sloped down, finishing at the edge of a large lake. Its color reminded her of peering into a snow burrow when the white faded into a translucent blue.

Æri yearned to hold and lock that scene away somewhere safe, so different was it from the dim cell and oppressive walls of the Castrum.

Another jerk on her chains, and the spell broke.

The guards pulled them in the opposite direction, toward the slope's top. A massive, horseshoe-shaped house with a veranda of columns the color of golden cream rested on the low hill. Lacking the mighty height of her fortress, the dwelling's spans, which crossed the entirety of the hillside, made up for the absence of turrets.

Cuthbert and Æri's guards shoved them into an entrance at the estate's rear. A cool, spacious gallery greeted them with high, honeycombed ceilings. It was a hive of activity with servants abuzz, cloth and food loaded in their arms. And there, amongst the commotion, waited Brennos in his brilliant cobalt blue.

As they approached, Brennos signaled the guards to remove their chains. Æri wrapped her arm behind her, stretching the soreness from it, not wanting to reveal her discomfort to the Keeper. She didn't want to show any weaknesses.

"Welcome to the Villa Glorial." Brennos grinned at them as if they were paying guests, and he the host. Her stomach curdled at the notion.

"The same rules of the Castrum apply. You may roam freely among the villa's grounds but no farther. I have placed wards at its borders, so if you do try to escape, well..." He held out his hands. "All has been said before. Do you have any questions ere we proceed?"

More questions? Forming a proper sentence alone vexed Æri. Her limbs ached and her stomach griped with hunger from the morning's skimpy meal. Sensing a mild headache pulsating at the back of her skull, she shook her head, as did the giant.

"The king desires to speak to you individually in his tablinum. Æri, he has requested you first. Cuthbert, you'll wait here until you are called upon." He gestured to a bench pressed against the wall.

It resembled a small stool as Cuthbert balanced his rear on the bench's feeble planks, and Æri would have smiled if she were not so tired.

The gallery's plain floor transformed into elaborate mosaic patterns as Æri progressed through the open corridors, and the once unadorned walls now donned frescos of fauna. Painted life-like humans and plants livened the plastered stone.

Light bounced off walls, which often gave way to exposed doorways featuring unblemished skies. An occasional spray of mist coasted by the glassless frames, giving an illusion the villa had been built on a cloud.

What a beautiful prison. She pressed her hand to her thigh, stopping the impulse to trail her fingers along the colorful walls.

They passed courtyards with exquisite gardens of herbs, orderly shrubs, and more summer blooms. An iridescent bird strutted in one, its blue and teal plumes sweeping the pebbled paths as if it were one of the proud royals who owned the palace.

Caught up in awe, she nearly stumbled into Brennos, who had stopped in a large room.

"Wait here." He disappeared behind a set of curtains.

She idled behind. The square room was grander than the others they had passed. An open gap in the ceiling's center framed a picture of vivid blue. Below it, a shallow pool rested at the heart of the room, holding a finger's depth of water. It shimmered like polished crystal, mirroring the sky above.

"An impluvium," Brennos said as he slipped back into the room. "Water is scarce, despite what you may see. When it rains, we try to take advantage. There is a small drain there." He pointed to a corked hole in the corner of the pool. "It fills a cistern beneath."

Like in Særenfell, small inventions helped sustain the lands and livelihoods even in its wealthiest homes.

"Come, this way." Brennos disappeared again through the curtained-off doorway. She followed, passing two armed sentinels under the towering arch. The new space appeared to be some form of study. Much like the Castrum's training room, one of the walls opened onto a garden. Daylight spread into every crook, and soothing gurgles of an exterior fountain echoed in the quiet space.

A young man stood by its yawning archway, his attention focused on the garden. A thin golden band circled his head. Far less refined than the traditional sun-rayed crown, the gleaming band was almost indistinguishable from his golden waves. They glistened in the midafternoon light, momentarily distracting Æri.

Brennos cleared his throat. "King Remus."

The king turned to study them with keen bronze eyes, which probed her with that same glint from the Arena. Today, he wore plainer attire: a long cream tunic cinched with a golden cord to match his crown.

Brennos gestured toward Æri, nodding slightly in the king's direction. He did not bow or lower himself to the floor.

"I present to you Æri of Særenfell, one of the Lamiæn."

King Remus gave a curt affirmation, saying nothing.

Brennos lowered his head and proceeded out. As he left, Æri realized he had failed to educate her on how to acknowledge the king in these private quarters. Brennos had given a simple greeting, but his ranking surpassed her own. Uncertainty danced at the edge of reason. The rules may differ for Æri, and she did not wish to lose her head for a dishonorable gesture.

So, not knowing what else to do, Æri fell to her knees and bowed her head. She winced as they made contact with the inlaid mosaic, her legs still sore from the morning's journey. Her head spun as she stared at the spiraled pattern tiling the ground.

A laugh broke from the young king. The blithe amusement in it floated about the room. "Rise"—a smile in his voice while he spoke in her native tongue—"there is no need to bow. Though it might be common in your lands, it is not a practice here. But I am flattered."

Her cheeks immediately heated with embarrassment.

Eyes of brown, do not bow down. The rhyme intruded her thoughts.

Then what did one do?

She rose tentatively. The king had left his position by the opening and now leaned against his clawfoot desk.

"An address and single nod are custom. You should greet me as 'King Remus.'"

Æri nodded. "King Remus."

He grinned at this. "Delightful.

"I saw you admiring my father's likeness." The king strode to a marble bust on a pedestal opposite his desk. He aligned his own tall stature with the bearded man's head. "Do you think we resemble one another?"

"I—" Æri hesitated. An odd question. "I suppose so..." There was a bit of resemblance sans the beard.

"My mother thinks so, but I cannot see it." His lip curled while he studied the bust. He did not seem to like the comparison.

As if a switch had been flipped, the king spun around and stepped toward Æri, the shift so abrupt she grit her teeth to keep from flinching. He paused before her, then moved to a brazier in the corner. There were three of them positioned about the room for when the light dimmed. Each base was adorned by a trio of bronze-cast women supporting the unlit bowls.

"And these lovely women"—his unmarred hands hovered over the curved waist of one clutching a scroll—"did I see you take an interest in these as well?"

What was this? Such strange questions. Wary from the day's ride and the increasing headache, she did not want to be here longer than necessary.

"There are nine of them." He counted each of the women aloud. "Do you know who they are?"

"The Nine Muses." Would he get to the point?

"Exactly! They provide such gratifying inspiration." He strolled back to his desk to fiddle with an orb used to hold papers. Something dark floated inside of it. "In fact, they inspired this little game we just played. And I believe you lost."

Game? Æri's brows drew together.

"Haven't you figured it out?" The king watched her face, clearly entertained by her incomprehension.

With his last words, realization struck, and her stomach dipped. He had asked the question about the Muses in Fíronian—not her native tongue.

"Ah, there. I presume that is recognition on your face." King Remus palmed the orb.

"How did you know?" The pounding in her head intensified. She didn't like this game.

His impish smile vanished, and he matched her serious tone, returning the glass orb to his desk.

"Brennos had an inkling. And your armband...while my dwarves' specialties rest in gemstones, they do hold some knowledge in metalwork, and though they could not determine the metal's origins, they were able to inform me of its superior quality. You're obviously not of the lower classes, thus I gathered you'd be educated in our language, as we are in yours." He tapped his full lips, leaning toward her. "Now, the question is, why would you hide this information, and who exactly are you...Perhaps a spy sent by your queen?"

His eyes danced with the suggestion. "I don't take kindly to *spies* in my realm." Again, he watched her reaction with cool precision.

Angst crawled up her arms. She bit the inside of her mouth, straining to keep her face stoic.

"Regardless, you are under my ownership now, and rumor has it that the queen of Særenfell does not like having her things taken."

Her fist tightened. So this was the reason for her summons today. He intended to use her. But in what capacity?

"I'll offer you a deal, Æri of Særenfell—and we'll make it a game because, of course, I do love making things a tad more entertaining." He rubbed his hands together while keeping her gaze. "Win the Auctioning, and you may return to your homeland. Free as a bird."

The words hit her like a gust of icy wind. *Home. Freedom.* And she would not have to win in the Games, just this final round of the Auctioning.

The king's eyebrows arched, awaiting her response. An offer like that did not come without a price.

"What do you want?"

He didn't waver. "I want to fly."

"What makes you think I can help with that?"

His eyes crinkled with a knowing smile, and he clicked his tongue. "Come now...I saw that invention you made for yesterday's match. And your apprehension report stated you were in a flying craft before crashing. I'd like you to tell me how you did it—explain how you powered such a device."

Her pulse pounded in her neck, and she prayed to Skathi he could not hear her hammering heart. This want was not just a need to satisfy a mere curiosity. The king's attributes went beyond a pretty face, and he knew it.

His knowledge of her language, skills, and possibly heritage put not only herself at risk, but also her queen, her people. She had to think this through—measure her responses. If she was identified as the queen's sister, her value to him would mean Særenfell's undoing.

He raised his hand just as she prepared to deliver her answer.

"Sleep on it. No need to make any hasty decisions now. I'd like you to attend a banquet I'm throwing tomorrow. Bring me your answer then. For the moment, enjoy the grounds and have a taste of freedom while it lasts." He lifted an object on his desk—a bell—and a servant appeared. "Show Æri to her rooms."

What was she to do? Æri plunked onto the feather-stuffed quilt. The fresh linens let up a lavender plume, lulling her racing thoughts.

She thought to say no. What did the king plan for that kind of energy source, anyway? Use it for harm? For gain? Judging by her recent introduction to King Remus, she doubted his satisfaction would stop there if he obtained it.

He had deceived her. *Brennos* had deceived her. Should she have expected any better? Trust certainly had no place in Fíronbec.

The ceiling whirled. Æri had been taking shallow breaths.

Attempting to calm herself, she started to count objects in the room, beginning with the bed she lay upon. A welcome sight when Æri entered. She curled herself in its center. The wooden frame held more firmly than the pallet she'd slept on for the last few nights. Thin paneled doors revealed yet another courtyard garden, one of supposedly six.

Open doors that let in drafts were unheard of in Særenfell. Air flowed freely in this royal dwelling, whereas her fortress's stones trapped it. This room alone only had those screen doors and a set of flimsy drapes that blocked the entry.

She thought of the soft terrain outside, the rolling hills, and the view of the lake, which offered a morsel of relief from these bizarre weeks in confinement. How "free" was she really?

Marlena's words returned to her: the worthier the performer, the superior the treatment granted.

Or was this just part of the king's ruse, luring her in to say yes to his deal?

King Remus was...She could not put her finger on it, his character too complex to read upon their first informal encounter. Something murky hid under his jovial disposition. Like the Bogs' turf, he appeared stable and solid at first glance, but underneath, cracked with molten flame, ready to incinerate everything it touched.

It unnerved her.

Æri needed the time to think—time she didn't have. He wanted an answer by tomorrow.

What was the cost of helping the king? And what if she didn't win? What then?

She craved a place to clear her head, where walls did not hold her in. Exhausted, physically and mentally, Æri put the problem aside. She'd wait until morning to resolve it. Today she would rest.

Sleep on it.

As her eyelids grew heavy, the headache finally subsided, and her objective formed sharper in her mind. A languid smile stole across her lips. Tomorrow she'd run.

~ 12 ~

ÆRI

Her feet pounded the soft earth, reverberating through her legs. Its contact pushed her to go farther, harder, faster.

Fresh morning air rounded her lungs with every deep inhalation. A bilious bubble had formed somewhere between her chest and the base of her throat last night, but with every breath, she shoved it down, letting it settle amongst her lower organs where it no longer nettled.

She increased into a sprint, the short, succinct burst exploding out of her.

Running. Æri was running again.

Oh, how she missed this feeling, the barrier between pain and liberation—as if her legs could take her anywhere, maybe even back across the Bogs to Særenfell.

She couldn't, though—not this way. Yet *this*, just this bit of open air lent her a different kind of escape.

Yesterday's heat emitted from the earth, and sweat slid down her shoulders. Her flexible boots were surprisingly well suited for the early morning run. Their leather didn't chafe or dig into her skin but molded snugly around her foot.

Æri bound up the hill, reaching its top as a trace of orange-yellow light erupted along the horizon. Her muscles began to cramp, and she developed a side stitch from her initial burst. She'd have to find a well before turning back to the villa.

Prior to setting out, she'd located a sentinel on guard and asked about the estate's borders—a novice she overheard the others poking at while roaming the villa the day afore. Not one for brownnosing, she simply asked the young guard nicely. It turned out kind words went a long way. He provided her with a rough estimate of how far she could go, describing specific landmarks that indicated Brennos's wards.

Æri didn't plan on wasting her so-called "freedom" for one more second.

The grounds did not compare to the crisp mountain air and high peaks of Særenfell. Yet the rolling meadows and the vast aquamarine lake that spooled between them retained a distinct kind of natural beauty.

Jamming her fist into her side to suppress the ache, she steadied her pace and aimed for a small plateau. An edifice sat atop the outcropping—one of the landmarks the sentinel had specified.

The building had provoked a peculiar presence, bringing to mind Skathi's temple in the floating precipices of Særenfell. But instead of tall, shingled spires, this roof only exhibited the slightest of crests. The structure, circular with large pillars hedging its exterior walls, was created from the same golden stone used for most buildings in Fíronbec.

Nearing the stones, she found a pump with a shallow tub. Hoping it worked, she grabbed hold of the lever. Instead of clogged, clay-ridden water as she expected from an ill-used pump, after a few cranks, cool pristine water cascaded from the spout into its basin. Æri eagerly splashed it on her face and gulped several handfuls. It went down fresh and rejuvenating, an earthy-sweet taste reviving her from the inside.

Straightening from the basin, she examined the building, now able to see more of its details. It looked in need of repair; the stone steps bore chips, and a few red tiles on the roof were missing. Dulcet sounds of chimes lifted over a warm breeze. The source was an array of bronze figurines strung with little bells above the entrance. Light flickered through the opening. Æri ventured up the steps but tarried at its threshold.

Faint whispers stirred from within the chamber, just under the tinkering of the bells: a soft lyrical voice that danced on the edge of song—a prayer?

Æri quieted her footfalls.

Through the archway, a woman with flowing copper-brown hair knelt below a statue of virginal beauty, its stone eyes carved to gaze toward its hands, supporting a wide bronze offering basin. Tiny flames flickered from the cupped bowl.

Æri stepped into the space, and the praying woman's head snapped around. "Oh!" She jumped up.

"I—I'm sorry. I did not mean to interrupt." Æri spoke in Fíronian, holding out a hand in a placating gesture. Her feigned ignorance in the tongue seemed irrelevant now.

The woman's face matched the statue's beauty. Her deep sable eyes were big and shaped like almonds, her nose and chin delicately tipped. She wasn't tall—smaller than Æri. Her long tunic fell just above her ankles, fashioned to drape across one shoulder, a cord secured at her slender waist.

"Oh," the woman said again more steadily. "That is all right. I am almost done." She dusted her knees and stooped to pick up a woven basket.

"Is she a god?" Æri motioned to the statue. Some of their Særenian gods overlapped with the Fíronians', but Æri didn't recognize this one from any of the scriptures.

The woman hesitated, and for a moment, Æri believed she translated the words wrong.

But then she looked back at the altar. "Yes. Though, I think most have forgotten her...like many of the other gods." She added a few more herbs from the basket into the flame and bowed her head. A savory scent permeated the space. It reminded Æri of her fortress's kitchens—traces of bay leaves, rosemary, and thyme. Herbs that only grew indoors in her cold lands.

"She is Thesta, the goddess of family and hearth." The woman studied Æri for a moment, her eyes lingering on her attire. "You are one of the fighters for the Auctioning, are you not? The Lamiæn. I heard you put on quite a show the other day."

Her uniform made it obvious, and for all her reticence, an introduction bubbled from her. "I'm Æri."

"Camilla." The copper-haired woman dipped in greeting. Then, walking to the entrance, she angled her head to the sky, gazing at the sun. She curved to look at Æri. "Will you be accompanying me back to the villa? I need to return before the king rises."

Æri agreed, figuring she may learn something about King Remus.

"Are you part of his retinue?" She certainly looked as if she belonged there.

Camilla laughed. "Oh no. I'm one of the lady's maids. I tend to one of his wives."

His wives...as in he had multiple?

"How many wives does King Remus have?" Æri struggled to keep in stride with Camilla, who maintained a long gait despite her petite frame, skipping down the plateau to the gravel path.

"Only two—Ismene and Rosalind. It was not the custom to take more than one before—Well, before the realms separated. But he is determined to have an heir."

Entering a coppice of fruit trees, Camilla plucked a nectarine and tossed it to Æri. "Breakfast." She smiled and added more to her basket.

Æri bit into the fruit, and her mouth exploded with rich flavor. They rarely, if ever, produced fruit this size in Særenfell. It usually came in the form of small winter berries. She licked at the sweet juice, which trickled down her thumb. This had to be the best breakfast in Fíronbec by far.

"May I ask something?"

"Mhmm." The lady's maid nodded.

Æri wavered, knowing she broached a sensitive subject. "How did the old king die—King Lucius?"

Camilla paused her stride, examining the red-and-orange skin of the ripe fruit. "It was his heart. It gave out one day. He was walking in the gardens, and he just collapsed. We don't talk about it much. It pains the king's mother to do so." She flicked off a fat green insect crawling across its flesh and dropped the fruit in her basket. "You might come across her roaming the villa. She still wears her black veils. But...she rarely leaves her chambers these days."

"I suppose it is never easy to lose a loved one." Æri was reminded of her own mother's mourning, a permanent type of grief.

A flash of sorrow filled Camilla's features. A mutual reminiscence of living in a world where endless age made losses all the more difficult. The moment passed in silence as they continued on their way to the villa.

A light skittering and scratching from behind caught Æri's attention. A weasel-like creature—a polecat—followed some stretches back. Black fur covered its body, save for a white wisp on its chest and the tip of its tail.

"We have company." Camilla giggled blithely.

The polecat took this as an invitation to scurry closer. At first with caution, then with an urge of boldness, and to Æri's surprise, it leaped up her side to snatch the half-eaten fruit from her hand.

"Wha—oh! That little rascal!"

"She's a clever one." Camilla's bowed lips curved.

"How do you know it's female?"

The animal sunk its teeth into the fruit's meat.

"She's small. We have a few about the villa. They keep rodents away."

The polecat tossed the pit aside and reapproached Æri, weaving in and out of her legs.

"She appears to have taken a liking to you."

"Because she got her grubby little claws on easy food." Æri tried to shoo her away, but the polecat kept following, hopping in step with the two women.

"Well, I'd better prepare for Ismene. Her temper becomes surly if she doesn't get her morning meal on time." If one could roll one's eyes gracefully, Camilla managed to do it. "I presume you are attending the banquet later today?"

"I don't think I have much choice." Æri kicked at some loose stones.

"Ah, right. Then you should try the baths." Camilla pointed toward the bathhouses next to the lake.

"Do I smell that bad?" Æri grimaced as she remembered Camilla eyeing her sweaty tunic in the temple.

Camilla burst out in a trill. "I was referring to that long run of yours. And after the days of fighting, I imagined the baths may be welcomed—so, yes, I suppose, for the 'smell' as well."

Æri chuckled. Her first proper laugh in a while. A soak did sound lovely. She hadn't taken one since she'd left for the hunt.

"Not many attend at this time of day..." Camilla mused. "You ought to have the place to yourself. Extra towels and robes are already prepared." She waved Æri in the direction of the lake. "You should go."

"All right."

Æri thanked her for the fruits and bade goodbye, glad she'd found a friendly soul in this peculiar place.

The polecat loitered in the orchard, watching Æri as she made her way toward the baths.

The bathhouses occupied a good portion of the lake's eastern shore. The sun was shining brightly—likely close to mid-morning.

Servants milled in and out of a lower chamber, wheeling barrels of dried turf molded into bricks; the dirt looked black enough to have come from the Bogs. Perhaps it had.

This must be the furnace to heat the baths, Æri guessed.

Thick smoke spewed from another end. The black cloud plumed out into the clear sky like an inky stain, its dark particles dispersing. No one would know the air was tainted with it.

Upon entering the building, Æri was greeted by a female servant. Her thin, loose robe did little to hide her shape underneath.

Feeling bashful, Æri looked away, her cheeks warm. The servant paid no heed, ushering her into a changing chamber.

Camilla was right. At this earlyish hour, the baths were completely empty. Besides the servant, no one occupied the room.

Hesitantly, she allowed the servant to peel off her sweat-drenched clothes. She tried to shield her breasts with her right arm, her face going hot with embarrassment.

Since arriving on Fíronbec, Æri had difficulty distinguishing between those who were just doing their job and those who "helped" out of pity.

In her fortress, the maids had grown accustomed to her snaps and sharp retorts. They knew not to insist when dressing. When Æri lost her arm, she sought to learn tasks independently, to do things as anyone else would. Not easily at first—tying laces one-handed had been one of the most challenging tasks—still, she did it. She fought through the initial swelling and agonizing pain of where her arm and hand used to be and eventually learned to do everything on her own. Yet here, she didn't have much say in the matter.

The servant quickly rid Æri of her soiled uniform, tossing it into a hamper.

"You must sweat first." The woman hustled her into an adjacent room.

A cloud of intense steam engulfed Æri, reminding her of the Bogs' sweltering heat. However, the aroma lingering in the air smelled pleasant, not rotten—more like pine resin. The room brought to mind the steam huts constructed near the glacial lakes of her homeland. Granted, they smelled of wood, and their steam was created by emptying water over hot stones in a hearth. Plus, the sheer size of Villa Glorial's bathing chambers dwarfed those little huts.

Here, thick grooves etched a vaulted ceiling, distributing the condensation into a concealed duct and preventing it from dripping onto her head. She took relief from the heat in a cooling basin at the center, splashing away her perspiration.

When she emerged from the steam room, Æri's eyes rounded. The servant held a set of cleaning tools. One resembled a sickle more than a washing apparatus.

"What do you intend to do with those?" Æri started to back away.

"You cannot enter the pools without a scrubbing. It's forbidden."

Æri debated if she really needed a bath. She surely didn't smell *that* bad. But after lifting an arm to sniff, her nose flared...and if she smelled it..."All right, fine."

She cringed as the woman scraped her skin until it bloomed pink. The servant brought the sickle back up for a second round, but Æri shook her hand. "I think one scrub is more than enough."

Even after the cleaning, her tanned skin, marking the hem of her uniform, remained. She examined the contrast between dark and light. Two skin tones dominated in Særenfell: one fair, sensitive to the sun's rays; and one that would tan dark like the bark of their pines, this trait deriving from the seafarer folk, whose blood mingled with the land's natives.

Æri forwent the offered massage and grooming, wanting to be left alone. Her skin hummed from the scrub. The servant shrugged, looking just as frustrated as Æri felt, and handed her a robe, indicating the way to the main bath.

A marbled pool occupied most of the regal space. Private alcoves branched from its rectangular body, each separated by embellished arched pillars. A ceiling dome flaunted a fresco of a blue sky, which unlike the sky outside, bore great, billowing clouds. They moved slowly, changing shape as if created from the actual heavens of Vallantheia.

A little thrill of delight ran through her. The space was blissfully vacant.

Glossy mosaics led to the pool steps, depicting sea animals; arcing dolphins and dashing fish guided the path into the water—representations of a bygone world.

Æri stripped from the robe and placed it on a bench by the entrance.

Sliding her toes in one by one, she descended. Tepid water folded around her ankles, and then her legs, until Æri fully submerged herself into the pool's depths.

The transition from the steam room to the cooler pool was nowhere near the extreme temperatures her people subjected themselves to. For after spending an hour or so in the huts, they bravely dived right into their frigid lakes.

This pool felt cool enough—like a breath of fresh air.

She glided deeper into the bath and flipped onto her back, floating on its placid surface. Her breasts bobbed above the water line, and her exposed nipples pebbled in the cool air. Hair fanned her face like a halo, the strands a buoyant wave in the subtle slosh from her kicks.

In the fresco, the clouds really did seem to shift and pass overhead, forming frothy swells, sometimes even mimicking sea creatures: a whale or a seal, a shark or an octopus.

What sort of trickery enthralled it?

As she watched the shapes disperse and reform, her mind settled. She'd have to find Camilla later to thank her for this suggestion. Spreading out her limbs, Æri melted into the water, forgetting the uncertain world outside. With her ears immersed, all seemed at peace, the only sound released from her soft inhalations. Water lapped, soothing her body like a lullaby.

She stayed like that for several minutes, letting her mind float in a place between wakefulness and sleep.

The light shifted and she lifted her head. Her ears perked as muffled voices resounded from outside the chamber—the servant and an unidentified guest.

Quickly, Æri reversed and swam into an alcove, calculating. She didn't have enough time to swim across the pool to leave.

The other voice was deep—a man's. She inwardly groaned, her fleeting peace now over. Æri peeked out from the shelf dividing the alcove, and her stomach twisted into a giant knot.

Rione.

Her mind scrambled for an action. She certainly did not want to share a bath with *him*. No. Ugh, *no*.

Besides a measly alcove wall, she had nothing else hiding her. Her heart thudded in her ears. She was completely exposed—*naked*.

Could this be the forgotten gods' cruel trick for interrupting one of their worshipers this morning?

Rione strode from the entrance to the pool's edge; a wrapped towel concealed his lower half. She diverted her gaze before he removed it, sinking beneath the water as quietly as she could muster. When she re-emerged, he had waded in, water now up to his waist.

His torso and arms showcased lean, sinewy muscles. Ragged whitish scars scored his bronzed skin, both small and large. One across his lower abdomen looked faintly new, still pink and raised. Then she remembered their wrestle in the Bogs—another one of her marks.

Why had he not healed it?

The scratch drew Æri's eyes across his chest, spying the rest of his torso: a chiseled body well-disciplined for battling beasts and using the weapons that ensnared them.

He moved toward the pool's rim—and, to her relief, away from her—turning to rest his elbows on the shelf, his back muscles shifting under the inky spill of his hair.

A tickle shivered through her. *Stay focused.*

It was now or never. She sucked in a gulp of air and dove, kicking her legs. She reached out, touching the first step, ready to climb the pool's stairs. Her head broke the surface.

"No need to sneak." His voice sounded easy and casual—not at all the harsh reprimands from the Bogs.

By Skathi's spear!

Æri plunked her body back under the water. "Close your eyes," she demanded in Fíronian, her words coming out more desperate than she liked.

"You mean my *eye*. I only have the one. Likewise, I would not say *hands* for you."

"*Please*—just don't look this way," she said, scrambling up the steps.

"I didn't take you to be such a prude. These are the villa's *public* bathhouses after all," he said, chuckling. "Anyone in the villa is privy to them."

Æri dashed to grab her thin robe and towel. When she glared over, his face was angled away.

"Camilla said no one would be here." She bit the inside of her cheek, not intending to give a reason for leaving the bathhouse. Why should she?

"Hmm, so you've met Camilla..." His voice trailed off. "I suppose she didn't know I arrived late last night from Méritras. I usually train in the gymnasium next door at dawn."

"Well, neither she nor I knew." Æri huffed, feeling the need to defend the lady's maid. She secured her robe and threw the towel over her arms. "I wouldn't have come otherwise."

Rione crooked his head back to look at her as if sensing Æri was now decent. He didn't wear his patch and the sunken, mutated flesh of where the eye should have been seemed to bore right through her. It was as if every time he looked at her, he threw her careless actions back into her face. She was responsible for those scars.

"I see you've stopped pretending you don't speak Fíronian."

Æri narrowed her eyes into slits, gathering all the acerbity she felt into her voice. "How did you know?" She'd have to get better at hiding things.

"I suspected it." He pushed off the shelf into the pool's center and made a show of having the bath to himself. "And speaking Fíronian to the Castrum's chambermaid may not have been wise."

She averted her eyes. Restless ire built in her chest as her lips curled inwards. *Fabia.*

"She told you?"

"I spoke to her in passing."

"Why would you talk to her?"

"She attends to the fighters in Auctioning. It is in my best interest to know they are cared for."

"Like you care." Æri scoffed.

There was a light splash. Rione had immersed his head below the silver-blue.

Shadows from the clouds patterned the pool, making it difficult to see where he swam. Where had he gone?

Goddess, he held his breath well.

Against her better judgment, she edged to the pool's rim to get a better look. Her toes gripped the slick tile. "Rione?" His name felt peculiar on her tongue, new and unpredictable.

He resurfaced a stride from her.

"Holydraugsofhell!" She steadied herself, feet firm on the rim before she could topple into the water.

A smirk lined his lips. "Didn't think Særenian huntresses scared. Was that concern I detected in your voice?"

"That wasn't funny."

"I'm not laughing."

"I like to have eyes on my assailants."

"Assailant? A little harsh."

"Assailant or asshole? I can't decide which one suits you better." Now she smirked.

"Wait a minute, I caught you as you would have caught me in the Bogs. Fair and square. I followed my orders. You would do far worse if it were the other way around. You're here because of me." Rione's jaw tightened as if he hadn't meant to say the last words.

Whatever knavery she felt in their earlier banter evaporated. "Exactly. I wouldn't be here if you hadn't dragged me from the Bogs."

"That came out wrong."

"Don't deny it." Æri snorted. What was she doing, talking to this man? He had imprisoned her, and she despised him—*hated* him for it. "I need to go."

She turned, but too fast. Her foot slipped on a wet tile.

A weightless sensation hit her stomach as she fell into the pool, right onto Rione.

Skathi, save her. Gasping, Æri inhaled a mouthful of water as she went under.

A hard, warm chest pressed against her, solid arms embracing her own, pulling her back to the surface.

Dread rioted in her chest like the bubbles whirling around her.

"Don't—don't touch me!" She failed, kicking and pushing, managing to jab a foot backward into something soft. Rione made a pained oof. His arms slackened.

"What was that for?"

She coughed up water. "I'm capable"—a breath and a splash—"of swimming." She distanced herself from him. Like a drowned bird, she flapped back to dry land. Her towel floated ahead. The water had soaked her robe through. "If you hadn't distracted me—"

"*I* distracted you?" Rione trailed her to the stairs.

It struck her that he was still naked. Not that her sodden robe hid anything either.

"No...I mean yes. No." Her eyes roamed everywhere, trying not to look at Rione. Heat rose up her spine and to her cheeks as she slopped up the steps. She darted around for another towel. Only his lay crumpled on the bench.

"Arggggh."

"Take mine." More sloshes. He must have wadded back into the water.

Instead, she grabbed her drenched one, which lapped at the pool's steps and wrapped it about her torso. "I have to go," she repeated. Æri stalked out of the bathhouses without giving Rione a chance to respond.

~ 13 ~

ÆRI

Arriving at the entrance to her chamber, still somewhat dis-gruntled, Æri discovered Brennos waiting by the curtains with a wheat-haired housemaid. The walk back had dried most of her off, but her hair still dripped.

"Ah, good. You've taken advantage of the baths," he said in Fíronian.

Æri threw him a brazen glower. "I assume I have you to thank for disclosing my language abilities?"

Brennos's face remained indifferent, ignoring her chagrin. "This is Karena." He piloted the girl toward the doorway. The young maid cradled a bolt of cloth along with a basket of notions in the crook of her arm. "She will dress you for the banquet and remain assigned to you for the rest of your stay."

"Isn't the banquet this evening?" Æri had the impression main meals were served at sunset. It was barely noon now.

"Oh no. The affair begins shortly this afternoon. Which is why you must start preparing promptly." Brennos clasped his hands. Spotting a spec of dirt on his thumb, he attempted to rub it off. "I hope this doesn't disrupt your plans."

"My day was packed," Æri said dryly as she trudged into her chambers. She indeed hoped to have more time to perfect an an-

115

swer for the king, but she'd make do with ideas formulated that morning.

A twinge of longing for her sister bloomed in her chest. Æri wished Brynja were here to ask for advice. She was accustomed to seeing out orders, not making them, and her sister's talents for diplomatic matters had always surmounted her own in the past.

Karena followed her into the room as Brennos said, "I'll leave you two to it, then," drawing the curtains to block the corridor.

The maid placed the fabric onto the bed and unpacked her notions. She moved with a docile nature, her shoulders folded in and hunched.

"Are you to tailor me something for the banquet?"

"Just to adjust a gown already fashioned, miss." She bowed her head and motioned Æri to take off the robe from the baths.

Karena's eyes flicked to her underarms and then down. "Oh...you didn't get groomed at the baths...?"

Feeling bare, Æri wrapped the robe around her again and crossed her arms. "We don't do that where I'm from."

In Særenfell, she wore thick pelts and long-sleeved woolen tunics all day to keep out the chill. No one cared about grooming, and Æri didn't want to be prodded more after the abrasive scrub.

The maid's face reddened. "You must allow me to take care of it, miss. It will be remarked upon if I do not."

Æri kept her arms folded. She wasn't going to let anyone near her with a blade—be it for battle or for vanity. "What would happen if I said no?"

"It will be reported to the housekeeper..." Karena faltered on the rest.

"And?"

"And I will be punished."

Æri sucked in her upper lip, grazing her teeth against the skin. It occurred to her that this maid was not just a servant paid for her tasks but an indentured one. Seeing Karena's brown eyes, Æri had fallen back into her predictive assumptions. She should have known from the start. The housemaid carried herself differently than Camilla. Camilla looked as though she belonged alongside the villa's courtiers. Karena, on the other hand, with her head stooped and her wobbly fingers unwrapping the sewing supplies, bore a very different role in this household.

"Very well." Æri sighed. "But only under the arms."

"I'll be right back, miss." Karena dipped her head and scurried out of the room like a mouse promised cheese.

Within a few minutes, the girl reemerged with a soap bar, a shaving flint, and a wooden bucket slopping over with water.

Once Karena finished with grooming and fitting the garment, Æri understood Brennos's urgency to prepare early. It took well into the afternoon's hours to trim, pin, comb, and style her into her ensemble.

She couldn't remember the last time she wore a dress. Her sister often donned long wool robes, but Æri opted for the convenience of tunics and braies, even as a child. Long, cumbersome skirts held no place in Særenfell's barefaced crags.

Æri fanned the skirt. She also would've avoided the light coral of the gown, typically leaning toward neutrals, cool grays, or her black flying leathers over this vibrant hue, but Karena insisted the color made her blue eyes shine.

Silky fabric twisted at the nape of her neck to create a halter, then crisscrossed in the back to eventually cinch at the waist, emphasizing her midriff. A thigh-high slit revealed an ample amount of her leg—more skin than she felt comfortable flaunting.

"Are these really necessary?" Æri wedged a finger between a strap and her skin, attempting to loosen the binding. The golden sandals squeezed her flesh, zigzagging and lacing beyond her knee.

"You can't go shoeless, miss."

"Ouch!" Æri winced as Karena coiled a strand of her hair around a heated rod.

"It's best that you stop fidgeting, miss."

The maid secured the spirals with a bandeau of matching coral.

Though Æri protested the use of pigment on her face, Karena promised she'd apply just the minimum amount, dabbling a pinkie-sized dot of rouge on her cheeks and lips. The maid finished by lining her eyes with a charcoal paste, swiping delicately across each lid.

When Karena brought Æri before the full-length mirror, she hardly recognized herself. Gone were the sharp lines, replaced by flowing waves of fabric. However, her shoulders still jutted out, the one thing betraying her strength. The upper arm muscles were defined and smooth, albeit not at their peak due to the weeks of inadequate food and movement. Karena finished by dusting a thin layer of shimmer on them.

"You look lovely, miss." The maid loosened a curl from her bandeau.

Æri debated if this was true. She never allowed herself to take part in all this strange preening and pampering at Særenfell, not entirely understanding the flurry around it. But as Karena sprayed a light lavender mist over her skin, even she was taken by its lavishness. Æri supposed she could endure it for the day.

"Now, *that* is a pleasant change." Brennos' eyes shone satisfactorily.

Even Cuthbert who typically remained silent, gestured in approval, his lids blinking slowly over his green eyes.

Eyes of green are serene.

The rhyme repeated in her memory. Odd that a giant would be considered serene. At first glance, one would think the opposite of the massive mortal. However, after some consideration, Cuthbert's overall countenance—unflappable and even-tempered—did indeed fit with the childhood rhyme.

Dolled up as well, Cuthbert re-adjusted the silk sash at his waist and patted his combed dark blond hair, seeming as uncomfortable as Æri. They had found a tunic big enough to fit past his knees, matching his green eyes. The giant's chamber was not far from her own, but unlike Marlena, Æri had little time to get to know him. She'd said only a few words to him, knowing minimal Jotnarthian, and Cuthbert often kept to himself, saying little in return.

"What part of the villa are we in?" Æri fiddled with the fabric tie at her back as the small party set out down the corridor.

"This wing is reserved for winning fighters invited by the king after the Games. On rarer occasions, he invites fighters from the Auctioning." Brennos prudently took her nervy hand away from her coral knot and instructed Æri to fold it in front. "Remember the bidding rules are still upheld here, and you should not speak to others who outrank you unless spoken to first."

He led them through a maze of passageways until they reached a more extensive courtyard. Low-hanging trees with summer fruits provided shade from the afternoon glare. In the middle of the sage-green foliage, a fountain trickled, its tiered base large enough to swim in. A handful of guests gathered about it, leaning or sitting around its marble rim. The king was nowhere to be found.

Her perusal halted on a familiar face.

Camilla loitered close to a lofty woman with a dark complexion in an elegant seafoam gown. A golden band entwined about the woman's coiffure, reflecting the afternoon sun, and matched her pendant-drop earrings. The layered and linked oblong gems, draped about her neck, nodded to the realm's wealth—though, this kind of adornment was not as openly seen on the king's ensembles.

"That is Consort Ismene." Brennos turned to Æri, identifying the tall beauty.

"Consort—not queen?"

"Queens do not exist in Fíronbec. It is against the custom."

So, in this regard, the Realm of Man wasn't just a title.

Cuthbert and Æri stepped in time behind Brennos, the lead in their trio.

"And there is Consort Rosalind." Brennos indicated the king's second wife, a young-looking woman clad in a rose-pink gown. Soft fabric flowed about her in wisps, like the wings of a bemused fairy. She meandered at the opposite end of the courtyard, encircled by her three lady's maids.

The two consorts couldn't have been more different. Where Consort Ismene was striking and bold in her presence, Consort Rosalind was delicate and ethereal.

Why had the king chosen such contrasting women? It fed Æri's curiosity.

Her eyes traveled over the growing assemblage and snagged on Rione. A sleek tunic enhanced his tall frame with a patterned leather belt. The sienna fabric looped and rested over his shoulder. It appeared a sophisticated shift from his dog-eared Bogs gear and casual clothing from the Auctioning, and, well...A blush crept into her cheeks, recalling their unrobed exchange this morning.

His mouth pressed into a white slash, eye passing over her face. He gave no other acknowledgment nor greeting, returning to his frigid, standoffish nature. Good. His sociable demeanor unsettled her in the baths.

A male servant approached the trio, carting a steaming bowl. Offering wet cloths, he motioned for them to clean their hands. The scent of roses lifted from the perfumed water as Æri rubbed the soft towel between her fingers. More servants rotated throughout the gardens with platters of hors d'oeuvres: figs wrapped in smoked meats, exotic plump eggs, and wine-marinated olives.

As the trio ambled through the gardens, the chatter quieted to whispers. Æri sensed the patrons' brown eyes upon her back—assuming a giant, a Lamiæn, and a mage were not such a common sight in Fíronbec. Discomfort sizzled through her; she was oblivious on how to behave at such an event. A guest, yes—but still a foreign slave, masked in the finery of satins and a painted face. A farce—they had dressed her up to be paraded and gawked at. She fought the creeping urge to smear it all off.

"Brennos, my old friend!" A lanky man with slate-colored robes approached the trio. As he lifted his arms in greeting, an opalescent appliqué glimmered along the hem. It whirled like ink in water. Unlike the typical tunics worn here, his collar was high and stiff, reaching just below the jawline. Behind thin, round-rimmed frames, his eyes shined silver, paralleling his peppered gray-and-black hair.

"Hello, Cormac." Brennos smiled in return and bowed his head in greeting. "May I introduce Æri of Særenfell and Cuthbert of Jotnarach." He turned back to them. "This is Reverend Cormac of Dianeane, the priest responsible for the archives in the Grand Libraries of Méritras."

Eyes of silver long remember.

Preceding the Split, priests and priestesses from Dianeane—the Realm of Gods and Goddesses—were sent throughout Glasterra to care for the realms' temples and their libraries.

An idea formed as Æri thought of the Blodlyst and her queen. This priest might have some answers. Following the set rules, she directed her question to Brennos.

"Are we permitted to visit these libraries?"

Reverend Cormac did not wait for Brennos's guiding gesture, his eyes crinkling at the corners. "Yes, the libraries are open to all, but only if your owner permits. In your case, you may have to wait until the end of the Auctioning."

Æri bowed her head in respect. "Thank you, Reverend."

It would be something to consider. Even in the years prior to the realms' separations, Særenfell was too northern to be regularly appointed a priest or a priestess. The last had died long before the Split. Here, she'd have access to new scriptures. Perhaps the priest or the documents he guarded held a key.

Æri's ears detected an identifiable voice, pulling her from her reverie as it carried over the festivity's babble, and she whirled toward its direction.

Marlena guided an elderly court member into the gardens at the north entrance. Her uniform resembled the sentinels' but with less bulk and she wore a long sword sheathed at her hip. Thick leather greaves shielded her feet and legs.

Æri's chest lightened with the sight of her acquaintance. She twirled back to Brennos. "May I approach her?"

Brennos's steady gaze went toward Marlena's, and he gave a curt nod. "You may, but be aware, she is on duty and will need approval from her owner to speak with you."

Doing little to hide her excitement, Æri dashed away.

Marlena's features lit up when she noticed Æri, cursorily turning to the noble beside her—a woman with fine lines and an upturned nose—who gave a silent sign of consent.

"Æri!" Her grin grew wide and infectious as she approached, then stopped to look her up and down. "Why, don't you look fashionable."

Æri waved off her compliment. "Marlena...how"—she began in Særenian, then decidedly switched to Fíronian—"how are you here?"

Marlena's eyebrows rose with the change in tongues, and she motioned to the woman she arrived with, who now conversed with another courtier. "Lady Lavina's husband won my bid and assigned me as her protector." She shifted the subject back to Æri. "And I'm assuming you're either a quick learner or...you knew Fíronian this whole time." Placing her hands on her hips, Marlena looked a tad peeved.

"I'm sorry...I had hoped it to provide some sort of advantage—against all of this." She chewed her cheek. "But apparently, I am not as good at hiding things as I thought."

Marlena chortled. "You sure fooled me."

Æri rolled her eyes and laughed. "I think you might be the only one who didn't know..." Wanting to digress from the topic, she asked, "How is your new position?"

"It's been good so far. Their household staff is fair-minded."

Only two days had elapsed from the second round, but Marlena's eyes already appeared more rested, the weariness of the Auctioning no longer there.

"I'm glad to hear." Æri spoke in earnest. She'd fretted over where they took both Marlena and Oisin after the match. "And what of Oisin?"

"A Venator chief purchased him."

Her stomach clenched. "Did he have an eyepatch? A scarred face?"

"I don't think so..." Marlena considered this, mouth screwing to the side. "No. He had two eyes. Light brown hair. Not very tall."

Not Rione, then. Æri puffed out a sigh.

A bell rang, the clear note pinging from the other side of the gardens.

"That would be your cue." Marlena jabbed a thumb behind her back. "I have to stand by the doors while everyone eats."

"I wish you could join us."

"I'm sure I'll see you around in Méritras. If my owners allow it and I get some time off, maybe we can share a meal after your last bidding round?"

"Yes, perhaps." Æri didn't know where she'd be after the final fight, but she had a feeling this would not be the last time she'd see Marlena. She bid her friend farewell and hurried toward the banqueting hall.

"You'll be sitting with me tonight." Camilla had hooked Æri's elbow and was dragging her through the sea of courtiers.

An expansive table shaped like a large U occupied the enormous dining area. Its hollowed center allowed servants to bring various dishes back and forth from where an impressive array of cuisine lay atop the alabaster marble, creatures' heads of varying shapes and sizes festooning the ends. Dishes burst, bowls overflowed, and pitchers brimmed—a far more ostentatious feast than the one she consumed after the Auctioning's first round. Æri only recognized a small portion of what was presented: a stuffed grouse or swine's head, but not much more.

What a strange way to dine. No chairs or benches lined the table as expected, and in their place, lounges.

Brennos and Cuthbert were already idling on a corner of the U—Cuthbert taking up two spaces—near Consort Rosalind, but Camilla towed her in the opposite direction.

"Camilla...I am not sure if this is allowed. Shouldn't I be with—"

"Hush, of course it is." Her lips lifted whimsically at the corners. "Ismene has requested your presence. Besides, the meal would be rather boring if I had no one new to talk to."

After Camilla finished the proper introductions, Æri stayed awkwardly upright as she waited for Consort Ismene or Camilla to give her further directions.

Was she to lie down next to the consort? Or to take the lounge adjacent?

"Tell me about your mountains, Lamiæn." The consort ushered Æri to recline beside her, tossing an emerald sateen cushion aside.

Æri faltered, but Camilla fluttered her hand, motioning for her to join the consort. Camilla took the lounge propped closest.

Consort Ismene's slender hands curved to cup her ceramic goblet. As she took a sip, her red lips left a burgundy imprint along the rim. The rouge reflected the mahogany of her heavy-lidded eyes, framed by thick lashes.

"I have heard many tales of Særenfell's alps, but never from the mouth of one who hails from them." The consort's tone was more of a command than a request, and Æri couldn't see how to avoid it.

She began hesitantly. "The mountains of Særenfell are much like the ones in those illustrations." Æri pointed to a lifelike mural on the wall. "However, ours are covered with a dusting of soft snow. And winds lash up scents of pine and winter berries in the mornings." Her head filled with images of the Northern Fells and the steep inclines of the Midland Valleys. "The best views are from the Ophinyne Cliffs, where our ancient griffins used to nest. Sometimes one can hear the howling of elk from their summits. Or, if the night is clear, wolf packs will cry to the three sister moons." As Æri spoke on, remembering home, her eyes started to burn. It had been too long since she felt the mountains' pull.

"What a divine place." The consort tilted her head back, studying the mountain mural. "Here, our realm is flat as an alia dulcia. The hills around the Villa Glorial are the closest we get to mountains. But perhaps someday I'll pay a visit to your fells."

An odd statement to make. Æri doubted Consort Ismene could go. Surely not now. Unless...

Camilla cut in. "Ismene, why don't you tell Æri about the painted sky." As she said this, Camilla gestured to the ceiling. Vaulted walls mimicked a setting sun, with purple and pink hues reflected in wispy, cirrus clouds. Like the baths, they moved ever so slightly.

"Yes..." Ismene drew her gaze to the changing ceiling. "That is Sulivan's doing." She identified a man decked with a large amethyst on his left index finger, the purple stone matching his eyes. Æri recognized the man as the advisor who sat next to King Remus during the bidding round.

"His magic is based on the manipulation of objects. Paintings at the villa are altered to make an onlooker feel like they are part of the image. It gives the sensation of moving along in the space, does it not?"

The ceiling did appear identical to an outdoor sunset, and the longer she stared, the more sugar-pink clouds intensified in the darkening sky.

What a great power to possess—to alter what one saw, Æri ruminated. And how fitting for King Remus to have an illusionist as an advisor.

Her attention moved back to the meal, wondering if this too could be an illusion. The table was laden with food oddities: Purple jellies and maroon stews housed in extravagant bowls of silver and gold. Exotic birds of different sizes stuffed with dates and spices.

"Is that one of the—?" A form looked suspiciously like the iridescent blue bird that had been roaming in the smaller courtyard.

"A peacock," Camilla said, grabbing a leg. "It's rather satisfying. They taste a lot like chicken."

Æri thought she'd pass on the peacock, finding it pitiful that they slaughtered such a beautiful creature for the indulgence of a feast.

Food was moderated in Særenfell, even for the noble classes. Yet here, it looked as if they took half of the realm's food to feed a handful of the court.

"How does this all get eaten?" She tore at a round disk of bread. At least the bread resembled bread.

"Whatever is left over goes to the servants of the household. It usually isn't wasted...however, some tend to eat a little more than they ought."

Consort Ismene chimed in. "I do dislike those who overindulge...quite repugnant."

Camilla tittered. "I would not be surprised if one of the lords used the vomitoria this evening." She languidly inserted an olive into her mouth.

"Vomitoria?" Their gossip repulsed Æri as much as the sound of the vomitoria.

"It's where one might go...if you find your head doesn't quite agree with your stomach. Just through the hall, there." Camilla indicated the exit.

Æri scrunched her nose, hoping she would not find herself in need of a visit.

Her gaze wandered back to Sulivan, then passed to the regal lounge beside him. Vacant. Where was King Remus?

She turned back to Ismene. "And what of the king? What are his appetites?"

"He likes to indulge himself in things other than food." Ismene's tone was laced with ice. Æri comprehended the topic was to end there.

"Speaking of the devil..." Ismene lifted her goblet.

A set of horns blared from the courtyard's threshold where the king made his entrance.

The room fell silent as King Remus joined his retinue. His traditional spiked crown replaced the gold band from earlier, and his bulging crimson shawl twisted about his shoulders and waist. If gods still roamed these lands, King Remus could be one incarnate.

"Don't stop the festivities on my account." The king addressed his courtiers with a smirk. "Eat, drink, laugh, and be merry." He raised his goblet while finding a reclined position and slung back its contents with gaiety. The room burst into a boisterous cheer, and the chatter from before ensued.

A servant shuffled through the space, carrying a large dish of blackened meats, and proceeded to place some of its contents on their plates. Camilla pulled a charred piece off with her fingers and deposited it into her mouth, chewing vigorously.

Æri leaned in to look at her own plate, bringing her nose close to take a whiff. The meat held a sour, pungent smell somewhere between vinegar and garlic.

"What is this?"

"That's one of the Bog beasts...I think we call it deinoplore?" Camilla licked her greasy fingertips.

Æri surreptitiously nudged the plate away. "Is this the beast we defeated in the second bidding rounds?"

The lady's maid emitted one of her light laughs. "No...Oh no. We would have eaten that the day of. The sentinels killed this one today."

Æri felt the blood drain from her face.

"It does take time to grow accustomed to it." Camilla passed her a double-handled goblet, brimful with sweet mint sorbet. "This might settle your stomach. Actually, this has been one of the king's tamer banquets. Do you not agree, Ismene?"

The consort's eyes twinkled with remembrance. "Oh yes. Just last week, all the food was dyed green. And one year, he put tombstones with the guests' names inscribed on their seats. It scared off all hairs from their necks. But it is his way—to jest."

Well aware of how much King Remus liked "to jest," Æri decided she wasn't one to enjoy his larks. This festivity seemed bizarre enough, and the sight of green food would not aid a tipsy stomach.

Shortly after the deinoplore was served, a band of five musicians arrived, picking up a boisterous tune. Their instruments—a collection of strings and brass along with a couple of percussionists to keep the rhythm—bobbed up and down with the jaunty melody. It did not escape her notice that some players' ears finished in prolonged points.

As they listened, tapping to the upbeat tune, Æri's stomach slowly settled. She had not heard much music in recent years. Brynja had learned the harp from their mother, who, in turn, learned the instrument from her music tutor—a Fae from the Isles of Erynelleth, hired by Æri's grandparents preceding the Split.

Æri never bothered to learn. Far from being musically inclined, she spent her time climbing weathered cliffs or dancing in falling snow. But Brynja stopped playing after their father died.

Camilla's handclaps faded on the lounge next to hers, her body going rigid. The lady's maid's head angled away from the band, and Æri followed her gaze.

Rione was in conversation with the king, standing a respectable distance from the royal. He shook his head fervently to something the king said.

King Remus locked eyes with Æri, trapping her stare. Without delay, he motioned to one of his servants.

Draugs. Æri's stomach flipped.

The servant weaved around the lounging patrons and soon faced her little party, rubbing his hands down his brown tunic. He nodded his head to the consort but only spoke to Æri. "The king wishes to speak with you, Æri of Særenfell."

Her stomach roiled again.

Would not Ismene or Camilla invent some excuse?

Ismene simply nodded.

"You are obliged to go." Camilla's voice had lost its serene mannerism.

With little alternative, Æri followed the servant. Her fingers curled, the skin of her palm turning dewy as she anticipated the reasons behind the summons. She breathed in deeply. There should be nothing to fear. The two men couldn't do anything to her here—not in a room with so many people.

As Æri edged nearer, King Remus rose from his grand settee. Twice as large as the other lounges, it featured the same cardinal red as the brocaded garment wrapped around him.

"Æri." He smiled winsomely at her as though she were an old companion. He then halted briefly, scrutinizing her gown, his gaze on where the slit exposed the smooth flesh of her upper thigh. "You clean up quite nicely. Almost...pretty."

His comment made her skin crawl, and she hastened to hide her leg with fabric, grateful her dress bore a high neckline. Other gowns courtiers flaunted that evening did not intend to hide such assets.

"King Remus." She nodded, waiting for him to continue, acutely aware of Rione standing an arm's width away.

The king motioned toward the Venator. "I am sure you are familiar with my lead strategist, Lord Rione Aulius."

Aulius? Why had King Remus presented Rione by his last name?

Throughout the nine realms, individuals were introduced by their surnames only if duplicate prenames existed or their birth origins lay unclaimed.

"I am acquainted." She managed to get out the words while turning briskly to acknowledge Rione. "Lord Aulius."

Æri stared at a spot just below his ear, unable to look into that face. His brown eye tore into her to the point where her pulse quickened.

"Æri of Særenfell." A terse bow of the head in return.

"Excellent." The king clapped his hands in delight. "Æri, now that you are more formally acquainted, you can assist me with a little dilemma. I have requested Rione to play for us tonight, but it seems he does not want to obey my wishes."

Her shoulders loosened a fraction, the tension between them receding. His summons was not about yesterday's proposition.

Rione shook his head again. "King Remus, I simply do not think it is wise. Your musicians have rehearsed every day this week. I am out of practice."

"Nonsense, Rione, you are the finest lyre player I have." The king batted his hand. "The only reason you're not there with them now is because of your hunting abilities."

A minute flinch crossed Rione's features, his nostrils flaring. A hidden jab, but she could not decipher what in the king's words made it so.

"This is where I need your assistance." The king motioned to her once more. "Please convince him to play for us."

"Me? I—I am not sure how—"

"Power in numbers, my darling. If there are two against one, we are sure to convince him, are we not? Or perhaps we need three?" The king pressed, playing another one of his games. Æri got the canny feeling she was merely a pawn, ignorant of his moves.

"I see that you've befriended Camilla, Æri. Shall we ask her for an opinion as well?"

Rione's voice was immediate. "Remus, you win. I will play once the musicians have finished. There is no need to involve Camilla."

Æri caught the slight in the title. *Remus?* Not *King?*

However, the king took no notice. "Ah, what I wanted to hear from the beginning! Thanks for being a fine sport, Rione." He signaled to the band's conductor, who quickly altered the current piece; the performance ended abruptly. "Perfect, it seems the musicians have finished. Fetch your instrument."

Rione only bowed his head and stalked away. If Æri did not know any better, she would have wagered his habitual cool temper bordered close to boiling.

"Sit. You'll enjoy this." The king patted the space next to him.

Her sweaty fist clenched tighter as she sat, thankful for such a large settee. As if supported by prickling needles, she held her body ramrod straight and refrained from lying down. She shot her gaze to where Consort Ismene lounged. Camilla had left.

Some moments later, Rione emerged, an oval string instrument and bow in hand. He rested himself upon a stool, placing the lyre upright on his thigh. Not waiting for the room's noise to settle, he dragged the bow across the strings.

An unnerving sound filled the room, and the walls rattled with the long-held note.

The ambient revelers quieted.

What flowed was not perfect. His instrument reverberated rough and low, swelling then thinning as the bow dragged back and forth, Rione's nimble fingers gliding along the strands. Still, it was pure, the rhythmic chords holding the audience as if in a trance. They fell deeper and deeper as long tones produced a melody so dissimilar from the lively canter played minutes before. Æri couldn't tear her eyes away.

She had never heard anything more moving—until he began to sing.

The lyrical ode resonated, its timbre echoing in the banqueting hall. Like honey melting in a cup of tisane, the verses calmed her tight chest, swaddling the heart. Strangely, the words were not in Fíronian. He sang them in Fae.

Her fingers uncurled, and her nose stung, foretelling tears that loomed close to the surface, elicited by an emotion she did not know existed.

A darker memory flashed of milky-white fingers plucking harp strings like hairs on a scalp. Shaking her head to wake her from the daze, she realized Rione had finished his song. Æri wiped at an escaped tear with the back of her hand.

A pause ensued. A breath held, lingering between shock and awe.

Then the king clapped, and his tranced courtiers joined. Slowly at first, then growing, some even stood from their lounges, the claps rising into thunderous applause.

Rione found her stare. Something vulnerable refracted.

She swallowed, her hand trembling; Æri took the opportunity to excuse herself. The king was too occupied to notice her departure. She aimed for the courtyard, escaping the room of too many eyes.

Warm tears now poured. The charcoal makeup blackened her fingertips as she smeared the salty drops. That song...his voice, unlatched memories she'd buried, memories of her childhood—of her mother and father.

Her throat ached with the withheld sob. She needed to find that place again, the place of balance. These last two days in the king's court had made her irrational. And Rione's melody—*What had it done to her?* The steadiness she valued for survival was slipping away like the ash between her fingers.

She walked through a maze of pruned hedges—the night air cool compared to the stuffy interior of the banquet. Only one moon shone bright, a waning gibbous, its light guiding a path.

Listen, smell, feel—a trace of an evening flower blooming, the crunch of gravel under her sandals, the soft cadence of crickets. She scraped for control again, inhaling. The budding sounds of the night gradually dissipated the echo of the haunting song.

Her head whipped up to a bird crying above.

Gyr? She reached out, searching.

No, just a night owl hunting for dormice. One skittered from the path and out of the predator's sight.

Her left elbow throbbed, and her palm itched. She moved to scratch it, but her fingers met air. She rubbed the rounded limb, then tapped the skin, hoping to quell the phantom sensation.

Now alone in the night with its comforting stillness, she wandered farther into the gardens, yearning for more of that calm—that place where she locked her memories away.

A sniffle came from behind one of the olive trees.

Rounding the corner, she discovered Camilla cradling her head in her hands. Had she, too, been provoked by Rione's music? But before she could approach the tearful lady's maid, audible footfalls thumped from the other side of the hedge—someone running on the gravel. And there was Rione. His arms banded around Camilla's middle and he scooped her up, her toes dangling just above the ground. They remained in a tight embrace.

Æri sprang behind the bend, hoping neither of them saw. Her feet found the path soundlessly back to the entrance of the banqueting hall.

Æri did not know what to make of the encounter. It looked so...intimate.

Could Rione and Camilla be lovers?

The idea floated in her thoughts as she tried to find hints that suggested this: Camilla's unease as King Remus spoke to Rione at the banquet and Rione's sudden change of heart when the king mentioned her name. But why keep it a secret?

Something rapped her shoulder.

Out of instinct, she threw out her arm, ready to defend herself. The scrawny man's eyes popped out in shock as she held him to the wall, crushing her forearm against his windpipe.

She immediately loosened the hold, shaken by her derailment. The man bent over, coughing. It was the same servant from earlier.

"Sorry—I'm...sorry." The walk appeared not to have helped much after all.

He flailed a hand, flapping it up and down as if to gesticulate it happened all the time. "The king—he wishes to speak with you again."

Æri moved toward the banqueting hall. Music from the band had started up, and a fool danced to a cackling crowd.

The servant shook his head, gesturing in the direction of the corridor. "Alone."

~ 14 ~

BRYNJA

Something hummed at her fingertips as if music played within the chamber. Brynja hadn't felt the vibration of chords for years, but a noise had drawn her to the door of the music room. She risked damnation to herself and her subjects by leaving the keep's tower. If her court discovered an unguarded way out from the tower, they'd escape, jeopardizing Særenfell. Those afflicted with the Blodlyst had decimated half the population during the last civil war. Containment was key. They were only permitted to leave with an accompaniment of guards, and never outside the fortress. Brynja had decreed this herself. But on occasion, when her restless mind could no longer find peace in her stone prison, her feet found their way to the West Wing of the keep—a place that existed in memories and sorrows, and the shut doors of her childhood.

Her hand rested on the music room's door, bolted and locked. She dared not enter. Where had that hum come from? Ghosts playing her harp from a yonder year? No, she didn't believe in ghosts. The wind, perhaps. Only pain, dust, and faded stains would greet her if she opened those doors. Instead, she continued down the hall to her old chambers she had shared with Æri.

Darkness and the wind's whistle shrouded the old rooms. Unrepaired windows leaked the cold, and cobwebs netted corners. No torch guided her, just her enhanced senses; safer to leave nothing, safer to walk in the cover of the night than bring unwanted probes.

Her finger drew lines in the dust on the bedside table, circling the storybook of fairytales. She and Æri spent hours into the night rereading them after Father had already finished reciting a dozen. It was before the Blodlyst had transformed her completely, when her hair was still a mismatch of white and dark brown. Her hand touched the brittle white that covered her head. The desire to turn back time made her throat ache.

She peeled open the cover of the storybook and located her favorite tale, "The Maiden in the Tower." The one where a knight saved a princess locked high in a tower and the only way in was by climbing her hair. She stroked the illustration: a charming turret, crooked and kinked, morning glories scaling its walls, and the sun, bright and gleaming on the maiden. As a child, she dreamed of a knight coming for her one day, whisking her to another realm without snow. Now she was locked in a tower, but no knight would ever save her. Her prison looked nowhere near as serene as the illustration. And Æri, Æri had been taken from her.

She slammed the book shut, scowling. Fairytales were for little children who had dreams.

When she snuck back into her rooms, an earsplitting scream traveled from the adjacent chamber. A deep, sick sensation ate at the pit of her stomach like gnawing wolves on bone marrow.

One of us succumbs. The voice told her it was time. Out of all those afflicted, to her knowledge, Brynja was the sole person who could hear the voice inside her mind. In all others, the Blodlyst took the form of pain and torture, driving its host to insanity.

Her door trembled with the knock of fists. "Your Majesty! We need you. It's Dahlia." Ildrid's voice carried through, marked with panic.

Brynja hastily draped her morning robe to cover her clothes, which would give away a night spent not in her chambers but out, and rushed to the neighboring room.

Dahlia lay bound to her bed, her body contorting against the restraints. They had tied her limbs to keep her from ripping herself to shreds.

Two other courtiers scurried with buckets and rags to clean her body.

"Did you give her the elk blood?"

"Yes, Your Majesty, it didn't work."

Black blood dribbled from a corner of Dahlia's mouth. Brynja didn't have to pry it open to know the tongue inside had turned black too. Her end was imminent.

"The Blodlyst is taking control."

They required human blood to slow the progression. She and Dahlia had been two of the longest afflicted; however, the illness progressed differently in all of them. Two years ago, another court member had succumbed to the disease but had been the latest to show the signs. Due to their long lives and the Narkryes' control, dying from the Blodlyst was rare, subdued by the blood they procured. But animal blood was erratic; it satiated but did not delay the development. They needed ironbloods. Wasn't Dahlia proof?

A moan keened from Dahlia, a plea in her expression hollowed Brynja's stomach, emptying it to a quarry. Red obliterated whatever blue remained in her courtier's eyes.

Brynja recalled Dahlia's request months before. *When it turns, do not hesitate. I do not wish to suffer. Will you do it for me, My Queen? Help me pass on into Vallantheia with your strength.*

What she asked from Brynja was mercy. Brynja had given it before and had a duty to give it again. None of her court should endure as her mother had. The Blodlyst robbed her of a dignified death and destroyed her. She had suffered in agony for years before it had ended her. Though this act, an act of fatality, ate at Brynja's soul every time. It was her duty to become reaper.

"Stand aside." She withdrew her dagger, Banisleif, from her belt. The weapon had been in her family since their creation; tales said a mage imbued its blade with the magic gods of Larkærseim. Once unsheathed, it must take a life—the cost of owning such a weapon. The blade banished any cowardness she possessed. It ensured death.

The room stilled apart from Dahlia's painful sobs. The voice that prodded Brynja's skull day in and day out too silenced, as if it comprehended. It's one leniency.

"Ildrid, it's time. Say the words."

The courtier began to chant, reciting an old song to comfort those passing into Vallantheia. The notes of Mother's harp playing strummed Brynja's thoughts. A profound sorrow entered her heart.

When the metal tip pressed under Dahlia's chin, amity passed over her loyal courtier's face. Brynja sliced the edge across her pale neck. It felt as if she had slit the blade over her own.

White smoke ascended from the keep's tower. A sign from the queen that one of her own had died. The practice had been custom since the civil wars, providing confidence in the monarchy. It reassured Brynja's people that those with Blodlyst were not immortal and that they, too, faced death.

Perhaps Æri would somehow see the curl of smoke against their gray clouds, a reminder that her queen, her sister, and her people still needed her. An impossible thought. Brynja was responsible for bringing Æri home, not the other way around.

She and the rest of her courtiers collected Dahlia's ashes and tipped them into the holy well designated for those afflicted, back into the ground of Særenfell. The ashes tumbled like snow from their skies until the darkness consumed them.

~ 15 ~

ÆRI

King Remus sprawled across his study chair, legs stretched open and torso arched. It gave him an air of ease undeterred by the rigidity of the curved seat, like a swathe of silk draped over a woman's shoulders.

Something aromatic and cloying clung to the air...incense?

The desk separated him from the rest of the study; a bowl of fruit sat on its marble center. The three braziers smoldered in the room's crooks, crackling and hissing, and the Nine Muses swayed beneath their low glow.

King Remus dismissed the servant with a leisurely swing of his hand. Then it was just the two of them.

Gooseflesh peppered Æri's shoulders, and she pinched the soft skin under her arm to steady her nerves. After his lewd look earlier, the subdued lighting and hypnotic scent in the room did little to ease her suspicious mind. Despite the king's sentinels and Brennos watching her like hawks, she wished she'd swiped some kind of defense at the banqueting hall—a butter knife would inflict more damage than her trimmed nails.

A smug grin dallied on his lips as he plucked a strawberry from the bowl. He fondled it with his fingers before biting into the red flesh.

"Surprising what a tidbit of rouge can do." His eyes teased her, assessing. "But it looks as though you've gone and smudged some of it." He tossed the fruit's calyx into the courtyard and paused a beat, waiting for her reaction. "Oh, don't stand there like I am going to ravish you—regardless of how appetizing you look tonight. If I wanted, I'd have sent you to my sleeping chambers, *not* my tablinum. Anyways, I prefer more willing subjects."

Did he think those words appeased her?

When she didn't move from the entry, the corners of his mouth flattened and his face turned somber. "Æri, have a seat. We are here strictly for business." King Remus gestured to a chair opposite him, on the other side of the desk. "I will behave myself."

She remained for a moment, evaluating, then proceeded cautiously toward the desk. Her legs felt heavy as if they were made from ore, her body a bundle of nerves.

Æri balanced herself on the chair and eyed the king as he scrutinized her mannerisms: the way her spine didn't touch its back, how she sat at the very rim, ready to take action—flight or fight—not yet convinced on which to choose.

"I am aware that my reputation may not be to your liking. However, as long as you're forthright, I too will be. Given this, I am eager to hear your answer." Something sparked in his eyes. They were dilated, the round blacks ebbing out the rim of golden brown. Had he taken something?

She should watch her words—careful to frame them in a way sure to satisfy. The king made no promises. Her reply to his "request" pushed at the tip of her tongue. He offered her freedom.

Æri was ready to use it to her advantage—the one thing she had to barter. "I will agree to your proposition...however, I have a condition."

"Ah, a bargain." The king rubbed his jaw. "Go on."

The gesture lit a small kindling of hope. "I will agree if you, in turn, help me find a cure for my people."

His discerning eyes refocused on hers. "I was unaware your people suffered from an illness."

Æri took in his gaze, clenching her hand on her lap to keep it from quivering. "Not all of them have it, just a select few. But if you aid us, my people should not need to hunt for your men. We'd both win."

When she left Særenfell, only one source of nourishment remained. What if Signe failed to hunt additional feed in time? What if her queen's court had escaped the tower and another civil war had been triggered in her absence? She stared at the king, willing herself not to express her fears. She would return to them.

The royal's mouth twisted to one side. "How are there any winners if no one loses?" He did not wait for a response. "I'd have to know more about this 'disease' first if I am to help you in any capacity."

Æri delayed, deliberating how much to reveal.

"It is a disease of the blood. The skin and hair turn white, the senses become altered, and it's progressive. We know a lack of iron in the body causes the cravings, but ordinary food alone cannot alleviate it. Blood is the only nourishment we've found that can satiate the afflicted...particularly men's blood, but not limited to. What draws them is a *type* of blood with increased iron—typically those born male just happen to have this trait. It's rarer in women."

"Interesting..." The king's face was inscrutable. Surprisingly, he didn't ask how she discovered this—how Otta spent years comparing blood samples under their magnifier to deduce these results. Instead, he drew in his lower lip, studying her as if he already knew she had more to say. "And you believe I could provide answers for a cure?"

"There's a possibility, yes. I need access to the Grand Libraries in Méritras." The sooner, the better, so she said, "Tomorrow."

Æri was pressing her luck, but she had to try. With any success, she'd unearth something worthwhile, no matter the results on the final bidding day.

The king's lids narrowed marginally, seeming to read her thoughts. "This...research would be strictly to find a cure?"

"Yes."

A long pause ensued. Of course, he made her wait on purpose.

Eventually, King Remus leaned across his desk, took up a stylus, dipped its quill into the glass orb to soak up the floating liquid, and scratched some letters on a leaf of pressed paper. After sprinkling sand over the page to dry the ink, he sealed the parchment with a wax signature using his signet ring. He lifted the handle of a golden bell and swung.

A servant scuttered in.

"Please deliver this to Reverend Cormac."

Only when he turned back to Æri did he address her deal. "*If you win the final round at the Auctioning, I will grant your freedom and help you find a cure. Yet, only on the pretense that you teach us how your aircraft work.* Consider that letter the first part of our deal carried out. Reverend Cormac is expecting you tomorrow. Before this, however, I'd like you to pay a visit to my Inventorium. Brennos will know what to do if you have any further questions."

The king blinked languidly at her, his hooded eyes falling to her mouth. "Now, I would like to move on to more pleasurable things..." He waited, letting his words trail off.

If she were smart, she'd stay quiet, but the impulse to throw the words back at him niggled her intentions. "I'll pass the message to one of your wives. I'm certain they'll help you with what you have in mind."

The silence in the room stretched. The taunt had bemused the king, but his reaction was quite the opposite of what she expected. His full lips arced upward.

Æri wriggled in the chair. "May I leave?"

"You are dismissed."

She had done it. Æri struggled to contain her triumph as she left the study. In spite of her success, she managed to keep her features to mild disgust, masking the giddiness building inside. An agreement Brynja undoubtedly would be proud of. Though the prospect of divulging her flying knowledge gnawed, the chance to find a cure for her sister and people outweighed the conflict riling in her chest—and she'd be free.

"Oof!" She collided into something solid...and warm. Sienna fabric? Retreating, she saw what—who it was. "For the love of gods and goddesses. Not you."

Rione, broad-chested and still in his clothing from the banquet, obstructed the exit from the king's chambers. His eye flew over her, looking visibly disturbed. Upset King Remus hadn't invited him to the meeting?

"Æri, are you—"

"Off to bed. Here to visit your master like a faithful hound? He seems to be in the mood to play fetch."

He scowled. "What did he want?"

"None of your business." She folded her arms. Why did he care about her discussion with the king? "Please move."

Rione wavered as if he had more to say but then stepped aside. As Æri strode out, the hairs on the back of her neck bristled from his watchful gaze.

A cool breeze flowed from the lake, tousling her loosened curls as she walked along the veranda. Her thoughts pinwheeled around her like the dizzying fall from her Skimmer. Was Rione following her? What loyalties did he have toward the king? She worried her tongue over her chipped incisor and she let out a puff of air. She didn't want to think about the Venator.

Unexpected hope loitered from her discussion with King Remus. She'd have access to the libraries. Something in the texts might give answers to the Blodlyst.

The air went unexpectedly still around her, the night noises silencing. Ahead of Æri, an aging woman shrouded in black wandered through the pillars, weaving like a dark specter. A lone wail hovered, chilling Æri to the marrow of her bones. All other thoughts whisked from her. She remembered that sorrow all too well.

She hurried to her rooms, leaving the king's mother to lament a husband long gone.

~ 16 ~

ÆRI

Pale, translucent rays diffused through the amber screen as peacocks' trumpeting squawks resounded in the courtyard outside Æri's room, making their presence known in the morning's early hours. She tugged on her bidding uniform of grays and laced her boots, almost grateful to be wearing them instead of the coral dress and gold sandals. Her legs ached from yesterday's run, but she embraced the sensation, knowing her muscles were stronger.

Karena had woken her at first light to prepare for the long ride back into the city. Æri beheld the meek girl one last time and wished she had something to give—a token of her gratitude—but she carried nothing save for her appreciation.

"Thank you." Æri squeezed the maid's scrawny hand, hoping she had been granted some excess food from the banquet.

Karena offered a humble smile.

Æri wanted to swoop the girl up and take her along—an impulse to protect the maid from the cruelties of her position. But how? As a slave herself, Æri had used up what little negotiating power she possessed for her people with the king's bargain.

"I won't forget your kindness." Her parting words to the girl felt flimsy, like dried reeds. Perhaps she would return for the maid when she won her freedom. Demand that she too be set free. If only Æri held that power now.

She walked out reluctantly into the sentinel's chained embrace, bound and blinded once more.

Brennos removed Æri's blindfold at the Inventorium's gates. Situated just outside the walls of Méritras, the facility lay on a flat stretch of plowed agricultural plots. The scent of manure blew toward them as a sentinel helped her dismount.

The buildings resembled the Villa Glorial at first glance, with a row of low-rising structures and an impressive façade of columns. However, its terrain held no rolling hills or cerulean-blue lake, and it looked more akin to a prosperous farm than an opulent palace.

Brennos slunk closer to her as they neared the gates.

"I feel like your dog," Æri grumbled. "I'm just missing the leash."

"There's one. You just can't see it," Brennos said, his voice flat and void of any humor.

"Wouldn't it be wiser to have watched over Cuthbert? He is three times my size."

"The king believes I'll be more use here than with Cuthbert."

Only Brennos and one other sentinel accompanied Æri. Apparently, this satisfied those in charge.

"He predicts I'll do more damage than a giant?"

The corner of Brennos's mouth twitched. "In a facility that manufactures the most valued innovations in Fíronbec—it is beyond doubt you'll do more damage."

A man with a round, sagging belly greeted them at the gate. Patchy wisps of hair stuck out from his ears and fringed a balding head, and his rosy cheeks gave him an amiable albeit ridiculous appearance. Eggshell-blue cloth covered his arms and legs, and hefty leather work boots protected his toes.

He thrust his hand out in welcome, taking Æri's before she could offer it. She bristled, the unwanted touch evident as she cringed, but the man seemed oblivious.

"Oh! I'm so delighted you're here! You must be Æri." His pudgy fingers gripped hers and squeezed with exuberance. A gushing smile matched his shining eyes. "Yes, yes, the king informed us that you would aid in one of our endeavors. My name's Gratian, the director of the Inventorium. Come, come, this way!" He walked forward as if bouncing to a jig, belly swaying along. "There is so much to see and, alas, so little time. One day simply could not cover a kernel of our work."

Before heading into the main building, Gratian bobbled his head to several stone-faced guards stationed along the gate's entrance, a silent acknowledgment foretelling his confidence in the security within the walls.

He guided Æri and Brennos through the gates, leaving the sentinel who had escorted them outside with the others. "To set the rules within the Inventorium, you may ask me as many questions as you desire. The ranking regulations on this aspect do not bind us. However, your questions must only concern the project you've come to assist us with."

Æri nodded, curiosity already coiling around her.

Other projects? What other projects? Perhaps the Fíronians had manufactured the road from the Bogs here? If so, what other innovations did these walls hold?

After discussing the bargain with the king, Æri had vowed to do everything in her power to help her people—that her sacrifice for disclosing the information would be offset by what she obtained in exchange. So, she agreed to teach what she knew to those at the Inventorium. However, the king had not specified an amount of time, and though it may delay her return home, Æri also needed time to research the disease. For what good was she to her sister—to her people—if she arrived back in Særenfell with no answers? Yet, she could not predict what that delay would mean for the Blodlyst. The decision weighed heavy on her, and she hoped the Narkrye managed to slow the spread for just a little longer.

Gratian directed Æri and Brennos through a spacious courtyard with various sized garden allotments, reminding Æri of Særenfell's greenhouses—though those seemed like plain compost heaps compared to what grew here. Carefully labeled fruits and vegetables matured within each organized bed.

"Our experimental plots—how we develop our food for our sole season. They appear to be doing well this year," Gratian explained.

They moved through unadorned stone and stucco passageways containing the sharp chemical odor of a space cleaned repeatedly. Impenetrable doors lined the corridor, blocking out contents within. Save for the raps of their feet, the halls were silent.

When they emerged out the back, several enormous barnlike structures, aligned in succinct, even rows, took up surrounding land.

"These are the Magcontinens. Our largest workrooms." Gratian strode to one in the middle.

A tickle riled in her throat.

The king had not told her his reasons for wanting to fly. Instead, she listened to his chosen words, carefully picking them apart and finding half promises. Things unsaid between the lines of his conditional offer—her freedom only given if she won the bidding rounds *and* helped create a flying contraption. But *why* he aspired to fly? The possibilities were endless. She needed the time to solve this answer too.

Brennos's face remained neutral as they ducked through a small door cut into the side of the building.

She had to blink several times to grasp the gist of what stood opposite her.

Inside, a rowing ship, with its extended hull and curved prow, echoed the ancient ships that roved the seas before the Split. However, instead of mast and sail, a streamlined hood arched over its deck, and long winglike fins jutting from its sides replaced the oars. She counted six on each flank. Propped timbers raised the vessel and allowed workers to access its underbelly.

Æri approached one of the strange oars, observing the lengthy blade.

"May I?"

At Gratian's nod, she reached out. To her astonishment, the material flexed under her push, firm but not completely ridged like her Skimmer's wings.

"I was under the belief you did not have aircraft—that the king wanted me to teach you how to build one."

"King Remus tends to be vague with his requests," Gratian said, his tone matter-of-fact. "We've been working on this one for a while now. Meet the Specuformae."

Æri ran her fingers over a sanded board on the hull, smooth as sculpted ice. "A scouting ship?" She identified the term in its name.

"Its main purpose would be to scout, yes. That is if we ever get it off the ground."

Scout what exactly? Æri wanted to ask, but she didn't know if he would answer. "How heavy is it?" she said instead, recalling that the old ships were quite dense despite having a hollow interior.

"It's not as heavy as it looks. We cultivated trees to be especially light without sacrificing their durability, and little iron is used in the framework. As you may have realized, our access to metal is scarce in Fíronbec. We only have what we obtained from before and have to reuse what is left."

Their agricultural innovations must be bountiful to farm trees with such a purpose, but having limited access to ore indeed restricted inventions. They boasted plenty of it in Særenfell's mountains. The most precious, arium, was used to create her Skimmer and many of their hunting tools.

"How is it supposed to fly?" She examined the lengthy propellers once more.

"Oh, I'm delighted you asked! Follow me. I'll show you."

An immense domed-shaped cage neighbored the Magcontinens. Sweet singsongy chirps emerged from the small gaps as they drew closer.

Gratian stopped next to the aviary, peering through its mesh. Birds swooped and fluttered, diving in and out of the jungle of trees within.

His gaze homed in on one. "There! Do you see that little fellow?" Pointing through the wire fencing, he selected a bird no bigger than Æri's thumb. It skirred in all directions, iridescent wings blurring and vibrating around its small frame like a floating gemstone. "Our oars are designed to move like that."

Æri focused on the bird, trying to catch its movement. She had yet to see the vessel work properly, but if they intended it to move like *that*—it was ingenious. Biomimetics had always fascinated her—she designed her Skimmer's body after Gyr's diving form—however, to mimic this tiny bird in flight must have taken ages. Their engineering and intuition far outranked Særenfell's. In her workshop, only she and Otta scrapped through design after design, failing over the years until they finally succeeded. But here...

"Surely you need a viable power source to lift the ship off the ground—to compensate the fuel-to-weight ratio. How do you plan on doing that?" Æri probed, anxious to get to the meaning of all this.

Gratian's eyes twinkled. "That's exactly my point! We *need* power. Procured Bog peat used for basic operations doesn't produce enough energy to lift the Specuformae. The fuel alone would weigh down the craft. It isn't feasible. Now, the reports stated your aircraft ran on a unique type of power source." He paused as she absorbed his explanation.

One of the Venators must have taken note while she flew the Skimmer in the Bogs. She doubted anything remained from the wreckage.

"It wouldn't work here," she asserted candidly. "You need storms to harvest it."

Gratian's face fell. "Oh...hmm...yes, that is unfortunate news. We do have the occasional rain shower, but rarely any storms." He piloted both Æri and Brennos—who'd stayed quiet for most of the tour, his concentration no doubt on her every move—back to the main structure.

"That being said, my scitators—engineers here at the Inventorium—say that they've detected two types of power sources from your realm."

Æri's jaw tightened. There was only one way they knew this. Icy-cold foreboding trickled down her neck.

They may not have it, she told herself. *Stay calm.*

Gratian escorted them into a room with long wooden tables set with an array of objects. Workers, the scitators presumably, in the same long-sleeved, pastel-blue tunics as Gratian, manipulated parts. The murmur of tools sawing and humming filled her ears. On a table in front, a scitator operated on a giant wheel, attaching a ribbed material to its outer rim.

But Æri's eyes faltered on the adjacent table, her body shaking as pure fury washed through her. Brennos's hand immediately moved to her right forearm, and a light prickling sensation radiated from his palm.

Stand down, it wordlessly said.

There, beside the monocle, lay her bionic arm, opened and splayed like a cadaver. They had dissected it into small, scattered pieces. It felt like an icicle to the gut to see her arm like that—first taken away and now torn apart. She'd never be able to reach Gyr now—nor have that sensation of a working hand again.

Her throat clenched, and her breaths staggered out of her. She wanted to scream at Gratian. To yell and shriek at his round, marmot-like face. How could he have done such a thing? His minions destroyed it, that vital part of her. She loathed Rione even more for it. *He* had stolen her arm. *He* had been the one to give it to this man.

She took a rattling breath and closed her eyes, trying to keep her chin from trembling, and focused on the tingling sensation emitting from Brennos's hand.

Æri reached for that numbness to help her think—that place where this rage could not control her. A calmness blanketed her.

"And what, Gratian, did you find after taking apart my arm?" Her words were smooth and steady, but there was also steel behind each syllable.

Gratian took no notice of her intonation; he circled the table and selected two items. Raising the small cylinder-shaped object first, he said, "This we believe to be the fuel cell. Where the energy of the gas you obtain from your storms is converted, but"—then holding out a thin black iridescent sheet, the color resembling a raven's feather, bowed to fit within the exterior shell of her bionic arm—"this is not from your land, is it?"

"No."

"Some of our scavengers have encountered this material in the Bogs. It's not common but by no means rare. What interests me more is how you used it to power this machine." Gratian poked at her disassembled forearm. "We know it utilizes the sun's power, transferring its energy to the same fuel cell, but we don't know *how* you did it."

He looked at Æri with pleading eyes.

She gnawed the skin of her left cheek, debating what to say. Æri had not expected this—any of this. She thought the king wanted to fly, not create a power source. Providing them with this information raised the stakes.

"It was a prototype." She sighed. "We were testing it out on my arm. You'll need much more of it to power your Specuformae. Particular tools are needed to melt and cut the ore. It's a lengthy process...and there is no guarantee it will work in the end."

"But you *will* try?"

Æri considered Gratian's plea.

This was all he cared about, this man of science: the invention, to create something entirely new. He did not see the human who once possessed that arm nor the consequences of such a power, of what the king might choose to do with it if she succeeded.

She struggled to formulate a plan to both satisfy the king and not betray her people—a way to gain her freedom without giving King Remus additional power. She wished now more than ever to have Brynja by her side to tell her what to do.

Still, Æri committed to her promises. Though not as truth-abiding as the Fae, her people prided themselves on their loyalty. And how else was she to save them if she did not agree?

"I swore to King Remus to show you what I know, so that is what I will do."

~ 17 ~

ÆRI

She might not have enough time at the libraries after all. The sun drooped well past its peak when Brennos once again covered her eyes with the blindfold. Her worry increased as they rode away from the Inventorium.

With the bouncing of the horse, Æri's doubts nibbled at her thoughts. Had she made the right choice? The king never specified how long she'd have, nor did she allocate the time for herself—in both the libraries and at the Inventorium. Yet another reminder of her flaws in diplomatic dealings.

Evening neared when they arrived at the Grand Libraries' illustrious steps. Brennos untied her blindfold, and the guarding sentinel, Sinio, guided their horses to a local stall.

Méritras thrived with the hustle and bustle of people ending their day's work. Food and clothing vendors crowded the city square, haggling with their patrons. Women with painted faces moseyed from one potential customer to the next, their draped robes cut to reveal the curve of a breast or an upper thigh. An old pair of comrades laughed boisterously, engaged in a game with two-colored stones, the checkered board etched into the rock they roosted upon.

At the top of the rising stone steps, the prodigious façade of the library towered. Two carved beasts came into view as Æri ascended the milky stone, worn with years of use. They glared down over the entrance.

Their heads maintained a lion form, but their bodies were neither feline, bird, nor serpent—rather a meld of all three, reminding Æri of the griffins that roamed Særenfell long before her people inhabited its mastiffs. Melancholy edged up her throat with the thought of her homeland. Æri tried to shake it off, focusing on what she came here to do.

"The Leo de Volucribus—the winged lions," Brennos said as he noticed her staring at the stone animals. The sculptor had set the beasts' bodies in a crouch, their mouths open to expose four daggerlike canines in a menacing snarl, ready to leap upon any uninvited guest. "One of the many guardians of the archives, embodying wisdom and knowledge."

"One of?"

"Reverend Cormac can answer more of your questions."

The library's atrium, majestic yet simple, held an extended version of an impluvium, creating an emblematic border like a moat encircling a castle. Soft gold light was cast down from the rectangular opening.

Footsteps pattered from one of the numerous archways, and Reverend Cormac entered. Though less ornamental than the previous night, that same thin strip of luminous needlework lined his dark gray robes.

Brennos bobbed his head. "I will go find a bite to eat while you're in the libraries. Sinio should be more than enough security."

The sentinel reappeared when he said this, pacing at the entrance.

"I put a warning ward around the building, so don't get any ideas." Brennos leveled his eyes with Æri's.

Offering him a skeptical look in return, Æri had long given up formulating a plan to escape on her own. The tracking device made it all but impossible, and her bargain was the most viable option now.

As Brennos slipped out, she realized he had bestowed a gift, providing her space from his guard. An act of kindness? Or pity?

He knew how much that arm meant to her. She sensed a change at the Inventorium when he touched her right arm in warning—a slight softening in his generally cold eyes. Whatever his intentions, Æri silently thanked him.

"I could not help but overhear your inquiry about the libraries' guardians." Reverend Cormac led Æri past the impluvium and through a carved archway.

"Just that Brennos implied there are multiple..."

"Ah, yes. There are countless, actually." One gray brow lifted as he inclined his chin—a tutor more than happy to inform. "From the winged lions down to the smallest house cat. Some are grander than others, but most come from legends, faded into myths, and are now only known to us by tradition or depicted in stone.

"Our two guardians there"—he pointed back to the winged lions—"were selected ahead of the Grand Libraries' construction. We've modified the building over the centuries, but those beloved lions stayed with us."

"Why do the libraries need so many guardians in the first place if they only act as a symbol?" Æri had never been one to consider myths as truth. She believed in what she saw, in what was presented before her.

"In Dianeane, knowledge holds supremacy. Faith comes in as a close second. They both need protection—should the guardians be real or symbolic."

They advanced into a reading room with long wooden tables. Arched windows allowed light to pour through. Thinking of Fíronbec's forever summer, she grinned. Some of her worry dissipated. Light would remain until well into the evening, providing her with ample time to read.

Seven stone figures watched over each open arc, their silhouetted heads tilted, gazing toward the floor.

Perhaps more guardians?

Large, low-lit braziers glowed at the base of each pillar, separated from the dark halls that led from the main reading room—their shadowy passageways lined with endless shelves of parchment.

Dust, leather, and old ink filled her nose. A comforting scent that brought back her time with Otta. To Æri's surprise though, the lofty space was entirely devoid of people.

"Where are the other scholars?"

"Given the unusual request, we closed our doors to the public today. It is uncommon to receive such an order from the king and have a bidding fighter enter on the eve of their final round. We thought it wise to eliminate distractions."

Or potential problems, Æri inferred.

Reverend Cormac guided her to a leather upholstered chair adjoining a table piled high in codices, tomes, and scrolls. "Here is what my acolytes gathered on blood diseases—before and after the separation of the realms. If you need anything else, just press on this." He tapped a lever attached to the end of the table. A single chime resonated throughout the reading room.

Æri settled in the chair and spread out her research. "Reverend Cormac," she called out, stopping him before he disappeared into one of the dimly lit hallways. "How long do I have...in the libraries?"

The fine lines around his eyes creased. "You may stay as long as you wish, my child. Although, I would advise against exhausting the whole night."

Æri started at the top of the pile. The medical scroll written in Fíronian described a blood disorder, where the patient bled out uncontrollably if the flesh was cut. She put it aside and took up the next one: a disease that manifested and killed from within, relatively common in Fíronbec, but the cause was unknown. The spleen or liver would enlarge, and a rash sometimes emerged on the patient's skin. Again, not the disease that ailed her sister. She put that aside as well.

The hours slipped by as she carried on with her search. Most of the documents were penned in Fíronian, a few in Dianeanian, and one or two recorded in elvish prose. The Fae often spoke in riddles since they could not lie, but none of their poems, written with characters, alluded to her sister's symptoms. Frustration started to build, a restless tickle growing in her chest and throat. The documents were no more helpful than the ancient ones in the fortress archives.

Æri groaned. How was she supposed to find a cure when she had no lead? Her deal with the king felt like a waste—being trapped in this realm a curse.

She took in a breath and set the medical journals aside, wrestling with the whim to toss them all to the floor.

Her eyes stopped on an old tome wedged at the bottom of the stacked codices. Fingers clasping the leather edges, she yanked it out. Its binding cracked, flaking old paint as she peeled back the cover, the velum within translucent with age. The tome's letters arced and swirled in a myriad of cryptic symbols.

To her luck, she found most of its pages were illustrated.

Æri's flips slowed as she studied the images further. The space between her shoulder blades pulled, her stomach hardening, and a disconcerting sense of something ominous took root.

The tome's pages were laden with haunting forms and apparitions. In one image, a man lay prone on a pallet; an arachnidian creature with long bristled legs clawed from his mouth. She turned the page and lingered, her fingers shaking. On the vellum, a striking beauty stood erect, entirely unclothed. Her eyes were sketched so that they lanced through the page, gazing straight at Æri. At her feet were heaped bodies of men, women, and children; a thin line of blood trickled from her mouth. The red lips were pulled back in a stretched sneer, displaying a row of needle-point teeth. But the woman's hair flowed an ebony black. *Not* white, nor did her sister possess those awful teeth.

"*The Shadow Tales of Hælsgade.*"

Æri jumped at the low voice.

"I wonder how that got mixed up in there." Reverend Cormac cocked his head in reflection. "I will have to have a word with my acolytes." His hands cupped a steaming bowl of stew and a fresh loaf of bread. It was just now Æri noticed the glimmer of words printed on the Reverend's fingers. They scrolled up his arm and beyond the hem. The tattoos matched the iridescent shine of his robes' stitching. She had forgotten that the holy folk carried the words of gods and goddesses on their skin. She must have missed it at the king's feast.

He set the bowl at the far end of the table. "I thought you might be hungry. It does not rival the food from the banquet, but we wouldn't want you to fight tomorrow on an empty stomach, would we?"

Steam floated from the bowl, reaching her nose, smelling of hearty meats and greens. Æri's stomach growled.

"As long as it isn't Bog beast." She gave Reverend Cormac a tight smile.

"We typically do not allow food in the libraries, but I think I'll make an exception tonight. Just keep the scrolls on the other side."

Æri placed the book flat, pages open. The image of the dark beauty with spired teeth stared back. "You said this book was called *The Shadow Tales of Hælsgade*? Is that not the ninth realm? I thought it was overrun with renegades and pirates."

As the most remote realm of all nine, people went to Hælsgade when they didn't want to be found.

"Yes, it has been for a while, or what we knew of it prior to the separations." Reverend Cormac pulled a chair close to sit. "However, before that—in yesteryear—another kingdom ruled the realm." He patted the book. "And these are their legends. The collected myths of monsters that roamed their lands and neighboring realms."

"Can you tell me what it says?" Æri pointed to the strange texts on the opposite side of the illustration.

"Let's see here." The Reverend slid the tome over, positioning it in front of him. He withdrew his silver-rimmed glasses, rubbing them clean with his shimmering sleeve before placing them on his bowed nose. "It states that these are the Vampryne, creatures of the night that feed off human blood. They are neither dead nor alive but somewhere in between."

Æri's own blood went cold with his translated words. There were more similarities in these ancient tales to the Blodlyst than in any of the medical scriptures. "Does it say anything more about where they originated? How they were formed?"

Reverend Cormac flipped to the front. "The tales say the god of darkness himself created these beings—crafted from another god's nightmares as an act of vengeance for not heeding his demands. The god of darkness wished to be revered as he was by all beings in a world once formed by shadows. But because the other deities forbade it, he made his own subjects from the darkness to follow his command." The Reverend paused, ruminating over the writings. "It is important to remember this is an interpretation. Not fact nor truth. These are oral legends written by a scholar, perhaps a set of scholars, who sought to preserve the old tales."

Æri's tongue skimmed the chip in her tooth. "Do you know where or from whom I can garner more about these Vampryne?"

Reverend Cormac closed the book and moved it to the side. "Besides going all the way to Hælsgade?" He let out a breath and shrugged. "The Seven Sages might know. They hold most of the answers when it comes to our ancient gods." He pointed to the statues in the great windows. The sky behind them had now cooled to a sapphire purple.

So those were who the statues represented.

Æri had forgotten about celestial rulers but was somewhat aware of their history. The original Seven Sages were the founders of Dianeane. When one died, a vote ensued to elect their replacement. It had gone on like that since the realm's formation. Supposedly the wisest of all the priests and priestesses, the Seven Sages were closest to the Holy Serenity—the creation of all—other than the gods themselves.

"I'd have to find a way to get to Dianeane first," Æri said, half joking.

Reverend Cormac's eyes glimmered sadly, but he attempted a smile. "Your stew is getting cold." He gestured to the steaming bowl.

Her stomach made another gurgle as she dragged her chair toward the end of the table. Tearing at the loaf, she dunked in the chunk to soak up some broth. After another day with little food, the stew surpassed anything offered at last night's banquet. She closed her eyes, savoring the flavors. Spices slowly budded on her tongue, warm and comforting.

"Mmmmm." An unintentional sigh escaped her lips, and she felt her face color with embarrassment.

The Reverend chuckled. "Glad to see it was not wasted. Our cook will be pleased to hear that someone enjoys her food."

Reverend Cormac folded his glasses and prepared to rise once more, but Æri didn't want him to leave just yet. Whether it was his profession or just his nature, Reverend Cormac's company soothed her.

"How long have you known Brennos?" Æri tucked a loose strand behind her ear before dipping another piece of bread into the stew.

His eyes warmed at the mention of his friend, and he settled back in the chair. "Oh, since he arrived here. He held a curiosity for the libraries, like you, though he did not come until after his final bidding round." Reverend Cormac's thoughts seemed to stray. "I know he appears detached at times, but his heart is in the right place."

As well as his loyalty to the king, Æri thought. And what of Reverend Cormac? How loyal was he to King Remus? After observing the two men together, she suspected he and Brennos might be more than just good acquaintances.

"How long have you been here in Fíronbec?"

"I arrived ere the separations. I'd say about ten years prior...so I assume I ought to be calling Fíronbec my home." Again, that wistful look appeared in his silver eyes, and he absently traced the marks on his hands.

"Would you choose to go back—if you could?"

"Ah, well, that is up to King Remus. I suppose I'd go if he allowed me to leave, but the journey might be long...and I am unsure what is left for me in Dianeane. My life's path sent me here, so my duty to the gods and goddesses remains in Fíronbec."

Æri pushed a braised carrot. The topic edged closer to another related question that had nagged at her for nearly a thousand years. "What is your theory...on the separations...of what happened to Glasterra?"

"Hmmm. The answer everyone wants to know..." He drummed his fingers on the table's wax-polished wood. "Alas, I am not one of the Seven Sages. Again, I believe they may know more than I...but I've had some time to reflect. As I am sure you know, time here is not what it was"—he looked at Æri—"and I think that you, too, have your own beliefs. Tell me, Æri, before I give you my theory, what of yours?"

Æri blinked a few times, flattered that he, a scholar of Dianeane, expressed an interest in hearing her opinion. She mulled over his question, thinking back to times when she sat alone in her chambers, reading over scrolls, hunted in the tranquility of their ancient forests, or flew the Skimmer over Skathi's temple.

"I think something displeased the gods...something angered them...to make them tear the world apart like that. I've seen temples abandoned by the people here. The same is true in my lands...but perhaps the gods abandoned us first."

Reverend Cormac's mouth curved in satisfaction. "Yes, but the greater question is why?"

"Do you know?"

But as he prepared to answer, a ginger cat jumped on the table, knocking Æri's empty bowl to the floor with a loud, echoing bang.

"Titus! Come back!" A young girl ran into the reading room dressed in similar dark gray robes as Reverend Cormac, save for the embroidery. Æri bridled her bewilderment. The girl was waiflike. Her height reached no taller than the third or fourth bookshelf.

The cat, perking his ears at her voice, darted toward the end of the table where the scrolls were piled high. Reverend Cormac caught the fleeing creature by its scruff before it knocked the ageless documents to the floor as well.

"Pia. You should be in bed." His tone was firm but not scolding as he addressed the little girl. Reverend Cormac beckoned her forward and deposited the mewing cat in her outstretched arms.

"Titus saw a mouse and ran out of my room. I can't sleep without him," the little girl said, whistling through a gap in her front teeth. She stroked the cat, who went limp in her arms. Her big brown eyes widened when she saw Æri. "Oh..."

"Pia, this is Æri. I am assisting her with some work this evening. Æri, Pia."

Æri smiled down at the child, astonished. This was *a child*. The first she'd seen in Fíronbec. "Nice to meet you, Pia. May I pet Titus?"

The doe-eyed girl nodded, and Æri stroked the cat's head, already purring in the girl's arms.

As Æri petted Titus, Pia's mouth shaped into an O again when she sighted Æri's limb. "Where's the rest of your arm?"

Æri leaned forward to whisper in the child's ear, and her eyes sparkled, growing even bigger. "Wow! You killed a Bog beast?!"

Reverend Cormac looked at Æri, seeing through the fabrication. Æri drew her shoulders up in admission. She had to tell the girl something—even if it wasn't fact. She didn't even know if she could voice the truth. Delving into the real reason caused Æri's chest to constrict and throat to close. If only she had truly lost it in something as heroic as killing a Bog beast.

"Pia is my youngest acolyte. Her mother works as an indentured servant. She entrusted her to the libraries for safekeeping."

How strange...Æri schooled her expression, not wanting to show her alarm. Didn't an indentured servant's child belong to the owner, not the mother? The rules might have possibly shifted with the servitude's reintroduction...

"Off to bed, Pia." Reverend Cormac shooed the girl toward a back exit of the reading room.

"Good night! Nice to meet you, Æri," she called as she scurried out, Titus in tow.

Reverend Cormac's smile faded as the girl left. "I trust you will keep this information between us. Brennos knows of the girl—but the king does not. And any child born must be registered with the Curia—the king's advising court. Pia's mother did not want her father to know. He is not a sympathetic man."

Æri bowed her head in understanding. "I won't mention it."

So Brennos did indeed keep secrets from the king. For his friends, at any rate.

"Thank you."

A yawn escaped Æri's mouth, and Reverend Cormac's grin reappeared.

"It seems Pia isn't the only one who should retire for the night."

"I suppose you are right." Æri was torn between leaving the library and going to bed. She needed sleep, requiring all her strength for tomorrow, but she had barely scraped the surface in her research.

The Reverend bent to retrieve the overturned bowl. "Brennos will be waiting for you in the atrium."

"You've been more than generous with your time and knowledge, Reverend Cormac." Æri turned, but he stopped her.

"You asked me why I thought the gods had left..." He hesitated, seeming to think over his words. "I believe the fates have dealt us the wrong card."

Æri's brows knitted in confusion.

"Perhaps I should reframe my answer in a way that would help your path: Seek an elf here in Fíronbec. If you can find the time, you may unearth more answers with them."

Æri digested his words as she exited. A clear direction. Despite the enigmatic meaning, it partly made up for her lack of luck combing through the library's scriptures.

~ 18 ~

ÆRI

Stars winked through the gauzy curtain. Its fine netting blocked buzzing insects from entering the chamber, their wriggling silhouettes defined by moonlight. Two moons were visible through the veils: a sliver of a waxing crescent, the other waning into its last quarter.

She should sleep—she *had* to sleep, but the anticipation of the final match churned in her gut, her nerves eddying like cold mountain winds, the restlessness not entirely due to the upcoming fight. The priest's parting words perseverated.

How could an elf give her answers he could not? Why didn't he, a scholar of the Dianeane, just tell her? And what of those shadowed creatures? The dark things from in-between. *The Vampryne.* Could they still be myths and legends? Or were her sister and her people part of this dark god's vengeance?

No. She wouldn't believe it.

Too many questions bubbled inside, and she admitted the library visit might cost her in the morning hours. Æri needed to relax. Cuthbert's maneuvers were easy to guess after the last two bidding rounds. Yes, he had strength on his side, but he moved slowly—his actions bulky and predictable. She would win. She'd win her freedom, find a cure another way, and go home.

Her morning routine for the final round was different from the start. The guards had not returned Æri to her old cell the night afore but rather to a much roomier chamber, and it was not Fabia who woke her but a new sweet-faced maid who delivered her laundered gray uniform.

Was she even in the Castrum?

The stone walls appeared to be the same, yet that said little—identical cream-colored sandstone covered the city.

When the guards guided her to a different training room, it became clear she did not reside in the same secured building. Though smaller than the one at the Castrum, the room was well-ordered, and its supplies were in fairer condition: the mats less worn and stained, the weights organized in neat rows instead of a jumbled stone pile. Besides her guards, she was the only fighter who occupied the space.

While warming up, Æri attempted to steady her mind and push the unanswered questions aside. Her muscles ached from the ride back to the city, so she concentrated on areas that gave her agile movement, recalling the methods Oisin had briefly instructed her and Marlena on before the second bidding round.

Oisin...*Oisin!*

Eyes of blue and yellow tell of tomorrow.

How could she have forgotten the rhyme for the Fae?

Despite trying to block out Reverend Cormac's advice from the libraries, she pictured the elf, his knowing bow of the head essentially handing her the win at the second match. Perhaps *he* had answers. Reverend Cormac did say to speak to an elf, did he not? And Oisin was the only one she knew in Fíronbec.

She'd seek him out once all this ended...somehow.

Æri had just finished stretching when Brennos entered the training room. "I imagine this will be the last time I'm honored with your morning welcome."

"I suppose it will." Brennos's lips twitched imperceptibly. "Follow me. I will explain the last bidding round while we prepare you."

"Prepare? Wasn't I just doing that?"

Brennos continued to walk as if he had not heard her, leaving Æri to trail after him. All his niceties from the night afore seemed to have evaporated with the formalities of bidding day.

"The second round was a challenge of wits and creativity. You were also given the day to make a weapon familiar to you—the bow and arrow. However, in this next round, familiar weapons will not be permitted. Rather, this final phase of the Auctioning will test your adaptability."

They curved around the corner, and Brennos directed her into a room. Rows of spears, crossbows, and swords of all shapes and sizes monopolized the walls, all the necessary combat equipment showcased like a confectioner's shop.

A tabletop displayed a selection of three weapons: a longsword, a great ax, and a mace. However, her attention quickly shifted to another object. Placed next to these three battle instruments was...her bionic arm—not in pieces, but whole.

"I"—her eyes jumped from Brennos to what lay on the prepping table—"I don't understand."

"A gift...to even out the playing field." Brennos gestured for her to try on the mechanical limb.

A gift from King Remus? This wasn't part of the bargain.

"I thought you said we were not to fight with familiar weapons."

"We've made a few alterations, and the blades are deactivated. It is purely a tool to make the fight fairer."

Æri snorted. She was well prepared to go against the giant regardless of her lost limb.

"I am just following instructions from higher up." The corner of Brennos's mouth contracted, but he made no other movement. "Nothing more."

Besides the missing harness, her bionic arm looked unchanged. In its place, a new material lined the interior compartment.

When she hesitated, Brennos explained further. "It's a type of vacuum suspension that extracts air from the socket. This can hold the limb without disrupting fluid circulation. There is no effect on the wiring sensation or the hand's functioning. You no longer need the connecting sleeve. It is all built-in."

"I'd like to know who instructed you to say all that." Æri smirked as she slipped her residual limb into the compartment. A soft and smooth gel-like substance molded around her arm, sealing the extremity in place. The memorable tingle wound up her arm, jolting the senses through her shoulder and undulating down her spine. She tested its movement, pronating and supinating the elbow, deviating the wrist, and flexing and extending the fingers one by one.

A swell of joy erupted through her. It tugged at her features making her almost grin. She'd kill to have a word with the scitator who worked on the updates when this was all over.

The Keeper's lips quivered, and did she detect...a smile? Brennos twisted away, gesturing toward the selection of weapons. "As you might have already deduced, these were selected based on your skills."

Æri let out another sarcastic snort. Or lack of.

Her talents excelled in snaring and shooting, not ax swinging and bludgeoning—especially not with these weapons' outrageous dimensions. The ax was twice the size of her arm. So it ruled that one out. Now, to choose between the mace or the longsword.

"What is the aim of this round?"

The last two had been different. The first's goal was to knock the opponent to the ground, the second was to disarm.

"To end with a killing blow"—Brennos paused—"without, of course, killing your opponent."

Æri ran her finger along the blade of the sword, taking a closer look. The edges were, in fact, dulled.

Hmmm...what would Cuthbert be wielding?

Based on her assumption, the mace, which held a heavy ball on a chain, was out of the question. Furthermore, it looked nearly as burdensome as the ax, which left the longsword.

She picked up the blade. Not as dense as she first believed. With some effort, she could maneuver it in both hands. It would also be long enough to deliver a blow from a decent distance. The others required closer combat.

Æri possessed some basic abilities in swordplay, a requirement for all the elite in Særenfell. It wasn't her strong suit, but that didn't matter. All she needed to do was deliver a blow judged to be lethal. She'd worry about her agility with the weapon another day.

"Now that you have your weapon of choice, you may select one form of defense." Brennos lifted an arm toward the wall composed of suspended shields. Most were made of leather or wood, but some held hints of bronze in the fastenings.

Æri had no idea where to start. The longsword already acted as both a weapon to block blows and a weapon to give them. I It all came back to Cuthbert's choice.

After reviewing her limited options, she managed to select a shoulder plate that attached to her upper arm, directly above her bionic one. It would act as a shield, blocking her face from any side blows from arrows and leaving her hands free to wield the sword.

Equipped with her bionic arm, longsword, and armor, she was ready for battle. Energy and suspense hummed through her limbs, her goal of freedom and answers to the Blodlyst in sight. Yet instead of going out to the Arena, Brennos led her to another door.

As he opened it, floral and citrus aromas floated from the entrance. Two maids arranged a raised pallet, towels strewn atop.

"You are to be prepared as if you already won the battle. The custom here is to massage the muscles ahead of the Games."

Æri took one look and understood. Though it may relax most individuals, it would do the opposite for her.

"No," she insisted, backing out of the doorway. "I'd rather not." Like in the baths, she did not trust people to touch her. Maybe she'd deal with that fear later...after winning the bidding rounds, but not now.

Brennos merely bowed his head. "As you wish."

Given the morning's preparations, the sun's scalding orb reached high noon as the guards finally paraded Æri and Cuthbert in front of the king's court.

In the Arena, spectators crowded the entire bottom tier. Even a few lower-class citizens had made the trip and were perched in the upper rows. A dizzying sensation came over Æri, like a fish trapped in a bowl with hundreds of eyes staring in.

What would it be like when the stands were packed on a Game day?

King Remus, only arriving marginally late this round, boasted a grossly disproportionate fanfare to the last. Trumpeters lined the first tier of the Arena, and her ears rang long after their blaring concluded. Sulivan was seated at his usual posting, his blue-black hair slicked from his face while his sharp lilac eyes sifted the pit. However, Rione was notably absent.

Perhaps he stayed at the villa? One less hindrance. She didn't want to think about the Venator.

Bringing her awareness back to Cuthbert, she confirmed the sword was a sensible choice. Cuthbert held a net in his mammoth hands, and she hoped it did not have the same jolts the Venators used in the Bogs.

But the shield he balanced on his other arm...Her throat bobbed as she surveyed the curved sheet. It nearly spanned the length of Cuthbert's body from shoulder to below the knee, covered end to end in spikes. Though dulled, he would be manipulating that shield as his weapon more so than the unfamiliar net.

"Hold your marks!" the official shouted.

Æri tried not to think of the giant's barbed shield. Instead, she redirected her concentration to what she remembered from her sword training.

Use your weight to throw blows. Dictate the tempo. Never overreach.

The high-pitched pipe of the horn sounded, and Cuthbert trudged forward.

Æri maintained her distance. Neither of them had instruments of long-range combat. She would need to approach him at some point, but there was no use wasting energy.

She kept her feet light, skirting close to the perimeter, avoiding Cuthbert's throwing range altogether as the giant lumbered at her.

"Don't bore us, Æri." The king's voice was amplified over the sandy pit.

Her cheeks heated from the chiding, not just a scolding remark but a warning. King Remus knew she was avoiding the offensive. If she were to win this round, she would have to attack the giant, and Æri preferred not to battle another Bog beast.

She stepped into Cuthbert's range. The giant towered over her as she maintained a wide stance, squaring her feet. Drawing her shoulders back, Æri threw her weight into the first blow—her back muscles rippled—a straight cut aimed for the giant's side.

Draugs! She immediately regretted the blow. The move was novice, and it threw her off-balance. He blocked her blow with that jagged shield. Tinny sounds of metal and wood clanking echoed in the Arena.

Æri pulled back before he could thrust the shield into the sword. She tried again, aiming for the shoulder.

Another wrong move.

It opened her position, and she tilted off-balance. His shoulder was too high for any heavy blows, and she had to take several backward strides for balance. Wielding the sword with two hands was more cumbersome than expected. She had misjudged the type of weapon. Though it resembled the longswords she was accustomed to, it was clearly not meant to be maneuvered in the way she had been trained.

The giant took advantage and pitched the netting, attempting to catch her off guard. Her longsword deflected the oncoming snare, tossing it to the side.

With his net gone, an opportunity opened.

She went in, watching her balance of the sword, this time aiming for the giant's exposed lower legs. Using the forward momentum of the swing, she drove her sword down. Its dull blade hit his shinbone with a thud. Cuthbert bellowed with pain.

That would leave a mark.

The crowd cheered and hooted as the giant stumbled. Still, he did not fall.

Grunting, he swung with the shield, directing it at her head. She ducked low, just dodging the barbed edge.

He might as well be manipulating a sledgehammer. This was a battle to the first deadly blow. If Cuthbert hit her in the head with that thing— What were the consequences if he did indeed smash her brains out? Would the official call the match before it came to that?

Perspiration glistened off their faces in the midday sun. Puffs of air sawed in and out from their dry mouths, crust forming in the cracked corners. Neither of them had landed a blow close enough to end the match.

Think, Æri. *Think.*

Her head ached, and her muscles strained from holding the longsword high in defense.

If she just managed to dart around the giant...Yes! There! He was exposed. A quick blow to his lower back could win the match. But he guarded it well. She'd need a distraction—something to get him to turn.

A bird screeched, and her head whipped up to the cloudless sky.

Gyr! Gyr, appearing as if he heard her pleading wish, and Æri remembered that with her arm returned, perhaps he truly had. Her heart soared. The glint of home and hope renewed her resolve to win this match.

Snow-white feathers blurred by as he swooped into the pit, crying again. The giant turned to look, giving Æri the perfect opportunity for an exposed blow. Her core hardened, preparing to lunge with the sword.

But as she aimed her attack, an archer in the king's dais broke her attention. Her eyes widened in horror and her stomach plunged. His bowstring was drawn taut as he pointed an arrow right for Gyr.

"Stop!" Æri yelled. Too late.

The sentinel's bow already made that dreadful vibrating thud.

Her eyes darted skyward.

The arrow's shaft struck through Gyr. He paused mid-flight, hovering above the pit, then tumbled downward. His lifeless wings flapped as he plunged.

Everything slowed. Her skull hammered, each thump of her heart booming, whether from exhaustion or her lost connection with Gyr, she didn't know. Æri dropped her sword and ran toward her falling falcon, endeavoring to reach him before his body slammed into the earth.

She was almost there. So close.

Something flew over her, blocking her path, her legs and arms entangling in a fine webbing, and she, too, fell.

Less than an arm's stretch away, her falcon collapsed with a sickening crunch on the sand.

The official's call dimly registered as Cuthbert raised his shield above her.

She had lost the match, and with it, her chance at going home.

The last thought didn't occur to Æri until the king summoned her before his dais—her mind solely on the friend who came to help only to be instantly slain, shot from the sky like a stalked game bird.

Æri's vision fogged, and her throat tightened as she fought the urge to run to Gyr. He lay motionless in the middle of the Arena, crumpled and broken.

"It seems our little bargain is void." The king's words vaguely registered through the roaring in her ears. "Let the bidding begin."

Void? *Void...*

Just like that, she was sold. A slave forever in this arid realm. It all happened so fast. Her head continued to hum, the sounds around her muffled as if submerged in a rushing current. Distantly, she felt the pressure of hands steering her away. She passed Cuthbert as he approached the dais, the king setting a woven wreath of laurel upon his head.

Forced from the pit floor and down that same exit hall Marlena and Oisin disappeared into only a few days prior, she was directed by the guards to where her new owner awaited.

Her right wrist stung.

One of the guards held a mechanism to her inner arm—the same one from that first day.

"A binding to your new owner," he said, grunting.

New manacles were shackled to her arms, just as a precaution while the new binding in her wrist engaged. She was now the property of this man, whoever he was.

Sold.

"Cosmos," her new owner introduced himself, saying nothing else. His thinning hair and white whiskers did little to conceal the tanned age spots that bloomed on his scalp. He was probably some rich merchant or lord...though he gave no title.

She numbly followed him from the Arena's gates and into the sprawling city.

Nearing the evening meal, street vendors rolled out their stands of sizzling foods and spices. Some of the traders called to them, haggling prices in hopes of reeling them in as they passed.

Farther from the public space, the streets tapered, and tall rickety buildings materialized, blocking the sun.

"Catch!" a voice shouted from an open window, a basket tossed from one sill to the next.

"Keep your crowns up!" another yelled out, and Æri narrowly missed a bucket of slop sloshing onto her head. It splattered at her feet.

The stench swelled as they continued to trudge through constricted alleys. Assuming her owner was wealthy, Æri thought it odd they did not take the main streets and ride on horseback or trolley to his dwelling. Instead, they dodged rubbish and sewage.

The man looked over his shoulder. "We are almost there."

Where? she sought to ask, but her tongue felt leaden, bloated in her mouth. Too dry and swollen from the fight and unshed tears for her falcon. Worse yet, without her freedom, without a cure or way of finding it, without any possibility of helping her sister, Særenfell was lost. The idea scraped her raw.

They halted their trek in front of a row of shops. A pottery boutique was positioned to Æri's right and barbers to her left—their wooden shutters and doors sealed for the evening. Rather than entering one of these, the man withdrew a sizable wrought-iron key from around his neck and unlocked a large door in the middle of the row. Figurines with bells, much like the ones above Thesta's temple, jingled as he opened the door.

He shepherded her through an entrance hallway, minimally decorated, but the intricate tiles and painted walls gave away the owner's means.

The hallway opened onto a room that echoed the villa's atrium; an impluvium sat at the center, and aureate light streamed in from the roof's opening.

Cosmos removed her shackles. "Stay here," he muttered, leaving her to study the room in more detail.

Where was she?

An ornate bronze urn was propped high on a pedestal, and a lounge butted against a glaucous blue wall accented by a white frame. More light drifted in from a courtyard beyond a set of carved screens.

Unconsciously ignoring her new owner's instructions, she wandered over to a tapestry next to the urn. The elaborately woven yarn depicted a woman wading into the ocean. Waves circled her waist, a family of seals beckoning her to stray farther into the watery depths, leaving the land behind to join them.

Æri recognized the story: the nymph, Salarán, who abandoned her human form and family to join the sea. A sad tale but also one of survival and sacrifice.

She recalled the iconography in the bathhouse—the lost sea creatures etched into the floor and walls.

For a people who once worshipped the sun god Hesól, Fíronians devoted much of their time to the sea deities. Æri supposed that before the Split, the ocean must have been as much a part of their livelihood as it was for Særenfell.

The room darkened, and a rare summer shower trickled through the open roof, water sliding off the red tiles and into the center well.

Drip, drop, drip, drop.

Such a lulling sound. Had she heard rain here before?

The light drips, the passing shadows, and the painting's roving waves created an underwater experience.

But that drip...no, not the rain anymore but footsteps. Hairs on her neck lifted.

"Hello, Æri."

She did not have to turn to know to whom that rough voice belonged.

~ 19 ~

SIGNE

The Bogs

Finally, some movement.

A seeker.

Signe recognized the man's attire: the thick padding on his knees, a pickax, and a hardhat strapped to his back. He rested on a holm, his body propped against a mound of pumice rock. Pulling his breathing cowl past his chin, he guzzled from a flask.

Only seekers wore the artless joint coverings—how the Narkrye easily picked them out from the skies. But not all of them carried rounded helms. This one seemed more cautious than the others, aware of the dangers the Bogs had to offer without proper gear.

As second-in-command—temporarily first, she supposed—it rested on Signe's shoulders to lead the hunt. Disa and Eydis were running patrol around the island. She had dutifully sent a signal to them once she spotted the man—a new rule enacted after what happened with Æri and Yrsa.

Send a signal to the crew if a sighting occurs.

Signe had little time to think of her lost captain. Once the news of the Narkrye's missing leader reached Særenfell, the queen had ordered Signe to take command without delay.

Take control and plan.

Her duties, first and foremost, were to serve her queen and, thus, the people of Særenfell. She'd been on the hunt ever since, only taking a brief respite to restock on one of the holms and head out once more.

It was not something she enjoyed.

Hunting she loved, yes. Flying she could not go without, but the wait and stalking of *this* particular prey...She'd prefer the wild beasts of her mountains to men any day.

And the monotonous days of hearth-worthy temperatures and scouring baking black turf had yielded only this *one*.

The seeker began to move again, hopping from holm to holm. Watching his movements, she confirmed he didn't have any unwanted company with him—another new rule.

A blue light flickered on the Boar's dash. Her crew were less than an hour's ride away. Time to strike. She lined up the Boar's net release with the seeker's position and fired.

Gotcha.

They never looked up, doubtlessly more preoccupied with what lay beneath their feet than what awaited them in the skies. Nevertheless, Signe expected him to be a little more alert, considering the amount of gear he wore.

She landed the Boar, going for the pickax first, kicking it from his pack. The seeker writhed on the small holm like a fly caught in a spider's web—clearly not a fighter.

Muffled whimpers emanated from the bound trap. A pool of urine leaked from beneath him, winding its way through the rocks' small crevices.

"Please. Please," the man pled in Fíronian. He started to hyperventilate.

"Save your begging for when it might save your sorry ass," she said in his tongue.

Signe made out two blurred figures zooming toward her and the holm on the horizon. Better to knock him out for the journey,

Signe mused. He'd be no use if he died of a heart attack along the way.

"The queen wants to speak with the prisoner." Ildrid looked paler than usual. Even her lips bore a sallow appearance, disappearing into her porcelain-white face. Her bright eyes displayed flecks of scarlet slashed in her irises, the color bolder today, juxtaposing against the blue.

The queen had sent one of her courtlings to the barracks—not a servant—so it must be important.

Signe considered this. She did not particularly feel like attending to the queen this evening. After weeks of flying in the unaccommodating Bogs, all she wanted to do was take a long, hot bath and sleep.

Æri possessed the fortitude for dealing with the queen's unruly tempers. Signe, on the other hand, despite her confidence in leading the Narkrye, tended to cower in front of the snow-white monarch.

"He's still unconscious." Signe peeled a flake of dead skin off the back of her hand. The Bogs had been uncommonly sunny. Rays diffused through the cloud cover and burned her fair complexion. "I suggest she wait until morning to speak with him. He'll have food and rest by then, and may be more willing to talk. Or if she doesn't plan on talking...*taste* a little better."

Blue-purple smudges, austere under Ildrid's eyes, alluded to her hunger. The queen's court had not enjoyed human blood for several weeks. Elk and bear sustained them, but they did not keep their tempers at bay. Animal blood resembled water to their finest cask spirits, and it only held the Blodlyst back by the barest of threads.

"Fine, morning then. When the sun rises. No later." Ildrid's heels dug into the cold stone as she turned, marching stiffly out of the communal hall.

Signe slumped in a chair next to the roaring fire. Her eyelids, like snow-laden boughs, drooped. Falling asleep in the hide-covered wingchair would be so easy. She'd just have to close her eyes. Her bones ached from riding the Boar day in and day out, sleeping fleetingly on marked holms, on bedrolls that barely blocked the slicing rocks beneath. But it would not help her sore back if she spent the night in the chair.

"You look like elk dung."

A corner of Signe's mouth quirked as Toril's boisterous gait echoed off the walls.

"Smell like it too."

Toril held two pewter mugs frothing over with ale. She shoved one into Signe's hand before plunking down in the wingback chair opposite and propping her feet on the low footstool. Toril had brushed out her characteristic half braid for the evening, and her rebellious golden tresses caught the firelight.

"So...should I be congratulating or consoling?"

Signe took a sip of ale; thick bubbly liquid coated her raw throat.

"Neither. After this drink, the best thing you can do is ask Hælga to prepare a bath in my room."

"Will do." Toril gave a larkish salute, putting a smile on Signe's weary face. "Disa left for the evening. She wanted to spend some time with her family in the Eastern Fells."

Tucked among the high caves of Ror and inclines of Austrker was a small mountainside settlement. Disa had not visited for several months. In Særenfell, they valued family above all else, and the trip offered a pleasant change from the fortress's icy walls.

Signe, too, wished she bore family elsewhere—to have a valid excuse to escape these cold ramparts for a few days—but she had none. Most of her family died before the Split. The Narkrye were her family now—had been for centuries.

She fixed her gaze above the fire mantel, where a crest of two large griffins bordered mountains and a swirling sea—the crest of Æri's ancestors. A now familiar ache pricked her throat. Æri...she missed her so much; her sharp smile, the small freckle under her eye, how she touched Signe's jaw just below the ear with long, calloused fingers.

"Do you want to talk about it?" Toril ventured, catching her gaze on the crest. "I know there hasn't been much time to...And you and Æri were close."

Signe shook her head, taking a large swig from her mug. Dancing flames licked the walls of the hearth. "I'm not ready."

"Okay." Toril took her gaze off Signe to drink her ale.

They sat there in the cavernous hall, listening to the embers' pops and crackles.

Later, when Signe settled into the copper tub in the privacy of her rooms, heat from the water loosening her joints, she let her tears fall.

Brynja

The fool trembled in the middle of the stone floor. Not a hunter. Fíronian huntsmen did not shudder, nor did they fear for their lives like this seeker. He smelled awful; the scent of his dread mixed with unwashed flesh—as if her Narkrye had pulled him from a pit of Bog beast feces. Holding her breath, Brynja circled the man, taking in his rough hands, sullied clothes, and the thick padding at his knees. The waxed cloak he wore over his shoulders; the foreign, fine-woven tunic underneath; his cropped brown hair—the pulsing of his throat.

Despite his stench, she sucked in her bottom lip, rubbing her tongue against it, almost tasting the blood's brine.

Taste him, the voice crooned.

Brynja stepped back from the man, squeezing her hands so hard she felt the bones between. She would not think of that.

Control yourself, Brynja.

Turning her head to look at something other than the seeker's beating pulse, she found a fly skittering around this morning's breakfast. Her court had yet to remove the bear carcass. A breath unfurled from her lungs.

She would get answers.

There was a shuffling of feet and a suppressed cough. The red-headed Narkrye waited for her commands in the doorway. Her rigid stance spoke of her unease in this room, of everything around her.

"Well done, Signe. You are dismissed." Brynja tried to ignore how quickly the provisional first-in-command spun on her heels.

Brynja suspected all the Narkrye held some sort of fear of her. Most avoided the tower. Even Æri did at times. She understood their underlying trepidation of the disease, the fear it may spread—smelled their lingering apprehension in the air. She didn't blame them; it was for the best. Her head muddled when too many of the unafflicted remained in her company.

At the very least, they respected her—followed her commands. But for how much longer? When would her mind, too, fade like her mother's? Her people left to chaos, and she left alone to rot.

She squeezed her hands together a second time, pressing out the anxiety, and refocused on the cowering man.

He was neither tall nor short, his arms and legs stocky. A man used to labor.

The booming of his heart caused her concentration to waver again.

By Skathi's spear, had they given him a tonic?

Those captured were typically treated with something to calm their nerves—an herbal concoction developed by their healers. It made feasting on their blood a little less uncomfortable. She may kill, but she did not take pleasure in inflicting pain.

"What is your name?" Her voice was choppy and disjointed as she addressed the seeker in her neglected Fíronian. Signe had reported the man was uneducated, not understanding their tongue. She also indicated he'd do anything to survive.

"Atticus of Fíronbec, Your Majesty." He bowed his head low, dropping to his knee.

Excellent. They had instructed the seeker on how to properly greet her. Brynja's lips twitched, pleased at the gesture. "What is it you do in the Bogs, *Atticus*?" She paused before adding, "Speak truthfully, for it may determine your life's fate."

He swallowed, his Adam's apple bobbing as he spoke. "I collect rocks...minerals...sometimes turf...anything worth selling back in Fíronbec."

Brynja released an imperceptible sigh. No affiliation with the hunting pack, then. "For how long have you resided in the Bogs?"

"Three weeks, Your Majesty."

Her heart fell. Too long. If Æri had been brought back to Fíronbec, this man would not be aware of it. Regardless, she probed for more, hoping to wring something out. "Did you come across any of your kind during your time there?"

He faltered. Not in his favor. If he intended to lie, she would know.

"I will remind you once more not to hold back."

The seeker nodded, his fingers scratching at the hem of his worn cloak, fraying it further.

"I passed a Venator procession—a troop—on their return to Fíronbec."

"Go on." At last, something useful.

The seeker exhaled slowly. "The chief's well known...the king's most esteemed hunter. Goes by the name Lord Rione Aulius."

"*Not* 'of Fíronbec'? Why?"

"I don't know, Your Majesty."

"Describe him. Is he from Fíronbec?"

"From what is told of him, yes. Wears an eyepatch. His uncovered eye is brown. Besides his long hair, he seems to be as much Fíronian as I, Your Majesty."

"Did they say anything about what they carried back? Of their"—Brynja scoured her brain for the right word in Fíronian—"their bounty?"

The man shook his head. "They only stopped for a brief salute."

She cursed. Brynja had no way to be sure these huntsmen were the ones who took her sister, but they had no other information.

"You encountered no other procession these last three weeks in the Bogs? No other hunters?"

He shook his head again. A shudder ran through his body as he seemed to sense her anger rising. "Please, Your Majesty, I have a family back home. They rely on me."

Despite the room's frost, a sheen of sweat dappled the seeker's brow. She let the clinging smells of fear float away so she could sense what lay underneath. Truly an honest man, and as Signe reported, this seeker would do anything to survive. She'd be sacrificing her feed, allowing the Blodlyst to rile inside her and her court, risking it scratching deeper on her sanity's doors. This would be for her sister. A sacrifice worth the hardship. They could hold out with the animals for a time.

"Your freedom is granted. You may return to your family."

Sobs burst from Atticus's mouth. "Thank you, Your Majesty."

Her glacial gaze locked on his, and Brynja didn't let a trace of compassion enter her voice. "But you must do something for me in return, Atticus of Fíronbec."

Signe

Her Boar zoomed over the Bogs, Disa flanking her side. Signe could not believe what she'd agreed to.

The orders from the queen were clear: *Drop the seeker as close as you can to Fíronbec's borders.*

All that work and more than a month of combing through the brutal landscape just to give him up.

After they cut his bindings, the seeker scrambled toward an invisible road, claiming it led to Fíronbec.

"I hope our queen knows what she's doing." Disa rotated her Boar in the direction of their island.

"As do I," Signe ceded.

~ 20 ~

ÆRI

"Hello, Æri."

Her body tensed as if pressed against a million shards of crystalline glass. *That voice*—that rough lilt in his Fíronian lingered in the air like the evaporating dew from the momentary rainfall.

She slowly turned her head.

"What are you—" She stopped herself, clamping down on her tongue, well aware that he was far above her ranking. Æri fought back her original retort and rephrased the question. "Where is Master Cosmos?" A coppery tang coated her mouth. She had bit her tongue too hard.

"*Master* Cosmos?" His scar stretched with the upward movement of his mouth.

Æri turned around fully, drawing her back closer to the tapestry. The cogs ticked into place, her mind quickly grasping the situation, *her* situation.

"Cosmos works for me."

She shook her head vehemently, right hand instinctively lifting to protect her bionic arm. "No. No...that means—that I'm your—No."

"I am not sure how pleased the king will be when he discovers I was the one who won your bid, but I think he'll recover with time."

"But—but why—How could you?" She wasn't able to stop herself from stammering, the mix of shock, fear, and hate invading her system.

Rione crossed his arms over his broad chest.

Her eyes frisked his attire, looking for a weapon. He wore a simple white tunic and long brown trousers, his feet bare. Dark hair unfastened about his shoulders. It hung long and damp like he'd just bathed or spent time outside under the light shower—no visible knife.

"I am not obligated to tell you my reasons." He dallied on his words as if he intended to continue, but instead, he stopped and waited for her reaction. His eye examined her face.

Æri's stomach flipped. Cold, undiluted dread filled her. *Trapped*, she was trapped again.

"You're a jackass." She scowled at the Venator, not caring anymore about the ranking rules. Damn those cautions to hell and its Draugs. She wanted to rip that self-righteous smirk off his face. If he came any closer, she would, master or not. He was a horrible human for doing this to her—as if it were all a game—always these awful games.

Maybe he bore the same impulses as the king...Was that why he bought her?

Another wave of fear crashed through her, and panic set in, needling through her arms and legs. The room tilted. She wanted to leave, but his form blocked the way.

She breathed in, pressing herself against the wall to steady the spinning.

"Did you buy me to feed your perverse fetish of dominance? Or was it just petty revenge? You already captured me, made me a slave, and you had to own me too? Am I to be like, what? Your sex warrior slave?" Her tone was laced with acid as she spat the words at him.

"What—no. Not at all." To her surprise, Rione stepped back. He seemed affronted by her retort—disgusted even.

He dropped his arms. His face didn't soften per se, but that smirk disappeared and something in the rigid features loosened. He let out a long sigh, combing a hand through his dark mane.

"I didn't—" He shut his eye, struggling for the right words. "You weren't meant to be part of the fighting rounds in the Auctioning."

Æri's brows furrowed, face scrunching. Her anger toward him continued to simmer, but his words made no sense. "Why, then, am I here?"

He examined her again, rolling his lips between his teeth while seeming to wrestle with what to say next. It looked like he wanted to say something but fought against it, subduing an inner battle.

Assuming he must be sizing her up while he debated his next actions, Æri stood on guard, like a raptor, ready to strike and leave a mark if he came closer.

Still in her bidding uniform, she resembled a mangled wreck. Dry dirt caked her knees, and scrapes of dried blood cracked on her elbows. Her brown-black hair was mussed and fell out of its tie, scrunched and blocking half her sight.

With the slightest shake of his head, Rione looked away. "It would have been a waste for you to go into the Games. Many of the Auction winners don't make it out. They're made to fight until they can't hold up a sword or spear to defend themselves. Rarely do they win their freedom." He found her gaze again.

"I made a deal with the king," Æri said, hissing back, and folded her arms, the room finally settling. He wasn't going to attack her, so she arced her head toward the courtyard, unable to look at him.

"Do you really believe the king would have honored your *deal*?" Æri heard doubt in his voice.

No. The king was a lying, scheming scumbag, and she knew it deep down. In all likelihood, he had been the one to orchestrate her defeat. But the bargain gave her hope—granted her some time, something to hold on to. She had obtained access to the libraries...spoken to the priest. The king hadn't lied about that. Æri could not rule out these small triumphs. Though ultimately, Rione spoke the truth, and Æri hated him for it. How likely was it that the king intended to grant her freedom after winning—after she handed him the power source to fly?

Her posture slumped marginally, and she angled her head just enough to see Rione's face out of the corner of her eye.

He gave her a sharp nod, gesturing to her rumpled clothes. "Let's have you cleaned up. Take a bath and get some rest. You'll get a week's hiatus with proper food and sleep. Then your training starts."

Training? What training? Hadn't she been through three rounds of "training"? Æri meant to tilt her head in further confusion, but her attention snagged on a maid loitering in the archway.

"Ofelia, very timely. Will you take Æri to the baths and show her to her room?"

The maid dipped and turned in response to Rione's order. Æri did not attempt to follow.

"Æri, go." Rione bit down on his words, his voice harsh. A command. As if in afterthought, he added, "We will speak later."

Æri ignored him, refusing to move. Why should she listen to him? What would he do? Lock her up? He'd already done that. Slave or not, she wasn't going to take orders from him—not like that.

Rione huffed, exasperated. "Fine, stay here if that is what you wish. The evening meal is at nine. I expect you to be there. *Clean.*" He left through the opposite entrance, his feet heavy on the tiled floor.

"Miss...?"

Ofelia peeked her head through the archway.

Æri unfurled her palms, her fingers stiff, knuckles white, and let out a long breath.

Her head started to spin again with all the revelations, the emotions making it difficult to comprehend what or who was around her. Was Rione truly her *owner*?

"Miss?" Ofelia approached with care.

Æri blinked a few times, then closed her eyes and inhaled, attempting to settle her nerves.

"The meal is in an hour, and I assume you want to rest up beforehand? Put on some tidy clothes..." Ofelia's voice came out uncertain. "The master of the house means well...He can be a little insistent at times...but that's his nature."

Her statement did little to placate Æri's feelings toward the Venator. The maid with nut-brown hair streaked with strands of gray dithered just beyond the archway.

"Are you a slave too?"

"Me? Oh, no, no, no..." Ofelia fluttered her hands. "I'm the housekeeper. Lord Rione doesn't keep slaves." She pursed her lips. "Well, he hasn't before."

Æri's mind thrummed, and she braced herself on the wall again.

Then why did he buy her?

Maybe she did need a bath and a place to lie down. She'd refuse to go to the meal, of course. The thought of sharing a meal with Rione nauseated her; a mélange of revulsion and dread twisted her insides.

At last, Æri got her feet to move.

She trailed the maid farther into the house, weaving in and out of open corridors until they reached the washrooms.

They were small: a separate room for undressing and an adjacent chamber with a sunken square tub took up most of the space.

Curling scents of lavender and sage floated from the vapor, beckoning.

Filled to the brim with steaming water, the tub opened onto a quaint garden and joined a fountain with a deep pool. A low stone barrier was all that divided the interior bath from the exterior one. Thankfully, the garden walls stood high, sheltered by emerald-green plants, creating a terrarium-like environment.

For all of what she'd felt earlier, the scene offered a serene ambiance—an oasis from everything that had just happened.

Ofelia left her a towel and robe folded neatly on a bench.

Removing her bionic arm and resting it next to the towel, she rubbed at the distal end of her limb and wondered if she had worn the contraption for too long. She hadn't applied any ointment, but no redness or blistering marred her skin. The arm and hand worked well—apart from the time Gyr came. Gyr...

A ball formed in the back of her throat, and her chest squeezed...*His feathered body on the sandy pit floor.* She swallowed, blinking back tears.

Æri descended into the water, trying to block out the day's events, trying to relax and let the warmth and the calming aromas of the pool unwind her.

But she couldn't.

She couldn't turn off her brain. Thoughts still whirred like a swarm of angry bees stinging her every time they drifted to the last hours. They stung irately at first. Soon, her mind became numb—numb and swollen with suppressed memories.

Æri tried to keep her attention on scrubbing herself clean, washing off the blood and dirt built up from the day. When she finished, the water had turned murky.

Grabbing her arm and the towel, she pulled the bathrobe over her body and left the washroom, not knowing how long the thoughts would stay down.

Ofelia obediently waited outside, ready to escort Æri to her new room.

"How long am I to stay here? In this house?" She hoped the housekeeper would divulge some information about what Rione planned.

"It's best you talk to Lord Rione about that." She fussed over a clean tunic for Æri, unfolding it in her arms. "The evening meal is in a few minutes. You can talk to him about it then. Now, we must dress you. Lord Rione often strives for punctuality."

Æri took in a breath and shook her head.

Ofelia tutted, her big brown eyes assessing warmly. "Oh dear...you aren't going to make this easy for him, are you?"

"I don't want to get you in any trouble...I just—Not tonight. Could you tell him I'm too tired?" Æri swallowed her dread. It was ridiculous to be afraid.

"Deary, I won't get in trouble. But if it is what you wish..." She eyed Æri, who nodded her reply a little too vigorously.

"Very well." Ofelia's shoulders lifted, and she clicked the door shut, leaving Æri the clean clothing.

The door had a lock, and Æri rushed to turn it before surveying the room. A real bed—not a cot or some hard pallet—lay in the center. A dressing table at its foot, with a jug of water and a washbasin on top. Simple, but she didn't need anything more.

Sinking onto the surprisingly comfortable mattress, she emitted an extended groan.

How could she talk to Rione? *Why* would she? Escaping this horrid house and being caught by the king's sentinels sounded more appealing.

Her head dropped with a flump onto the pillow, and Æri closed her eyes.

Bang!

Jerking up rod straight, Æri wiped at saliva pooling from her mouth. She had fallen asleep on the bed, still clothed in her bathrobe.

Where was she? Not the Castrum...no. Her mind jumbled. It took her a moment to reacclimate, and the evening filtered back.

"Æri." Another bang shuddered her door. "Æri? I told you to be ready." Rione's voice was commanding but not loud, and layered with discontent. "I know you're in there."

She kept quiet, avoiding her problem.

"Look. I'm not good at these kinds of things."

"Not good at what? Keeping me captive?"

He paused. "Negotiating. Come out. You have to eat."

"I am not hungry." The retort fell out of her mouth, and she prayed he didn't hear her stomach shriek in protest.

An audible huff came from outside. "Æri."

"Just leave me alone."

"Fine. Stay in your room. But you'll have to come out at some point."

Again, she fell silent.

Another huff as he muttered, "Senseless, stubborn girl." His footsteps receded down the passage.

Girl? Senseless? Æri stuck out her tongue at the door. Hah! She was almost one thousand. Probably older than he was.

Æri rolled her eyes. Right, maybe she did act a bit childish, but she wouldn't change her mind. Not now. Not after what he'd done.

A few minutes later, a quiet tap sounded. "Deary...it's me, Ofelia. I am leaving a plate here. It's best to snatch it up soon, or the dormice might get it."

Æri's stomach made another deep gurgle, and she sighed, giving in to her needs. She guardedly pried the door open. The hallway was empty, save for a tiny mouse that scurried into her room.

A plate sat by the entrance, stacked with spiced meats, sautéed vegetables, and some hearty buttered bread wedges. Traces of garlic and oregano teased Æri's senses. Her stomach grumbled louder. She dragged the plate in, then relocked the door.

~ 21 ~

ÆRI

*W*hite feathers drifted into the sandy pit. Like flakes of snow, they covered the Arena floor. Plumes piled on top of each other, drawing in at the center, forming...a bird—Gyr. His blue eye a flare in all the white. He unfolded his snowy wings, readying himself to soar into the sky. Then, as he lifted himself from the earth, the arrow flew, and red bloomed. The fatal target increased, its circumference expanding at his heart. A blink. A shift in forms. It was no longer Gyr on the pit floor but one of her Narkrye—Yrsa, her eyes a lifeless blue.

Æri's eyelids snapped open.

A small feather rested on the coverlet. Somehow it had escaped from her goose-down pillow. Subtly curving upward, the feather rocked back and forth with her uneven breaths, bobbing like a boat. Inhaling and holding the air, she watched the feather's movements ebb. Finally, in one gust, Æri blew it off the bed.

She rubbed at the sand in her eyes. They felt itchy and dry, though she had shed no tears the night afore.

Maybe it was the dream?

Æri hadn't bothered to change out of the plush bathrobe. The night was warm, and exhaustion had settled in quickly. After eating, she'd fallen asleep directly on the duvet, discarding the wooden plate at the foot of the bed.

Sunbeams diffused through latticework shutters. Carved in floral patterns, they left twirling shadows on the tiled floor.

Æri rose indolently, moving to unlatch the shutters, which swung open onto the square courtyard. A trickling fountain shimmered at its heart. It wasn't groomed like the Villa Glorial's; instead, the flora grew somewhat wild and, comparable to the garden next to the washroom, emanated a sense of serenity—such a contrast to how she felt.

Birds chirped, flipping and fluttering their wings in the shallow pool, and traces of thyme and rosemary filtered into her chamber. The sun was sinking below roof tiles in the west.

Gods and goddesses above...had she slept all day? Æri couldn't remember the last time she'd been granted the luxury.

Hesitant to leave her room, Æri paced the chamber for several minutes, weighing the likelihood of running into Rione. She should find Ofelia and thank her for the meal...and return the plate. She'd do her best to avoid the master of the house.

Æri tiptoed through the short corridor, her feet silent on the gray-and-white marble. Rays from the accompanying garden provided pockets of light, guiding the way.

No exterior windows lined the walls. Her room rested at the back of the house, but even here, where she assumed it must butt against an alley or another city street, no noises hinted at the boisterous metropolis beyond.

She edged along the courtyard's veranda. Heady-scented wisteria climbed the posts, its flowers cascading like purple grapes, framing the untamed garden.

A whiff of baked bread suffused the flowers' aroma, making Æri's stomach grumble. She followed its scent. A pleasant humming and the flow of running water arose from a doorway a few steps ahead. Turning the corner, Æri found herself at a kitchen's entrance. A young woman with a sweet face bent over a basin and scrubbed dishes while a bearded cook zealously chopped root vegetables. Ofelia, the one humming, animatedly swept the floors as food scraps tumbled from the table.

"Oh! Nynth's ghost!" Ofelia's hand flew to her chest, and she dropped the broom with a clatter. The others stopped their tasks, halted by Ofelia's exclamation. "Deary, you gave me such a fright without a sound like that. Oh, come in, come in." Ofelia fanned her face as she picked up the broom.

Æri bit her lower lip to keep from smiling. Ofelia's oath to the night sky goddess was rather endearing. "I'm sorry. I didn't mean to scare you." Fiddling with the rim of the plate, Æri held it out to the housekeeper. "I wanted to return this."

Ofelia moved her fanning hand to Æri, waving off her apologies. "No explanations needed; I am always a little jumpy. Just ask my husband." She gestured to the cook, who resumed chopping.

"Don't let her near the knives," the large man rumbled.

"And it's why I'm the one washing up," the woman at the basin added.

"Oh hush, you two." Ofelia planted her hands on her wide hips. "I said jumpy—not clumsy." She waved again at Æri. "Come sit. Would you like anything? Perhaps water?"

Æri nodded shyly at the offer. "Yes, water, thank you."

Ofelia filled a cup from an earthenware pitcher and handed it to Æri as she settled on the kitchen bench. "This is Leta, my daughter." She motioned to the petite woman washing the pots and pans. "And Jonas, my husband."

Leta and Jonas, who shared the same golden-brown hair, cast friendly smiles but did not move from their work.

Ofelia gazed back at Æri for a moment. A look of forgetful surprise took over her features. "Heavens, where are my manners! You must be starving, having slept all day and missing the morning meal."

"Has it really been the entire day?" Æri replied, still dazed she had slept for so long.

"Yep, the evening meal is in less than an hour." Jonas tipped the vegetables onto a skillet, and the stovetop sizzled.

"Lord Rione requested you sit with him tonight." Ofelia passed Æri's old plate to Leta.

"Oh..." Æri rolled the water inside her cup, letting it slosh up the sides. "Could I eat something while I'm here?"

Ofelia and Jonas exchanged looks.

"All right..." The housekeeper sighed. "But perhaps tomorrow you'll sit with him?"

The warmth sapped from Æri's face, and she forced herself to take a long gulp of water.

Ofelia offered her a sad smile. "He's a different kind of soul, that one...Give him some time."

Æri wanted to deny her words, saying that Rione held as much spite as his king. However, something in Ofelia's tone gave her pause, the grief in it. What caused such care?

Ofelia, Jonas, and Leta smiled and laughed throughout their work while Æri munched on her food. They seemed happy.

With the cordial discussion, she discovered that they and Cosmos—who, as it turned out, was Ofelia's father—were the only hired staff living in the house.

"Lord Rione kept us together. We would've had to work in separate estates if not for his kindness," Leta said over her shoulder.

His kindness only went so far, Æri thought, feasibly extending only to his own people.

"Why don't I show you around the house tomorrow?" Ofelia proposed once Æri finished eating. She held in an immediate reply, then agreed, supposing it would do her some good. If anything, it could give her more information about her new surroundings.

Again, Rione knocked on her door that night, demanding she'd join him for the evening meal.

"I already ate," she yelled back.

"When?"

"In the kitchen an hour ago." She had devoured a whole loaf of the doughy bread, slathering a generous amount of herbed butter on each wedge. With the added fruits, greens, and spiced meats, her belly was bursting.

Rione puffed out a response and stomped away, his mumbled curses following him.

Æri met Ofelia in the kitchen the next day. The housekeeper and her daughter laughed over cups of steaming tea. Their inviting voices filled the space. Something about it reminded Æri of her Narkrye in the early mornings—the companionship.

A pang of homesickness tingled her senses as she took the offered cup of hot brew. With the urgency of the Auctioning, Æri had hardly any time to think about her crew. Would she ever see them again? And Yrsa...A knot developed at her chest's core, and a surge of grief seized her. She didn't allow herself to grieve for her lost sister in the Bogs nor during the bidding rounds. Even here, she could not let it fester—the same went for Gyr's death. Doing so would weaken her guard and leave her vulnerable. Instead, Æri concentrated on Ofelia's words, listening as the maid now guided her through the spacious house.

"This domus has been in Lord Rione's family for years, though he's made some changes to suit his tastes."

"Domus?"

"It's the house, deary." Ofelia explained that it was a name given to houses situated within the city's limits.

They entered the blue atrium from the first day, the space appearing bigger now without Rione in it, through the study, and into the library, a decently sized room with shelves stacked high in scrolls and codices. The majority of titles blared hunting techniques.

"You might be able to find some leisure tales amongst all that muddle." Ofelia motioned at the floor-to-ceiling shelf of documents. "I've seen one or two hiding in there."

Were all these Rione's? "Is the master in?"

Ofelia shook her head. "No. He had matters to attend to outside the domus."

Surely the king being one of them...And what of King Remus? Æri ruminated on this. Did he have any say in her newfound circumstances? She highly doubted he would let it rest. Her time at the Inventorium said otherwise.

"Does the king know I'm here?"

"Oh, I assume he does, deary. Not much goes beyond the king's notice."

Dismay sunk in her belly. How long did she have until he called on her?

Completing the tour, they passed a set of large sliding doors at the very back of the house near her chamber.

"Where do those lead?" Perhaps onto city streets or a quiet alley?

"Those go to the palestra." Ofelia wrung her hands. "That's the one place you're not permitted without the master."

Palestra—what Marlena had titled the training yard at the Castrum.

"Why am I not allowed there?"

Ofelia smoothed her hands on her apron and gave a little shrug. "It is best to ask Lord Rione that. It isn't my place. You are free to roam the rest of the house on your own."

Æri hid her scowl. Most of her questions had been directed Rione's way thus far.

Ofelia shepherded Æri back to her room but halted at the door. The housekeeper's face quivered with excitement. "I think a friend is waiting for you in there." Ofelia's telling smile left Æri flummoxed. Friend?

However, as she opened the door, Æri's heart nearly stopped with disbelief. For there in the room, balancing on a bowed perch was...

"Gyr!" Æri ran forward, immediately sensing their link.

A small chain anchored him to a post, and he wore a leather hood hiding his eyes and ears. Despite the covering, he squawked at her in greeting, his yellow feet moving side to side. Gently, her fingers found the hood's latch, then moved to untether the chain around his leg. They trembled with shock, her gaiety overwhelming her motions.

Æri held out her arm, and he clicked his sharp talons along the metal frame. Drawing her finger across his back, she lightly stroked the space between his wings, right where he liked it. Gyr chirped and cawed in delight, his blue bionic eye blinking back at her.

She swirled to Ofelia.

"But how—" At a loss for words, Æri's eyes welled as emotion reflected in her voice.

Ofelia tipped a shoulder. "Lord Rione has his ways. Instructed us to look after your falcon for some time..." She wagged her finger, her mouth creasing at the edges. "That bird's a feisty one. Wouldn't let anyone near him the first few days. Still won't let us touch him. Jonas had been feeding him. He's the only one your bird's taken a liking to."

"How long has he been in your care?"

"Oh, I'd say a week or so now."

A week? Rione had him this entire time? What about the bidding round? There in the Arena, Æri saw Gyr fall—and that arrow. It was impossible.

Ofelia noticed Æri's eyebrows knit together, attempting to make sense of the differing time frames. "If you'd give Lord Rione a chance, I am sure he'd clear things up for you, deary."

Æri sighed. Another question on the growing list of things she ought to ask Rione—about Gyr, about the palestra, about her role here—*if* she ever brought herself to do so.

Rione did not knock that night, nor did he knock the day after, and she didn't see him about the domus or its courtyard when she took Gyr out to stretch his wings.

She began to think he'd left the house altogether. However, the next morning, just as the sun's rays illuminated the red-tiled roof, a shadow passed her shutters from the garden beyond.

Noiselessly, she propped the screen open.

Rione sat at the far end of the courtyard, settled on a stone bench, his good eye shut. The other, absent of his eyepatch, displayed a hollowed pocket of scar tissue stretched over bone. The scar trailed beyond his mouth and down his strong jawline. The tension that usually ticced there was gone. His back was upright, hands resting on his knees, and his bare feet were rooted as if they grew from the earth.

His chest moved with each inhalation, taking deep, rhythmic breaths. The beat of them drew her in. Her body eased, the coil inside unwinding. It felt as if the world stopped, sounds and movements all focused on the Venator.

The one eye opened, and his gaze careened into hers.

His face hardened, and the tranquility bolted out of her, jarring her into consciousness. She ducked beneath the sill, her pulse quickening.

It was like the night at the banquet when he sang that elven ballad, but then that utter callousness when he locked eyes with hers. *Draugs.* This fear and hate mixed in with what? *What was it? What of that sense of peace?* The calmness and ease that gripped her wholly were what? She found no reason for it. The sentiments did not fit, scrambling into chaos.

Frustration overwhelming her, Æri snatched a pillow from the bed and pressed her face into it, wanting to scream. But it didn't come. She gasped for breath, seeking that constraint. Instead of finding it she just felt that bubble in her chest grow again. Æri wadded up the pillow and threw it at the door.

She sensed his presence about the house. His scent had returned. It covered places he frequented: the library...the courtyard...and that back door. Something citrusy lingered in it, but not sweet, like bergamot. And another underlying base note—woodsy, but she could not pinpoint the kind. It was unlike anything she had encountered before. None of the trees nor thickets here in Fíronbec smelled like that.

On the sixth evening at the domus, Æri wrestled with her thoughts. For all she knew, Rione would let her spend eternity in this house, mulling about. She lay across her bed and counted the geometric patterns on the ceiling, methodically composed to make the form of a large sun.

Gyr clucked in her direction from his perch, sensing her unease.

I know, Gyr, I know. It's not wise to avoid problems. They only get bigger.

Since his return, Gyr hadn't left her side, and to her relief, the insistent buzzing caused by their separation had ceased. Æri took him out daily to stretch his wings and fly above the domus. Though, without the monocle, she couldn't use his bionic eye to obtain a better view of the city's terrain. Æri desperately desired to see beyond the domus's walls and into the training yard. Despite her freedom to move about the house, she felt cooped up, stuck in this pattern—just moved from one prison to another.

And avoiding the Venator got her nowhere. She recognized her current actions were thoughtless, selfish even. Just because she feared him did not mean she should give up. Æri may be enslaved to Rione, but he had shown generosity to his staff. Perhaps he would permit her to return to the libraries...or find Oisin? If only she managed to be civil enough in his company...

Logic finally won over. Æri needed to face this fear—as long as she lived in the Venator's house, it was pointless to avoid him. She bore greater fears, some she dared not think about, but this one Æri could master. She would sit down or lie down, or however he ate his meals here, and get some answers.

A genuine, albeit brief, look of surprise passed over Rione's face when she entered the dining area. He was already eating, the table set for one. Unlike at the Villa Glorial's banquet, and to her relief, he ate his meal upright. Rione clasped a letter, but when he saw Æri, he promptly folded it away. She glimpsed the sender's name before it disappeared into his pocket: *Camilla*.

Her thoughts strayed to that night when she saw them together. It seemed like such a clandestine moment. The king must know about their relationship to wield it against Rione the way he did at the banquet.

A weakness.

Love could be a disadvantage in a realm like this—with a ruler like King Remus. He'd exploit it, use the connection to his advantage, twist something that once was beautiful into a weapon. Æri expected the huntsman to have hidden it better, if not avoided it altogether.

"I'll call for Ofelia to bring in another plate." He rose from his chair as she gave him the slightest of nods. Æri chose the seat farthest away.

Looking chipper, Ofelia practically bounded into the room. Her wonted benevolence amplified as she set a plate of food in front of Æri. "Is there anything else I can bring?" Ofelia directed the question to both of them. Her broad smile was meant to be reassuring, but the question just made Æri feel awkward. Ofelia functioned as an employee of the domus. Her role was clear, but then what did that make Æri? Certainly not a guest.

Æri shook her head while fumbling with the provided serviette.

"No. That is all. Thank you, Ofelia." Rione bowed his head, and she took this as her cue to leave.

No wine or posca accompanied the meal; Rione only held a ceramic water cup. Æri didn't recall seeing him with a goblet at the banquet either.

Like the previous meals in her room, Ofelia had arranged some barnyard fowl and grains on her plate, along with a smattering of braised dark greens. She moved the contents around with her spoon, evading his gaze.

A small chirp sprang out of Gyr, and Rione's eye snagged on the falcon. Gyr perched on the chair's top rail—drumming it with yellow feet. His blue eye blinked, scanning Rione in return.

"Not sure if falcons are appropriate meal guests."

Was this Rione's poor attempt to make conversation?

"He stays." She lifted her eyes from the food, sending him a shrewd glare—sharp like tiny slivers of ice crystals. She hoped it gave him the impression she'd easily send Gyr to poke out his other eye if he objected.

"He can stay."

They ate in silence for the remainder of the meal. Rione occasionally cast his eye in her and Gyr's direction. She had found the nerve to walk out and sit at the table with him, but her many questions remained clamped between her teeth. Another night, she'd loosen her tongue when she wasn't so unaccountably flustered around this man.

The following day, Æri swore to herself to get one question out. *Just one.* It shouldn't be that difficult.

Upon her arrival at the domus, he had told her she would have seven days to rest. It was the last day. How could she prepare herself for what he planned tomorrow if she didn't ask?

Æri approached the table with less apprehension this time. Her hands did not ball as tightly as they had the night afore, nor did her mouth feel like dry wool.

Tonight, the table was set for two, the second set much closer to Rione's end. No doubt Ofelia's doing. Æri picked up the plate and water cup and again placed herself at the opposite end.

"Do I stink?" His eye twinkled, but his mouth remained a thin line.

Æri narrowed her eyes into slits.

"Okay"—he held up a hand—"sit where you like."

She ripped off a chunk of bread and started to chew on it, deliberating how to ask what tomorrow entailed.

Mercifully, Rione broached the topic first.

"Training starts at dawn. Will you be able to rise that early?"

"I got up earlier during the bidding rounds."

"Right..." He looked at her while taking a gulp of water, then set his cup down without a sound. "Just make sure you get enough sleep. We'll be training all day, and it might be...challenging."

"I think I'd sleep better if I knew what I was training for."

His thick brows arched. "You never asked."

"You never offered," she retorted. "Me being your *slave* and all, I'm not supposed to ask. Those are the rules, aren't they?"

Rione winced, the words striking a chord. Evidently, he did not like her referring to herself as "his slave." Well, he should get used to it. He did buy her, after all.

He tapped the lip of his plate as if deciding what to say next. "Fine. Let's clear this out. After this evening, I grant you the freedom to ask any question you wish. We won't be bound by the standard Fíronian rules of slave and master."

The words *freedom* and *bound* hung heavy. Of course, Rione said them intentionally.

"Can I get that in writing?" She meant it as a joke, but her tone came out serious.

"Yes. I'll have Cosmos add it to the papers tonight. You can watch me sign if you wish."

Æri tipped her head in reply. She ran a fingernail along the table's wood grain. Æri still didn't have an answer.

Just get out with it, she chastised.

"What is this training for?" There. Done.

Rione reached for his cup again, turning it with dexterous fingers, then enclosed his large hand around it and brought it to his lips. His throat moved up and down as he drank, meeting Æri's restless glower. After placing it on the table, he sucked his teeth.

His reply came candidly. "You are to be a Venator."

~ 22 ~

ÆRI

"**C**hoose one." Rione leaned against the large sliding doors, his arms folded. She hadn't realized how tall he was; she never gave it much thought before, and the last few nights he had been seated. His head almost touched the top frame. He wore his hair plaited back in rows, merging into one coiled twist down his back.

Why did he not cut it short like the rest of the Fíronian men?

Æri had unenthusiastically dragged her feet out of bed at the early hour, despite telling Rione she'd have no qualms about it the day afore. The past week lent her time to savor rousing late in the mornings.

Spectral blue light hinted dawn approached, and dark shadows and shapes flickered in the passageways of the domus. She followed Rione's instructions to meet him by the palestra doors, and now he was offering her a choice—albeit a choice between staring into space or running. Nevertheless, it was a *choice*.

"Run. I'll run." Meditation never appealed to her.

His brow arched, a sly look passing over his features.

"You know what I mean." She wanted to punch his side for taunting her with that expression, but she kept her distance. Even with the last two shared meals, she was still uneasy around him, and though he had altered their contract, it did little to change the power he held over her.

Rione stood straight and unbolted the doors. A loud scrape resounded. They slid to make a gap in the plastered wall. She let her eyes adjust, impatient to see what he kept hidden. Though not quite dawn, the three moons shined bright enough to reveal a vast field with a track stretching wide and long, hedged by a barrier of connected structures. Ropes, bars, and rings rested at one end set up like an obstacle course. The domus's tall walls had concealed this enormous open space in plain sight from the cramped city streets of Méritras.

"This is our training facility, where my troop prepares for the Bogs. You'll meet them some other time." Once they stepped into the palestra, he slammed the doors back into place.

Her mind flashed to the pack of men on the day of her capture. Hating to admit it, she again agreed with Rione, thinking she'd likely attack or flee in their presence. Æri still struggled to control the urge not to do so with Rione, but she had yet to find a way to seek out Oisin, and being at odds with the Venator wouldn't be wise.

On the subject of Oisin...

"Do all the Venators train here?"

Other than themselves, no one else occupied the space.

"No, just my troop. The others have their own facilities."

"Right..." Æri scrubbed her tongue across her broken tooth, thinking. She didn't want to sound too obvious. "And do we ever train with the other troops?"

"No." He leaned to the side, stretching his torso, then pulled his right foot behind, lengthening the thigh.

"Compete?"

A beat passed. Rione cast a guarded look in her direction. "We have an annual tournament. It usually determines where we will be allocated in the Bogs—the hunting zones. But it's more for show rather than a competition."

"When is it?" Æri bit on her tongue, causing her to muffle the last syllable. She said it too fast, her voice too eager. "I mean—would I be competing with your troop?" Attempting to sound banal, Æri hoped he did not notice the enthusiasm in her previous question.

"It depends..."

"On what?"

"If you're ready in two months."

When Rione told her she would be trained as a Venator, her initial gut reaction was to rebuff the order. She'd never commit to it. Doing so would be traitorous to her people—to her queen. They were the very people her Narkrye hunted. But then it occurred to Æri that Oisin, too, had been sold to a chief Venator. If all the Venators congregated at the competition, it could serve as the perfect cover to meet. Still, *two months*—granted, if Rione even allowed her to talk to the elf—seemed so far away.

"Try to keep pace." Rione didn't give a signal. He just started running on the track that encircled the field. By the time she registered she was to trail him, he had already sprinted several paces ahead.

Neither of them spoke—which Æri preferred. They continued at a steady jog, then gradually Rione increased his stride.

By Skathi's spear, he was fast.

The rhythm of their feet on the dry track diverged, becoming more and more uneven. Her steps doubled his, legs pumping, as she attempted to keep up—the thudding of their feet the only sound in the eerie quiet, like the pulsing of an irregular heart.

After the twenty-fourth or maybe the twenty-fifth loop around the field, Rione slowed his gait. Æri, who had matched it until the sixth lap or so, came to a stop a few minutes later, the sun's glow just now breaking above the red tiled roofs.

She limped to the water pump, where Rione drank from a four-handled jug. Her chest heaved and a nagging cramp formed at her side. Face flushed, Æri groped at the sticky hair plastered to her forehead and neck. Her tunic stuck limply to her skin. Sure, she ran in her mountains throughout Særenfell and that time at the villa, but not at the pace Rione had set.

Æri bent over and placed her hands on her knees, attempting to get air into her lungs. He thrust the earthenware jug into her line of vision. Grudgingly, she accepted it, avoiding where his mouth had touched. Sharing the jug was enough to make her want to toss it back at him. She would have if she hadn't been so thirsty. Just the thought of his lips on the clay rim...A feverish sensation licked up her body, recognizable and not unlike—she coughed on the first sip.

No, that'd be absurd. It must have been from the run.

Rione gave her a slight frown. "Don't drink too fast."

"I'm not." She faced away and lifted the jug again. The fresh liquid jostled as she chugged, splashing down her neck and chest and soaking her tunic's collar. It cooled the heat and cleared her head. After the last gulp, she shoved it into Rione's hands. He looked amused.

Her cheeks burned. "What? Did you expect me to run like a snow leopard? I've hardly had the chance to get outside." Looking at the earth, Æri gawped at Rione's feet. He ran the entire thing barefoot. Was this man even human?

"I was about to say you did well. But after that remark..."

Her teeth ground together. Flipping Rione a rude gesture, she turned her back and started a cool down, lightly tapping her feet side to side on the track's pavement and stretching her tingling limbs.

Rione ignored her slight. "This week, we'll focus on regaining your stamina." His voice was as steady as if he had taken a stroll around the palestra—not a twenty-five-lap run. "But now we eat."

She released her boot onto the ground. "*That* sounds like something I'd be more than happy to participate in."

Æri regretted the statement once she saw the morning meal.

"What is this?" It tasted gods awful. She pinched her nose to swallow. The eggs she stomached, but the strange thick green juice, bitter and chalky, made her want to gag.

"Mostly proteins. Some blended greens." Rione slugged his straight down in two quick chugs.

"It tastes like grass *after* cows stomped on it." It congealed in her throat, and she had to chase it with additional mouthfuls of water. "I think you're trying to poison me."

"Get used to it. It's what we have every morning."

Æri made some more grumbling noises as they returned to the field. She missed Særenfell's nut rolls.

"Heads up!" Rione tossed a leather ball. Crude sutures held the skin together, preventing the heavy stones within from falling free. The sloppy stitching brought back memories of when Æri's nursemaid attempted to teach her how to sew pelts together. It did not go very well.

They threw the ball to and fro until their stomachs fully digested, then Rione put her through interval sprints, placing hurdles at random markings. It went on like this for the remainder of the day, short instructions followed by endurance training and strength building.

Æri slogged off to bed with her whole body aching. Every bit of muscle burned, and the tissues tingled and twinged as she stretched herself across the sheets. But she had never felt so alive. Æri let herself revel in that pure exhausted state. A relief that didn't come with anything else—well, *almost* anything else.

She thought of the redhead, her second, so far away. In her half-coherent daze, her lids drooped. Æri fell asleep with Signe's name, a whisper on her lips.

If Rione pushed her to the cliff's edge the first day, the next day was falling off said cliff.

When she woke, her joints were swollen and stiff, and her legs refused to move. Like stone pillars, she lugged them to the palestra.

Before the run, Rione held out a sturdy arm, halting her steps, and pointed down. "We start by taking those off."

"Are you crazy? I'd cut my feet." Æri was pretty sure she sounded as old as she looked—the characteristics of a petulant teenager finally matching her forever eighteen-year-old face. Back home, she never complained, just sucked it up and gritted through the hurdles, but she couldn't help it with Rione. Something about him made her want to gripe.

Eventually, she pulled at her boots, deliberately showing her annoyance. Her facial expressions didn't need much exaggeration. The motion of bending to yank them off alone sent a ripple of pain up her thigh, causing her to groan.

"I didn't think you were such a whiner." Again Rione's eye sparked. "It's unbecoming."

Her lips thinned, rolling inward. Sadistic prick—her suffering entertained him. She threw her boots at his chest and started the initial pace.

The track's turf wasn't exceptionally soft, but not rocky either. Just tolerable.

It began like this, leaving her shoes off for the first few laps, then the next day a little longer, the next, a little more, a little farther, another lap.

Her skills lay in tracking. Survival on Særenfell and in the Bogs relied on keen eyesight, quick thinking, and quiet stealth. Speed too played a vital part, but because they usually flew, good aim was prized over swiftness of the body.

Training to be a Venator was different.

Not only did she need her tracking abilities, but she had to out-run or, at minimum, outmaneuver a Bog beast. It would mean the difference between life and death.

Into the second week, Rione incorporated agility into her drills: explosive jumps to increase her pace while running, combining turns and precision footwork into the routine whilst watching for distractions or heeding orders. His voice carried over the palestra, bellowing out instructions again and again. "If you want to survive the Bogs," Rione explained, "these exercises are better than any kind of close-combat training."

He never fatigued through all these drills, never once sat on the terrain to rest as she did on multiple occasions. His stamina seemed innate, born into action under a blistering sun. But he was also fair, letting Æri take the long respites when she needed them.

She understood why his troop triumphed over the other Ve-nators in Fíronbec—Rione's leadership and devotion indeed the cause.

Soon, Æri discovered the buildings enclosing the palestra held a specific purpose, being tied directly to the training and care of the Venators. Rione's private chambers, too, were located at a remote end of the gymnasium. No doubt why she could liberally roam the main part of the house without running into him.

"What's wrong?" Rione had noticed her limp following an af-ternoon drill.

"Nothing. Probably just a blister."

He glared at her, doubtful. "Let me see."

Æri rolled her eyes but lifted her foot.

Surprising her, he got on his knees and took her foot gently in his hands, resting it on his bent leg. He ran a featherlight finger over the injury. His position of supplication, the tipping of his head, and his tender hands baffled her, the action so at odds with the man who had kidnapped her. She didn't think Fíronians bowed down like this.

Rione put her foot on the ground and stood to his full height, breaking the brief thrall.

"Looks like a blood blister—go have it checked by one of the healers." He pointed to the buildings toward the back.

Her heel did look rather gruesome; a reddish-black lump protruded from the sole. It dumbfounded her further. Why would he even touch it?

In the infirmary's airy room, heady-smelling fennel, chamomile, and yarrow dangled from the ceiling joists like an overturned meadow.

A woman with knobby fingers aptly cleaned the wound and applied an adhesive. She wore a thin bronze ring on her right hand, and Æri wondered if the older healer could be Cosmos's wife. But she refrained from asking, oddly too shy. The healer's touch was soothing and cautious, and they shared quiet smiles.

"There, now, good as new." The woman patted her heel, and when she sent Æri back out to the palestra, her blister no longer smarted.

Regardless of the happenings outside, Rione's domus functioned as a world of its own—a well-oiled machine for the people who dwelt inside. However, for all the time spent in the facility, Æri never once saw the rest of Rione's Venator troop.

Why? Nearly three weeks had passed. When would he deem her ready? Impatience tickled her thoughts, but she did not press him, and instead focused on gaining her strength back.

By the fourth week, Æri was able to match Rione's pace in bare feet for almost the whole hour on their morning runs. The blisters healed over, and now rough callouses covered the soles. Her energy, too, returned, the muscles becoming used to the daily strain.

She spent her days jumping through hoops, balancing on logs, and scaling thorny walls, the infinite calisthenics only ceasing when Rione determined they were through.

Yet, the most arduous training for her to endure, which Rione surreptitiously snuck in after the second week, was meditation.

"A cooldown," as Rione called it, insisting they do the breathing practice ere the evening meal. It consisted of counting in and out or roaring like a lion—tongue extended—this one she tolerated because she could direct it toward Rione.

However, the steady inhalations made her fidget. She only breathed like that when she couldn't control her thoughts and emotions, when they took her to a darker place. Associating it with a cooldown didn't feel right, and the noises of the garden—the fountain, buzzing of bees, or the cooing doves—distracted her.

Æri was too exhausted to speak at mealtimes, usually scarfing down the food, then darting for the baths, her eyes falling shut the minute her head hit the pillow.

She did, however, overcome her fear of Rione—pushed past it and numbed it like she numbed previous fears, forcing herself to function. Yet, it also numbed other feelings...about her homeland, how much she missed her Narkrye, Signe, and her sister, and that odd mix of sensations when she caught Rione meditating that first week here.

Of course, it was a temporary fix—a binding waiting to be torn off, and maybe she'd explode...or cease functioning altogether. But for now, it worked.

"Tonight, we play Game of Mercenaries." Rione slid a board in front of his plate, then poured a set of circular black and white stones from a clay jar, placing them gingerly on the checkered slat.

He cast an eye at her. "But you'll have to come a little closer."

Was this some kind of trick?

Rione's face remained blank. No flash of amusement there nor that subtle, wry expression he offered when he found pleasure in her impatience.

The board resembled the game the two older men played in front of the library, but this one was crafted in wood in place of the stone.

She let out a noisy sigh and reluctantly pushed her plate toward Rione, plopping herself in the chair kitty-corner to his. A sizable gap still fell between them. Gyr promptly followed, moving in buoyant hops along the table's rim.

A smidge of satisfaction shone in Rione's eye.

Was he gloating?

As quickly as it appeared, the trace vanished.

"Is this supposed to be your version of bonding time?" Æri said with a scoff. She started to play with some peas from her meal, lining them in a row behind her black game pieces.

"Venators don't battle many human enemies, but we do fight beasts in the Bogs...and some are not as brainless as they look. Playing these kinds of games can help with making calculated decisions."

She sighed. Of course logic undermined any fun in Rione's book, but he added, "It also passes the time," and offered her a small smile.

The game's objective was to blockade all opponents and, finally, the king's pieces.

To Æri's vexation, Rione won the first two rounds.

"Stop only looking at the board. Watch me—how I move and think. It will help you determine my next play. See this?" He pointed to one of her black stones. "When your eyes move over the piece, I can guess you'll try to capture my pawn. Thus, I have to move it." He picked up his white stone and placed it several squares away. "Try to predict my moves before I make them."

"Easier said than done..." She reflected on his advice, trying to move past her initial gut feeling to reject it. "I suppose it is like sparring."

"Yes, a bit like that."

After the third game, she grew more acquainted with his tells, how his hand hovered, deliberating a move, or how he scratched at his neck when he planned to block versus attack, and how she could flank one piece there, encircle another here.

The game reminded her of one she'd seen Otta and sometimes Signe played when the storms raged, making it too dangerous to hunt or fly outside. However, instead of two kings, their game consisted of one; the alabaster pieces collected at the center, and the dark pieces lined the board's perimeter. Still, the goal was the same: to capture the opponent's king.

Midway through their fourth game, Æri caught Rione staring at her limb. His gaze darted back to the board. She'd started doffing her bionic arm during meditation in the garden, allowing her skin to breathe.

"Just ask." She scowled at him and moved one of her stones, plunking it on the board with a thump.

"Are you ever going to tell me what happened?" He leaned back in his chair. It creaked under his weight.

"No. Moving on."

"Why'd you tell me to ask?"

"So you'd stop staring." She sent him a fleeting, sarcastic smile and pulled some meat off a cold chicken leg. Enamored with the board game, Æri had forgotten about her food.

"You'll have to start trusting me if you want to be successful in the Venator troop."

She eyed him again, attempting to keep the mood light, nevertheless meaning every word. "You know those fall exercises? To build confidence in the other person..."

"Trust falls?" Rione's eyebrow rose.

"Yeah, those. Well, I wouldn't get near you even if you were covered in a million feathers and rabbit pelts." She bit into the meat held between her fingers.

Rione's mouth quirked, and a flash of mirth crossed his face. "I prefer larger prey to chickens and rabbits. Perhaps you'll try if I'm wearing puma and leopard furs?"

A corner lifted on Æri's mouth at the jest, giving the smallest of smiles.

His brown eye glinted again, gaze sweeping over her face and touching her mouth where she smiled.

When he lifted his eye to connect with hers, Æri hastily looked down at the board to avoid staring. She straightened her mouth, focusing on her final move. There, a win. With her three pawns, she trapped his king against the rim of the board.

"Well done." He gave her a congratulatory grin. Gyr cawed from his perch. He, too, was pleased with her triumph. Rione's smile remained as he motioned to her bird. "What about his story?"

Æri deliberated if she should keep that a mystery as well but then considered against it. No harm or fear was attached to Gyr's past.

"I found him as a nestling. Abandoned atop an Ophinyne cave near Kastald—our tallest mountain. His feathers had just started coming in. I think he was the runt. He never grew to his full size." Her lips curved in memory. Æri had spent the whole day climbing the ancient cliffs and was preparing to stay in the cave overnight before rappelling down the next day. She heard his insistent chirping from above the cave mouth. As she pulled herself up to the nest, this little white puff squawked back at her, flapping blindly. His tiny eyes were red and crusted, and he looked so vulnerable.

Æri watched throughout the night to see if his mother returned, but she never did.

"Both his eyes were damaged. Once I nursed him back to health, only one cleared. The other was too far marred, so we replaced it."

Rione nodded in thought. "'Seems like you've been through a lot together."

"We have," she said matter-of-factly. "He's saved me on more than one occasion in the Bogs. I don't go anywhere without him. We're connected...It's hard to explain. Even before I replaced his eye, we shared a bond."

Rione scratched at his clean-shaven jaw, musing over her words. "Well, then, Æri of Særenfell, that will be my next challenge."

A beat passed while she thought about what he implied. *Trust.* Trust would be wasted here, in this realm. "Is that why you're keeping your troop away?"

"Partially, yes." His face turned serious again.

"Where are they?"

"They're training elsewhere for now."

A soft throat clearing came from the room's entrance. They both cocked their heads. Cosmos stood under the eve.

"Lord Rione." The man bent his head.

Æri had learned Cosmos handled most of Rione's routine business dealings. Hence, his attendance at the final bidding round in lieu of the Venator. He also took charge of messages to and from the domus, settling most of the administrative tasks.

"There has been a summons from the king."

Rione's eye turned somber, and he nodded. "Ready my things for the morning."

"It is not a request for you, my lord." Cosmos extended an arm toward Æri. "It's for her."

~ 23 ~

ÆRI

If she ever thought the king held modest tastes, that vanished upon her arrival at Solistra Belisaur Palace. Extending across a third of Méritras, the palace's estate had been erected by the late king on a slight incline so that the structure dominated the city, its golden columns visible from the lower urban streets. In juxtaposition to the grand collection of buildings, the Villa Glorial appeared rustic, a raw nugget compared to this polished gold crown. Its absurdity did little to assuage the mounting tumult in her head.

Why had King Remus summoned her after weeks of silence?

Æri stayed on the older man's heels as they walked through the entrance. Rione's absence at her side felt strange, like when the official removed her torc—a ghost of something that ought to be there but wasn't. Odd that both were something she was reluctant about at first...But King Remus requested Æri alone, so only Rione's liaison, Cosmos, chaperoned. With some finagling, she convinced Rione to allow her to take Gyr—though on the condition he remained tethered to her at all times.

They had forgone shackles, her whereabouts known by both Rione and the king through the device implanted in her arm. She was still unaware of how it worked, the buzz of it running through her veins. Perhaps the tracker worked on magic, like Brennos's wards? Or more plausibly, innovation...

"It's been some time since I had the pleasure of visiting the palace. Icarus, please tell me how you managed to keep it looking like the day King Lucius completed it?" Cosmos had picked up a conversation with the servant who guided them through the massive galleries.

"The palace needs constant restoration. We inspect each room on an annual basis."

Stories of the Solistra Belisaur Palace had reached her mountain fells well before the Split. Of how the previous king commissioned a handful of dwarves from the Isle of Hártolf to aid in the interior construction, inlaying the ceiling and walls with dazzling gemstones.

Unfortunately, most of the crafted work was hidden today—paintings, statues, windows—all of it was covered.

Had the king just returned from his villa?

Large braziers lit the passageways despite the daylight hour.

Icarus, clad in dark grays and blacks, ushered them into an antechamber where they were to wait, indicating an engraved bench to sit—the embellishments so elaborate, it looked painful.

"Æri! Cosmos!"

Their names bounced harmonically off the room's vaulted arches. Under the entry, beside a veiled statue, stood Camilla. She, too, wore a dark ensemble, the gown wrapping about her like an inky cocoon.

"I received word you'd be here." Her gait was graceful and smooth on the marble slabs as she approached.

"Lady Camilla." Cosmos bobbed his head.

Lady? Æri did not realize the lady's maid was a true *lady*.

"I'd like to borrow Æri for a few minutes, Cosmos."

"It may have to wait, my lady. We'll be meeting King Remus shortly."

"At what time?"

"High noon, my lady."

Camilla scrunched her face and tutted. "Then you will have plenty of time. You know well enough of King Remus's punctuality." She looped her arm through Æri's, Camilla's bare skin brushing against her own, and tugged Æri toward the entrance.

"We will be in the front gardens. Send a servant when the king calls." Camilla whisked Æri away before Cosmos could protest.

"This is much more satisfying than waiting in that bleak old palace, is it not?" Camilla let out a sigh, stretching her free arm to the sky.

Æri had to agree. The palace's imperious walls appeared solemn compared to the fresh air of the manicured gardens. Floral scents of summer lilac and rhododendron floated in the air, reminiscent of the villa's meadow. From the subtle elevation, she could just make out a river curving along Méritras's borders.

Gyr chirped a few times and, forgetting about the chain tethering him to Æri, he shook out his wings. The small pull quickly reminded him he was bound. Æri wished she could let him fly, but she feared what would happen if she did.

Arm in arm, they strolled through a low maze, the hedges topped with lavender.

"Should I address you as 'Lady,' then?"

"Oh, don't be ridiculous." Camilla batted off Æri's suggestion. "You may address me as Camilla. That was how I introduced myself before, and that is how I shall remain."

A smile tugged at the corner of Æri's mouth. Camilla was likable in that way, as sophisticated as any high-born yet remarkably down to earth.

They made their way about the gardens and to the open vestibule of the palace. As Æri and Camilla wound through its columns, the shadow of a colossal bronze statue overtook the two women. A glistening figure of a man wearing the sunray crown gazed out over Méritras. Focused on the king's summons, Æri had entirely overlooked the impressive statue upon her arrival.

"Is that Hesól—the sun god?"

Camilla grinned and regarded the effigy, shading her eyes from the sun. "I'm sure if he lived, he would have liked to be called as such, but no—that is the late King Lucius."

"King Remus did not want to have it replaced?" It seemed out of character for the new king.

"Oh, he did. He wished to have its face recast to mimic his own, but the Curia recommended against it."

"Why was that?" Æri thought it must be strange to see the looming face of one's father depicted in such a godly manner every day. She recalled the bust in his study at the Villa Glorial. King Remus had plenty of reminders of the old king about Fíronbec. A sharp ache coiled in her chest; Æri was suddenly jealous—she had nothing to remember her own father by.

"King Remus is still a new king—if one can consider fifty years 'new.' His father ruled justly for such a long time before. Most people adored his reign."

"And what of King Remus? Do the people like this new king as much as his predecessor?"

Camilla seemed to weigh her response, and after a moment, she said, "I believe the people tolerate his reign, but they mourn for their lost sovereign." Her reply was guarded, purposely deflecting the focus from the king.

As they wandered from the vestibule and bronze statue, Camilla fell into silence, and Æri became aware of the shift in her posture, her arm growing tense with apprehension.

"Æri...I must confess my true reasons for taking you from Cosmos. It is essential you know before your audience with the king." Camilla looked at her with sad eyes. "The king's mother is dead."

Æri halted in her tracks, releasing Camilla's arm.

"Excuse me—wait. I'm sorry, what?"

"Dowager Jocasta Adriana Belisaur has passed away," Camilla repeated.

The slight tinge of sorrow resurfaced. She recalled the lamenting woman in veils wandering the villa's halls. Why didn't Rione tell her of this news?

"Oh...King Remus must be devastated." Æri said this mostly out of reflex. She did not know if love was lost between the king and his mother or if the relationship resembled what she had endured with her own. Regardless, a parent's passing could be distressing.

Camilla linked her fingers, twisting them together. "The palace and the court are in mourning, hence our drapery." She motioned back to the palace, which displayed dark banners between columned entries, the gloomy decor obvious now.

How did she not connect the dots?

"When did this happen?"

"Several weeks ago. The procession and burial occurred shortly after."

Perhaps the reason why King Remus had not demanded her presence sooner.

"Why was this kept from me?" Did Rione intend for her to meet the king oblivious to what had occurred?

Camilla paused again, considering her words. "Lord Rione did not think it wise to inform you. He believed it might interfere with your training and deemed it unimportant to know at the time." Inspecting Æri's face, Camilla added, "I imagine he did not think it necessary for you to know until the king called upon you."

"So he asked you to inform me instead? At the same hour I am to meet the king—did he want me to look like a fool?"

Camilla shook her head adamantly. "No. I do not believe those were his intentions...but I agree. He should not have withheld such information. Lord Rione strives to be a man of logic, though sometimes I think it may hinder his sentimental judgments."

"Do you know him well enough to say that?" Æri's tone came out bitter, feeling like he left her out intentionally. She knew it was a strike at Camilla as well.

Camilla's eyes darted away, looking as if she wanted to say more. Ultimately, she cast Æri's remark aside and took Æri's hand, clasping it between her own. "Please accept my apology on his behalf. I do hope he is treating you well besides this...latest information. If he isn't, well, I'll give him a proper tongue-lashing."

Æri's eyes softened, relaxing the strain in her neck. How could she hold resentment for this woman who had been more than kind to her? Rione's negligence was not Camilla's fault.

Gravel crunched from behind. One of the bleakly dressed servants walked in their direction, and on the palace steps, Cosmos waved his arms for her to return.

Following the grim news, Æri suspected Ofelia also knew of the bereavement. She had insisted Æri wear a gown of deep navy blue for the summons, and though reluctant to don the sheer and flowing material at first, Æri was now glad of it. At least she looked the part to meet a royal in mourning.

Candlelight rippled against golden walls, producing a distorted picture of the imperial throne room. The king sat alone on his gilded throne, his retinue nowhere in view besides the two sentinels flanking the stately doors, their tall lances clutched close. A fresco behind the sovereign mimicked the rays of a sun, looking as if they emanated from the throne itself. Like the bronze statue, it spoke of the relationship between Fíronian royals and their lost devotion to Hesól.

In light of the circumstances, the king did look less radiant today. Sooty smudges framed his sore eyes, marring his handsome face, and his burnished hair hung lackluster and limp. He wore a tunic black as night.

King Remus dismissed Cosmos, leaving Æri to stand before the elevated dais. Gyr tapped nervously on her shoulder.

"Nice dress. You appear to be...well." His bronze eyes dropped from her falcon to linger below her neckline. "Though the ensemble would be better without the bird."

Her face heated under his rakish stare. She had fleshed out after a month of hard training. Her bones no longer jutted from poor nutrition, and though far from shapely, the dress's style, like the coral one at the banquet, emphasized the curve of her waist and accented her small breasts.

"I offer my condolences, King Remus." She dipped her head, trying to ignore his apparent scrutiny.

"Ah, it appears Æri of Særenfell has developed manners *and* that your owner informed you of my sad news after all." He toyed with the sash that cinched his tunic. "I missed you at the funeral. You've been hidden away from me all these weeks; I began to think Lord Rione did not want to share."

Æri's attempt to keep her lip from wrinkling in disgust failed. "Share" sounded like she was an object to be played with, tossed like a doll from one owner to the next.

"It is no matter." His singsong voice interrupted her thoughts. "This mourning period keeps us from enjoying certain pleasures." He released an exasperated sigh. "And it would be so rude to my dear late mother."

King Remus tested her patience. Grief had not changed this.

"I suppose we should get to the point, despite being charmed by your stoic presence." He tarried again, perusing her body from head to toe.

The look sent a shiver through her bones. Her instincts pushed her to turn and leave that ostentatious, oversized throne room. But she stood firm.

"You are to work one day a week at the Inventorium until your task is complete. I've already spoken to your master. He is aware of these requests."

"And what if I refuse your generous offer?" she said, scoffing. Then immediately bit into her cheek.

Draugs.

She just had to say that, and she'd been doing so well. Why couldn't she hold her tongue?

Not that she enjoyed taking orders from this man who made her skin crawl, but she had a plan. It would be stupid to deviate from it just to get into a spat with the king—especially on his first summons after the Auctioning.

Though every fiber in her screamed to rebel, he was not her queen—nor Rione, for that matter. Rione tolerated her brashness and encouraged it sometimes...but to defy *this* king outright would be...

His lips curved upward. "I'm sure we can arrange less hospitable living circumstances and still have you train as a Venator for Lord Rione." He refocused his gaze on Gyr, who gave a shrill little squawk. "Alas, you would not be able to take your bird, nor your arm...both I hear you are rather attached to."

Æri released a snarl. "Fine."

She had nothing to negotiate with. Æri would agree to do as he said—for now. He again did not specify a time. Good. She planned on making him wait. In any case, it would take her away from the grueling days of training.

"Excellent. I knew you were a person of reason. You'll begin this afternoon." He snapped at the sentinels to open the doors. Taking this as her dismissal, Æri turned to leave.

"Oh...and before you go. I'd like you to deliver a message to your new owner." The king's tone shifted again; that playful little jibe in his voice returned.

Æri swallowed the unease rising as she curved back.

"Let Lord Rione know he did well to suggest using Sulivan's powers during your final bidding round. I do love a little theatrics in these contests."

The muscles in Æri's throat knotted as she took in the king's supposedly flippant words.

His brow furrowed, seeing through her attempt to hide the hurt across her face. "He didn't tell you? I assumed he explained since he gave you back your bird."

Æri gritted her teeth. "He failed to mention it."

Then, in afterthought, she pulled her lips back, plastering on a smile.

The king picked at a corner of his throne, peeling the gold paint, and rambled on as if he didn't hear her. "It really did create a more entertaining match. At first, I was a tad disappointed at your loss—you would have been a unique asset in the Arena. But in the end, Cuthbert does make a better contender for the Games. I've heard he's already won the last two. If he goes on like this, he'll earn his freedom and return to Jotnarach before the year is up."

Æri's hands curled into claws, her fingernails digging into her right palm and feeling the half-moons in her skin. She understood what the king played at—rubbing salt into the wound. King Remus may be a nasty piece of work, but she *knew* she couldn't trust him. He made that clear with his gibes from the beginning. Rione, on the other hand...Rione just pretended. He pretended to be self-righteous by bending the rules, providing her with comfort and care, and speaking of *trust*. Yet, he had kept these secrets from her and deliberately sabotaged her only opportunity of escaping this gods' forsaken realm. What Rione withheld from her chafed at her insides. Why would she dare to trust him after that? Trying to suppress her anger—and to avoid handing the king one more thing to crow about—she exhaled, nodded to the royal, and pivoted out of the throne room.

~ 24 ~

OTTA

Særenfell

Blistering winds lashed past Otta's well-bundled ears. The coverings of her fleece-lined hat flapped as sharp ice crystals scraped against her raw cheeks, and the inside of her nose throbbed with the bite of cold. The whistling squalls and howling gusts of the Northwestern Fells of Nordan were some of the most treacherous in Særenfell.

Tall metal rods hummed in the frozen lake, like a woodland of bizarre leafless trees with only their towering trunks remaining. High- and low-pitched vibrations sang from beneath the thick sheet of ice, its reverberating cadence a warning. An ether-filled sky was drenched gray.

Time to seek shelter.

At a brisk trot, she aimed for the stone lodge. Her cleats' small arium-coated spikes dug into smooth ice—a lifesaving invention used on these desolate peaks.

As she reached the rim, the first lightning bolt struck. A clap of thunder boomed simultaneously, and another form of thunder echoed below her feet. Her head darted toward the compressor and storage tanks close to the lake's edge. A red light winked back at her.

Fantastic, the reloading process was functioning again.

Fresh snow crunched as she scudded around snowdrifts to the stables. There, attached to the rear of the stone shelter, she checked the doors and latches of the elk's stalls. Sometimes the elk became spooked during the ether storms—all locked. Jodi proved their worth well.

Otta had hired on Jodi after the queen deemed the progress of the new Skimmer too slow. Despite having spare parts from earlier trials, and the new hydraulic trip hammer, Otta struggled without help. She needed more arium ore from the Brokrann mineworkers, and once she obtained that, she had to melt and mold it into the desired shapes.

At this report, Queen Brynja took immediate action. She called upon the blacksmiths of Særenfell to assist Otta with the production. While seeing out this summons in Marr, a local mining village tucked away between the Glyllstald quarries and the Brokrann mines, Otta came across Jodi, one of the blacksmiths' children.

Their homely workshop was littered with minute creations: a cart with iron wheels chugging on its own here, a windup flying bird leaving trails of shimmery dust there—or her favorite: a hand-cranked mobile light source, its flame shielded by a sheet of crystal. Rainbows of light streamed from its prismed lens.

However, what astonished Otta the most was the creator of these inventions: a reedy, unkempt adolescent, their appearance not yet fully set. They looked perhaps fourteen or fifteen.

"You can take them. They'd be more use to you than tinkering their life away in this ol' shop," Jodi's mother—the blacksmith—said when Otta made the offer. Jodi's eager smile confirmed their agreement. Though they had been cared for, the small shop visibly limited their potential.

With Jodi and the other blacksmiths throughout the realm to help, the fabrication rate of the Skimmer quadrupled. At the accelerated speed, they'd have two finished aircraft within the next three months.

Yet, the queen continued her demands, requiring Otta to harness as much energy as possible from the glacial lakes. And though Queen Brynja did not mention the specifics behind the urgent uptake, Otta believed this too had something to do with Æri.

Since her disappearance, the fortress felt gutted, as if Æri was its heart, and everyone within the ramparts slowly drained of life without her—the queen suffering the most.

Otta flung the shelter's door open and slammed it behind her. A wooden bar thudded into place as hail clattered down in hurried sheets, tinny on the shale roof—like marbles rattling in a metal jar.

The shelter—once the hunting lodge to the Summer Castle—had been in near ruins when Otta first started hiking to the Northwestern Fells. After the Split, when summer disappeared, the castle fell into disuse, as did its lodge. Otta fixed up the shelter with the assistance of the Narkrye, using it as a home when she came up to harvest. Due to raging ether storms in the Fells, Lake Mærrain served as an ideal place to capture the tempestuous power.

In the hearth, a hearty stew boiled in an iron crock. A crane held the pot above the fire's crackling tips.

"That smells delicious. Do I detect pine nuts?"

A meaty aroma filled the room, making the shelter almost cozy—if one looked past the slew of parchment, scrolls, and modeling kits on the tables and floors—half-finished concept plans and doodles of an idea that passed the long hours indoors.

"I hope you don't mind. I added some mountain herbs." Jodi reclined their rickety chair, balancing on the two back legs. Hair sprung from their head in an array of twisted ash-black ends. They twirled a curl around a small finger, the tight spiral coiled perfectly. "Given what we have access to…"

"I'm delighted to take any variation on the humdrum rabbit or venison." Otta readjusted her spectacles, rubbed the condensation from the lenses, and strode over to the hearth to help herself to the bubbling concoction.

"The rods seem to be faring well." Jodi leaned forward again, motioning their head to the lake. Their chair thumped with the movement, and Jodi scooted into the large worktable that butted against a crystal observation window. Three fingers thick, the glass provided protection and served as viewing access.

Together, they watched the tempest brew over the frozen lake—one of Otta's favorite moments in the harvest. Warm and shielded, she pulled up a chair next to Jodi to enjoy the light show, falling snow and hail kicking up in swirls over the ice. Brilliant electrical currents extended from turbulent skies, striking the rod forest.

"I think the maintenance we did yesterday paid off. The arium rods are conducting more efficiently." Jodi pointed to the large dial fixed to the wall that displayed the energy input of the storage tanks.

"Encouraging." Elation was evident in Otta's voice. She pulled off her gloves and cupped her hands around the pewter bowl. Its warmth seeped into her numb fingers. "This means we can return to the fortress tomorrow."

They had lodged upon these peaks for over two weeks, and though she enjoyed the solitude of the lake, Otta fretted she spent too much time here. She needed to get back to complete the Skimmers. Some of the best blacksmiths in Særenfell oversaw the legwork, but she worried about its execution.

"How many tanks do we have for the return trip?"

Compressors installed next to the storage tanks converted bubbles from the lightning storms into a highly pressurized gaseous form. After sealing the tanks, they would transport the lot back to the fortress.

"Ten. Do you think the elk can handle that many?" Jodi's eyes held a sliver of concern.

Otta chewed the question over as wood snapped in the hearth. The compressed fuel tanks easily measured half the size of a human. She typically carted seven to eight in the sleigh. Ten would be a stretch, but they could manage. Even if one dropped from the sleigh, the risk of combustion in the tightly sealed tanks was rare due to their high concentration and the lack of a flame. Snow and ice cloaked their lands.

Otta and Jodi woke early, harnessing the elk to begin their tread down the mountain pass.

With a full sleigh, the ride would take over a fortnight, the first day's descent the most dangerous.

The pair treaded on a road built wide and flat where switchbacks spared them from any steep declines. Otta had climbed up and down this mountain trail for years. This was Jodi's first trip.

Snow piled the tops of evergreen trees, knifelike icicles clinging to their bows. Otta and Jodi walked alongside the wagon, steering the trained elk. Their snowshoes and the sleigh left tracks cut into the fresh powder.

A rustling in the thicket beyond seized Otta's attention. Two long ears popped out from the brush, and a snowshoe hare skittered across the path, its white coat blending in with the powdery trail. She exhaled but kept her guard up.

Far from any villages, she anticipated a bear or snow leopard sighting. Though she didn't have the Narkrye's penchant for hunting, she had to kill on more than one occasion. Another reason why she cherished Jodi's presence. A crossbow and dagger only did so much.

"Replacing the trail with a pulley system would be more efficient, don't you think?" Jodi's nose and cheeks had turned a rosy pink, nipped by the cold despite their layers of wool. Jodi went on to discuss their future transportation plans, utterly engrossed in the topic. "We can have a frame or container to haul the tanks up and down from the lower fells and use the shelters as checkpoints." One of the elk neighed as if it were listening. "Yes, I think it's an excellent idea too, Tuck." Jodi grinned while the elk leaned into their scratch. "We can use the energy from the lake to power the pulley and take advantage of gravity when we send tanks down."

This idea was the best suggestion yet, and Otta was just about to say so when a warm wind lifted, flowing past their sled. Shadows formed on the glistening snow, the rays of the arctic sun disappearing. The pungent, metallic scent of ozone wound up her nose. Dark billowing clouds verged on the blue sky.

"Storms are forming too soon in the day." Her head whipped back up the mountainside to gauge how far they'd traveled—less than halfway. They needed to get farther down the trail, past that old fir. The tree stood stark like a spear, lancing the clouded sky; its rust-colored pine needles scattered the snow under drooping arms, which lacked the packed white of the others. Just past that, the trail curved south. If they cleared the bend before the worst of the storm, they'd be all right, safe from the stronger flurries.

Otta clicked her tongue, signaling the elk to quicken their pace.

A crack of thunder resonated from atop the mountain, and Tuck barked in distress.

"Shhh, there, there." Jodi patted his bristled side, whispering soothing words.

Again, a flash and the echoing rumble, closer this time. They were still several hundred strides from the bend. More barks came from the elk.

Another ribbon of light extended from the roiling sky, so bright it left Otta blinking. Forcing her eyes to readjust, she faltered. The flash had struck that old fir below the slope, and the tree, withered and dry, burst into flames.

Startled by the fire and crack of the tree's limbs, the elk has-tened their trot. Otta's breaths came out in heavy gasps, struggling to keep pace. The sleigh tilted under the acceleration, shaking the contents within.

Her legs burned as she tried not to trip over her snowshoes.

"The rail! Get to the rail!" she yelled, but Jodi was only slightly ahead.

Tanks rolled, and the sleigh teetered, balancing on one ski. Ten was too much. *It was too full.*

Otta and Jodi grabbed hold of the rail on the opposite side and pulled with their weight, but not in time. One of the tanks slipped from the top canvas, thudding onto the snowy earth, then tum-bled down the steep mountainside—right for the alight tree.

Otta allowed herself the briefest of seconds to watch before her brain kicked in. *If* it hit the flaming tree and *if* the pressure relief valve failed—and air entered the tank—it would just take a tiny spark...but what troubled Otta more than the explosion was the af-termath. Months of snow, in compact layers, covered the craggy slope above.

"We need to get around the corner, fast." Her voice sounded unreservedly calm—an attempt not to alarm Jodi or the already frightened elk. She pushed Jodi to move faster while keeping the sleigh balanced.

They had to get beyond that boulder which would block the south-facing side—trusting it would protect them.

With a thump, the tank landed at the burning tree's base. Otta's chest pounded. No flames had reached it yet. Maneuvering the elk around the turn, she and Jodi held tight, gripping their leather reins.

Not two minutes later, an explosion boomed over the valley. Then the ground rumbled with the deep quake of the mountain-side.

~ 25 ~

ÆRI

Her hand came away black and coated in soot. Crisp singes ran up the skirts of her navy dress. She shook the fabric, and tiny flakes of ash fluttered to the floor. Æri had stepped too close to the furnaces.

"Well, I won't be wearing this again," she mumbled to Gyr. Æri wasn't particularly fond of the gown, but it seemed a waste. Unlatching the clasps, she let the fabric slink to the floor and slipped on a simple night shift.

Æri had returned late from the Inventorium—too late to speak to Rione. Anyhow, she had little energy left to confront the Venator. Her anger had weaned out into exhaustion, fordone not only from the long day but emotionally from Rione's continuous betrayal. This place reeked of dishonest society, and he was the worst of them all.

Following her chat with the king, she'd been sent directly to the laboratories, where Gratian updated her on the energy source's progress. The scavengers—what her crew called the seekers—were just now filtering back with the black rock collected from the Bogs. Having a scant choice in the matter, Æri set to work, instructing the scitators on how to roast and smelt the raw material, the facility's furnaces already prepped for the lengthy process. Once they extracted a sample of the Bogs' ore, she taught them how to layer the material into thin sheets so meticulously that it took the rest of the day and into the night. By the time she returned to Rione's domus, the household was idle with its dozing inhabitants.

Æri's fists gripped the sheets; her body wound into a tight ball. Images of Gyr and Yrsa's deaths replayed even after her eyes opened.

Idling away time, she ate breakfast in silence. Æri still fumed over what Rione had done. The agitation hadn't abated after sleep.

"Ouch!" *Quit it, Gyr! You ate.*

He, her sole companion for the morning, pecked at her hand until she passed him some bread. Today marked their biweekly day of rest, and Rione, the person she needed to vent her frustrations to, wasn't to be found, conveniently opting to be elsewhere.

Let's see if we can find one of those leisure tomes Ofelia mentioned earlier, hmm? Might be entertaining.

If not, at least the library would keep her mind off the absent Venator.

Attached to the study, the library took up a small corner of the house. Both the Grand Libraries of Méritras and Rione's collection differed vastly from her fortress's archives. Særenfell's umbral rooms exuded damp and echoing spaces, its only viable light source, the lambent torches mounted to its stone walls. Here, a lattice-cut screen welcomed natural light, casting a warm glow over the parchment.

Æri perused the shelves, searching top to bottom for a title that alluded to a leisure tale. With no luck, she settled on a scroll labeled *A Bestiary: The Anatomy and Dissection of Bog Beasts*, wanting to familiarize herself with some of the creatures she'd be fighting.

Not five pages in, her stomach churned—reminded of the sour meat she almost ate at the banquet. The images of beasts, so finely rendered in colored inks, looked tangible on the page—*including* depictions of the beasts' innards. She charily rolled and placed the scroll back on the shelf.

Æri yanked down a newer tome: *The Rules and Regulations of the Royal Venators Tournaments.* Now, this was something worthwhile. She had roughly a month before the contest, and it wouldn't hurt to know a little more about the affair—especially if she planned to find Oisin there.

Propping the book on her knees, she scanned the contents page: "Gameday Protocols," "Spectator Regulations," "Scoring, Bog Territorial Allocations"—ah. "Troop Participants and Registration."

The top fifteen Venator troops of Fíronbec compete in the tournaments. Individual competitions are also organized for Venators with excelling talents. Registration is based on troop membership and the permission of the troop's chief. Ceremonial receptions are held before and after each match for participating members.

Okay...this was good.

Æri tried to dampen the fluttering inside her chest. It would take maneuvering on the tournament day, but the task wasn't impossible—she just had to register for a match where Oisin was a participant. Grudgingly, she also realized if she wanted a favor from Rione, she'd have to rein in her temper around him.

"No. Not in Draug's hell is that happening." Æri crossed her arms and took a step back from the mats. There was no way she'd lay under Rione in that position again.

They had moved into the palestra's interior rooms. Rione wanted to teach her some defense skills, and to Æri's dismay, he started with a hold very similar to the one from the Bogs.

"It's vital you learn this technique, Æri. You already have a good aptitude for defense—you demonstrated as much at the bid-

ding rounds—but I doubt you've escaped a hold like this before."
He knelt on the compact mats, ready to begin the exercise.

She sank her teeth into her lip and shook her head, retreating
another step. It made absolute logical sense to learn how to overthrow a man twice her size. Of course it did. But did it mean she
was eager to put herself *back* in that situation? Hell no.

"Okay." Rione let out a long exhalation. He rose from the mat
and strode toward the doorway. "I'll get Leta to demonstrate."

Æri's arms remained folded when he returned with Leta by his
side. She had changed out of her house dress into their typical
training gear.

"Are you comfortable, Leta?"

"As good as I'll ever be in this position." Leta laughed.

"Good." Rione's face was stern in contrast to Leta's playful disposition. He hovered over her, instructing. "There are a few positions of defense from this point."

Æri's chest squeezed, and her throat went dry as she observed
the pair—this stress brought on by simply *watching*. She fought to
numb the feeling, pushing it down and telling herself she was in
no danger.

"First, if someone attempts to choke you in this position"—Rione placed his body between Leta's legs and his hands moved to
her neck—"this is the best thing you can do."

Æri wanted to tear him off of Leta, but again, that voice of reason held her back. *He is trying to help.*

"Leta—explain it from here."

"I control the elbows." Her voice sounded unruffled and clear
as she crossed her thin arms, binding Rione's muscular ones. "And
I push on his pelvis." Then Leta raised her legs to his shoulders,
wrapping them around his neck. "At this point, I would shove
down." Leta stopped before she did any damage.

The move was effective. If Leta pressed her hips with enough
force, she could break the elbow joint.

"Excellent, Leta. Let's do another one."

She released Rione, adjusting her body underneath his.

"This one is more effective if you can't break the arms..." The next position began similarly to the last, but instead of locking Rione's arms, Leta performed a maneuver that twisted his torso to the side and off her body. Again, she locked one of his elbows.

"Now we'll try another situation."

Æri tensed, body prickling, as she recognized this mount to be the one used to immobilize her.

His voice bit through the air, educational and sharp. "Your goal is to get on top so you can stand. First, you don't want me to pin your arms—keep your arms tight and close to your body. Good, Leta. Move your elbows and arms to block me from getting to your neck. Like this." He demonstrated the move from the Bogs, pinning Leta's arms with his upper legs. "You also don't want me to keep my base low." Rione scooted back to the original position, his two legs straddling Leta's. "Try to trap one of my arms—so I can't post and move my center of gravity over you. And make a fast bridge. It should be as big as possible while you twist your body."

Leta executed the move.

"Make it explosive— Yes, that's right, Leta. You want to bring your hip up and take a big step over with your right leg. And..."

Leta kicked over her leg. Instantly, Rione lay supine.

Looking pleased with herself, Leta stood and reached down to help Rione from the ground. Then she turned to Æri. "Want to give it a go?"

Æri weighed the possibility. She had tolerated watching.

Leta noticed her hesitation. "You can practice with me—if you think that might help?"

Rione stayed quiet, letting Æri think it over.

Æri chewed her lip some more, tearing at the skin. If she wanted to overcome her fear once and for all, she'd just have to get this over and done with.

"No." She shook her head, closing her eyes to take in a breath. "I can do it." Who knows, maybe she could land a punch in Rione's face while she was at it.

Leta winked and stepped aside. "He's a great teacher," she said. "Taught everyone in the house."

Æri returned Leta's encouragement with a nod and squared her shoulders, too focused to think what her words implied.

Numb...numb...numb. Be numb.

"Are you okay?" Rione said, his voice softening and solicitous. "You can choose to tap out whenever you feel uncomfortable."

Giving him the go-ahead, she stared pointedly at that spot below his ear as she reclined on the woven mats.

"Which one did you want to start with?"

"The last."

She followed Rione's instructions as they did the bridge twist, slowly at first. He didn't resist her push, allowing her to practice the moves several times before proceeding.

Æri focused on the steps, the steady command of his voice. And only that. She numbed everything else out, willing all her thoughts and feelings not to interfere.

After they practiced each defense maneuver several times, Leta wandered back into the main house, seeing they no longer needed her.

Æri felt good, empowered even.

They took a quick break and drank water from the jug Leta left behind.

"We'll test with more force now. You should be able to overpower me. I won't be holding back." Rione tossed her a small towel to mop the sweat. The air in the room had become thick from their practice. "Are you ready?"

She could do this. Æri responded with a determined nod.

"We're going to move from standing—try to run from me." Rione's authoritative voice returned.

Æri inhaled. *Be numb.*

The first time, he couldn't catch her. All the fear and trepidation she expressed at the beginning ebbed, and a tiny smirk appeared on her lips. With the weeks of Venator training, she had become faster.

Rione's brows lifted at the sight of her small smile. "Don't get too ahead of yourself. Stay on guard."

"That's if you can catch me." Æri slipped past him again.

"What would be the point of training you this morning if I couldn't catch you?" Rione's tone was dry, though his eye started to dance. The mood shifted into something playful. His catlike prowl re-emerged.

She leaped from his lunges, Rione acting as the pursuer. Finally, he waylaid her, his firm hands latching onto her shoulders. She jerked away, the movement causing her to stumble and she fell, her back hitting the ground hard.

The calm cracked.

It was so quick. With his arms pressed against her, he was poised to trap her again. The sensation did something, splintering that numb feeling. Her head swam, becoming too heavy and light at the same time. The heat in the room made Æri's skin tight, like something wanted to combust from the inside. All that suppressed terror and hate teetered on a precipice. It just took one tiny push.

Her breath quickened, and panic set in. Everything learned from that morning evaporated as quickly as moon spirit. She didn't know what to do. She was stuck. She was going to be tossed in that cold cell again—and that darkness—pain surged from her arm. A cry of horror rammed into the forefront of her mind.

"Get off of me!" she screamed. Her hand lashed out, and she dug her nails into his neck.

Rione immediately released her, stepping back with a hand at his throat. He drew his fingers away. They were splotched with red—blood.

The smell of salt and iron clogged her nose. She remembered the blood on that day, so much blood. It *couldn't* be real. Not now. *Not real. Not real. Not real.* Yet everything was red; pain pulsed from her arm.

"Æri...?"

Her breaths came in fast—rapid and shallow. She swallowed and curled her body, drawing her knees close and tightening her arms around them. Æri squeezed her eyes shut and began to rock back and forth, trying to tame the fire within.

*Numb...numb...numb...*She was numb.

"Æri?" Rione repeated more urgently, taking a step closer. He extended his hand, then flexed it into a ball.

"Don't come near me."

Concern stamped his brow, and his frown showed something that looked like sorrow. He stood motionless, watching as her breaths slowed.

Æri's hand drifted to her side, roving over the woven mats. She focused her attention on the divots and nubs of the coarse texture. How some of the loosened fibers poked and pricked her fingertips, the slight sting when it caught the nailbed.

At last, her breathing regulated.

Rione picked up the empty jug and moved toward the door.

"Why did you have your mistress tell me?" Æri called out.

Rione paused, facing the entry to the palestra, then turned back.

She got to her feet, her glare a dagger of ice aimed directly at him.

"You didn't notify me about the king's mother—instead, you had your *mistress* do your dirty work. *Why?*"

Rione took in a breath and examined Æri. A flat expression concealed his inner thoughts. Her fear of him now manifested into some kind of resentment, and her lips drew back in a snarl. "Tell me, do you prefer Camilla to relay all your problematic messages, or the king?"

Guilt flashed behind his brown eye, and Rione flinched.

It was a sharp dig. A part of her knew he had his reasons, but another part was fed up with his secrets. He deserved her spite, her frustrations crushing—a heavy stone she wanted to hurl at his chest. "You claim you bought me to protect me from the Games' fate...but maybe you couldn't handle the king having what you wanted for yourself." Each of her words hit its mark, stabbing deeper. "If you're so generous, you'd have let me go—released me. But you won't, will you? You're just as cruel and selfish as he is—"

"You know nothing of me nor my actions to assume that." Rione broke her monologue.

She lifted her hands in exasperation. "You're right. I don't know a thing about you, Rione. So why don't you tell me? If you want me to trust you, that would be an excellent place to start."

He pinched the bridge of his nose. "It's not that simple."

"Fine, then I'm done until you figure it out." With that, Æri skirted past, leaving him in the training rooms.

~ 26 ~

ÆRI

"**G**et up."

Rione's silhouette blocked the doorframe to her chamber, and candlelight seeped in from the hallway. He balanced at the threshold, not daring to enter the room. She'd forgotten to lock the door.

"I'm not training today."

Æri needed to forget, to find something to get her mind off that splintered memory and push the recollections of yesterday back into their buried box. She couldn't find any wine in the storage cellar. After storming from the training rooms, Æri had torn through all the crates, looking for anything to lose herself in, but there was nothing—not a single cask of ale or jug of posca.

So, instead, Æri ran.

She ran and ran around the palestra's track until her feet turned pink and began to bleed and blister, the pain a distraction. Then she took an exceedingly long bath, letting the sound of running water calm her thoughts. She drained the last of the scented oils into the tub, hoping the potent perfumes would mask her turmoil.

The idea of sinking under the water, of fogging her mind with that scramble for air, floated through her thoughts—but no...that wasn't an escape she'd choose.

After watching the lathered water swirl down the drain, she shut herself in her room, Gyr her only company.

Left to her own devices, she took to counting the triangles and squares on the fresco above: one hundred; then the circles: forty-five; then the carved leaves on the shutters: thirty-two, and spots on Gyr's wings: four hundred fifty-three—anything to keep her mind present.

Some part of her wanted to hide in this room forever. She intended to spend the whole of the next day doing just that. Yet here was Rione, requiring she get out of bed at the cockcrow of dawn with that authoritative tone of his.

"Go away."

She flipped, shoving a pillow over her head to block out his muted outline.

"You said you wanted to know more about me...so get up."

She didn't budge.

"Please, Æri."

Not an apology, but probably the closest she'd get from him. A breath passed, and he sighed. Her door clicked quietly. His footfalls faded.

Gyr emitted a loud squawk, and she shot him a louring glare. He chirped back, tapping his feet side to side on his perch, unaffected by her look.

Æri released a huff and grabbed her tunic, stumbling out of bed. What in gods' names was she doing?

"Rione! Wait!"

Æri twisted her hands, looping the reins around her fists as she tried not to yank out the horse's hair while staying balanced.

"When you said 'explain,' I didn't realize it entailed riding bare-back through Fíronbec's countryside." Her horseback riding skills were mediocre at best.

Rione looked rueful.

In Særenfell, they tamed elk, not horses, and they sure as hell didn't ride them. Despite keeping her fiery core and thighs clenched against the horse's flank, she struggled to stay upright. But Rione had promised her answers, and she naively took the bait. He'd barely given her enough time to dress and tie her hair before they rode off.

Riding bareback is part of your training as a Venator, he had ratio-nalized when she agreed to hear him out, saying he'd rather *show* her than tell her.

Apparently, answers also implied frolicking in meadows. Draugs, she wasn't complaining about that. This was the first time in weeks she'd left the city walls besides her guarded trips to the Inventorium. Æri tried not to grumble as she attempted to stay atop her stallion. The beautiful beast didn't make it easy, though. He had picked up a canter behind Rione's mare the second they departed Méritras's main gates.

Gyr glided on a light wind, cawing in delight ahead of them. Eventually, Rione slowed his onyx mare, Juno, to a trot. Æri's fin-gers ached, stiff from clinging to her reins. For most of their jour-ney, Rione had guided them through small paths and trails in lieu of taking the main roads, avoiding towns.

Æri stroked her horse's chestnut mane.

"You learn quickly." Rione gestured to her stance. "I thought you said you never rode bareback?"

"Is that supposed to be a compliment?" Æri ignored his imme-diate frown at her jest. "I don't have any experience with horses, but they're not much different from straddling the Boars."

Rione choked. "You rode *boars* in Særenfell?"

His candid look of surprise made her smile, and she rolled her lips between her teeth to suppress a laugh. "Our light aircraft...we call them Boars. But I guess you can say it's like riding a real boar—that hovers in the air. They take a while to master; balancing on them takes skill, and they do look like boars, minus the legs and snout."

Rione's brows drew together.

Æri openly laughed then. "I don't think I've seen you puzzled."

"Maybe you're just not very good at describing things."

"I take it compliments are over, then?" Æri raised an eyebrow. The fresh air of the countryside relaxed her—an unexpected reprieve from the overwhelming emotions. The wild horse under her; the tall yellowing grass, blowing lazily in a warm breeze; the winged beetles' unbroken chorus; scents of animals, straw, and dry earth drifting about them, all gave a semblance of freedom—a perfect distraction.

Rione steered his horse off the path, signaling a close to their light conversation. Something else preoccupied his mind.

"Are you going to tell me where you're taking me?"

"It's better you see for yourself. We are stopping just beyond that copse of trees." He pointed at the eastern horizon where a thicket of green marked their excursion's end.

The sun advanced to its pinnacle, and its intensity fell over her skin like a hearth-heated pelt. She eyed Rione's packs. Æri relied on his careful planning for food. All she took was her water skin, thinking they'd be going on a short outing.

As they neared the gathering of trees, a thatched farmhouse came into view. The area around it, once a smallholding, appeared abandoned. A portion of its roof had caved in, revealing old timbers beneath. Woolly moss grew in patches over graying straw, and a family of doves cooed from the opening.

Regardless of its dilapidation, the rundown cottage and its surroundings emitted a quaint sort of charm. How the trees bowed over its crumbling walls, the cheerful warble of birds, and the calming burble of a brook close by made it feel like it had sprouted from the pages of Æri's childhood fairy tales.

Rione dismounted and tied his mare's reins to a broken fence that bordered a knotted vegetable garden, then removed a bundled object from his sack. His movements were measured as he approached the house, his mouth a solemn line.

Æri followed, tethering Ajax—her borrowed stallion—next to Juno.

The Venator stopped on the weedy path that led to an entrance, the door gone; a twisting of ivy replaced its frame.

"This was my home." Rione's mouth slid to the side, pressing his lips together. "I grew up here."

"Oh..." She waited for a beat, her fingers tracing her collarbone. "Are they alive..." she ventured cautiously, "your family?"

He turned and gave her an inviting smile that did not reach his good eye. "You already know my mother."

Æri scrunched her face in bemusement. "Ofelia?"

Rione laughed. The first time she'd heard it like that—a pleasant laugh. Low and appeasing, reminding her of his singing voice. It yielded an unrecognizable sentiment within her, bittersweet and something she didn't think she needed until now.

"Hah. No, not at all. But she does act like it sometimes." He raked his hand through his hair, freeing some of the shorter strands from the braids. "My mother is Camilla."

Æri opened and closed her mouth, then finally stammered out, "I—I thought Camilla and you..." Her face burned as she admitted her mistake. "But she looks so young—and I thought—"

"You thought we were lovers?" Rione did not look shocked by her suggestion.

"I saw you two—in the courtyard at the villa...and I assumed..."

Rione stepped away from Æri, his eye probing.

"No...she stopped aging at the same time the realms separated. I was born long after it struck Fíronbec."

Like a glacier plunge, shame and embarrassment flooded through Æri's veins. She raised her hand to hide her gaping mouth. Her own mother didn't age, but she had been older when she gave birth to Brynja and herself.

Camilla didn't look a day past twenty.

"We don't tell many people...Some assume we are cousins...but the king is aware. That's why he keeps her close. He likes to retain those who've mothered children after the separations in his court...for several reasons."

Acid scrubbed her throat, remembering Camilla's comment in the villa's orchard. *The king is desperate for an heir.*

No wonder Rione became so vague when he talked of Camilla—and she of him. Æri's nausea intensified with yet another realization.

"Is the king—" Æri cleared her throat, trying to get the words out. "Is King Remus your father?"

"Thank the gods, no," he said, letting out a sigh and then squeezing his eye shut. "If anything, he's more like a brother. We grew up together. This farm edges the Villa Glorial's estate. And my mother's family was part of King Lucius's court years before I was born."

"Then who is your father?" She failed to hold the bubbling question back, her curiosity rising with each new piece of the puzzle. He must favor him—Rione looked nothing like Camilla.

Rione glanced away, his face blank, and instead of answering, he unwrapped the bundle and handed her a bow. He held his own with a sheaf of arrows and gestured to a footpath that ran behind the house.

"Come, let's see if we can find something to eat."

The air changed in the thicket. Cool and moist under sheltered trees, the overhanging canopy trapped water from the burbling stream.

Rione studied the small trails made by creatures inhabiting the place. The hunters crouched, concealed by bramble. Their knees bumped while they waited, a strangely private moment with just the two of them and the quiet sounds of the forest, their arrows ready. How natural it felt to hunt by his side. Still, this man perplexed her. He was the same hunter who had taken her prisoner in the Bogs, but she saw him differently now. Her skin prickled this close to his, with the eagerness of the hunt, and...not fear...Yet it aroused a similar heightened emotion—something unidentified. She exhaled. Her concentration refocused on the forest floor.

Soon, the underbrush stirred at the water's edge, and a cottontail peeked out to sniff the air.

Whip!

It scarcely had time to lap from the stream before Æri's arrow struck, her cheek stinging from the bowstring's snap. Though she had overdrawn, her accuracy remained flawless. The shaft protruded from the animal's small head. A swift death. She didn't like to make things suffer, even on a hunt.

Æri shrugged and waded across the shallow bank to retrieve their food. Its soft brown fur was matted with sticky blood. She tried to look past it, concentrating on the task. Before pulling the arrow out, she touched her middle and index finger to her forehead, then to the creature's. "I see you, and Skathi thanks you for your gift. Your spirit goes into the sky, to Vallantheia, and your body becomes part of us."

A tradition after every kill. Without this prayer, the old scriptures said the soul would wander Glasterra, plaguing the one that took its life.

Æri and Rione worked together to skin the rabbit.

As they prepared their meal, Æri thought that perhaps she had pried too deep when she asked about his father.

But when the carcass was clean, he spoke, breaking the natural silence. "My father was enslaved by the old king—a musician in his court."

Æri promptly pieced two and two together.

"He was Fae," she whispered.

A single dip of his chin confirmed her deduction.

It explained so much. Why she struggled to read him. Elves were known for their aloofness and reticent dispositions. The way Rione behaved, his mannerisms—notwithstanding his intermittent surly temper—all spoke of a Fae heritage...even his uncanny ability to play the bowed lyre.

Rione immersed his hands in the stream, the flow of water washing away the red. "My mother fell in love with him the first night he performed at the Villa Glorial. And when they wished to wed, her family disowned her." Rione looked absorbed by the tale, as if he recalled his own memories. "They meant to run away together...but once the old king heard she was with child, he permitted them to stay, offering this farm. It was close enough to the villa. My father could continue playing at King Lucius's court—and it ensured the young prince would have a companion as he grew."

A breeze ruffled the leaves in the small forest, and a sense of peace settled behind the house. Squirrels chattered in branches, and rays of light scattered the dry forest floor.

Æri wanted Rione to go on, abandoning their rabbit carcass for now. Her ears perked, listening to every detail.

"Which is why I have a different name...I am titled after my mother's family here in Fíronbec. I'm not permitted to take the origin name."

She had suspected as such, recalling how the king formally introduced him at the banquet. His tale exposed another revelation. "Are you and King Remus...still close?"

"We were for many years. Remus wasn't always so..."

"Rotten?"

"Apathetic...but he changed after his father died. His heart froze—" Rione blinked before going on, as if waking from a daydream. "But these are things for him to share, not me."

Æri wavered, debating whether to inquire more about the king. Rione didn't seem inclined to continue on the subject, so she moved the topic back. "And what of your own father? Is he still at court?"

Rione's gaze grew distant. He picked up a smooth green stone from the creek bed, rubbing it between his forefinger and thumb. "He left."

Straightening, he chucked the stone downstream and watched it clunk and recoil against the larger rocks. A haunted look passed over his features. "He was released from his contract and returned to his people—or so King Lucius told us."

A short pause ensued as Rione edged the stream's shore, scuffling his boots while searching for another stone. "This was many years ago...I had just settled—stopped aging—and I made some poor choices after he left. I didn't understand why he had abandoned us. I thought that maybe *I* was the reason, being associated with Remus...I fell into the wrong crowd, started making wagers...It led to other things...gambling...drinking. The worst things you can think of—I did them."

A hollow laugh escaped his throat. It reminded her of his cackle in the Bogs. Not an ounce of joy in it, no charm nor reconciliation. He tipped his head back, looking at the rustling canopy above. "When you caught me in the Bogs—I was drunk. I functioned to a point...but in the end, it nearly cost me my life."

Æri's chest clenched. "Do I remind you then—of that time in your life?"

Rione pursed his lips and picked up another stone, throwing it farther than the last. "Yes...and no...It was more of a wake-up call for me." He pointed to his face. "*This* has been my reminder for years. You know, if I hadn't been captured, I wouldn't have changed. I realized that day I wanted to live.

"My mother beseeched me for years—tried to get me to change before I killed myself out of recklessness, but I wasn't ready, not until I put myself in that kind of palpable danger." He offered Æri a sad smile, his eye roaming her face.

"I also vowed I'd capture the Lamiæn who took my eye. One part of me wanted to prove I could defeat the demon that had manifested inside for so long. Another part wanted to acknowledge the Lamiæn for saving my miserable life. It's why the troop was so close to your realm when we caught you. I've been leading the hunt closer to Særenfell for years. Telling the king it was to explore new territory. He never questioned it as long as we brought back beasts and mapped out more of the Bogs.

"Searching for you gave me a purpose...I started to see I wasn't only destroying myself, but the people around me—people I cared about. If it wasn't for you, I would have died—or worse, killed my troop out of negligence. That's how I was caught—through my own stupidity. I haven't taken a drink since." Rione steadied his gaze, locking his eye with hers. "And in the end, all that time hunting in the Bogs paid off...After you crashed, it felt like the gods had listened. I found the Lamiæn I'd been hunting. I captured *you*. But that gratification—it didn't feel right. I knew I was meant to find you, but you weren't what I thought, and, well...you weren't intended to be in fighting bids. Remus would have never known about you...so that brings us here." He rushed his words at the end, leaving out something vital.

"So getting Sulivan to trick me about Gyr...what was that about?" Æri tried and failed to grapple with this information.

"Like I said, the Games would have killed you before you earned your freedom. Maybe not right away since, as a Lamiæn, you're too valuable. But...King Remus would've forced you to fight. The

Games aren't like the Auctioning." His features hardened as if recalling an unpleasant memory. "I wanted to get you out of the king's direct control."

She attempted to ingest all of it. Instead of clarifying, it just confused her more. A bit of her still struggled not to snap at him. What if she had won the Auctioning? Maybe the king would have kept his deal and she wouldn't have had to fight in the Games. She'd never know now. He made that choice for her. Yet she knew he was honest, that if he believed the king lied and she wouldn't have survived, then...

"Rione...if you say all this...then...then why am I still here...why am I still your slave? Why not free me today? Here, now?"

His fingers tugged at his lower lip, and he exhaled. "The rules are not that simple. The king himself must free you." He indicated the small line on her right wrist—the tracking device. "If I let you go—freed you now—you'd be hunted again by another Venator troop, and I wouldn't be able to keep you from King Remus."

Seeming to notice the hope fall from her eyes, he added, "There is a loophole. We can have Cosmos remake the contract. Once you become a Venator—you can become a hand of the Crown."

"Will that allow me to return to my people freely?"

Rione swallowed. "No, but you will no longer be titled a slave. You'll be able to make a living here, and it will permit you to have some freedom in Fíronbec. However, the king would maintain power over you in some form."

Æri glared at Rione. "Is that the best you can offer?"

Rione cocked his head, thinking. Then he shook it, strands of dark hair falling into his angular features. He held back an alternative—a more logical option.

"What? What is the other possibility?"

"You wouldn't agree to it."

"How can I agree or not agree to something I know nothing about?"

"No," he said, attempting to gather another stone. "It wouldn't work."

"Spit it out, Rione. You owe me that much for bringing me to your gods' forsaken island."

He flung the third stone. It ricocheted off a tree, bark splintering under the impact.

"Marriage."

Her eyes widened, and she released a chortle of air, sounding more like a strangled wheeze than a laugh. He was not serious. "You mean between you and me. We'd be at each other's throats."

His face did not twitch, the expression on it sober. Rione *was* serious.

"Likely, but it's the only other option. Marriage is a business contract here. It would give the spouse protection and rights, regardless of whether they were a slave before. And I'd be able to free you from your bondage to the king."

"And be bound forever to you. I'd be trading one bondage for another. That's not an option."

"Technically, it is..."

Æri rolled her eyes and started counting off on her fingers. "So my choices are: *a*, stay a slave and be bound to you *and* the king; *b*; become an authorized Venator—which is what I was already doing—but have the title changed so I am not necessarily a slave but an employee under the Crown and, well, you; or *c*; I marry you—in which I'd be trussed to you by the laws of the land. Essentially, I am still enslaved in all of these options, and in none of them am I allowed to return to my people."

"I'd allow you to return."

Æri held in a breath, studying Rione's face.

Could this be his way to atone? Without saying it outright?

"Why?" She needed to hear it.

"I owe it to you. A life debt."

"I planned to feed you to my queen. You call that a life debt?"

Rione lifted his shoulders. "An unintentional saving. And...you've earned it."

Æri paced along the stream, hands on her hips. "You don't want to marry me. We don't love each other."

"It isn't about that here. Marriage must benefit one or both parties involved—financially or by title. My parents weren't married because her family did not sanction it—so there was no advantage for them."

"And Camilla will?"

"I haven't asked her." He mirrored Æri, placing his fists at his sides. "But she won't object."

Her eyes narrowed, and she changed her position. "What makes you so sure?"

"She likes you." Rione's mouth quirked up into a half smile.

Æri regarded him for a second, chafing her tongue against her chipped incisor. They were having a staring contest. She inhaled. "Hypothetically, let's say I do agree to it." Now she started picking up and throwing stones. She understood why he tossed them before, putting her frustration into the throw. "How do I know you'll be true to your word? That you'll free me?"

"You have to trust me." He rocked back on his heels.

She needed time to think, to make a rational decision. Other things preoccupied her mind—like speaking to Oisin and finding a cure.

"How long do I have to decide?"

"There's no time limit. But I wager you'll want to return to your lands on the next Bog hunt—which is five weeks after the tournament."

That, indeed, was plenty of time.

Rione started toward the horses.

"Where are you going?" She had more questions, and if she intended to consider marriage to this...gods, this man or demi-Fae or wh—

But he cut off her thoughts. "I'm giving you space."

"You trust that I won't run away?"

"After what I told you" —his shoulders lifted, and he extended his arms—"it's your choice. If you're ever going to trust me, I'm going to have to trust you first."

With that, he swung his leg over the mare. "Hand this to any official or sentinel if they intercept you on the way back into the city." He held out a thin scroll with his seal embossed on the front. "So you won't get tossed in prison. I'm sure you'd rather spend a night under the stars than in those cells."

As she took the documents, Æri's fingers grazed his. The touch sent a zing through the tips to her core like a mage's current. She recoiled, pulling the scroll to her chest.

Rione's eye moved from her hand to his own, which closed tightly around Juno's reins. His jaw flexed. "See you at the domus tomorrow afternoon." He clicked his tongue, tapping his heels into Juno's side, and she advanced into a gallop.

Æri rubbed her fingers absently, trying to grapple with what had transpired. He planned this whole day, expecting she'd say yes to the journey all along. Stunned into wordlessness, she watched as he rode away, becoming a black speck on the wheat-colored horizon.

~ 27 ~

ÆRI

Æ ri slept under glittering stars that night. A night of freedom from the walls of Rione's domus and the confines of the oppressive city. A taste of what he offered.

Outside in the tepid air, Æri camped a stone's throw from the abandoned smallholding. Locating a patch of earth where the trees gave way to fields, she cleared a space for the bedroll left by Rione, flattening knee-high shoots and brushing away prickly heads of the golden grasses. Gyr perched watchfully on a tree's bow nearby as crickets played their evening refrain.

Æri crunched into an apple from the provisions, having finished their hunted rabbit, and gazed into the cobalt sky. Twilight faded to a navy blue, and she imagined her nights back in Særenfell. As snow clouds often shrouded her skies, it was rare to have clear nights such as these. But the stars in sky shined the same—little pinpricks of light peeking through the velvet. Constellations gradually emerged as the blue darkened. Skathi's Spear twinkled, a straight line of ten stars pointing north. Then, there, winking from the lapis, the Last Griffin's Talons—a constellation shaped like four claws. Legends said Skathi herself slayed the last of the mythical beasts from the Ophinyne Cliffs out of rage for aiding her betraying lover's escape.

The three sister moons, Urdris, Verida, and Skulnas, were to the left of the talons, depicted as three distinct crescents. Verida curved to beam a smile down upon Æri. The others, just two tiny fingernails, hovered in opposite directions as if being pulled away from Verida.

Strange how some things about Glasterra continued: the moons' monthly cycles—from full to gibbous, to quarter, crescent, and the new—and how days darkened. These things existed in constant motion. They stayed unbroken even after the Split. Only age itself wavered, and how their realms affixed to one never-ending season. Yet, these consistencies, the moons and the passing days, helped make time feel like it still existed.

Time. This was what Rione also granted her—the time to choose.

Perhaps he did not mean for her to meet the king, intending her to be a house slave so he could free her from the king's court without trouble...or, more likely, he didn't have a plan after he seized her in the Bogs, his goal fulfilled, and thus content to never see her again—if not for her little mishap with the official. But then, why did he go to such lengths to purchase her?

Assuming Rione stayed true to his word, she recognized that if she wished to see her homeland again, his last proposition was the most sensible. But she didn't know if she could trust him—forgive him for everything he'd put her through. Forgiveness was riddled with old scars, and Æri wasn't sure if she knew how to take the next steps forward.

Why did she need to rush into a decision tonight?

Deliberating through the choices only made her head hurt.

Æri gnawed the remnants of her tart apple and threw its core to Ajax. He whinnied happily, munching on the treat. Gyr squawked.

"I haven't forgotten about you, bud."

She tossed him a last bit of meat stuck to the bone and went back to staring at the stars.

When Æri returned to the palestra the next day, she found not one Venator but four.

Wearing his customary steely expression, Rione softened after he saw Æri walk through the palestra doors.

A test. It was a test, and she had passed.

However, she would not become an official Venator until she completed the first hunt, when Venators received the branded *V* on their forearm. A mark each of the four men before her held with pride. And though her stomach knotted to see their faces anew, it was less unsettling than in the Bogs.

The troop shuffled around outdoor training equipment, Rione making no move to introduce them. So after a few moments of awkward gazes, one stepped forward.

"Welcome to the troop. I'm Tyegrieve—but everyone calls me Tye." The Venator with russet hair saluted Æri. "And, uh...I owe you an apology for the netting's sting...back in the Bogs."

Æri frowned, remembering the zinging currents that wrapped her body. "That was your doing? How?"

Tye lifted a palm, where tiny purple sparks skipped between his fingers. "I can enchant chains and nets if I'm in proximity. My father hailed from Larkærseim. It's nowhere near as strong as Brennos's wards, but the sting isn't pleasant."

Æri flicked her eyes to the other two men. "Do you all have a parent from another realm?"

Their irises bore the Fíronian brown, making it difficult to tell, but Tye had a faint violet halo; the other two possessed green or gold flecks that circled their brown. Even now, pausing on Rione, she made out the slightest rim of teal.

"Does she always ask this many questions?" the smaller man quipped toward Rione. He wore his black hair short, and it spiked straight out, giving him a prickly appearance—somewhat like a porcupine. He twisted a small hatchet in his right hand.

"Why don't you ask her yourself, Sten?" Rione redirected.

Sten—the wiry man who led them into that ravine. This Venator may take a little longer to warm up to.

"Me father's a dwarf." Sten picked at some dirt under his nail with the hatchet tip. "Refuses to acknowledge my existence. Still works for the king. Me mother died in childbirth. Anything else ye want to know, Æri?"

Well...it seemed he, too, wasn't so keen to get to know her.

"Give the lass a break. If Rione says she's trustworthy, then she is," came a baritone voice from the man who was not quite a giant but soared over the rest of them and bore biceps the size of ale casks. His expression spoke contrary to his size; a cornsilk beard framed a benevolent face.

"Well met, I'm Knjal." He brushed chalk off his fingers before holding out a massive hand. "I'm sure you've guessed—I'm half giant on my mother's side; my father's a stonemason in Ebix—a smaller town by the eastern edge of Fíronbec."

Æri tentatively shook his hand, recalling that part of Jotnarach that bordered Fíronbec before the Split.

"Don't get too charmed by his manners," Sten said, sneering. "He's gotta soft spot for Leta."

As if on cue, Leta emerged from the domus's back doors with a rolling tray of refreshments, and Knjal did indeed blush, the tips of his ears pricking scarlet.

"Glad to see you're doing well, boys. We missed you here."

Knjal was the first to dash off to the veranda and take one of the earthenware cups. He and Leta slipped into a hushed conversation.

"Fell for her when she flipped him to the ground," Tye whispered.

"Leta flipped him?"

The petite woman erupted into giggles as the demi-giant murmured something into her ear.

"Yep, flat on his back." Tye chuckled.

Once they all sampled some of the sweet-sour juice, Rione clapped his hands. "If we're ever making it to the tournament this year, we'll have to build rapport with Æri at the same time as training. Come on, let's get back to it."

As Leta returned to the house, she flashed Knjal a winning smile with a quick wink, and Æri swore his cheeks turned as red as lilliock berries.

"So...is this a hybrid-only group?" Æri jogged after the lightweight ball. It had rolled toward Rione, who refereed from the sidelines.

The troop was finishing a game involving two teams and a goal. Thankfully, Rione had paired her with Tye. She didn't know how well she'd fare with Sten. He kept grousing under his breath and throwing her death glares.

"I'm selective...but I accept anyone and everyone who's passed my initial training routines. If they can show tenacity, they can join. Besides, you're not demi."

"Well, I didn't have the luxury of choosing to join..."

Before he countered, Tye came to his defense as Æri passed him the ball. "Rione offered us an opportunity we couldn't get elsewhere. Most Fíronians don't take too kindly to demis. They consider us 'half-breeds' unreliable. I was out of a job before Rione offered me a spot in the troop. We're lucky. He's the best troop chief out there."

Æri cast Tye an incredulous look. *Lucky. Really?*

"I'm not sure." Sten kicked the ball away from Tye. "Rione didn't hesitate to beat the gods' nonsense from ye when ye called in sick that training day ten years ago. He bagged ye in the tavern trying to pick up...what was her name? The one with big—"

"Sabia. And she had other fine attributes. So shove it, Sten. I don't care to be reminded of all those dragon walks. Rione made me crawl for a week straight wherever we went." Tye rubbed his upper arms in recollection.

Æri pressed her lips together to hold in a laugh—she understood exactly what he meant. One did not tell fibs to Rione and expect to get away with it.

"Hey, Æri, do you want to hear a joke?" Tye swiveled toward her after kicking the ball from Sten, landing a goal through the two posts.

Sten immediately butted in. "Oh no, ye don't, Tye. Yer puns are crap."

"Don't torture the newbie," Knjal added, running for the ball, now bouncing off the field. "She deserves better!" he yelled.

"You might want to shield your ears." Rione had left his directive position and was hovering a tad too close for her liking. His words tickled her neck.

"You lot just don't appreciate a bit of humor, that's all. Let's hear from Æri, shall we?" Tye's eyebrows waggled.

Æri didn't see the harm in it, so she shrugged. "Why not."

How bad could it be?

Tye held his arms out to the other Venators. "The lady has spoken."

Turning to Æri, he rubbed his hands together, letting violet sparks fly. "Okay. So why does the Venator go to the tavern every night?"

"Save us all." Sten rolled his eyes and walked toward the stall bars.

"Ignore him." Tye batted a hand and continued. "Where was I? Right. Why does the Venator go to the tavern every night?"

"For some posca?" Æri guessed.

"Because he's so Bogged down!" Tye looked at her expectantly. "Good, right?"

"See, his jokes are crap!" Sten called from across the yard.

Æri blinked at him slowly, then a wholehearted guffaw tumbled out, shocking even herself. "That was pretty terrible," she said, wiping tears from her eyes.

Rione looked at her in stunned silence. Tye just grinned from ear to ear.

She couldn't remember the last time she had laughed that hard, even in Særenfell—a proper belly laugh. With that mirth came the feeling she'd get along just fine with this Venator troop of wood-woses.

~ 28 ~

ÆRI

The moons cast silvered light through the carved screens while the house slept. Awakened from another nightmare, Æri tiptoed from the library into the study, dewy sweat still evaporating from her back and thighs. It was a week before the tournament, and her nervous energy seemed to be mounting. Nonetheless, giddy success tingled through her. Æri had finally sleuthed out one of the leisure tomes.

Reading the title in her hands, she stifled a frenzied laugh. It had to be Ofelia's or Leta's. Rione would never purchase a tome with such a garish name.

Æri placed the oil lamp on the desk, its light just bright enough to read by. She decided to remain here rather than retreat to her room; she needed time away to forget the lucid dream.

Gyr sprung from her shoulder to settle on the tabletop. Rione rarely used this study, and she suspected he had another that looked over the palestra. However, Cosmos regularly occupied the space—a messy stack of day-to-day lists cluttered the desk.

She nestled into the chair, holding the tome open to the lamp's flame.

Balbina Gabinus was neither extremely bright nor beautiful but solemnly believed she was destined to find true love.

Oh, by the goddess. No wonder this book was hidden.

Æri continued to leaf through it, mildly intrigued to see where the story may lead, until Gyr started pecking the papers.

Shhh.

She waved a hand at his feet. He flapped his wings and skipped, and the stack fanned, spilling to the floor with a whoosh.

Gyr!

He clicked and tapped his talons, tucking his head to preen feathers under his wing.

Her chair scraped the marble floor as she bent to collect the dispersed papers.

Rione's signature stared back at her from an equipment receipt, circles and lines seeming to war with each other. She traced his scratched design with the pad of her finger and, before she thought better of it, folded the parchment, stuffing it into her night shift's pocket.

Another page drew her eye—a letter addressed to Cosmos from Gratian.

As requested by Lord Rione Aulius, we have returned the mechanical device to its owner with the enhancements indicated. We respect his decision not to consign the falcon to our facilities for further study, though, as our protocol commands, we have notified His Royal Highness of this refusal.

Our sincerest and utmost gratitude,

Gratian of Fíronbec

Principle Scitator of the Royal Inventorium

She reread the letter, ensuring she hadn't misinterpreted its words in the vacillating light. All this time, she thought the king or Brennos had been the one to return her arm before the final match...though reflecting on it, neither man seemed likely to do so.

Should she feel gratitude? Rione had seized it from her after all...staged the idea of her defeat, kept Gyr from her—something she still struggled with despite his explanation—but to defy the king's command...Why hadn't he told her at the farmstead?

A creak from the stairs startled her, and Æri quickly finished restacking the papers as Ofelia entered the study, oil lamp pinched between her index finger and thumb.

"Deary! What are you doing up at this witching hour?"

"A bad dream." She realigned the parchment's corners, casting a veiled smile. "I think I'm anxious about the upcoming tournament...Did I wake you?"

"No, no. Wanted a ladle of water from the kitchen, and I saw your light."

Æri studied Gratian's note on the pile, skewing her mouth to the side. "Why didn't Rione tell me he was the one who returned my arm? And about Gyr? He protected him, didn't he?"

Ofelia's expression settled somewhere between somnolent and consolatory. "You need to ask him, dear. He's not one for boasting about the deeds he does. He just does them."

But Æri *had* asked him, hadn't she? Perhaps not so directly...

"Join me for a bit of brew, will you? I have the perfect infusion for night frights." Ofelia moved her hand to cover a yawn, then blinked, tipping her head to look at the tome left facedown. "Oh, you found *Balbina and the Boobie Charmer*! That's one of my favorites."

As the troop entered the Ludisaren, a vast park where the Royal Venator Tournaments took place, Æri's stomach oscillated with nerves. She had agreed to leave Gyr in the care of Jonas for the day, and the temporary separation exemplified her jitters, that gnawing buzz in her skull returning.

"Our team's gone unchallenged for twenty years straight," Sten said while they waited by the registration tents, avoiding the intense morning rays.

Her eyes shot around the vicinity. Most of the other troops consisted of men. In fact, as far as she could tell, she was the only woman in a Venator uniform.

At least the king wasn't here.

This assuaged her angst a hair. King Remus had one more week of mourning. The laws forbade the sovereign to attend any gaming events until two months had passed following the death of a family member. She was glad of it—one less pair of scrutinizing eyes to deal with.

"Here, tie this around your arm." Rione handed her a red sash.

"What's this for?"

"Colored tags are assigned to distinguish the troops." He identified the other troops' arms, which sported similar sashes with varying shades of whites, blues, greens, and purples. "Those who won the majority of last year's events wear the representing color of Fíronbec."

Æri twiddled with the glossy burgundy-red strip in her hand. She had yet to decide on Rione's proposal. For the moment, Æri tucked that choice away with all the other irksome questions; the past few weeks had been filled with last-minute trainings and devising a strategy to approach Oisin. She had little room to think of anything else. With any luck, her troop would be matched against Oisin's in one of the events, and all she would have to do was locate the elf during an opening reception.

Troop members clapped backs, greeting their fellow rivals—no sign of Oisin yet.

"Are there any rules about using people from other realms in the competition? Or women, for that matter?" Æri and Tye shambled forward in the registration line.

"Nope. As long as half your troop is from Fíronbec. And techni-cally, we are all from here. You're the exception. Oh, and in rarer cases, rules are in place for magic wielders." Tye shoved his hands in his pockets as if to help keep the sparks at bay. "It isn't allowed. If I'm caught using it during the event, our troop will be disquali-fied." He angled his chin toward a group with purple armbands. "I think that's why Nicomedes's troop bought the Fae. So they'd have a leg up against ours."

Nicomedes, a short, broad-chested Venator with greased hair, stood out from the other three men. His leathery skin looked like he spent too many days in the sun, and his face twisted in a smug expression that made Æri want to retch—still no Oisin.

"Where is the elf?" Æri attempted to quell her impatience.

Tye shrugged. "The Fae's a slave. Not sure if his chief's letting him out until the events start."

"*I'm* a slave."

Tye gave Æri a knowing look in return, and she understood what his pert brown eyes conveyed.

A space opened at the tables, and they moved toward the entry codex. Æri scanned the giant ledger for their troop's events. Lining her finger with the names one by one, she let out an exasperated huff.

She signed next to her printed name, confirming her participa-tion, then marched up to Rione. "Why am I only in two events with the troop? They're registered for five." Oisin and his troop weren't recorded alongside either of her events.

"You aren't ready for the others—they require more teamwork, and we didn't have time to train you. The events you're registered for will be a good challenge, especially the equestrian."

"Then what was I preparing for in the last month?" She fisted her hands at her hips and scowled.

"Our troop's been training together for years. It takes some ad-justment for us too." Rione's tone was resolute.

"Fine." Æri didn't see the point in pressing him further.

So she wasn't participating in as many of the events as she first thought. But how would she find Oisin now?

Æri returned to the register to search for Oisin's name. She paged to the back, where it listed individual events.

Ah-ha! There. His troop's chief had signed him up for target archery at the end of the day.

Rione was engrossed in a conversation with another chief, but the rest of her troop roved about the tables. They'd notice if she picked up the stylus. Æri sucked at her teeth in thought. She needed a way to divert their attention just for a moment—

"Æri! Hey, Æri!"

A familiar voice carried over the hoard of people entering through the park's front gates. Marlena waved her hand high, her tall frame easy to spot amongst the jostling. Æri smiled in disbelief and raised her own hand in greeting as Marlena approached the registration tables.

"My owner gave me the day off to watch the tournament." Her eyes brimmed with enthusiasm. "When I heard you were part of Lord Rione Aulius's troop, I wanted to try to catch you before the events. Thank the gods I found you amid all this chaos."

"It's nice to see you too, Marlena—" Æri winced, knowing she forgot to contact her after the Auctioning ended. "I meant to send a letter," she said sheepishly.

Marlena swatted aside her apology. "Oh, it's no bother...you must have trained for weeks. Give a whirl. Let me see your new regalia."

Æri reluctantly did a little turn. In all honesty, she disliked the hype. Part of her felt ashamed for wearing the uniform, as if donning the burgundy tunic and leg coverings epitomized a direct betrayal to her realm. She reminded herself it was temporary.

"Oisin's here too...but his troop chief isn't allowing him to roam." Then, with a stroke of inspiration, an idea popped into Æri's head. "Hey, Marlena, can I ask you for a favor?"

"Sure, what do you need?"

When Æri described what she wanted, a wicked grin played on Marlena's lips. Without another word, Marlena spun from Æri and walked straight over to her troop members.

A shrill squeal hailed from Marlena's mouth. *"Oh my gods!* Are you Lord Rione Aulius's troop? I'm your biggest fan. Can you please, please, *please* autograph my pugillares codex?" She dug into her satchel and held up a small notebook.

Æri snatched the stylus and hastily signed. Perfect. It was done.

In keeping with their previous years, Rione's troop went unrivaled. Though Æri did not show the best of her abilities at the chosen events, they did well, managing to place second in the equestrian as a team. However, the equine showjumping concluded directly ahead of the target archery, and Æri realized too late that she had missed its opening reception.

So she improvised.

"I have to take care of...some lady things!" She faked a cringe while pointing to her lower gut and shoved the horse's reins into a groom's hands.

"Things? Oof!"

Sten elbowed Tye's side, and his eyes widened in realization.

"Why don't we get some snacks?" Knjal suggested. "I'm starving. We'll save you something, Æri."

The troop became decidedly interested in a stand selling roasted chickpeas across from the stables. None of them followed as she slipped away to the archery field.

The officials were allocating bows and arrows when she arrived. Twelve round targets decorated the field, aligned evenly with the archers' posts, their red cores visible from the entrance.

Scurrying to the admittance booth, she gave the official her name.

"You're late."

"Sorry—the, um, the previous event ran over." Æri panted the words, trying to catch her breath.

He gave her a dubious glare, then looked at his ledger. The official's eyes dallied on the signature—not hers but Rione's. The one she had forged. She willed herself to stay calm, taking measured breaths.

After procuring a sample from Cosmos's study, Æri had scrupulously examined Rione's signature over the last week, practicing the smooth loops that abruptly cut through with a line strike or corner of a Fíronian letter. It was guileful, especially after what Rione offered her...what he had done—but the knack ended up being useful.

At last, the official jerked his head, letting her through the gate. Her held breath escaped in a sudden puff.

A squire guided Æri to stand before the third target. The field's yellowing grass had been clipped short, stretching out until it stopped at a wall of cypress trees in the distance.

She leaned to peer down the row of archers. Oisin faced the twelfth target—not close enough to talk. She'd have to wait until the finishing reception.

The elf's hair was now crudely shorn, and her throat cramped with disgust for his chief, Nicomedes. Given how proud Oisin seemed of his long black locks during the Auctioning, Æri assumed it had been done against his will.

She expelled a sigh, trying to shake off her animosity and refocus. Okay...she made it here—might as well make it count.

Well aware of her talent in archery, Æri straightened her spine and leveled her shoulders. Why should she hold back?

Glancing at the flapping flags that marked the wind's direction, she nocked her arrow.

The repetitive whoosh, then chunking of arrows landing on their targets played like drumbeats, echoing the stomps of the rowdy crowd. She struck the bullseye every time.

Her arrow first hit the thirty-five-pace mark, then the forty-five, fifty-five, and so on for seven more rounds until just she and Oisin stood facing their ninety-five-pace targets.

The official's red flag fell, and she let the arrow soar. Both their arrows flew, landing in each of their target's centers simultaneously.

"A deuce!" yelled the official over the crowd's cries.

This didn't bother Æri one bit. She wasn't here to win. Æri bounced on her heels, quietly reciting her prepared questions—remembering Reverend Cormac's advice. It was all she could do to keep herself from running over to Oisin while they stood on the podiums, anxious that his chief would lock him away before she had the opportunity to reach him.

As the squire ushered her off the winning stands, an invisible tug toward the crammed benches halted Æri. Her head whipped to the top row. There, a Venator with a darkened brow and scarred face glared down.

Æri ignored Rione's frown; she'd deal with the Venator after the reception.

She and the elf walked side by side, the squire leading them into an outdoor plaza. People mingled around an assortment of food and drinks on long tables, and glittering lights wreathed the olive trees. The lanterns burned brighter as daylight dwindled.

"Oisin," she murmured. "I must talk with you."

His chief, Nicomedes, liaised with another noble across the plaza. But instead of directing them to the chief, the squire permitted them to wander.

Oisin's ears twitched and his eyes slipped toward her. "Ah, the Lamiæn speaks the Fíronian tongue. Do you speak Fae as well?"

"Some." She learned Fae as a child, but a while had passed since she spoke the melodic words. She suppressed a jitter. His sidelong look unnerved her.

No one noticed as she and Oisin veered toward a secluded corner framed by the glowing trees.

Oisin's eyes narrowed perspicaciously. "Do you think it unwise with so many eyes and ears about, *princess*?"

Æri's mouth went dry. She darted her head around, hoping no one had overheard, despite the elf saying the words in his native tongue. Seeing no one, she attempted to make her tone flat. "I don't know what you mean."

"It's no use playing coy. You reek of royal blood." Oisin's head tilted sinuously to the side. "Are you not the daughter of King Arne and Queen Freydis of Særenfell? I see them in your face"—his eyes swept over her—"though, I believe you take after your father more, princess."

Damn the Fae and their heightened senses. She forgot that some controlled a rare ability to pair origins—and *princess*. She wished Oisin would stop calling her that. She detested the title.

Æri didn't have time to dwell on how he knew, but she found herself saying, "Have you met them?"

The elf's eyes flicked over her features, her high cheekbones, and small but strong stature. "I visited your realm by orders of my queen just months before the separations—treaty parleys. Your mother was heavy with child. Her aura still curls around you..."

"Why didn't you say anything before?" Æri couldn't hide the waver in her voice. "If you believed I was their daughter—"

"Doing so during the bidding rounds may have revealed your heritage to the king's informants. I didn't want to risk that."

"Is this why you let me win the second round? Because you knew?"

The elf bowed his head in answer. "I've been sent here for other reasons. I did not need to win the Auctioning to achieve them. Why not give another a fighting chance?"

Oisin's words were earnest.

A boisterous laugh erupted from a nearby group, and Æri reminded herself of the goal. Still no sign of Rione, but she hooked Nicomedes's glare, his eyelids thinning in suspicion. So without preamble, she jumped to the point. "Reverend Cormac said I should find an elf—that it might uncover more answers about my people and their disease if I sought a Fae."

"He is of Dianeane, is he not?"

Æri bobbed her head.

"The priests and priestesses of Dianeane generally give more articulate answers than the Fae, but I assume he would require more of his companions to provide exact answers for you." Oisin's mouth twisted. "I will do my best. Give me your hand."

Her heart thumped as she placed her calloused fingers into the elf's slender ones. Oisin's touch was cool. Not cold, but light and fluid, as if water flowed beneath his skin.

"Now, think of your question, and I will see what comes." He closed his golden-blue eyes, his breaths slowing with every inhalation.

Æri enquired voicelessly: *A cure, how do I find a cure for my sister?*

A long moment of arrested silence passed, save for the rhythm of their steady breaths. When Oisin's eyes opened, his lids remained hooded. He narrowed them further in thought. Casting a glance about the area, Oisin reached and snapped a twig from a leaning olive branch. He started to draw a set of lines in the dusty earth at their feet.

"Our divinations come to us in the form of our talents. For some, it is a poem or a song; for myself, they come in images—symbols."

Oisin stepped back to view his work. There, etched into the dirt, lay two sets of drawings. In each image, the symbols were the same yet rearranged. The first depicted a crown at the center bound by a circle. Atop this straddled a great tree, its roots fastening around both the crown and the ring. In the second sketch, the circle was broken into three segments and the tree split, its two halves toppled by the crown, which loomed above both destroyed objects.

"What does it mean?" Æri could only guess what each symbol represented. Her pulse accelerated in anticipation as she waited for the elf's answer.

Oisin's ears turned down as he worked his jaw in contemplation. "I have seen this vision in my dreams...and sometimes in my waking thoughts. The image comes when I question the separations. There may be a connection between this and your people's illness."

Æri had speculated this already. No other illness came before or after the Split with such gravity.

"But that is all I can gather. I do not know what the symbols represent."

Her heart sank. This was not the answer she hoped for.

A heavy hand clamped onto Æri's shoulder, its pressure making her flinch, and her stomach dropped.

"I think you've had enough time playing rogue with your friend."

She swallowed the disquiet as she turned to behold Rione.

Oisin quickly scratched the drawings out with his foot. "I should be finding my chief as well." The elf bowed. When Oisin's head rose, his eyes halted on Rione's face. His ears lifted up and forward, regarding the Venator raptly. Time seemed to pause for a moment between the two. Then Oisin dismissed himself, departing before Æri could thank him.

Rione's grip tightened as he steered her from the reception plaza by her elbow.

"You can let go of my arm. I'm not going anywhere," she said, growling. His uninvited touch made her skin itch as if grazing against thistle leaves. She moved to pull away.

He loosened his hold but didn't let go. "Do you think that was funny?" Rione's nostrils flared, and his incipient ire simmered under his skin, on the brink of a rolling storm.

A spark of savage satisfaction swelled from within—relishing that she had caused a reaction in him—and as if something possessed her, she said, "What? I thought you'd be pleased. I managed to get the troop more points, didn't I?" Sarcasm laced her voice. Perhaps not the best words to placate his mood, but she couldn't help it. She excelled at archery. Why hadn't he placed her in the event in the first place?

"There's no honor in winning when you know there's no challenge. And the goal was to work with the troop as a unit, but that's beside the point."

They halted abruptly along the main walkway. Concession tents signaled the path out of the park. People passed, heading for the exits, paying them no heed.

He spun her to face him. "You *forged* my signature, Æri. I should have you dismissed from the troop for that. Can you imagine what the officials would have done if they discovered the signature wasn't mine? They'd disqualify the whole troop."

Rione scowled, and embarrassment spooled into her chest as he went on. "It would have turned out worse for you. Do you know that? They'd throw you back into the Cells. Is that what you want? To be starved again? To have to go through another bidding process and be sold into hard labor under the king? Or worst, the Lupanar?" Rione let his words sink in, finally releasing her arm.

She didn't move. She just stared blankly at him, her anger draining. He was right.

He rubbed at his temples. "Why didn't you just ask me?"

She swallowed; her throat felt as though she'd shoved sand down it. What could she say to that?

Rione let out a frustrated sigh. "If you just told me you wanted to speak with the Fae, I would have understood. I would have let you."

Her arms tingled, waking as though they'd fallen asleep. She'd failed to trust Rione. Æri had been so concerned about finding a way to talk to Oisin she'd dismissed the most straightforward solution. The feeling sunk cold and deep as she gazed at Rione, his eye reflecting her betrayal.

~ 29 ~

ÆRI

The dark shadows and lambent braziers that inhabited the throne room during the mourning period had vanished, and today, it seemed as if Æri stepped into the sun itself. Daylight spilled in from arched windows and bounded off the gold-leafed columns and coffered ceiling. Illuminated rays beamed behind the dais through slashed windows—overlooked on her first visit—making the painted ones blaze. The red marbled floor was so polished her sullen reflection glared back.

Æri slid her eyes past Gyr resting on her shoulder, and over to Rione. Back straight as a board, feet apart, his eye didn't so much as twitch in her direction. He'd stopped speaking to her after the tournament. Not that he said much to begin with, but when Rione had something important to say, he would say it. And Rione's wrath was quiet, the kind that didn't require words.

Her incessant thoughts kept alluding to his expression that day where disappointment and recrimination filled his face. Over a week passed since the tournament, and she had not uttered one repentant word. She hadn't apologized—hadn't dared approach the Venator—and knew she was a coward for it.

Æri rocked on her toes, relieving the spasms in her calves. They throbbed from yesterday's one-legged squats. Sten required her to maintain the low position for over an hour on each leg. Rione had been out of the city for a few days and on his orders, left her least favorite troop member in charge. If she thought Rione's demands were callous, Sten embodied the ruthlessness of a Bog beast.

The king's footsteps echoed off the chamber's gilded walls, and Æri adjusted her stance. He passed them, eyes fixed on a fruit bowl next to his dais. Fingers perused plums and peaches before selecting a bunch of grapes.

He finally turned his gaze, surveying them with nonchalance. "You both look like you could use a day at the royal baths. Perhaps together...it would certainly defuse whatever vile tension is going on between the two of you."

Gyr's feathers ruffled, and heat rolled up Æri's neck. She forced herself to keep her eyes on the king. He lowered himself into his golden throne and sucked on a grape, rakishly grinning at the two of them. "But I have more important subjects to discuss than getting involved in your little dramatic tiffs." The king swallowed and plucked another oval from the vine.

"You've been invited here to receive your next assignment into the Bogs." He looked at Rione. "Given the exceptional results from the tournaments, this next mission requires my best." Then the king turned his gaze to her. "And it involves Æri, which is why I've summoned you both. This season will be different."

Rione's expression didn't alter; only his heels shuffled.

King Remus rose from his throne and snapped his fingers at a man leaning against a set of doors. Not a sentinel, but perhaps an assistant or advisor. Of average height and build, the man possessed hair the color of parchment—unlike her queen's, which retained a cool white like the moons, his had a hint of gold. His scooped cheeks gave him a gaunt appearance, the bones there prominent and almost skeletal. Menacing mahogany-black eyes stared back at them, assessing.

"Odoacer, do you have the map?" The platinum-haired man inclined his head, though he said nothing.

"Very good. Follow me." King Remus instructed Rione and Æri to trail him through the doors where Odoacer loitered and into a lesser, adjacent chamber.

Anchored at its center was a large, well-built table, signifying the room's purpose: a strategy chamber, whether for the hunts or the realm's long-ago battles. It was devoid of any other furniture.

"I, too, want answers," King Remus said, a flare in his eyes. "And I have you to thank for awakening my new curiosity, Æri."

He commanded Odoacer to unfurl the map on the enormous stone table.

Æri recognized the curvilinear lines and shapes immediately—Glasterra before the Split. This map must be ancient. Beautifully detailed, with the four great oceans and their adjacent seas enveloping the nine realms. As a Fíronian map, the subsequent realms branched off Fíronbec—its focal point. Place names were less familiar to Æri; however, the silhouettes of the realms replicated the maps from her archives: Særenfell in the high north above Fíronbec, once connected by a strait titled the Petraynese Range, now just floating pieces of rock and mountain around the outskirts of Særenfell. Dianeane lay to Fíronbec's northeast, and Jotnarach below that—the Realm of Giants resting above the equator. The Isles of Erynelleth and Isle of Hártolf lay in the Gulf of Tynethin. Larkærseim and Bolcán stretched farther east. And lastly, Hælsgade—detached and alone in the Quadrarian Ocean.

"It has come to my attention that we do not have proper representations of our new world—only these old relics." The king pointed to the artwork before him as if it showcased a rudimentary drawing. "Yet, we no longer live in a world connected by water and land. And we merely have crude sketches of the Bogs where our roads extend, but that is all. For too long, we have relied on these as being enough. What of the fellow realms? Where are they now?" He placed both of his hands on the table, arching his fingers to hold the ends of the curling paper. "It is high time we have proper maps that reflect this."

His attention refocused on Rione. "Your and your troop's new mission is to find and chart the current locations of the realms. Your tracking abilities are exceptional, and I won't have any other Venator troop lead the expedition. No more guesswork, no more suppositions. And we will start with Dianeane."

Æri's eyelids contracted. The king was not telling the whole truth, and she suspected the reasoning behind this sudden appeal was not only to map out the lost realms. She meant to question his interest, but Rione beat her to it.

"Why Dianeane? Særenfell and Jotnarach were the closest realms before the separations. Even the Isles of Erynelleth are more reachable from our southern borders." His finger outlined Fíronbec's southern peninsula.

"Rione, my dear friend, I do not think I have to remind you of how welcoming the Lamiæn are to our people." The king's eyes grazed back to Æri and passed to Gyr. "I've heard from a little bird that Dianeane may give us some solutions—a clear reason to what caused the separations. With the great knowledge possessed there, they may even hold the locations of all the realms, saving us the trouble in mapping them out ourselves."

Æri felt the blood drain from her face. She tried not to let the king's words affect her. *Little bird.* Her father used to call her that.

Little bird, my little bird, the words rang.

The attempt to control her features waned, and she hoped he'd think it about the separations. His statement did trouble her—how he knew about her conversation with Reverend Cormac. Perhaps through Brennos? Or, more unsettling, could someone else have been in the library with them, unseen? Æri didn't believe there was much to hide—she hadn't revealed her connection to her sister—but the conversation seemed personal.

As if the king had read her mind, he said, "My eyes and ears are everywhere, Æri. And I thought—since you've been so diligent with your work at the Inventorium—I'd grant you this little favor and help find a cure for your *queen*."

"How do you propose we get to these realms? It would take months if not years with the caravans," Rione cut in, seeming to ignore the new information divulged by the king and asking another question of logic.

An inkling of amusement and surprise teemed in King Remus's bronze eyes. "Has Æri not informed you of our special project in development at the Inventorium?"

No. Æri hadn't told Rione. She hadn't told Rione about her sister, her people, her need to find a cure, nor of the power source the king wished her to create to run his aircraft. And apparently, the king had not told his lead strategist either.

Rione showed no hint of her further failures to trust him as he stated, "I was informed of some new transport, yes. But do you deem it to be ready? Is there time to test it? The Bog hunts begin at the month's end. That's just over three weeks from today."

"Why don't you ask your clever *slave*, Rione?"

Rione's face flushed crimson. King Remus broke the Venator's steady composure with that single word, hitting the intended nerve.

Æri interceded. "We've almost finished replicating a prototype, but the process takes time. Three weeks may not be feasible."

This was partially true. She had deliberately slowed the development of the power source in fear of what King Remus might do with it when she finished. But to go to Dianeane...she may have to rethink her indecision.

"Then it is too risky." Rione shook his head, again looking deceptively calm—but she sensed a storm rising. His arms crossed his chest like a shield, containing whatever anger roiled inside. "Unmapped territory in the Bogs, new forms of transportation—we haven't properly tested these aircraft. It's a fool's errand, and I won't endanger my troop like that."

King Remus chuckled, his hand finding a hold on Rione's rigid shoulder.

"Don't be such a bore, Rione. Learn to live a little. Ever since you got that gash across that beautiful face, you've acted as though you have a Bog beast's femur up that tight ass. What is eternal life worth without any risk?"

Rione's mouth thinned, chafing at the comment. "I won't put my troop in danger. Test the aircraft first. Then we'll talk."

The king sniffled. His golden curls fell across his forehead, resembling a scolded child.

How could these two men ever have been childhood companions?

Æri strained not to gape. With a snap of his fingers, the king held Rione's life—*all* their lives—in his hands. Yet, Rione seemed to have no fear of this.

He rounded on his heels, not turning back as he delivered a parting command. "Æri, come. We're done here."

A sonorous melody wove from the domus's courtyard into her room.

Æri finished combing her wet strands after taking a much-needed bath. Despite the king's peeving taunts, she admitted he was astute. The soak did indeed help her relax, lending her the time she needed to clear her head and make at least one decision.

Her skin felt fresh from the lemon-verbena soap, her hair loose, its ends now dry and brushing against her neck as she padded down the passage, edging toward the otherworldly music.

Æri found Ofelia and Leta leaning against one of the pillars that framed the garden—out of view from the musician. They, too, had been drawn from their tasks to watch him play.

He had his good eye closed; the other was absent of an eyepatch. Long inky hair draped, unbound, over his shoulders, obscuring part of his face. Purple coneflower and wild lupin blossomed about the bench where he sat. Their fragrant redolence mingled with other herbs in the garden, honeyed and alluring.

That bittersweet nostalgia curled in her chest like hands wrapped around a hot cup of tea or lost hours from a summer's afternoon—now that she knew what summer was. Æri cleared her throat. It helped dispel the emotion and warn her company. She had learned not to sneak up after that first day.

Ofelia turned, placing a finger to her lips, and beckoned Æri to join them.

"Only plays when he's deep in thought," Ofelia whispered. "Something must have happened today to make him take out that lyre. But gods blessed the man who plays it; such a shame he doesn't do it more often."

Rione drew his curved bow over the strings, his arm swaying along with the slow tune. The Venator played on like that for a time, and when he eventually set his instrument aside, a sense of peace floated in the air.

Ofelia released a long sigh. "Well, I ought to be getting on with my chores."

Leta turned to do the same, but on the way, she gave Æri a tiny shove. "Go talk to him, you goose. You've made him wait long enough."

With the push, Æri stumbled onto the cobblestones of the courtyard. She tried to walk off the unexpected trip, but her attempt to be suave faltered when Rione looked up. His brown eye scrolled over her face like he was reading words on a page, and she felt her cheeks redden.

Æri raised a hand awkwardly as if to wave, then thought against it, interlacing her fingers to prevent them from making more spastic movements.

"Er... hi—" Her words tangled.

How was she supposed to do this? Rows with her sister simply faded with time, and her Narkrye usually came to a mutual agreement when arguments arose. To say sorry to Rione was...Let's just say apologies were never her forte.

Rione's mouth twitched, but his expression stayed downcast...No, not downcast—nostalgic. He blinked, patiently waiting for her to say more.

"You...um...play well."

"Thank you."

Another tongue-tied beat passed. Her chest pulsed like the wings of the butterflies that fluttered by, and her fingers twisted tighter.

"Do you want to sit down?" He moved his lyre from the marble bench.

Æri resisted the urge to refuse, knowing it would be rude. She came here to avoid doing just that. So she sat on the cool marble. Heat radiated from his body despite the hand's width of space separating them. That heady aroma of citrus and wood drifted up her nose again. Rione smelled...comforting? Safe? The scent perplexed her.

Trying to distract herself, she gestured to his lyre propped against the leg of the bench. "Did your father teach you?"

"He did." Rione took up the bow again, and on closer inspection, Æri noted a delicate design of circles and knots etched into its handle. "This is his instrument from Erynelleth."

"They let him keep it?"

A nod.

"Is it difficult...to play?"

"It took many years to master, so yes—"

"No, I mean..." She shook her head. "Does it remind you of him?"

Rione pressed his mouth together and inhaled. "Yes, every time. All the time."

Æri thought this was all he planned to say, but after a breath, he went on. "It also helps me tolerate it—to cope with his absence. It's as if I have a little piece of him with me. The good parts...one of the reasons why I don't play in front of others." A corner lifted from the side of his mouth. "Not intentionally."

Her face burned, knowing he had been conscious of the small audience that gathered by the pillar.

"I understand now...why you were so reluctant to play at the banquet."

"Yes, well, the king usually gets what he wants." An exasperated sigh escaped from his mouth as he rotated the bow in his fingers.

"And what of today? The king didn't get what he wanted at our meeting."

Rione moved his gaze toward the gurgling fountain. "I stand by what I said." He lifted his shoulders. "We'll see what Remus does."

Unsaid words hung between them. It also depended on what she chose to do. She could speed up the process.

Æri gnawed on her lip, debating how much to tell Rione. Maybe just this little part? He had exposed details of his past—laying them bare—and explained his reasons, yet she had done nothing of the sort in return. Admittedly, she demurred, unable to fully trust him even after what he said, that small piece of her still not willing to let go. And now there was the possibility of going to Dianeane with the troop. But what of home? She had little time to weigh the ramifications of it all, to weigh the choices and know where their paths led.

"I—I delayed it on purpose." Her voice came out in a quiet stutter.

Rione angled his head toward her, his brows creased.

"I mean..." She took a moment and spoke again. "I've *been* delaying the production of the power source on purpose." Looking at her hands and away from his gaze, Æri decided she owed him this truth, this segment of the whole.

"They have all the materials in the right order, but I've been finding snags, having the team re-fix parts—just little things. I thought if I stalled its production, I could buy more time to learn what the king intended to do with the ship—prevent him from doing any harm. But with the opportunity to go to Dianeane—knowing this is what he intended—it changes things." Her words didn't explain everything. Though the matters were indirectly connected, she still had to tell Rione *why* she disobeyed his orders at the tournament. Æri tried to keep the regret from her voice. "I sought Oisin—the Fae Venator at the tournament—to seek answers for my queen, for an illness threatening my realm."

Æri paused so she could gather the right words. His stare scorched the side of her face. Gaining the courage, she looked back at him. "I'm in the habit of doing things on my own."

Rione's eye stayed on hers, encouraging her wordlessly to go on.

So she told Rione of the strange tome found in the library and Oisin's cryptic symbols but omitted her royal lineage, not yet ready to share that secret.

"The symbols mean nothing without words or a story behind them. I needed Oisin for answers, but all I got were more questions. Perhaps the Seven Sages in Dianeane might know how to interpret Oisin's message or more about the god of darkness who created the Vampryne. This is the closest I've ever been, but if I choose to go, I'd be prolonging my return to Særenfell, and with the Blodlyst spreading again...I miss it, I miss it so much." Æri opened a floodgate of words, lost in her indecisions. "And if I go to Dianeane under King Remus's command, it would be a betrayal to my queen. I don't—" She stopped. Her rib cage squeezed like ropes pulling tighter and tighter, and her head droned with building frustration.

Æri took a breath and let the silence grow. The ropes slowly loosened.

Rione rubbed his thumb against his lower lip. "It sounds as if you care for your queen greatly. Enough to sacrifice what you truly want." He took a breath. "Do you not want to go home?"

Æri considered his words. Brynja would always be her sister—her twin; they grew up together, went through their burdens together. She was her queen, her people's queen. How could she not put that first?

"I don't know what I want."

Rione nodded thoughtfully, leaning forward to prop his arms on his knees. "I can't decide for you. I can assist, but it must ultimately come from you alone."

She understood, but she had hoped for an order—a command to follow; she wanted someone to tell her what to do. Brynja always made the decisions—at least the ones that held the most gravity.

Her eyes stung. This was not what she expected to feel—she hadn't been expecting to feel anything at all.

Rione tilted his head to look at her again. "My father once said...no matter how little or grand your choices may be, they are yours to own. They belong to you, and no one can take that away."

Æri closed her eyes, and something wet trickled down her face. She moved her hand to wipe the tear, but Rione caught it first. His coarse thumb moved over her cheek. To her surprise, she didn't shrink from his touch. Instead, her skin tingled where the stroke of rough and wet skin met. A small tug came from her core, but it felt different from before. Not many ropes, but a single thread—that same sensation in this garden weeks ago and at the banquet...yet no fear or hate manifested. Somehow, they had all vanished.

Her eyes roamed across his face, the narrow lips and bent nose, the scar, and the teal-rimmed, chocolate eye; his skin was set aglow by the dipping sun. She imagined tracing her finger along the scar's rim, imagined following it to the shell of his ear and then to his mouth.

"Æri..." Her name a murmur on his lips, the whispered breath falling over her own.

Rione removed his hand, and the pull disappeared with it.

He stood to leave, but she found herself slipping her small rough hand into his larger one and tugged him gently back to the bench.

"Stay...a little longer. Please."

~ 30 ~

REMUS

The scavenger may very well collapse onto the marble floor. Remus hoped he didn't...then he'd have to send someone to shine it again. His bedraggled subject looked as though he'd trolled through a magma pit—and likely had. Crusted lips and reddened eyes indicated dehydration, and the clothes on his back, charred and tattered, were much too warm for this realm.

The two sentinels who had delivered him idled by the throne room doors.

"Found him at the realm's borders, down in the Bogs," one had said. "He wore those Lamiæn pelts, and we thought him to be their kind at first." Sentinels had trapped the man in their enchanted nets as soon as he passed the patrol line. Only after they dragged him in, bruised and scuffed, did they recognize his brown eyes.

"King Remus." The drained man's voice wheezed.

Remus examined the scavenger for a few drawn-out beats. He categorized him as a squirmer—no harm in having a little fun. Hesól, he needed some after his brush with Rione and his slave. His lip curled at how Rione had dismissed his orders; lead strategist or not, Remus was king. He claimed the last word. In the meantime, he had this scrap to dabble with.

Remus toyed with a plum from the fruit bowl, lobbing it between each hand and then decisively sinking his teeth into its purple skin. His fierce craving for fruit never ebbed. Sugar kept that itch inside satisfied. Swallowing, he wiped a drop of dark juice from his chin.

Finally, he drawled, "Atticus."

"Yes, My King."

"I presume you are here to tell me why you are wearing the clothes of my enemy?"

Remus already knew the answer. His sentinels relayed the information prior to hauling in the scavenger. But, ah yes, there it was, that delightful wriggle.

Atticus attempted to quell his shudder. "I was taken by the Lamiæn, My King."

"And they let you live...how kind of them. What did you do to gain their favor?" His voice was full of jocularity.

When the scavenger didn't respond, Remus snapped his fingers.

"Am I to make you dance on Bog peat to get the words out?"

The scavenger's protuberant eyes went as wide as his sentinels' parma shields.

Oh, all too easy to tease.

"Though that might be amusing to watch, I needn't waste my energy on such trivial matters. So, I will repeat: What was the favor, *Atticus*?"

His fingers trembled as he withdrew a sealed letter from his breast pocket and extended his arm. The tremor in his hand was so great Remus thought the man would drop the parchment.

Odoacer stepped forward to retrieve the message.

"The seal appears to be intact, and there are no traces of poison. Shall I read it aloud, King Remus?"

Remus inclined his head to his steward's query but kept his impish glare on Atticus.

Odoacer's toneless voice carried throughout the large chamber. As he read on, Remus's brow furrowed, and irritation made his jaw tic.

When the steward finished speaking, Remus's teeth gnashed, and his fingers had tensed around the armrests.

Riveting news indeed—and not to be taken lightly.

He was glad he toyed with the scavenger when he had the opportunity. He abhorred being serious. Remus grimaced; his father was always serious. His father...always wanting him to be something he wasn't. The thought of the former king pulled the corners of his mouth down further. He would not die like his father. *He'd* at least live to see his power flourish—Remus had ensured that.

The stillness in the room matched everyone else's restrained breath; even the dust motes in the sun's beams appeared motionless.

Remus tapped his index finger, mouth pinching with annoyance and deliberation. He eyed the bowl of fruit, wanting another.

"Summon the Curia." He tore his gaze from the fruit to address Odoacer. "Set the meeting for tomorrow evening—*after* the Games. I believe we have quite a show to put on first."

~ 31 ~

ÆRI

"**B** ut we spoke with him not two days ago."

Ghosts of wavy light glistened off the impluvium pool and onto the blue walls.

Rione paced the domus's atrium, his head and broad shoulders arched over the fastidious script. "I suspect this is his way of trying to persuade me."

His brows pulled in, expression bleak as he reread the decree aloud. "On behalf of the king, you are hereby requested to attend the Games in his royal dais."

"Are we both to join?" Æri exhaled loudly. She wasn't eager to make an appearance at the Arena, nor did she have the aptitude for spending an entire day with King Remus. From what she'd heard of the Games, they were nothing like the Royal Venator Tournament. The king needed his Venators in one piece for the Bogs. The Games, on the other hand...

"It's a royal summons. Not even I can say no to that." Rione rubbed his jaw, giving Æri a once-over. "Wear something light. It's going to be a long day."

The Arena thrummed with the cheers and shouts of Fíronbec's countless citizens crammed into the impressive space. Tiered seats gleamed gold in the mid-morning sun as thousands upon thousands of patrons saturated its stands.

"This way, my lord." An attendant guided Æri and Rione through the dais's private entrance. The king had yet to arrive, but most of his retinue were already seated.

One of his consorts, Rosalind, rested a level above the king's row. Still in mourning, she wore a dark indigo gown of heavy royal silk and waved a hand fan vigorously. Wan in the face, Rosalind must have been perspiring under the dismal fabric. Despite the low-hanging canopy and parasols, the Fíronian sun invaded every corner of the dais.

The consort's expression soured when she saw Æri's scrutiny, and she leaned to her companion's ear. Snickers ensued as the women eyeballed Æri.

Æri turned her head from Rosalind's leer, no longer sympathetic to the consort roasting in the sun. If her glower was about Æri's arm, the fact she was a Lamiæn, or Gyr roosting on her shoulder, she couldn't tell. At least Æri wouldn't be melting in the heat.

She had opted for a light sage dress fastening at her shoulders with two spiraled pins. The featherweight fabric billowed as she moved, allowing what little breeze there was to cool her legs, and for all her gripes, she found herself grateful again for Ofelia's persistence.

"Braccae would get you thrown from the Arena!" Ofelia had chided when Æri suggested them. Though Æri preferred her training livery, both Leta and Ofelia forewarned formal events such as the Games forbade the practical clothing on women.

Men, on the other hand, could dress as they pleased.

She envied Rione's well-tailored taupe trousers and diamond-patterned copper tunic, the design's shimmering threads catching the bold light. Æri rarely saw Rione wear such fine clothing. It didn't quite suit him, making the dais all the more uncomfortable, and she suddenly longed to see him in his accustomed training tunic.

Æri gazed back at the gathering of courtiers, searching for Camilla. She hoped the lady's maid would be here to keep the Games more bearable.

Rione picked up on her intent. "Consort Ismene does not prefer the Games, to my mother's satisfaction as well."

"Oh..."

"But you'll see her soon enough," he reassured.

She hadn't seen Camilla since the day at the palace. Had Rione told her about their meeting at his childhood farmhouse? If so, how much did he reveal of their discussion? Reminded of his offer from the month before, Æri pushed the thought away for later. She had not yet decided, still having several weeks left before the Bog hunts.

They advanced to their seats, two spaces on the right side of the U-shaped throne. Rione made to sit in the one closest to the king's, but the attendant stuck out a hand. "I am sorry, Lord Aulius, but the king bids Æri of Særenfell rest there today."

An odd request. They rearranged themselves as the attendant instructed.

Gyr hopped down to perch on the rail, and she tethered him to her chair, fearing to relive the events of the Auctioning. Despite it being an illusion, the deluded memory of Gyr's fallen form replayed unbidden in her thoughts.

Adjusting herself on the red cushion, she jumped at the contact of warm skin, and a surprised hum escaped her throat.

"Are you all right?"

Rione's hand had grazed hers.

"Yes, I—" There, that tug again, that slight tingle. *What was that?* "I'm fine."

All too aware something was emerging between herself and Rione, her mind failed to define it. It lacked clarity. Possibly friends? *No.* They were not friends.

Æri recalled his tentative touch the night in the garden, how his hand cupped her cheek, capturing her tear before it fell. How he had whispered her name as if his life was hers to take. After she reached out, he delicately circled his fingers around her hand, her heart skipping as his thumb skimmed the back of her knuckles.

Nothing else happened, just that touch and the unassuming silence enveloping them. He stayed with her until the sun faded into dusk and the moons climbed. The next day, they trained together like any other, neither acknowledging what had occurred.

Now the opportunity arose again—to reach out and hold his hand. He placed it next to his side, palm up, loose and relaxed as if to let her make the choice, to take it if she wished.

Her fingertips brushed his, just the lightest of strokes when the horns blasted through the Arena.

Æri snatched her hand back, curling her fingers into tight fists as they rose to hail the king.

Still decked in his emblematic black suit, King Remus strolled to his gilded chair; his golden tresses coiled around the sun crown, that crimson sash flaring like a bright wound across his chest.

"I am delighted you two made it on such short notice," the king said, his voice silky as he settled on his throne. With some rustle, the court descended promptly after. "I thought it high time you witnessed what you've missed out on."

Æri bristled, and the king smirked, enjoying the effect of his provocation.

Rione tapped her foot with his and slid her a warning glare.

Aware of King Remus's baiting, she didn't entirely appreciate Rione's extra caution. She exposed her teeth, stretching her lips into a smile and directing it at the king. "We are honored you thought of us, King Remus." Then she threw Rione a wry look. She didn't wait for his answering gesture, not in the mood to continue their wordless banter. Instead, Æri turned her eyes toward the pit.

The Games certainly lived up to their reputation.

Two enormous Bog beasts clawed at each other's limbs as blue-black blood gushed and dripped across the sand with every swipe.

Æri took small, judicious sips of water from her goblet as she attempted to steady her nerves and quell the broiling turbulence in her gut. She refused to eat or drink the bounty of wine and food offered, only taking a few pieces out of decorum and sneaking them to Gyr. But he didn't seem hungry either.

True, Æri saw her fair share of blood when hunting and cleaning up after her queen's court, but it had always made her stomach churn, and what the Narkrye sought was far from sport. Through their kills, they sacrificed morality for survival. This, the bloody brawl that unfolded in front of her, manifested a much darker craving.

The amount of blood soaking the pit was enough to make those with arium stomachs cringe—and these were just two Bog beasts. The vile creatures tore and shredded, their claws grating each other's flesh, all while a bloodthirsty crowd roared them on.

Æri recognized the smaller beast from the scroll in Rione's library. The acuslasor, with its needlelike teeth and limbs that bent at unnatural angles, pranced about the larger toadlike creature. It sprinted in and out of the other's reach, teasing.

In due time, the acuslasor went in for the kill, jumping on the bulkier one's back and clenching its elongated maw around its bulbous neck. The acuslasor yanked its head, ripping a giant chunk from the beast's neck.

Reeking blood sprayed over the spectators. They cheered as if it had been wine, their spattered-faces and teeth grinning out in a macabre tableau.

After re-tethering the winning beast, rakers scampered in to clear the remnants from the sand's surface, preparing the pit for the next round.

The Game's intervals weren't much of an improvement.

It took all of Æri's willpower not to stand and leave when sentinels towed two maimed men out: One lacked both his arms and the other his legs, ordered to combat one another with short swords. Each maneuvered with their remaining limbs. The audience's laughter alone made her despise the entirety of these people. Sour bile ascended, coating her throat, and its acidic taste filled her mouth. She was going to be sick.

This was their entertainment?

Rione wore his mask again, his face impassive, hiding his true thoughts beneath the guise.

"Is this common practice?" she bit out.

He nodded slowly. "It's worse when they add injured beasts to the melee." His eye went to hers. "Do you need a bucket?" She must have looked confused because he said, "They have them stored behind the stands."

Æri shook her head, trying to swallow the bitter flavor.

"Let me know if you do. It's normal, especially if you're not accustomed to the Games. I retched three times on my first attendance."

Whether it was the compassion in Rione's voice or his admission, the nausea in her stomach eased a fraction.

"A battle of brute strength!" an official yelled from the podium, and the throng hollered louder at the introduction of the second event.

A giant emerged from the pit's grated gates—Cuthbert.

Her nausea resurfaced. Æri couldn't help but picture herself down there fighting for her life. She hoped the giant earned his freedom in this match.

He strutted before the dais. Aptly armored, he wore a finned helm and a full chest plate; bronze vambraces and greaves protected his arms and legs. He hoisted a curved shield comparable to the one from the Auctioning. In the other hand, he held a club with a spiked iron ball at its tip.

Fans' cries mounted to a fever pitch when another giant entered from the opposite ramparts. Geared similarly to Cuthbert, the giant pumped his arms in the air to generate more cheers. In place of a club, a broadsword gleamed in his hand.

Æri spun to the king in disbelief. "They're of the same kind—the same realm. You'll have them fight each other?"

She sparred with her Narkrye for training and, at times, play; she had a sickening foreboding this would have a different end.

"On rare occasions," King Remus said in a tone dripping with impudence. He picked at his plate, finding a thin piece of cured black meat. "We usually save the giants to battle the larger Bog beasts. They're less likely to die that way. But since you're here, I thought I'd make it a special event." Gnawing on the meat, he waved toward the pit. "You'll miss the fun if you continue to watch me."

How did he do it—have such brutality unfold and still have an appetite?

She pressed her stomach to curb the sick that bubbled. Æri finally understood why Rione wanted to keep her from this, from fighting in the Games. She'd have to kill for sport. If not her body, her mind would certainly have given in.

The giants began their combat; they slashed and stabbed, and the clanging of metal against metal pealed over the crowd's howls.

Cuthbert blocked a heavy blow with his shield, then propelled the other giant's sword back. He stumbled but quickly regained his footing.

The unfamiliar giant angled his arm, catching Cuthbert off guard, and rammed his sword's hilt into Cuthbert's mouth.

A uniform gasp escaped from the onlookers as he careened to the side, spitting bright red blood. But the blow only seemed to steady him as he squared his stance and raised the club above his head, swinging it around and around.

He landed that swirling orb with a sharp crack to his rival's upper arm, right above his vambrace. Spikes burrowed into flesh. The giant's cry of pain tore through the Arena only to be drowned out by the din of the audience. His sword dropped to the ground. Blood spurted over the opponent's armor, coating his arm. It rocked limply at his side as Cuthbert advanced, gaining momentum. He knocked the giant's shield from his grip in two resolute swipes. The giant fell to the earth. Cuthbert raised his club again, about to slam a final blow, when the injured giant raised three fingers. Cuthbert's gaze shot toward the dais.

In a moment of suspense, the crowd quieted to watch the king's verdict.

"The sign for mercy. If Remus raises a fist, Cuthbert will end it," Rione whispered. His breath tickled against her ear, heightened by the tension in the air.

"What if he decides to spare the giant?"

Rione did not have to answer. King Remus raised three fingers in return. "It would be a shame to lose a giant like this in the Games." He shrugged dismissively.

Cuthbert lowered his club, and a team of sentinels ran out to assist the collapsed giant. A pool of blood had developed under his arm. Rivulets fingered from the source, snaking in the sand.

More yells and cheers rang as King Remus announced Cuthbert as the winner.

The king stretched his arms wide to quiet the horde as he rose from his throne. His golden-brown eyes mirrored their anticipation. "We have an extraordinary show for our final round today." His voice augmented over the tiers.

He gestured back to Æri.

Not understanding his meaning, she hesitated. His whetted gaze slipped to Rione, who gently nudged her to stand.

Her senses pricked, heightening as Æri approached the erect king. Gyr squawked—feeling her unease—but she bade him to remain by Rione.

The king readdressed his audience. "I am disheartened to say that my sentinels have discovered two spies on our land."

Æri's chest tightened, and she clenched her hands behind her back to keep them from shaking.

Spies?

The air stilled, the crowd holding their breath as they waited for the king's next words.

"And it is up to this Lamiæn to decide their fates."

Rione remained silent, his face cast in stone, unreadable, eye averted.

The king motioned down to the pits once more.

"Bring them out."

The Arena rumbled. From its heart, two trapdoors gave way. Sand at their edges spilled inward as two podiums rose into the sky.

Æri's breath accelerated as she beheld the two individuals tied to those towering posts.

The king twisted to Æri, his voice no more than a hissing whisper. "Who are you?" The mischief in his tenor snuffed, replaced by pure ferocity.

She gulped, struggling to get ahold of her uneven breaths.

The pale blonde thrashed at her bindings as the dark-haired Fae stood rigid against the pillar, his ears tucked.

Yrsa and Oisin were tied and gagged to those stakes. Her gaze flicked back to the king.

"What—I—I'm no one." Her voice came out strangled, the words sticking in her throat.

The king chuckled spitefully. "Oh, Æri. I don't believe you are 'no one.' I received news inferring otherwise. So you're lying. And like spies, I don't like liars."

News? Æri tried to calm her mind. A faint ringing started to build in her ears.

"Tell me who you are, or they *both* die."

She stalled, needing more time. Her eyes located Rione's, and for once, he stared directly back, the vigilance in his eye unmistakable, his arms tense, fingers gripping the sides of his seat.

"You have until the count of three." He held up his hand, and her head snapped toward the monstrous roars. Two Bog beasts bellowed from across the pit as dozens of sentinels wrenched at their bindings, restraining the crazed creatures. One stood upright on its hindlimbs, reminding her of the beast battled in the Auctioning—only bigger. Its two elongated arms forked into three lethal points, and its legs, thick and muscular, were meant for running. A ribbed dorsal fin fanned as its jaws clicked in rapid succession.

The smaller beast appeared more akin to a snake. Daggerlike fangs protracted from its mouth, covered in a slimy venom. Six sticklike legs pierced through its serpentine form, jutting out at abnormal angles, popping and cracking as it slithered.

"One." The king extended his thumb, and the sentinels lifted their swords to cut the bindings.

"Two."

They lowered their serrated edges.

"Th—"

"Don't!" Æri yelled. She had to save them. "I am her sister. I am the queen's sister." The words spluttered out of her in a rush. "I'm her sister."

Thousands of eyes fixed upon her, and she felt as bare as the blue sky that stretched above.

A guileful smile played across King Remus's red lips, and he lowered his hand. The sentinels sheathed their swords once more. "Now that wasn't so terrible, was it?"

Æri slumped. She did not know what the king planned to do with this information. A part of her sensed he knew all along, and he just wanted her to say it, to confirm his suspicion.

"Oh, don't sit down just yet. I'm not done." His voice was laced with a merciless charm, that roguish smile widening on his too-perfect features.

"Choose one to save." The king gesticulated a hand to Oisin and Yrsa.

Æri balked. *Choose?* How could she? By picking one, she condemned the other: the Fae who helped her or her own Narkrye. She couldn't choose.

"Don't do this, Remus." Rione abruptly shot up next to Æri. "She gave you what you wanted."

"Ah, Rione. I did not ask for your advice." The king's eyes narrowed. "Perhaps, you *have* developed a fondness for this little Lamiæn."

He directed his focus back to Æri.

"Choose one."

She turned to Rione for some sort of support—help.

But the king grabbed her jaw, forcing her to stare into his bronzed eyes. "Don't look at him. *Choose.*" He snarled, spittle flecking her face. She fought the urge to wipe it away. His pupils swelled to large black circles, brows angled inward, his lips pulled down. The handsome features ultimately gave way to cruelty, and a monster's face glared at her.

Æri squeezed her eyes shut. She didn't know what to do. Her insides tore at the seams with indecision.

His grip tightened on her jaw, and she opened her eyes, slamming them into the king's. Her voice came out in a rasp. "Yrsa..."

The king leaned in. "What? I didn't hear you."

"*Yrsa.*"

"Say that loud and clear—unless you want them both to die."

"*I choose Yrsa!*"

He dropped her chin. She felt the angry marks linger where his fingers pressed.

"Loyal to your own kind, I see." He pouted, eyes glittering. "Well, that's unfortunate..." King Remus raised a fist and said, "You chose wrong."

She watched in muted horror as the king's archer nocked an arrow and fired, straight at the thrashing Narkrye.

Æri's joints locked, stunned like a defenseless doe, the predator ready to devour her whole. She was reliving Gyr's death—Yrsa's in the Bogs. There was no way to halt that arrow. *Useless.* She was useless, just like before. The ringing reached a crescendo, and the world swayed. Her stomach dipped, and a sensation of falling through a bottomless chasm overwhelmed her. Æri clung to the balustrade, her knuckles turning white as the arrow rocketed through the air. It spiraled over the pit, ready to sink its pointed tip into her Narkrye's heart.

Then...it stopped.

The arrow hovered mere inches from Yrsa's chest. It floated for a second, the Arena utterly silent. And then it wavered, the edges blurring, and slowly, it dissolved.

Yrsa, who had stopped struggling, held the same odd blur as if Æri was looking at her through hot air. *A mirage.* Yrsa's body started to fade, dissolving like the arrow until a new shape appeared—one of the king's sentinels.

Æri darted her gaze to the king and then to the violet-eyed advisor by his left side.

Sulivan. His eyes still focused on the sentinel who was once Yrsa. How had she missed it?

"It's too bad the real one didn't last very long. A troop found your friend wandering the Bogs last month. Delusional from a septic wound on her side. But I figured she'd be useful to me after all. Or at best, an illusion of her." The king's blasé response hardly registered over Æri's internal screams. Building abhorrence scorched through her. Raising her arm, she aimed for him, her nails like talons ready to tear his beautiful face into tiny, bloodied pieces, just like the Bog beasts. But as she raised her hand, a white-hot, prickling sensation rippled up her right arm. She staggered back in pain. Gasping, the step away from the king immediately caused the ache to recede.

"I don't think that's necessary." He tutted. "Do you think I would be so foolish to leave myself unprotected next to a Lamiæn?" His eyes landed on the raised line at her wrist. "Come, now. We aren't finished. I did say you chose wrong, didn't I?"

Again, he signaled to his sentinels in the pit with another fist. And to Æri's terror, they started to saw at the Bog beasts' ropes. Their jaws snapped in the direction of the Fae.

"I have no qualms about losing a spy." The king's voice oozed with derision.

Oisin, still tied to the podium, *was* real.

"Remus. Don't do this," Rione interrupted, breaking his reticence; his words were drawn out and strained, sounding like he, too, was fighting through something.

The king tsked with sympathy. "Rione..." His expression tightened when he inhaled as if tasting a bitter seed. "You've been such a disappointment lately, denying me things that I want. You don't have much of a say in this matter. I've made up my mind."

"I'll buy the Fae out. We can return him to Erynelleth. Use him as trade."

"And how do you propose to do that? Do you have the funds in your accounts, Rione? I thought purchasing Æri here created a sizable dent in your coffers."

Vallantheia's Gates. Æri's mouth fell open. Her hand shook. What had Rione done to save her? And he was doing it again, bargaining for Oisin.

"I can credit it."

"On what? You refused my offer for your next expedition."

"I'll agree to the expedition." Rione gritted his teeth. "Just let the elf come with us."

"I'll tell you what." The king tapped his cheek. "I'll unbind the poor Fae so he has an allowance against the beasts. My people need a final show. But only if you agree to take your troop to Dianeane—and you will *only* be going to Dianeane. I do not need you paying a visit to Erynelleth to talk to your long-lost father along the way."

Like a sharp twist of a knife between the ribs, Æri guessed how those words cut. She caught the tic in Rione's jaw. Otherwise he remained unchanged.

The king went on. "You will leave by the month's end when the Bog hunts begin. Then I'll make it a deal."

"All right. But the Fae joins us."

The king flashed Rione a winning grin. "Agreed."

One by one, sentinels loosened the Bog beasts' ropes. Finishing, they ran to the grated gates, away from those lashing teeth and claws now freed. The sentinel who posed as Yrsa untied Oisin's bound wrists, then disappeared underneath the Arena floor with the podium.

At the king's command, another sentinel tossed Oisin a small knife. It rotated in the air, blade directed at the elf, and Æri's throat strained. But he seized its grip—the blade a hand's width from his face—and cut the rest of himself free, just in time to scurry down the podium and out of the Bog beast's reach. It roared, preparing to leap toward the elf. Saliva sprayed and foamed from its oblong maw, the jaw showcasing rows of razor-edged obsidian teeth.

Gods and goddesses above...

The other beast released a strangled screech, still writhing in the ropes. Its thin body corkscrewed as it tried to free its sticklike limbs.

How was Oisin going to survive this?

She squeezed her right hand and started when she felt a squeeze in return—Rione's fingers interlaced with hers.

When did she grasp his hand? Warmth spread from those clasped fingers, and her trembling abated. The comforting gesture reminded her she was not alone in this.

They watched as Oisin scrabbled for footing. Using his loosened ropes to his advantage, the elf looped the cords over his arm as he evaded the roaring beast.

But instead of eluding both, Oisin beelined toward the snakelike creature—now nearly free from its bindings.

What was he doing? Æri tracked the elf's actions with increasing realization.

The colossal beast hurled itself at Oisin. Not just toward the elf—but to the other beast.

Oisin dodged the oncoming jaws at his heels. Swiftly, he lassoed the rope back and around a hooked spike atop the bounding beast's head, using the momentum of his run to swing himself up and vault over the creature entirely. Now facing in the opposite direction, Oisin bolted.

The beast barreled forward and collided in a mass of teeth and talons with the other, ripping at black, nacreous scales. Fíronbec's audience roared with satisfaction as the creatures tore each other apart. Indigo blood leached into the sandy pit once more.

"It appears you now own two slaves, Rione" was all King Remus said.

And through her rattled thoughts, Æri remembered Rione's words of warning: *The king usually gets what he wants.*

~ 32 ~

RIONE

"**D**id you do it?" Rione slammed the Fae into stone, lifting him by his ragged collar. Decay chipped from the cell wall.

To his credit, Oisin's features remained deferential, unfazed by Rione's size and height difference. Rione loomed a few inches over the elf's lean frame.

Rione's agitation had intensified as he made his way to the Cells, fuming under his skin as blood pounded in his ears. The Games' events shoved him over the edge, his self-control hanging on by a thread.

For years, the king had coerced Rione into doing things he thought too hazardous or unreasonable, tempting him to play with fire. He was finished trying to predict his king's next move—trying to mitigate the repercussions—and so tired of being his puppet, of jumping when ordered to jump. He was no strategist but a marionette in the king's hands. His vow to King Lucius, made all those years ago, withered with each new twisted deed from his son.

He saw his old friend's face when he looked at Æri—the heartlessness that manifested in it. Lead strategist or not, Rione did not want any part of it—not anymore.

He pressed the elf against the wall, his head throbbing with the thought of Remus's games.

Rione had hoped a portion of his childhood companion re-mained inside that calculating mind—*prayed* to Hesól he was still in there, that he'd come to his senses and wake from whatever spell consumed him. But after today...Rione failed to shake the images from his mind. Æri's panic, her trauma—the king had tri-fled with it maliciously, and Rione had been powerless to stop it. Like the crack of a whip slicing skin, the pain of his friend's deceit stung.

Rione ground his knuckles into the stone by Oisin's ear, at-tempting to expel the anger.

Æri's confession had not been enough. Remus manipulated her for his entertainment. That shattered look upon her face when they returned to his domus coiled a tight knot inside of him. And *he* encouraged her to make her own choices. Hells below, she didn't even have a choice! What choice was there when Remus had already determined the outcome?

He remembered her hesitant hold—the clasp of fingers, so un-like the bite along his knuckles' ridge now.

When she grasped his hand with her own, he knew. Rione *knew* his king's guiles went beyond any vengeful game, and he needed to fix it—give her back the choice Remus had stolen.

But by the gods, to glean Æri was the queen of Særenfell's *sis-ter*—a princess, and the hand to the queen. If he'd known before, Rione would've never ensnared her in the Bogs—the diplomatic threat of it too great between the realms. This mess was irrevo-cably his responsibility; he fouled up, and now Remus held some-thing to dangle in front of her queen.

"Tell me how it happened," Rione said, growling at the Fae. He had volunteered to put his troop in danger for this elf, and if Oisin, in any way, exposed Æri's identity to Remus, he needed to hear it straight from the Fae's lips. He'd think about what to do with him after. Rione's fists squeezed tighter on the collar's fabric, the tunic sleeves cutting into the elf's arms.

Still, Oisin did not quail.

Rione was well acquainted with Remus's tactics. His old friend liked to see how far he could push—to dance on that line of right and wrong. Even before their ages settled, Remus persuaded Rione to help him outwit his father's advisors, set pranks on the villa's maids, or run amuck in the stables. It all bored Remus eventually—his privileged life, all of it too easy. Remus sought a challenge, games he'd win but only with an equal match. King Lucius was beside himself on what to do, so he made Rione swear: *Entertain him and keep his mind busy.*

He'd done just that. From the beginning, Remus would drag Rione to all the unseen revelry dens of Méritras. At times, Rione still craved that part of his past—the things they did when they snuck away from the palace: the forbidden parties, the drinks, the lovers. And when Rione's own father left, he fell hard and fast because of it—already exposed to all the pleasures that helped him forget.

Remus was different.

He moved on, again tiring of their corrupt routine, and took solace in yet another interest—the Grand Libraries of Méritras. Research and knowledge finally gained his attention, a place where Remus learned on his own terms. Rione would find his friend abandoned to the dimmed hallways and numerous codices of that sanctuary.

Then the old king died, and everything changed.

Oisin wheezed—the one thing that indicated he might be in pain—and Rione shook himself from his thoughts. He needed to fix this problem first, not get lost in the past.

"Did you tell the king who Æri is?" he said, snarling again.

The Fae's blue-and-gold eyes stared back at him, unblinking.

"No."

His words were firm—a truth.

Rione heaved out a sigh.

The king must have acquired it another way—but how? A guess? Remus possessed a talent for absorbing information and deducing a near accurate outcome. However, Rione had little opportunity to know for certain. Remus had stopped requesting Rione's presence at the Curia's council after he won Æri's bid. He believed it temporary—thought Remus would re-invite him to the palace to strategize for the upcoming hunt. But after today...

Rione released Oisin's tunic, letting the elf sink to the floor. Oisin expelled a long-held breath, running long fingers over his shaved head. His black hair had been cut in haste, scalp scabbed with nicks; his clothes were torn and splattered with blue-black blood.

Nicomedes had yet to provide him with a new set. Typical of the chief. Adequate food and clothing were the first things Rione planned to remedy.

"Are you a spy for the Fae Queen of Erynelleth?"

Oisin straightened, regaining his footing. "If you are referring to Queen Áina, then, yes, I am."

"Do you know who turned you in?"

"That, I do not know." Oisin attempted to brush dirt from his hem to little avail. "But I have my suspicions."

His ears precipitously flicked, then flattened.

Nicomedes banged a baton on the cell gate, his rough voice grating through its bars. "You have ten more minutes, Rione, or I'm locking you in with him for the night. The elf's still mine until you pay up."

"I'm almost done."

Under the law, Rione must pay not only the king but also Oisin's former owner, Nicomedes. Cosmos was currently procuring the bank's calculations, but the process took time.

Rione waited for the other chief Venator's footfalls to disappear around the corner to turn back to Oisin.

"Why did your queen send you here?" He didn't want to waste time solving the Fae's riddles. Æri's broken visage would not leave his thoughts, that stunningly alive face darkened by defeat. It was seared into his mind. He needed to return home to see if she was all right.

Rione had believed he'd hidden his nascent emotions—the draw toward her starting with her capture in the Bogs. At first, he thought he detested her for what she did, for what she represented, and how she failed to remember she had captured and maimed him. But something shifted after their eyes locked, the ice blue absolving, cleansing that hate. He followed the Venators' set rules, hoping they would quell the pull, but every time he saw her, a sense of vulnerability consumed him in a way he could not comprehend, and it frightened him.

Despite trying to reel himself in, the thoughts welled—even as he slept. When he woke, he fought to shove them out with logic, but it didn't work.

The more time he spent around Æri, the more his desire intensified. He started picking up things—noticing she didn't like being touched, seeing how she shrank back every time he forgot. Save for the fact that was *all* he wanted to do. He hoped she would open up on her own terms, in her own time, and she had.

Except the king knew Rione. He'd seen right through Rione's pretense the minute Æri stepped into the Arena, the attraction apparent enough for Remus to use it to his advantage, allowing it to persist. But for how long? How much longer until he grew uninterested and decided to end it? End her?

A shuffling came from the corner of the cell along with a sniff.

Rione's attention snapped back, realizing he had been distracted by his churning thoughts again. The Fae was piling some of the rotting straw, and a pitiful understanding jabbed into Rione; the elf meant to use this lousy mound as a bed. The hay stirred, and a rat surfaced, scuttling over Rione's boots and squiggling through the cell's bars. Rione's lip twitched in disgust.

After finishing with the straw, Oisin curved his head toward Rione, examining him the same way he had at the Venator tournament.

Something about that look unnerved him. Rione repeated his earlier question, not quite meeting the elf's eyes. "Why are you here, Oisin? In Fíronbec."

"My queen sent me to track one of our Fae. Another lost from our lands years ago."

Rione sucked his teeth, considering his words. "Continue."

"He left our island about three centuries after the separations to seek his own answers. This Fae means a great deal to our queen and she will stop at nothing to find him."

"Does this Fae have a name? There are many in the king's court."

"Ah, yes, he does." Oisin paused, seeming to select the words shared with Rione. Again, he gave Rione that curious look. "Are you loyal to King Remus? He is your...friend, is he not?"

Rione did not expect this turn of questions.

"I serve my people, and through this, I serve my king who rules them," he stated plainly. Though no longer faithful to his king, Rione's duty toward his people—his mother's people—remained. His loyalties lay in the soil he was raised upon and his vow as a Venator. "But I have not considered him my friend. Not for some time."

"Hmmm, yes, honor runs in our blood. But do you trust your old friend to do the same—to serve his people above all else?"

In these last fifty years, after Remus became king, the trust Rione held for his childhood companion waned. He suspected Remus's actions did not wholly align with his people's needs, and Rione saw something dark festering from the inside out. He blamed himself for it. But Rione wanted to believe Remus still cared, that he put his people first.

"I don't know," he said honestly, swallowing hard on the thought.

Oisin exhaled, nodding as if he had made up his mind about something. "What if I told you your father never returned to Erynelleth?"

Rione stared blankly at the elf. "What do you mean?"

"I seek Prince Uilliamu of the Isles of Erynelleth, the youngest son of Queen Áina Kuya. Your father."

~ 33 ~

BRYNJA

Særenfell

"I only said the one."

Instead, the king of Fíronbec had sent three. Two were sentinels, doused with tonic. Their eyelids drooped from the concoction but they managed to stand upright. Her letter explicitly stated the seeker should return alone.

More for us, then. Those arms and legs burst with muscle—well-fed. Give us some real blood. The voice pricked at her senses. She'd been able to temper it for a time, but the men's scent awakened the urge.

No matter. Her court needed to feed, so they would feed. And these men would do well to satiate their stomachs.

"Put them in the crypts." With a flick of her wrist, she ordered Signe to lock the two sentinels away.

Let us feast on them now! The voice cut into her skull, and she flinched.

Not now. Soon, she soothed. Æri came first.

Brynja pulled her gaze from the sedated men departing through the tower doors and toward the seeker.

Atticus did not appear much improved from their last meeting. He still stunk of the Bogs, though his clothes were less tattered, and perhaps his trembling had subsided a fraction.

"We meet again, Atticus."

The man took a knee. "Your Majesty."

"I assume you have something for me."

Atticus extracted the letter tucked in his satchel.

The dispatch looked crisp and luminescent against his ash-coated hands. A residue clung to the parchment. Brynja smelled it even from where she sat across the tower room, a sort of summer fruit with a musky undernote—no lacing of poison.

She curved a long, white finger toward Atticus, beckoning him to approach.

A vein palpitated at his neck, its rhythm increasing as he drew near.

Why not try him first?

No.

Please. Just a little taste.

Stop it.

Brynja endeavored to ignore the pulsing, focusing on the letter instead of the blood flowing beneath his skin. It had been so long since she tasted human blood. The primal instincts re-awakened and clawed through the layer of fraught control. Saliva pooled in her mouth, coppery and anticipant.

The letter fell into her outstretched hand, and she squashed the sensation down with her fervor to open the sealed parchment.

Instructing Atticus to stand away while she broke the burgundy wax, Brynja slid a small bone-carved dagger under the king's signet: a setting sun, its rays pointed like blades of a sword, and in the dome a wreath of laurel leaves looped downward, following the sun's curve. More of that scent wafted from the envelope—saccharine, like something on the verge of spoiling or having spent too much time in the heat.

In the room's cold silence, she read.

Written in Særenian—and though the words were borderline archaic—the fine penmanship took her aback. The king must have employed a scribe from his court, Brynja mused. She wet her lips as she scanned the parchment.

So her threat proved effective. Brynja suspected that if a Fíronian hunting pack had captured her sister, they'd likely take her to their sovereign. The realm's court would have discovered she held some worth by now. Although a distinguished hunter and engineer, Æri was not an accomplished liar, no matter how hard she tried. Even as children, their father saw right through her little tales. Except, perhaps, Æri's sentiments of the heart...despite Brynja's heightened senses, Æri veiled them well.

She loved her sister and Æri reciprocated, but they rarely displayed it to one another. They shared a cold, restless love, like flurries of snow clouds that refused to settle. Warmth between each other was something lost when their father died. Lost with an event that forged them both into what they were today.

Nonetheless, Æri had not forgiven Brynja for her mistake, Æri alone bearing the visible reminder. Sometimes, Brynja thought that if she had just stolen past the sentinels to visit her sister in the crypts while they waited out her quarantine those dark weeks after, things might have been different. But that time had passed.

Her eyes ran over the parchment again, and Brynja wondered if she had made another mistake.

Questioning ourselves are we? Remorse makes us weak. Release us. Let us take control, and we can make that guilt disappear. We can rule more efficiently without it.

No. *No.* She dampened the voice, tempting as it was to listen to it.

She had done the right thing.

Brynja dared not mention Æri as her sister to the king. Merely a court member she'd like returned—no need to give the king of Fíronbec more than he required. It wasn't a mistake. She only hoped Æri had attained enough sense not to reveal the snippet about her heritage.

The king acceded to her terms, yes—things were going to plan. He would not have agreed otherwise. Now she'd see if he was a man of his word.

She refolded the letter and meant to instruct Signe, but another Narkrye waited by the door. The golden blonde...what was her name? Something with an *E*...or maybe a *T*? Curse her rutted mind! Wait...yes. *Toril.* The impertinent one. She possessed a brashness that Signe lacked, evident by how she held her chin up when Brynja addressed her.

She smelled fear on this Narkrye, too—sensed it through her false bravado and reticent composure.

Brynja sighed. "Send for Signe. We need to begin preparations." In afterthought, she added, "Oh, and find this seeker a room. He's had an arduous journey."

Signe

Thunk.

"Nearly hit the heart with that one." Eydis tossed her blades.

Thunk, thunk.

They sliced through the shoulder of a straw-filled dummy. Tufts of hay scattered.

"Nearly."

Signe was throwing knives in the bailey with Eydis. A pastime reserved for expelling excess energy. Or, in Signe's case, heartache. She'd been in a sour funk since Æri's capture. Draug's blood, all the Narkrye had. At least she was alive; at least they had that.

"I left the seeker in one of the barracks' guest rooms." Toril entered the yard, flinging her braid over her shoulder with an exaggerated flare, then headed toward the small awning stocked with practice gear.

Signe refocused on the angle of her knife.

She hoped Toril had put him mercifully far, far away from the queen's court. With any luck, they'd have plenty to feast on after those two sentinels she'd just stored in the crypts.

Signe had half a mind to throttle the seeker from that stinking island—not that he, himself, did anything wrong; she just hated what he represented. But the queen wanted him alive to deliver her letters. Goddess knew what the messages contained. The queen refused to tell anyone and only relayed the basics to Signe.

"He's in dire need of a bath. Have you seen Hælga? Or perhaps Anneke. Her sense of smell hasn't returned since Yuletide...An arduous journey indeed." Toril muttered the last words.

Signe had seen Toril struggling not to cover her nose as they both accompanied Atticus to the tower room. A twinge of regret tickled Signe's throat. She should have returned to help Toril deal with Queen Brynja's orders.

Signe couldn't look at her just yet. She and Eydis remained absorbed in their target propped at the far end of the bailey.

The Narkrye had cleared the snow earlier that day, and now, only compact, frozen dirt remained. When was the last time she'd seen green grass in this yard? Or anything bloom for that matter—nothing since the Split. But fresh air gently caressed her cheeks, not the usual bone-chilling winds. And if she shut her eyes, it almost felt like early spring. Almost.

A gentle snowfall started up. Crystal flakes landed on her pelt-wrapped shoulders and knitted through her fiery hair. The light metallic scent of new snow ebbed and flowed in the yard.

After no reply, Toril shouted again. "You're welcome!" Another pause. "The queen demands your attendance again, Signe. It has something to do with that letter the seeker brought."

Signe released a long groan and chucked her blade. "I don't know how Æri did it—take orders from her and *not* go insane."

Eydis joined Toril at the table, her eyes roaming over various blades in the unrolled sheath. "I'm sure if Queen Brynja had a choice, she'd be happy to do some of the tasks on her own. She's lived vicariously through Æri for so long. The transition has to be difficult for both of you." Eventually, she picked a knife that suited her and wheeled around to throw it at the straw figure.

Signe closed her eyes. "It just gets...tedious."

"I'm going to have to side with Eydis on this one, Signe. I pity the queen. Definitely would not want to be in her shoes." Toril threw her dagger. *Thunk.* It landed in the dummy's chest. "It's not like Queen Brynja gets out much. She's locked herself in that tower. Probably got to her head, and she doesn't exactly favor council meetings. Remember what too many warm bodies do to her—even if they aren't ironbloods."

"And now you know what Æri went through." Eydis's scar broadened as she offered Signe a hopeful smile. "Maybe you can suggest sharing the load if we get her back?"

"Not if, when. *When* we get her back." Signe hurled her final knife at the dummy before marching off.

Bullseye. Right in the head.

Otta

"You're planning to give the king of Fíronbec what?" Otta's jaw felt as if it would sink to the stone floor.

"It's not like *I* want to hand over the fuel cells. These are direct orders from the queen." Signe's face looked haggard, the once subtle lines on her forehead more pronounced.

Otta walked back and forth in the drafting room. "Do you know how difficult it is to obtain and transport the gas tanks from the

Summer Castle? Jodi and I almost died last time. And we're going to give it away just like that—to this king?!"

Jodi had been shaken by the avalanche. True, they needed to learn. If they planned to be at Otta's side, survival skills started with experience, but Otta wasn't sure how willing they'd be to return after the scare.

Signe shook her head minutely. "We aren't giving it away. It's in exchange for Æri." A doleful expression passed over her face.

Otta stopped her pacing. She understood how much this meant to Signe. This was their chance to have Æri returned to them safely. "Do you have any clue what the king wants to do with it?"

Signe grimaced, seeming to steel herself for what she'd say next. "We're supposed to deliver one of the Skimmers."

Otta stared at her, gut calcifying. "We're not even halfway through the second one."

Signe's shoulders dropped, her voice betraying her exhaustion. "By the time we convene with the king, it should be finished. We can start training Toril to fly the second one."

Given the risks and skill it required, only Signe and Æri knew how to maneuver the Skimmers properly.

Otta plucked at her frazzled hair, knowing it made her look even more like a crazed scientist. "And he's agreed to surrender Æri if we exchange the Skimmer?

"Yes. He's agreed to negotiate."

Otta sat down on a workbench. Her staff's clanking and humming carried from the hangar, filling the silence. She heaved out a breath. "All right. I'll give the blacksmiths the orders. How many fuel cells are we to give this king?"

"I'd say just enough to power the aircraft. We'll need the rest for our own transport, and...well, the queen has something else in mind if things go haywire in the Bogs."

Otta's brows lifted in curiosity. Despite the additional pressures Signe had just unloaded, her eyes fixed on the first-in-command, ears pricked as she listened to the queen's plan.

~ 34 ~

ÆRI

A low, transcendent hum resonated in the skies. The small mass of scitators issued delighted whoops and cheers as the vessel hovered above the Inventorium.

"Well done, Æri! Well done!" Gratian's congratulatory voice oscillated as they lifted higher. He leaned treacherously beyond the rail, wreathed in smiles, displaying his tiny white teeth. His tufts of hair sprung out in woolly clumps, matching the occasional cloud puff.

After that vile day at the Games, Æri decided to no longer delay the production. If Rione intended to risk his troop with this contraption, she wouldn't endanger their lives with a half-finished aircraft and a faulty power source, nor let them occupy a vessel likely to crash if not adequately assessed first.

She'd finished installing the solar cells just short of a week before the deadline. Tomorrow, they planned to fly to the southern side of Fíronbec and back, testing the craft's durability.

Rione, expected to accompany her, would serve as guide and co-pilot, his navigation skills surpassing her own. Estimated to take four days, the journey included an additional day of rest in the realm's southernmost city, Kostros.

If all went well, they'd be ready for Dianeane.

But even with her attention focused on the Specuformae, Æri still felt reft, her actions now mechanical and automatic, her emotions all but drained from the nerve-wrenching events at the Games.

The king shattered her choices that day, and she was left to drag her messy pieces back to the domus. Hardly able to utter a word when they reached its doors, she somehow managed to explain to Rione why she kept her heritage a secret, why she didn't want the king to know—to possess that power over her. To her knowledge, Oisin was the only other being who held that information on Fíronbec. He and Yrsa...

A wicked sting lanced her chest when she thought of her Narkrye. Yrsa *survived* the crash, and Æri had abandoned her, wounded in the Bogs with the Blodlyst invading her system. Guilt ripped through her. She had broken her vow, forsaken her Narkrye, and now Yrsa's blood coated her hands.

She couldn't fathom what the king pried from her.

Had she told him? Divulged Æri's secret to the king?

No. Yrsa wouldn't have betrayed Æri. Perhaps King Remus suspected her royalty from the beginning—from that meeting at his villa—and all her efforts to keep her stupid secret were fruitless.

Doubts found their way inside and latched on. Her decision to save Yrsa had been a foolish illusion, and Oisin would have died if Rione had not stepped in. She had made the wrong decision. What if she made the wrong one again? Uncertainties plagued Æri as she thought back to all the reckless choices that bound her to Fíronbec—a slave *because* of those choices. .

And though she welcomed Rione's reassurances after the Games, they were brief. He needed to arrange the dealings for Oisin, leaving Æri with Ofelia and Leta at the domus. The women comforted her for a time, fetching a steaming pot of lavender and verbena tisane to soothe her nerves. Yet, she found herself counting the minutes and then the hours—*wanting* to see Rione, needing his steadiness amongst the chaos that broiled within her mind.

However, upon his return from the Cells, he had distanced himself, a foul mood rankling, evident from the loud thud of his boots on marble. Rione headed straight to the palestra, not stopping to look her way, and slammed the large doors. A clear sign no one should follow.

Since that night, his temperament had not improved. He withdrew from their evening meals, and although he continued to train with the troop, lashing out his usual orders, he kept away if it did not involve the Venators. Not just from Æri but from everyone. With that sliding door, he erected a wall, blocking himself from the rest of the world.

Desperate to know what had occurred at the Cells, she told herself his mood had nothing to do with her. And although her loneliness grew since he withdrew, he needed time to get through whatever irked him. Why should she prod? If he didn't want to talk, fine. And yet, again, that doubt wheedled its way in.

Had *she* forced this change?

As the days grew closer to their expedition to Dianeane, Rione found more and more excuses to be absent from the domus, and with Æri's own tasks taking her from the house, she never gained the opportunity to find out.

It certainly pleased Gratian. He did not comment on the miraculous advancement in production, simply marveled at the outcome. Æri admitted part of her too reveled, rewarded by seeing her endeavors come to life.

She adhered to the king's orders: to make a power source for one aircraft. Now it would be up to Gratian and his team of scitators to create more of it—if they could—and hope they maintained enough sense to thwart the king if he intended to use it for anything other than remapping the realms.

So, instead of dwelling on the concern, the doubts, and that tug—that little pull and spur of warmth between herself and Rione—she shoved it all down, like everything else out of her control, choosing to focus on something more tangible. For tomorrow, she would fly.

"Angle the rotors!"

Æri shouted to her crew as they scrambled across the deck to adjust the gyrating oars. They steered through the Fíronian skies. An experience both old and new, the cool winds swept her skin, and Gyr glided alongside—Æri was airborne again.

The Specuformae did not have the same speed as her Skimmer, but there were advantages to the large vessel. Able to hold a crew of twenty or so men, it could fly indefinitely, as long as the sun's rays shone on its rotating wings. Smooth black strips of the molded ore shimmered on the hull's flanks—the harvester she had toiled over these last months. It collected the sun's energy and stored it in the chambers below deck. If no light beamed, the fuel cells could power the ship for up to two weeks with no additional input.

Æri roped off the galver and called for a crew member to take the controls. Then she strode through the body of the ship to reach its bow. She was not going to miss the incredible view.

Kostros's creamy white walls curved like a crescent moon from this vantage, their alabaster ramparts protecting the luminous buildings within. A river roared below and then divided into a vast delta. It branched out like roots across the southern peninsula of Fíronbec, fringing Kostros. The trickling rivulets emptied into an elaborate system of moats that bordered the island's rim, preventing the precious water from plummeting into the Bogs.

"Mesmerizing, isn't it?" Rione joined her at the rail but kept a distance between them. "I've never seen it like this before."

Æri resisted the inclination to put her hand next to his; the desire to feel his warmth gnawed at her. Compared to his habitually composed self, he looked disheveled; stubble grazed his jaw and bordered on the beginnings of a beard, and bloodshot eyes hinted that he'd been forgoing sleep. He had hiked up the aviation goggles they all wore, mussing his hair, and strands fell into his face—not weaved into plaited rows. Instead, a single braid hung loose down his back. Something troubled him and, in turn, troubled her.

Beholding the city, Rione ignored her chary look. "Kostros was once the closest port to the Isles of Erynelleth."

Æri resisted the urge to rebuke him, listening as he spoke. He hadn't talked to her directly since the Games.

"They've managed to harness the water that derives from the Osar River over there"—his finger outlined the massive waterway flowing from the north—"so the city resembles a seaport village—when you're on ground level. The streets are all canals."

"Have you been here before?"

"Only as a child. The old king and his court often summered in the city..." The ship rocked, and his grip tightened on the rail as he lingered on the words.

Was it his memories or the odd sensation of flying that made him hesitate?

When the ship steadied again, his grip didn't loosen.

"Before the separations, the Fae frequented the port. It was a prominent stop along their trade routes. Only a handful of freed elves remained when we visited, and obviously, they no longer sailed from Erynelleth."

His words sparked a nettling question that dwelt in the back of her mind since her capture. "Why did King Lucius break the oath outlawing slavery?"

"To sustain our lands." Rione's answer came out blunt, and when Æri crinkled her brow, he continued. "The idea manifested when he offered an indenture to the Fíronian people. He originally intended the indenture for those who couldn't afford to pay their taxes or had lost their land from the separations. It enabled them to put food in their stomach, while in turn, the king gained subjects to work his lands."

"You make it sound as if it was a good thing." She leaned her forearms on the rail, stretching the new leathers that sheathed her arms. The warm breeze loosened her braid, her hair now long enough to twist into one.

"Many acts of power initially stem from good intentions." Rione angled his body to face her. "His intentions were moral to begin with. He needed to save his people and the land, and that was one solution. But...then he realized the prisoners seized in the Bogs carried certain talents and found use for them in other ways."

"Like in the Games?"

"Yes." Rione confirmed, his brown eye grave. "Another way to satiate a troubled population. King Remus merely capitalized on this after his father passed."

He tilted his head and offered her a long, measured look. One that tore away the days of silence—a calm and steady gaze of unsaid words struggling to surface. The depth of emotion in it consumed her.

She quickly turned to look up at Gyr, trying to block what that stare conveyed—before it nestled in. "It's too bad Oisin couldn't join us. Who knows, he might have been one of those seafaring elves."

Rione stiffened, and Æri knew she'd hit a nerve, the tension palpable.

"Yes, well, the king has him locked in the Cells until we journey to Dianeane. I just had the one night to talk." He seemed to grapple with his control, turmoil roiling within but not yet willing to share its burden.

She silently willed him to go on. Returning her gaze to his, she cautiously opened that door again.

His eye flickered, and darkness waved behind it. "I meant to tell you..." His voice trailed off. "I wanted to find a place away from prying eyes and ears."

It was an opening in return.

Æri gestured about the deck, swiftly placing her foot in the doorway before he slammed it shut again. "This is the best you'll get, Rione."

She had selected a bare minimum crew for the trip in case something went awry. At the moment, every member of the skeleton crew busied themselves, engrossed in keeping the vessel afloat. Just the two pilots took a respite from their duties, the only ones at the bow. With the wind lashing past them, their words would be lost to anyone nearby.

So Rione told her about Oisin and who the Fae queen sought.

"Your father never returned to Erynelleth?" Æri took in the information in stride but struggled to hide her astonishment.

Rione sucked in a breath, the topic plainly still raw. "According to Oisin, no. They've been looking for him for years. He said their queen refuses to give up. Somehow she knows he's alive."

Æri ran her tongue over her chipped tooth. So, the title of *Lord* fit Rione, after all. Not the son of a slave, but a prince. No wonder Rione's mood had changed so drastically. For years, he believed his father had returned to his homeland, only to discover otherwise.

"Do you know where he could be?"

Rione shook his head. "Neither do the Fae. That's why his queen sent Oisin here. They got wind he was residing in Fíronbec. It took years—decades—for them to attain that information. Even so, Oisin arrived too late. My father left long before Oisin arrived."

"So, what now?"

Rione leaned farther back on the rail. "I haven't decided. I can't tell Remus—that's clear."

Rione was right. He'd be in the same bind as her if the king learned of the connection.

A shout came from the crew member at the galver. He waved for her to return, interrupting their tête-à-tête.

More calls arose from across the deck. A calmer branch of the Osar's delta emerged below, the marked location outside Kostros where they'd arranged to anchor the vessel.

Rione and Æri took one last look at the approaching city.

"Camilla will be there." Rione gestured with his chin. "Ismene frequents the city. She prefers it to Méritras."

"Your mother will be in Kostros?"

A solemn nod in confirmation. "I meant to invite her to the domus, but with everything..."

"Have you told her yet? About your father?"

"No, but I will. She has a right to hear it."

With his assertion, an unexpected phrase flared through Æri's thoughts. *You are two sides of the same coin.* Ofelia had said the words to her a few weeks prior. Æri had thrown the remark aside, thinking it ridiculous. She was nothing like Rione.

But now, *now*...Æri understood what Ofelia meant by it. With this, she gained a glimpse into the demi-Fae's true self. Not the Venator or battle strategist of the king, nor all the other masks he bore. Like herself, he was a subject loyal to his family, to his people, and willing to do anything for them in return.

As if the gods guided her along, Æri saw her path. This choice was her own to make. Not some trick played by a jesting sovereign but given to her by a man who valued his promises above all else.

"I've decided." Her words came out surer than she felt. Æri didn't need to specify what she meant.

"Are you certain?" He regarded her, a determined glint in his eye. Something else also lay there beneath the stone resolve. Not the same dejection she'd seen at the tournament nor the worry from after the Games...an underlying drop of sadness, perhaps? Longing?

She bottled the uncertainty, shoving all her doubts inside. This was the next choice she would make. Æri inhaled. "Yes. I'm certain."

~ 35 ~

ÆRI

The courier forced down gulps of air, mouth agape like a fish just reeled from water. Having no horses to spare, he had raced on foot through the narrow city streets of Méritras and out to the Inventorium's fields where they prepared the launch.

"Rione?" The courier panted. "I have a message for Rione."

Æri looped her thumb to where Rione loaded food crates with his troop.

The Specuformae fared well to Kostros and back, and without any complications, they were prepared to leave that afternoon.

Beyond the gasping courier, a handful of spectators assembled at the temporary fence. Most were dwellers from the local town that skirted Méritras, but some had trekked from the city to watch the ship depart.

The morning sun's tormenting rays offered little relief for those hauling provisions. Æri mopped sweat from her forehead, glad Gratian had kept the fanfare to a minimum. Not even the king intended to see them off. He had departed the city the day afore, presumably to one of his country villas, leaving his steward, Odoacer, in charge of royal decrees. Not fond of either man, she was keen to get going.

A total of twenty-three would board—the five Venators, with an addition of twelve crew members to man the Specuformae.

The king also required two of his sentinels, an official, a cartographer, and to Æri's grievance, not Reverend Cormac, but one of his acolytes instead. Procul—proficient in the Dianeane language and customs—would serve as a translator when they arrived at the Realm of Gods.

Oisin was the last addition to the Dianeane group—whenever, of course, the officials released him from the Cells. Even after Rione secured his paperwork, they had retained the elf on the king's command.

Curiosity piqued, Æri followed the zealous messenger to Rione's side. The man bounced on alternating feet as if his shoes were fashioned of hot iron, heedless of his apparent exhaustion.

Others in the troop drew in, their interest, too, fueled by the dispatch's urgency.

Rione set down his crate, and the courier thrust the parchment into his freed hands. An insignia, stamped where the two folded ends met, foretold the letter's sender.

"It's from the Curia." He broke the seal in haste.

Rione's shoulder blades retracted, eye remaining fixed on the letter.

"What does it say?" Æri blurted, unable to take the suspense any longer.

Rione took a stride away from the group and inclined his face to the empty sky, avoiding others' eyes. "Oisin's dead."

The cords in Æri's throat strained. *Dead?*

When Rione looked back at them, his expression held that impenetrable mask again.

"Figures." Sten scowled, shuffling his feet back and forth, while Tye crossed and then uncrossed his arms, little sparks escaping from his fingertips. Knjal clapped a hand over Rione's shoulder as he shook his head in dismay. The air crackled and buzzed with the Venators' agitation.

"Does the message give any details?" Æri scraped at her mind to find a reason for it. She couldn't believe it—*wouldn't* believe it.

"No." Rione balled the paper in his fist.

Glancing back and forth between the hunters, the courier looked uncertain, his voice cracking. "Shall I send a message in return, Lord Rione?"

"I'll go myself."

Rione made for Juno tethered outside the designated launch zone, his hand hastily freeing her reins from the hitching post. "We're not delaying the flight. Adhere to the plan. I'll return ere noon."

Without another word, he kicked his heels into Juno's flank, tearing toward the direction of the city walls.

Just as the crew finished their checks and the sun had risen to a blazing beacon above them, Rione galloped into the launching zone.

"Leaving as scheduled?" Sten yelled as Rione re-tied Juno and thudded over.

"Yes."

"And Oisin?" Æri hoped he brought fairer news. Looking a little worse for wear, he nursed a slash across his cheek and a rip on his tunic's sleeve. Had he been in a fight?

"I've arranged a proper burial with Cosmos." Rione's mouth grew thin. His eye flicked around as he inhaled. Æri knew he was debating his next words, cautious with the other crew members hovering. "It took some persuasion, but they permitted me to inter him within my family's vault. He was under my ownership after all."

The reality of his confirmation knocked the wind out of Æri. Oisin was gone.

Her eyes pricked with tears threatening to spill. Though she held no genuine connection to the elf, a sense of sorrow wrenched through her, his death somehow reminding her of a past she liked to keep buried deep. Æri prayed his soul found Vallantheia.

The troop purposefully busied themselves in the final hour before the launch, their departure serving as a good distraction.

Æri stole glances at Rione. Nothing in his stance or booming voice betrayed his thoughts; his attention was solely focused on stocking the last of their supplies—including one large rectangular crate.

"Scriptures from the king's collection," he said. "A gift for the priests and priestesses of Dianeane." They needed something of value for the holy court if they intended to get suitable answers.

As the crew carried the crate up the accommodation ladder, Æri spotted a furry black-and-white tail. It whipped and weaved between the men's legs—the pelt identical to that of the villa's polecat. She rubbed at her sore eyes and blinked, but no animal scampered there, only the crew trudging up the rickety wooden steps with that cumbrous crate.

~ 36 ~

BRYNJA

The Bogs

"Ah, the queen of Særenfell finally graces me with her presence."

The king of Fíronbec had arrived late, and he opened with *these* words? Brynja seethed, clinging to the end of her tether. It irked her all the more his Særenian sounded near perfect, the words falling from his mouth with natural ease.

Despite draining the sentinel before departing the fortress, the Blodlyst pulsated under her skin. The excess of ironbloods addled her wits, their odor wending above the stink of brimstone. Restlessness welled.

Feed on them, taste their blood, the voice bade. It twisted like a trapped worm. Brynja attempted to snuff its scratching, clenching her fists and letting the bite of her nails maintain her reality.

Why did she agree to come here?

She had not left her keep in years. *Years.* The journey to the Bogs tired her to the bone. Brynja longed for the ice of her fortress, its cold more tolerable than this oppressive heat. Even with her light leathers, she held her arms from her body, her skin vexing from the rising warmth of the black stones. This holm they agreed to convene upon—an intermediate between her realm and Fíronbec—was in the middle of goddess blessed knew where, and this king had made her *wait*. If he weren't the king of Fíronbec, she'd have his heart by now.

Ten bulky sentinels were grouped behind the king, shoulder to shoulder, in orderly rows—all clad in the same protective black-and-red armor. The spiked candescent crown upon the sovereign's golden head was the only item distinguishing him from his brood. Well...other than the tall one at his side. His violet eyes and raked-back hair—as black as the rocks around them—clearly identified him as a man not from Fíronbec.

Æri was nowhere in sight.

Brynja's chest squeezed upon seeing the assemblage.

Negotiations indeed. She wanted to laugh.

The two realms looked prepared for battle as their convoys faced each other, an imposing gap separating them.

Two of her best Narkrye flanked her. The rest hovered on the Boars with a handful of their skilled underlings. Not an army, but—with their aptitude—she'd hoped it sufficient...Yet, counting the number of men he brought along...

"King Remus." Brynja sneered, her way of welcoming anything but genial.

To make matters worse, a sort of aeronautical device was suspended above them. It looked more like a battleship than an aircraft. Additional sentinels stood at attention against its rails, making her Narkrye slightly outnumbered.

With careless air, King Remus moved a hand to his floating ship. Her neck craned. The vessel's wings moved at such a high speed its pod-shaped hull looked as if it levitated in midair. Whirls of floating ash and a low thrum were the only indications propellers kept it afloat.

"Do you like it? It is a marvelous contraption. I would have preferred it to our chariots, but we're still testing this one out."

This one. Did this mean he owned others? More of these battle-ships? She suppressed the rising bile, not wanting to think of the repercussions—of what it meant.

He might be bluffing.

Brynja crooked her head to view the king's ground transport: a glossy onyx cart made to match the volcanic rock that sur-rounded it. Harnessed to the yoke were four massive horselike beasts, snarling and stomping on the earth; black scales crawled up their limbs. Their muzzles foamed with recent exertion.

Well, then, perhaps he did not bluff.

She squeezed her bare hands again, having forgone her gloves. Though now, a shred of her wished she wore the ore-clad instru-ments and her blade, Banisleif. Despite her fitted arium chest plate and the griffin head covering that replaced her thorned crown, Brynja feared she looked as weak as she felt. But the gloves acted as tools—not for negotiations, and Banisleif served one purpose: to relieve the pain of her own kind, not kill Fíronian men. She was grateful her Narkrye had donned their blue hunting paint, the dis-tinctive patterns etched across their cheeks and foreheads.

The king continued, seeming to enjoy the sound of his voice.

"You can thank your sister for the aircraft's completion. I so badly wanted to show you her hard work, and I fretted she wouldn't have it ready in time. But she fulfilled her task quite com-petently...with a little pushing."

Brynja's breath hitched, and the Narkrye emitted a collective hiss, hands poised over loaded crossbows and daggers.

So, the king had learned of Æri's relation. But why would she aid him in the first place? His words opened a slew of questions. Had he hurt her? Or worse...*Where was she?*

Brynja did not know this king—had never met him to assess his character, but so far, he had done nothing to gain her favor, quite the opposite. King Remus blazed with an arrogance that almost blinded her in the Bogs' haze. All air of diplomacy had reputedly departed with his late father.

She mentally counted to ten, her patience waning. No matter now how he identified Æri. She was finished talking to this...man, a semblance of a king. All she desired to do was leave this hell of a holm with her sister.

"Where is Æri?" Brynja jerked her hand to the Skimmer. "That stays with us until she is returned."

"Ah, yes. A valid question." King Remus tapped a finger to his lips and then fished in a satchel at his hip as if he had lost a pair of spectacles. Finally, he withdrew a silver-blue torc that matched her own—Æri's birth band.

Signe snarled louder. Her hand pulled at her dagger's hilt, but Brynja gestured for the second to stand down. It wasn't time. Not yet. If this boy-king wanted to play, let him play. Ending it too soon may make his actions shift. Spoiled little boys threw tantrums when they didn't get their way.

She waited as the king goaded them, flipping the precious torc between his tanned fingers the way one handled a cheap trinket. It was a mockery. He knew the value of that torc.

"Æri's off running a small errand for me. However, I am sure if she knew we were meeting, she wouldn't have missed it for the world. But not to worry, she's in good hands."

"Are you saying you did not bring her?"

"That is correct."

"Then you're wasting my time." Brynja strained to veil her indignation. A vein on her neck palpitated. She came here for nothing. "The deal is off. If she isn't here, we're leaving." She signaled her Narkrye to power up the Skimmers and Boars.

"Wait!"

King Remus took a step into that charged space between them as her crew turned away. A whiff of that sickly-sweet fruit cloyed her senses, overpowering the men's coursing blood. It made her want to gag. However, desperation lingered in his words, the mocking tone now gone.

Brynja slowly rotated back, willing her expression to remain cold.

"I would like to make you another offer." He held out the silver torc.

She made no move to take it. "I don't make deals with liars."

King Remus extended his arms, hands open in defense. "I haven't lied. In my letter, I said I'd agree to negotiate. To quote my words, *Æri of Særenfell will be released from my bondage in exchange for the aircraft and its power source.* I did not explicitly say I would bring your sister *here.* Anyhow, I've sent her on a mission that benefits us both. Lord Rione Aulius, my lead strategist, is squiring her, and I vow no harm will come to her as long as she stays with him. When she returns from her task, she'll be allowed to return to Særenfell."

Brynja snorted incredulously. "And you thought I would trust your word on that? Hand over our aircraft with nothing in return but your *word?*"

Why did his strategist's name sound so familiar...Rione. Should the king not have him by his side today instead of on some name-less excursion? She dug into her memory. This accursed Blodlyst affected that as well. A moment passed, and then it connected—*the lead huntsman from the Bogs*—recalling Atticus's description of him. Why would Æri agree to accompany the man who captured her? Too many pieces were missing to make any sense.

King Remus lowered his outstretched arm, his fingers tighten-ing around the metal band. "No. I hoped to make another deal to-day. A treaty."

Brynja crossed her arms, evaluating the worth of hearing the king out. The Boars continued to hum from behind. She had yet to call her crew to switch them off.

Signe went taut beside her. "I don't trust him."

Brynja ignored the second, rolling her lips back. "Make it quick."

King Remus nodded and straightened as though he had prepared this speech centuries ago. "I believe we are similar, you and I."

Brynja cocked a pallid eyebrow, hoping her face showed her cynicism, but did not attempt to stop him, a sliver of amusement sneaking its way in. She tilted her head, curious to see how far he decided to take this moronic speech.

"Two young rulers who want to do what is best for their realms."

True...on her end.

He waited for her attention. She realigned her head and nodded, ultimately giving it.

"The treaty between my dearly deceased father, King Lucius, and your past relations has faded with these wasted years. And since the separations, many of our rules have been lost. I want to propose a new alliance—one that would ensure both our realms' survival."

"An alliance." She meditated on this proposal. "Entailing what exactly?"

"A trade between our people. We will open our borders, share our resources, and in return, you will do the same for us. You may require some agricultural necessities—fruits, wheat, even livestock. We have these. Our soil is fertile. Yet, we do not have ore." He lifted the torc as an example.

Brynja knew her people could reap from such agreements, but she wasn't eager to agree just yet. "Again, there is no guarantee you will honor this new alliance. How do you propose to do so if I consider this bargain? You've shown little respect thus far."

King Remus swept a small bow in apology. "Forgive me, Queen Brynja. In Fíronbec, our greetings can be considered bellicose to outsiders. I am not yet practiced in your customs." He held out the torc again. "I can start by returning this to you—as a peace offering. Then we can discuss logistics. I am prepared to write an agreement if you so wish...?"

She made King Remus hold the silver birth band a little longer, letting him believe she may turn down his offer. His arm twitched with strain.

Then, surprising herself, she signaled her Narkrye to shut down the Boars.

"Signe, retrieve the birth band."

Unease flickered in Signe's eyes, but she obeyed, stepping forward. Tension rippled through the rest of the Narkrye. They dared not loosen their stances, their hostile glares remaining on the king's men.

Signe took purposeful strides toward the king's outstretched arm. She held her palm just below his fist, not risking closer proximity. His fingers uncurled from the silver circle, and it dropped into Signe's hand. Her arm bobbed with the weight of it. Once secured in her palm, she quickly pulled back to the cover of her Narkrye crew.

"One step closer to a resolution." The king's lips curved. "Shall I call my scribe to begin the documents?"

Brynja nodded curtly and took the reclaimed torc from Signe.

Her family's invaluable heirloom, her sister's possession, the esteemed item now returned. She studied the torc. A simple twisting of metal, like a cord. Three small loops decorated each end of the open circle, identical to her own. But something was wrong. The woven metal felt warm—too warm, growing hotter as she held it in her exposed hand—as if she touched an open flame. Pain blazed, and she released the torc on instinct. It clattered onto the porous rock, rolling toward Signe.

Nothing coated her palm. No visible burns, boils, or blisters, but her hand seared with agony. She fought against digging her nails in and tearing at the skin. The painful sensation licked up her arms, increasing with every thump of her heart. Collapsing to her knees, she ignored the stabs of the volcanic rock, the twinge nothing compared to what coursed under her skin.

"What—what did you do?" Her icicled stare targeted the king as her mind fuzzed, pain making it unbearable to speak.

King Remus didn't move as Brynja writhed. A smug grin darkened his beautifully wicked features; his eyes burned cunning and fox-like, the pupils dilated. He seemed entertained as the Narkrye gawked in stunned silence. It arose so quickly, their reactions too slow—too sluggish to do anything but stare. Yet realization gradually emerged on their faces.

Signe promptly took command.

Signe

She swerved around to her crew, signaling to aim their weapons high, prepared to wreak havoc.

Too late. The king's court matched their pointed arrows, bows taut and ready to fire, both sides in a deadlock.

King Remus's grin stretched, clearly enjoying the knife's edge. "Æri requested that I help her find a cure for your 'Blodlyst,' as your people call it. I looked into it when a troop brought in your comrade...Her name was Ycira? Yyra—"

"Yrsa!" Toril roared next to Brynja. "Her name was *Yrsa*."

"Ah, yes, Yrsa...Well, it seemed she possessed your 'Blodlyst.' Told me so much about your realm for just a drop of my men's blood. Coincidently, she was the perfect subject to help 'find a cure.' But instead, my researchers unintentionally created something that reacts with the skin."

Signe reflexively stuck out her hands. The king's hands were bare too. Neither of them wore gloves. How were they not affected?

"It's a peculiar substance." The king spoke to Signe, comprehending her unsaid words. "It won't harm just anyone. It wouldn't have even harmed your queen. But I took a gamble. The toxin only reacts when two blood diseases mix. You see, my people have another blood illness. It's harmless to most, but on occasion, it can kill. I thought it might have related to your Blodlyst, but they couldn't be more contradictory: Where one causes a craving, a need for more, the other expels it.

"However, we discovered—and unfortunately for Yrsa—if the two diseases overlap and the individual is exposed to this new substance, a reaction occurs. It's absorbed through the skin and rapidly flows within the blood. Though not a cure, I believed it convenient." The king clicked his tongue, shaking his head in feigned sorrow. "Pity those guards I sent with Atticus did not return with him. If your people looked closer, they might have seen the rashes."

"You're a bastard." Toril bared her teeth in a growl.

He held up a finger and pouted. "Actually, no. That would be unfitting. I am not a bastard. My father loved my mother dearly."

How could he be so flippant—so nonchalant when they were on the brink of war? Like a fox provoking a pack of hounds. Yet, the fox bore an army and did not fear being trapped.

Realizing the torc was still at her feet, Signe scrambled for it. Not knowing what to do, she fumbled with the heirloom, eyes flitting back and forth between the object and her crumpled queen. The invisible substance likely coated her hands, and the Narkrye dared not lower their weapons to help. In the end, she placed it around her arm, out of the way.

Brynja sent another keening scream as the toxin spread. Streaks of blood ran up her arms where her nails had broken skin.

"Make it stop!" Signe shouted, fearing to touch the queen in case of inflicting more damage.

The king's smile waned. "I cannot. She needs the antidote."

The queen thrashed on the ground, her screaming ebbing into whimpers. Tears streamed down her blanched cheeks.

"Can't or won't?" Signe riposted. Her core wanted to burst with how inept she felt. "Will she die?"

"No. Just pain."

"Then give us the antidote," Toril commanded, pure revulsion infusing her tone. Her crossbow pointed at the king's chest.

"Now, why would I do that? Anyway, it's not on my person. I left it in Fíronbec." King Remus skewed his head, studying the queen at a distance—his science experiment. "She'll have to return with us...or you could wait and see if the chemical leeches from her system, but that may take some time. And pain can do strange things to the brain when it persists."

"Why are you doing this?" Signe's voice shook. It took every muscle in her not to throw that sheathed dagger at her belt into the king's heart.

"You can say I take the threat of war very, very seriously." His mouth transformed from the satirical grin into a grimace, warping his empyrean features. "The note your queen sent made it clear what she wanted. No one threatens me, nor my realm." He fastened his stare on Signe, his smile larkish again. "Besides, I'd prefer it the other way around. I've never taken a winter holiday."

What had Queen Brynja done? Signe's jaw clenched. "If you think for an instant I'd allow you to take my queen back to your realm—"

"I thought you might say that." As he said this, he twirled his finger, gesturing for her to look around.

Movement stirred, and more sentinels materialized from the holm's rock.

But the Narkrye had checked the holm before. How was this possible?

Somehow they missed it. The men had lain in wait undetected, camouflaged in their black gear, and now they barricaded her crew.

Unabated dread went straight to the pit of Signe's stomach as she realized her mistake. The king had not arrived late. He only wanted them to believe it. A trap all along.

"Drop your weapons," he ordered.

None of the Narkrye moved, all waiting for Signe's final command.

Lost in pain, Queen Brynja had furled herself into a ball, helpless as a child. The king's men grossly outnumbered them.

If she reached for her dagger, how many of her Narkrye would fall before she threw it?

She couldn't risk it. Not now.

Having no other choice, Signe gave the signal, and her crew lowered their weapons.

"I am glad you can see reason."

King Remus motioned to the tall, purple-eyed man. "We'll give your queen a sedative to dull the pain until she reaches Fíronbec." The cloaked man approached them, a pointed syringe in hand. He injected her queen before Signe could object and scooped up her limp form as if she weighed no more than a griffin's feather, turning toward their floating ship.

"You don't play by the rules." Signe's hand found her dagger's hilt.

"Ah ah ah." King Remus wagged his finger, and she hissed as another sentinel snuck in from behind, bending her arm back to release the fisted blade.

"If I played by the rules, I wouldn't win, now, would I?" The king flicked at an invisible piece of dust from his vambrace. "And I like to win."

White rage poured into Signe. She held one more move. Her queen would not have folded so fast, nor would Æri. They'd fight till the end.

Signe locked eyes with Disa, the Narkrye closest to the Boars. Then shot her gaze to Toril. They were ready. It was suicide, but they had to try.

A slow smile formed on Signe's lips to mirror the king's. "Well, then. It's a good thing we don't play by the rules either."

Signe stomped on the sentinel's foot, her metal heel puncturing the leather of his boot while spiraling her arm away. She dove for her fallen dagger, and before the sentinel could comprehend what was happening, she swiped the honed blade across his neck. Dark blood spewed across her leathers. Chaos erupted around them.

Disa swung her leg over her Boar, immediately rising into the air. Toril tore for one of the Skimmers. Her crew fought tooth and nail against the black-suited men, holding their ground. They just needed enough time to mobilize all of the Boars.

Gaze whipping over her shoulder, she cursed. The purple-eyed man had loaded the queen onto the ship. Signe bolted for the remaining Skimmer, hoping to catch the ship in flight.

Disa was waving her arms, yelling at them above the madness—trying to warn the clashing Narkrye. Simultaneously, the rocky terrain trembled beneath their feet.

"Pull back!" Signe called to her crew.

As they ran for their Boars, the earth moaned again. The sentinels shifted their stances—some shared looks of confusion with the lost balance. Signe reeled around to look at the king one more time—his lips mutated into that devilish sneer. His fiendish eyes speared into hers as if he intended to slay her with them. Instead, his lip curved higher, and he winked—a fox taunting his hound. King Remus pivoted and fled for his ship.

Like a bolt of lightning, Signe gripped the hilt of her blood-stained dagger and threw. It sailed true, right toward his head.

The earth quaked again. Not waiting to see if the blade found its intended mark, she ran for her Skimmer.

Signe flung herself into the cockpit, the engine revved. Rocks swelled in a low wave. The land ripped. A roar erupted from the holm like a beast awakening from a deep slumber. The ground buckled. Fissures of molten magma gushed. Another reverberating crack and the world turned red.

~ 37 ~

RIONE

The Bogs

A black, lapidarian landscape stretched below the ship, out into the nothingness. Rione was used to the desolation, but not from this vantage. They passed the Bogs' thick shroud without much turbulence. Mists ebbed and flowed about the ship, accompanied by the sulfurous reek of a kindling earth beneath.

He supposed it ironic how, after vowing never to own a slave, he owned two within a few short months. Now he'd be losing them both within the same week.

Rione's thoughts strayed to the wooden crate below deck. He'd try to make this right, even if that meant defying his king and the Curia's orders. They seemed obsolete at any rate. The expedition to Dianeane would have to wait until he completed this undertaking. He owed it to Oisin—his father's friend.

After the dispatch from Odoacer, Rione rode to the Cells with one goal in mind. He resisted crediting the words on that page until he saw what happened to Oisin firsthand.

Based on the report, guards had found a crude knife beside the Fae's body, created from an earthenware oil lamp. The elf sliced right through his neck, severing the carotid artery. Though, what distressed Rione more was what Oisin had done prior—cut out his tongue and broke every finger in his left hand. Rione only held speculative guesses as to why.

Upon his arrival at the Cells, a maid was mopping the floor of the dingy chamber, the bubbles turning pink with her scrubs. A metallic scent remained in the air, heavy over its usual fetid stench. Initially, the warden refused to let Rione take the body, but after a persuasive "chat," Rione had carted Oisin's shrouded form over a shoulder and left that rotting prison. His knuckles still ached from the reluctant blows. Rione's stomach twisted. He preferred not to use force to get things done.

"Lost in thought?" Æri said from behind.

His muscles tightened, all too aware of how close she stood.

"Aren't you supposed to be steering?" He huffed, focusing on the bleak horizon.

"Tye's got it. He's a decent third officer—if one doesn't mind an electric jolt once in a while."

Rione cocked his head, tearing his gaze from the barren expanse. The corner of his mouth quirked, offering her a ghost of a smile.

"Thinking about Oisin?"

Rione gave a single nod. He had told his troop the details after they launched. However, he decided to withhold the information about Oisin's tongue and fingers, thinking it would raise too many questions on the ship. They shouldered enough with the journey ahead, and he didn't want them distracted by something he couldn't fix. Rione planned to tell them eventually, he just needed time.

Æri already insisted Oisin's death did not sit right, arguing the elf wouldn't take his life, that it was all too suspicious, too convenient with their departure. But the evidence stated otherwise. Save for Rione, the guards listed no other visitors, and he discovered no indication of foul play. Though, Æri had a point. Would

Remus sink that low? Surely the elf held more value alive. He couldn't believe Oisin inflicted such wounds on himself.

Rione examined Æri raptly, striving to memorize her resolute face, the line of her jaw, her small sharp-tipped nose, and those ice-blue, bird-bright eyes. Dark tendrils of hair danced in front of those eyes, and he resisted the impulse to tuck them behind her ear. Rione's throat clenched, and he cast an eye over the terrain again, knowing this part of the Bogs by heart. He intentionally switched topics, not wanting to dwell on the subject of Oisin or Æri.

"Are you ready? We're nearly there."

Æri

Æri rubbed at the pink mark where the tracking device used to be, unsure how to respond to Rione's words.

Was she ready? Even after what happened with Oisin? It hadn't changed anything...at least with what she chose to do.

She held out her bionic arm, signaling Gyr to fly in. He landed on the metal with a quiet click. Æri guided him to the vessel's rail, where he secured his talons. They were long past the borders of Fíronbec. Headed north as expected—but not toward Dianeane.

Rione raised his arm to Tye, motioning him to slow the rotors, and the Specuformae lurched, then started to lower toward the raw earth. The hull shook as the ship descended. Æri and Rione clutched at the rail, their fists momentarily touching, and she suppressed a shiver.

A bony man with a polished head bobbed from below deck.

"What is this? What is happening!?" the official yawped above the roaring hum, his hands flailing. "Why have we stopped? We cannot land here."

Rione stepped in line with Æri. "We can, and we will. Æri of Særenfell has requested to return home."

A weight lifted from her shoulders with those words, its lightness odd but welcoming.

"You are not permitted to free her. She is first and foremost the property of the king." The official adjusted the rucks on his maroon robe, but the wind untidied them again.

The two appointed sentinels edged nearer, leaving their positions at the end of the hull, alerted by the official's bleats.

"No, she is not," Rione amended. "Æri of Særenfell has been released from the Fíronian binding." He removed the authorized documents from his satchel.

The official's face scrunched as if he sucked on a lemon. He snatched the papers out of Rione's hands, inspecting them with his gangly fingers. His eyes tapered into thin slits. "And where is the band to prove it? I see no ring."

"It's here." Rione probed at his breast pocket, withdrawing a leather pouch. He emptied the contents onto his palm. A delicate ring rolled to the center. *Silver.* Metal was so precious in Fíronbec, silver even more so—a small fortune. How had Rione obtained the currency? The design was basic, hammered into a rough circle, bearing the resemblance of a twig bent into a slender loop.

Rione reached for her but halted, leaving his palm open. Struggling to quell her rapid heartbeat, Æri carefully placed her right hand into his. His calloused fingers grazed against her own as he positioned the circle onto her fourth finger, the cool metal sliding over the width. It fit perfectly.

Heat flushed through her. That warm, tingling sensation of skin against skin reawakened the memory, taking her back to a night less than a week ago.

Æri had tried not to let her trembling show as she stood in front of the Kostros official, her body enveloped in tiny gooseflesh—the truth of what she agreed upon sinking in.

Camilla, positioned quietly in the pews, held a small, wistful smile—their only witness. Scents of orange blossoms and lavender floated in from an open window, merging with Rione's woodsy one.

His tall stature stooped to reach her own, and their mouths met. His lips pressed against hers, the rough palms of his hands cupping her chin.

The single chaste kiss, a soft caress that passed at the end of their vows, officially marked their union. So brief and gentle, yet her body was electrified with it, everything pulsating, down to her very core and out to the tips of her toes. He tasted like bergamot and smoke, of firewood just starting to kindle. The sensation thawed the frost inside, her snow-covered mountains finally feeling the subtle warmth of spring.

Æri played it off as if it was nothing, ignoring that her bones purred with the light touch—an altogether new feeling. She sensed the compulsion to dive into that budding awareness—wanted to wrap it about her, lose herself in it.

But Æri knew it to be reckless and cursed herself for even allowing the fleeting moment. She hadn't permitted it with Signe; why should she with Rione? And letting others know of it—*especially* Rione—was out of the question.

Yet the word echoed over and over in her mind. *Marriage.* She had *married* Rione. A man she thought she despised—thought him to be her enemy, and here she was, having feelings for him, trusting him. Her one-sided emotions made it worse. Of course, he did not reciprocate. This marriage was a debt paid, a life owed, and nothing more. He had said as much that day at the smallholding. Even supposing he did return the sentiments, they were selfish—dangerous. It meant she cared, and caring for Rione was not part of the plan.

On top of all that, he was letting her go home. *Rione* gave her that decision, and she had chosen. Ever since King Remus's discovery, Æri was determined to detach herself from Fíronbec and the king's control. Once out far enough in the Bogs, she intended to reactivate the signal in her bionic arm, alerting her Narkrye. She'd return to her mountains, and things would go back to the way they were.

As Rione finished gliding the silver ring past Æri's knuckle, she sensed that tug again, as if one of those threads she desperately grasped linked her to him. It tugged just behind her ribcage, oddly strengthening when he lawfully bound his life to hers.

Æri pressed her eyes shut, fighting that incessant sentiment. She had chosen to return home. This was what she wanted—to find a cure with her Narkrye with Otta while sustaining her queen. That was her plan. Fíronbec held no more answers. Staying with Rione would eventually lead her back to the king, and she had to escape—to go home. It was simple. Yet the choice felt anything but.

Her mangled decisions yanked her in all directions. She grasped blindly, trying to find a thread that wouldn't break, other than the one tied to Rione. The sliver of doubt rose and threatened to slice the lines she held.

What of her sister? Her people? What of the Vampryne and the god of darkness—of Hælsgade? Answers to the Split. Did she just intend to return to Særenfell without a solution? And what would she return to—a crumbling queendom that survived only by carnage?

Journeying to the other realms did not guarantee answers, but they provided a lead—a direction.

Her initial choice now seemed...insignificant. What if that pull toward Rione was a sign from the gods? A solid thread to hold on to and follow, one that would not break.

Gyr squawked, drawing her out and bringing her to the present. The Specuformae had ceased its descent—hovering above the Bogs' crust.

Rione's hand still cocooned hers. His coarse thumb circled over the delicate skin of her wrist as if he, too, did not want to let go.

A sense of calm washed over her.

Why couldn't she go to Dianeane? She didn't have to go back to Særenfell right away. She secured her freedom, but it did not mean she ought to leave now. Æri could go to Dianeane with Rione and find a cure. She'd just leave before they returned to Fíronbec.

Her fingers curled around Rione's as she looked him square in the eye, her resolve hardening.

"I will stay with you."

His eye widened, and his brows arched in surprise. Something glinted. What was that? A spark of hope? The small bit of gold and blue shined more prominently, circling his iris.

"Until we get the right answers," she added quickly.

The spark winked out. Rione's brows schooled back into their neutral position. He turned away from the official. The sentinels had lost interest in the minor dispute and wandered back to the upper deck.

Rione's voice came in a hush. "You know what's planned. We are not going to Dianeane first. This trajectory remains in place. Can your sister wait that long?"

Æri raised to her toes to peek beyond his shoulder, ensuring the official wasn't eavesdropping. His head was still buried in the papers as he endeavored to find an error.

"I know, but in Erynelleth...the Fae may be able to help decipher Oisin's message—even without him to redraw it—perhaps put words to the page," she whispered. "Besides, what use am I to my sister without a cure? It may be my only chance. A few months more won't make a difference. As long as I have your word, I can go home once I've found the answers."

"I promised you freedom, and I meant it. My word is yours." Rione's response was automatic. His eye swept over her face. "Are you sure this is what you want?" Yet even as he said this, his grip tightened and his voice thickened with emotion. The affectionate gesture sent a plethora of prickling spirals down her spine. He, too, seemed to be struggling between his own indecisions.

Æri smiled up at Rione, her hand entwined with his. Their fingers laced together—a new bond of her own making. "There's only one way to find out."

POISONED PAWN

ACKNOWLEDGEMENTS

First, thank you to my loving and supportive husband, who read my work's first and last drafts. You are my anchor in life.

Thank you to my friends and family, who encouraged me to continue writing and never give up on a dream. Perseverance is what saw this novel through.

A huge thank you to all my beta readers and critical partners who helped me find a draft I was proud of. These include Maria Achihaitei, Jeanette Barszewski, Caitlin, and Jessica. A particular thank you to Pawan Helix Thaokar, a fellow writer and friend who has supported and believed in this book from its rough drafts up to its publication.

Thank you to my cousin, Charlotte, and twin, Sonja, who have listened to my rants and tirades, struggles and confessions, and tears and laughs while putting this novel together. You have contributed incredible amounts to this project!

Thank you to my developmental editor, Nicole McCurdy at Emerald Edits, and Misha, my copyeditor. Your professional feedback and direction made this book shine.

Lastly, thank you to April White, who has taken me under her wing and guided me through the independent publishing process.

I could not have made this novel happen without you.

ABOUT THE AUTHOR

K. L. Vincent is an award-winning author originally from California with a degree in theater design and anthropology from UCLA. She later received a master's degree in anthropology and occupational therapy in the UK. Following her passion for history, people, and travel, she dabbled in archaeology and spent a summer exploring Scotland while volunteering on a dig at the Ness of Brodgar.

She is an active Globe Soup member with accolades in their short fiction challenges and continues to pen stories whenever possible. She has short stories featured in *Marbles: An Anthology of Micro and Flash Fiction* and *The Book of Choices*. As a neurodivergent writer, she infuses her work with a focus on resilience and identity. Both she and her identical twin collaborate and bounce stories off one another even though they live in different countries. She calls France her home, and lives with her partner, baby girl, and furball.

Want to explore more in the Lost Sovereigns Series? Sign up to the Newsletter below for continued updates on what's next!

KLVincentWrites.com
@thebluestockingtrio

POISONED PAWN

K. L. Vincent

The Bluestocking Trio